TABLE FOR FOUR

A Medical Thriller Series Book 1

Chris Bliersbach

Smashwords

CHAPTER 1

There is no good or easy way to lose someone you love. How Curt Barnes lost his wife was beyond heinous. What degree of anger or mental instability was necessary to consider, let alone do such a thing?

After ten years of marriage, Curt and Calli's life together in Central Maine had become comfortable routines impervious to any major shifts or upsets. While not a perfect marriage, there was much more harmony than discord. As marriages around them disintegrated, Curt and Calli soldiered on. He was a healthcare consultant, and she had just received a promotion to manager at the local Lester's, a big box store in town. They successfully juggled their schedules to accommodate the kids' school and extra-curricular activities. They had dreams of moving to a warmer climate after the kids were out of the house. They were a typical, middle-class family with middle-class dreams. Living in a neighborhood where the most egregious thing to occur was the paperboy flinging the Dracut-Campion Star Ledger and missing the front steps. This is why August 20, 2008, came as such a shock, not only to Curt and the kids but also to the entire community.

When Curt and Calli had disagreements, it was usually over how to manage their children, Caitlin and Cade, 7 and 5, respectively, at the time of Calli's death. The kids could get into battles over virtually anything. On one occasion, while Curt and Calli were digging a new garden in the backyard, Cade and Caitlin were playing in the house. Cade, irritated by something Caitlin had done, got his Super Soaker and drenched his sister. In response, Caitlin called 911 and screamed to the operator that her brother had shot her. Cade started shooting her with the water gun again. Caitlin dropped the phone and ran screaming through the house with Cade in hot pursuit. The 911 operator had no choice but to follow protocol. In minutes, two police cars pulled into the driveway, and officers emerged, guns at the ready. As one officer rounded silently to the back of the house, Curt and Calli heard, "Stop right there! Drop what's in your hands and turn slowly towards us." It was unfortunate that the new garden looked more like the beginnings of a burial plot at that point. As Curt and Calli followed the officer's instructions, Caitlin and Cade burst out the back door screaming, "Mom, Dad, the police are here." They managed to sort everything out, and luckily, none of the police officers had itchy fingers. The kids got a stern lecture from Officers Dzideck and Schweikert. Mom and Dad imposed house arrest for two weeks, and Cade's Super Soaker and an air-soft gun ended up in the local landfill. At the time, it was a big deal, but Curt and Calli could laugh about the incident months later. They would tell friends that those were the most peaceful two weeks they had had in years.

On that fateful day in August, around 3 p.m., when Caitlin and Cade got off the school bus, smoke and flames had just started to escape from the upper floor of their house. They had the good sense not to enter the house and instead ran to the neighbor to call 911 – this time for real. They stood helpless in the front yard, waiting for the fire department to arrive. They heard not only their mother's screams but also the wild, unintelligible ranting of a man.

"Mommy," the kids cried repeatedly.

"Mommy."

Soon, Mommy screamed no more, replaced by the snap, crackle, and pop of a fire that was starting to consume the upper floor of the Cape nestled amongst a stand of white birch. Still, they heard the rants of a man whose screams were at first guttural and then would crescendo to an almost hyena-like laugh. Words, unintelligible at first, got louder and clearer.

As neighbors began to congregate and try unsuccessfully to calm the kids, Curt pulled into the driveway. He had come home early so that Calli would be able to work the late shift. He was unprepared for the scene. Caitlin and Cade ran to him. They couldn't speak and were only able to utter a choking kind of inhaled, huh, huh, huh, as if they were trying to catch their breath. The smoke, now reaching the neighborhood bystanders on the lawn, stung their throats and eyes. In the distance, the sirens of the fire department finally announced their imminent arrival.

"Ma, ma, ma, Mommy," Caitlin sobbed. "Sh, Sh, She, she's,"

As Caitlin tried to complete her sentence, the ranting man in the house crashed through the front door.

He stood on the front step with his arms raised in victory. In his right hand, a propane torch. In his left a can of kerosene. His left trouser leg and left shirtsleeve were smoldering, and parts of both his left leg and left arm were charred black and seeping something bloody and gelatinous. If he felt pain, he didn't show it. As if in a trance or responding to some stimulus only he could hear, he kept repeating "Yes" in rhythmic intervals,

"Yes"

"Yes"

"Yes"

The Fire Department and police arrived simultaneously. The firefighters moved as quickly as possible, but the flames had already engulfed most of the house. There was also the matter of the crazed man on the front step. "Drop what is in your hands and lay down on the ground," instructed the police, but he did not appear to hear them.

He continued, "Yes."

"Yes"

"We repeat, drop what is in your hands, and lay down on the ground."

"Yes"

"Yes"

Time was of the essence if the firefighters were going to try to salvage anything of the house. The police approached the man cautiously. They repeatedly instructed him to lie down. He continued, "Yes, yes, yes." The police reached him, and he offered no resistance. As they led him to a police cruiser, the gathering heard him shout, "Her fate is sealed. She is finally free."

The firefighters did the best they could, but it was evident that the home was a total loss. Only the garage would escape damage. Despite the grim scene, Curt held out hope that maybe his wife had been able to survive. The kids had witnessed their mother's screams and then their discontinuation. Cade was in shock, and Caitlin was delirious. Paramedics brought them to an ambulance where they lay Cade down, elevated his feet, and administered oxygen. Caitlin was inconsolable and combative, requiring restraint and a light sedative before she calmed down. Curt was anxious to get into his home, and firefighters repeatedly asked him to step away from the house.

"Calli," he shouted. No response.

"Calli" Silence.

The crime scene investigators and firefighters, despite repeated warnings, finally allowed Curt into the house. Escorted by one of the firefighters, Curt quickly wished he had heeded their advice. He smelt burnt flesh and the smoldering ooze of what was barely recognizable as his wife. He doubled over and deposited the contents of his stomach in an ash heap that was once their dresser. Each time he tried to straighten up and make it out the door, he would retch again. Leaving only when there was nothing more to expel. Paramedics met him as he exited the house. They brought him to the ambulance and administered oxygen and a sedative.

Neither Curt nor the kids recall the rest of that day. They woke up on the morning of August 21st in a spare room in his brother's house – about 15 miles from what used to be their home. To say it would be a torturous route to recovery didn't require an advanced degree in psychology. The horror of that day would only be the first insult. It existed like a bookmark in life, bisecting it into all that went before and all that occurred after.

CHAPTER 2

J ackie Selaney was bright, outgoing, and articulate. With stunning good looks, a supple, athletic body, long brown hair, dark brown eyes, and a 5'9" frame, she had been a high school basketball and a college volleyball standout. Growing up, Jackie was always tall for her age, and people often mistakenly thought she was older. Despite her height, she was still well proportioned and never considered gawky. She moved with grace, and even as a young teen, people called her elegant. In other words, she had it all. For the most part, people wanted to be in her orbit, minus a few of her female acquaintances who feigned friendship but secretly resented her. Through High School and before she met Stu, she attracted the attention of many men, young and old, but she never had a serious relationship. She was quite naïve about relationships with men. While many professed only wanting her friendship, all eventually tried to push well beyond that boundary. Invariably, she would rebuff their advances, and they would leave in frustration.

Jackie met Stuart Deno at Carter's Bar in 2002, her freshman year at South Temple University (STU). Carter's was a popular college hangout in South Temple, NY. Although drinking didn't appeal to Jackie, her friends had heard it was a bit loose about checking ID's. While her friends partied, she sat at a table in the corner, sipping a ginger ale. Stuart, who was from Barron, was working on a highway construction project on I-84 just outside South Temple. Stu had been a High School football star for the Barron Bears and had idolized former STU star cornerback Russell Carter who had made it to the pros and for whom Carter's had been christened. Stu, at 6'2" and 245 pounds, had been a linebacker in High School. His work on the road crew had only served to add more muscle and a dark tan to his rippling musculature, evident outside and underneath the tight t-shirt he wore. His snug blue jeans didn't detract from his athletic look or appeal to the women in the bar. While Stu liked his Jack and Cokes, he was no match for his maintenance crew buddies, who could put most folks to shame with their alcohol consumption. Taking a break from the boisterous bunch at the bar, Stu spied Jackie, and with the bravery that only two Jack and Cokes could provide, he approached her.

"You look pretty lonely over here," he opened.

"I'm not really into the bar scene," she responded.

"I'm Stu. Mind if I join you?

"Ahh, OK," she said.

From this lackluster beginning grew a bond that neither had experienced before. For the next hour, they conversed easily. Both felt as if they had known one another for years. Amid the din, they were in their own little world. Nothing going on around them mattered, and their consuming connection was only interrupted when one of Jackie's friends approached.

"Jackie"

"JACKIE!"

"JACKIE!" her friend repeated, almost falling into the table as she grabbed and shook Jackie's arm.

"WHAT?" Jackie said, looking up a bit perturbed to see her bleary-eyed, stumbling friend.

"Jeez, I called your name like 100 times." Her friend slurred. "We're trashed. Can you give us a ride to the dorm?"

Although Tower dorm was only a mile from Carter's, her friends were obviously in no condition to drive or walk back to the dorm. Reluctantly, she agreed to drive them. Stu, recognizing that the night might be ending prematurely, put on his best puppy dog face. It wasn't necessary.

"Stu, it will only take me 10 minutes to drive them. Are you going to be here if I come back?"

"Absolutely," Stu brightened, "I'd be crazy not to be."

Tower dorm was the tallest structure on campus but located the furthest distance from most of the classrooms and nightlife. Freshmen were usually relegated to living there, having to pay their dues before qualifying for the more desirable and conveniently located housing.

Jackie dropped her friends off and returned to Carter's as promised.

"Now you're the one that looks pretty lonely," Jackie remarked as she approached Stu. "Mind if I join you?"

"I'm sorry, ma'am, do I know you? I don't think my girlfriend would approve if I let you sit in her seat."

"Oh, really! What's your girlfriend's name?"

"Betty Sue," Stu shot back.

"So, where is this, Betty Sue?"

"She just went to the ladies' room to powder her nose."

"Well, I guess I'll just have to find another table then," as she started to walk away.

"Ahh, you know what? Perhaps you could join me for a little bit."

"Oh, I wouldn't want to upset Betty Sue."

"Well, she's got a big nose, and it takes her a long time to powder it."

Upon that invitation, Jackie reclaimed the chair opposite Stu, and they rekindled the life-changing conversation they had begun earlier that evening. As things started to get a bit raucous in the bar, Stu suggested they take a drive. Their conversation continued in the car, and in 30 minutes, they rolled up to Diamond Lake. It was midnight on a mild April evening with a full moon that glistened off the lake's mirror-like calm. It was the perfect accompaniment to a magical evening. They lay in each other's arms taking in the flashlight moon, the blanket of stars, and each other.

CHAPTER 3

I t took Curt and the kids a long time to recover enough from the shock to begin to piece their lives back together. Curt was interviewed by an endless parade of police officers and investigators. They asked him the same questions day after day, thwarting any attempt he may have made to start to insulate himself from the horror and move forward.

"What do you know about the fire?"

"Do you know Darius Scott?"

"Have you ever seen Darius Scott before?"

"Was everything OK between you and your wife?"

"Did your wife have any enemies or get into an argument with anyone recently?"

Curt and the kids knew nothing, but no matter how many ways they communicated this, the questions just kept coming.

"No, no, no, and no for the hundredth time," Curt said in an exasperated tone.

"No, I don't know the man. No, neither the kids nor I had an argument with my wife. And no, I'm not aware of anyone angry with her."

"I'm sorry, Mr. Barnes, I realize that this must be difficult, but we need to investigate this thoroughly. I'm sure you understand," said the Investigator.

"No, I don't understand," Curt fired back, "all I know is that my kids lost their mother, I lost my wife, we all lost our home and our belongings, and some whack job came out of my burning house with a torch and kerosene. How much more fucking clearer could it be?"

"I understand how upset you must be," said the Investigator trying to recover, "I only have,"

"You have NO FUCKING idea," exploded Curt, "so don't try that empathetic investigator bullshit on me. My kids and I am tired of these stupid questions. Now, if you don't mind, I'm going to get my kids, and we're going to find a new place to live."

Curt's accommodating, even keel personality had disintegrated over the last few days. The horrific loss, followed by a lack of sleep, no appetite, morose kids, and an investigation led by the Three Stooges, had exhausted his reserves of tolerance. He wouldn't have been surprised if Curly had walked in, saying, "Nyuk, nyuk, nyuk." Only to be followed by making that galloping horse sound by snapping his fingers and clapping his hands together repeatedly. He was on edge and needed to take steps to get himself back on his feet. Not to mention, rescue his kids, who were adrift in a very dark place.

Curt and the kids stayed in the basement of his brother's house. Robert Barnes was Curt's younger brother by two years. Everyone, including Robert's wife Melissa, referred to him as "BB." Robert had acquired this nickname early in life. No one was sure whether the origin of BB was Baby Barnes or Bob Barnes. Or, perhaps it was the incident at his 10th birthday party when he shot the neighbor girl in the butt trying out his new BB gun. It didn't matter. The moniker stuck.

The first time Curt and the kids left BB's home was for Calli's funeral. Curt doesn't recall being involved in any of the funeral arrangements. However, BB later insisted that he had consulted Curt a few times. St. Pius Catholic Church stood across from Lake Campion. Father Levesque married Curt and Calli at St. Pius in 1998. Curt and Calli had walked across the street after the wedding ceremony to have their wedding pictures taken with Lake Campion in the background. Now Father Levesque would preside over Calli's funeral. There would be no pictures today.

The funeral, and frankly the whole day, was a blur for Curt and the kids. Curt only recalled two things about the funeral, and neither of them was pleasant – the light and the smell. Emerging from their cold, damp, and windowless basement cocoon into the light of day caused them to squint and cover their eyes until their eyes adjusted. Curt hadn't expected that he would continue to smell the smoke long after it was gone. At first, he thought the smell was coming from the few clothes they had salvaged from the house. Even now, when they were outside and nowhere near the clothes, he not only smelled smoke, but he also smelled the charred remains of his wife. Haunted by the pain of his olfactory memory, that unforgettable, acrid smell grew so strong as to cause him to gag. Throughout the funeral, Curt grimaced and gagged. Observers forgave these expressions as reasonable reactions to the funeral, the touching eulogy given by Calli's sister, Father Levesque's supportive words to Caitlin and Cade, or the songs sung by a group of Calli's friends. Curt never heard any of the words or the songs; he smelled that awful smell. His gags were his battle to keep the contents of his stomach at bay. Somehow, although he doesn't recall how he got there, Curt stood before Calli's casket at the Mount Campion Cemetery. He suspects Psalm 23 was read, but he doesn't remember hearing it. The only thing Curt recalls was the irony that they were burying his wife when she had, for all practical purposes, already been cremated. It was all so senseless to him.

After the lost week that followed August 20, 2008, Curt and the kids forced themselves out of the shelter of BB's basement. Curt found a small, furnished apartment in Campion that wasn't elegant but convenient for families that had virtually nothing. The Terrace Hill apartments housed many of the same interesting clientele that you commonly find in Laundromats. Despite some of the colorful characters, the apartment immediately simplified things for Curt, who was struggling to wrap his head around being a widower with two damaged kids. The kids' school bus stopped just 50 yards from their front door. August 20th had been the first day of the new school year, so except for the first day, Caitlin and Cade had missed most of the first two weeks of school. He needed to get them back into the school routine and get himself back to work. The apartment had a playground and pool filled with kids Caitlin and Cade's age. It hadn't occurred to Curt, but losing their house, also caused Caitlin and Cade to lose access to their neighborhood friends. Curt only realized this when, upon seeing the pool and playground alive with children, the kids' eyes lit up for the first time in over a week. While Curt toured the apartment, he had let the kids go to the playground. They caught up to him 10 minutes later, breathless.

"Daddy, can we live here?" Caitlin pleaded, "My best friend Jordan lives here."

"Jordan?" Curt asked, "I don't remember you having a friend named Jordan."

"Well, I just met her," Caitlin replied.

Curt looked at the landlord, "Kids, they have a new best friend every day!"

"Tell me about it," said the landlord, "I have three girls, and it's a soap opera every day!"

"Daddy, they have a merry-go-round," announced Cade, "can you come down and make it go round real fast?"

"In a minute, hon," said Curt, "I have to do some paperwork so that we can live here."

Caitlin and Cade erupted into cheers and hugged Curt's legs

before running out the door on their way back to the playground.

"Wow," said Curt to the landlord, "that's the first time I have seen them happy in a long time."

Seeing that the landlord didn't quite understand, Curt added,

"Their mother died in a fire last week."

"Oh, I'm sorry," said the landlord touching his arm. "You mean that fire set by that crazy man?"

Initially taken aback by her knowledge of this, he suddenly realized that it must have been big news. Apart from the irritating visits and questions of the police and investigators, he had not read a newspaper or watched a newscast.

"Yes," he said, recovering, "Did you know him?"

"Hell no," she said, "but the paper said he's locked up in the loony bin in Harlow awaiting trial."

Curt had not thought until that moment that he would have to relive the events and perhaps face the crazed Darius Scott again. It shook his constitution. Seeing the color drain from his face, the landlord said,

"I'm sorry. I'm sure this is the last thing you want to hear or talk about. Let's get that paperwork done and get you and your kids settled in your new home."

"Thanks" was all Curt could produce, his mind spinning and trying to refocus on the task at hand.

Curt signed the lease and paid the rent and security deposit.

"That's it, Mr. Barnes," said the landlord handing Curt a copy of the signed lease, "Your new home is #316. I hope the best for you and the kids."

"Thanks," Curt responded.

Looking down at the plastic key fob that read 316, his mind

suddenly shifted to John 3:16. "For God so loved the world that he gave his one and only Son, that whoever believes in him shall not perish but have eternal life." He wondered if maybe this was an omen, hopeful that perhaps it was the beginning of salvation. He made a mental note to start attending church that Sunday with the kids.

As he approached the playground, he heard an excited, ping-pong conversation coming from a picnic table as Caitlin and Jordan consolidated their new BFF status. For a moment, Curt thought that this might work out. Collecting the kids from the playground, they went shopping for groceries. Curt had never overseen grocery shopping responsibilities, so his first excursion to the store proved frustrating. He had never paid attention to what groceries Calli would buy. Nor did he have any concept of how to plan a menu and purchase food for a week, let alone a day. He recognized some things in the aisles, and the kids certainly had an eye for their favorite, less than ideal food choices. Still, the grocery store was overwhelming to him. He eventually gave in to the kids who claimed they knew best from accompanying their Mom to the store. This, he would discover, was his first mistake.

The apartment was a long and narrow three-bedroom on the third floor. The apartment didn't have an elevator, only a walk-up. This was not a significant issue unless he had ten bags of groceries, which on this occasion, he did. The major downside of the apartment, from Curt's perspective, was the two small rooms side-by-side in the back of the apartment. Caitlin and Cade, close to one another, were a guarantee for conflict. Curt had held out some hope that the recent trauma or their delight with the playground and new friends might cure Caitlin and Cade of their sharing problem. He quickly learned this was folly. As Curt was lugging groceries up the stairs, the kids explored the apartment discovering the three bedrooms. As he got the last bags into the apartment and to the counter, Caitlin announced,

"Daddy, here's your room," pointing to one of the small back bedrooms.

"Well, honey, I thought you and Cade would take the back bedrooms, and I would take the front bedroom."

"Daddy, I want you to sleep next to my room," hollered Cade from the other bedroom.

"Yeah, and I need room for my horses," countered Caitlin, "and these rooms are too small."

There was no sense in negotiating, and Curt realized that his accepting a smaller room would eliminate potential battles. He wanted the kids to be as comfortable as possible. He relented, and Caitlin took the large front bedroom, relegating "the boys" to the smaller back bedrooms.

"What do you want for dinner?" Curt called from the kitchen.

"Chef Boyardee" sang both Caitlin and Cade.

Their first dinner in their new home was Chef Boyardee Mini Ravioli in Tomato and Meat Sauce. Curt, who still hadn't recovered his appetite, had a Diet Coke. After dinner, the kids settled in front of the TV. While Curt was cleaning up, the doorbell rang.

"Who could that possibly be," Curt asked himself.

"Surprise!" shouted BB and Melissa as Curt opened the door.

"What in the world?" Curt said, seeing BB and Melissa holding two large boxes.

"We have some housewarming gifts for you," announced Melissa, "We hope this makes things a little easier."

"We also have some dinners your former neighbors made for you," said BB, "I know how much of a gourmet chef you are!" he joked.

The commotion by the door had enticed the kids away

from the TV. Seeing the large boxes filled with things, perhaps some things for them, made them react as if it was Christmas in August. Curt stood silently as tears ran down his cheek. Melissa and BB hugged him and said that things would be all right. He began to sob. He had held it together well up until this moment. The kids chimed in and started to cry as well,

"It will be OK, Daddy," sniffed Caitlin while hugging his leg.

Ever the savior, Cade had run to the kitchen.

"Here, Daddy," said Cade handing Curt a tissue.

This made Curt cry even more, but in this instance, it was tears of gratitude that Cade had inherited his mother's compassion. BB and Melissa stayed until Curt, and the kids were back on a level emotional plane. The donated dinners looked delicious and filled the freezer. Fortunately, Curt's inept shopping had left plenty of room in the refrigerator for some of the overflow. The boxes were like Christmas with clothes, books, and toys for the kids and cleaning supplies and kitchenware that Curt never thought to buy.

It had been a long, emotional day, and Curt prepared the beds for their new occupants. The kids had precise bedtime routines, and with this, Curt was familiar. He read to Cade and sang him his favorite bedtime song, "The Star-Spangled Banner," of all things. His fascination with the National Anthem probably had something to do with its playing before his peewee hockey games. Not an easy song to sing, but Curt's rendition, even as exhausted as he was that night, did the trick. Cade was asleep by the time Curt reached "and the home of the brave." Caitlin was a different story. She primped and dawdled in the bathroom, impervious to Curt's efforts to get her to bed. When she finally did get to her room, she started to play with the Breyer horses and stable that she had received in the box of gifts. Curt, now acting more like a zombie than a human, trudged into Caitlin's room. He promptly stepped barefooted onto a stray section of picket fence from the horse stable set.

Painful as it was, Caitlin's gales of laughter at her Daddy's wounded expression prevented him from erupting in anger. Instead, he managed to overplay the pain hopping wildly on one foot while holding the other to his daughter's delight. This was all in service to trying to get his daughter to bed. After recovering from being impaled by the plastic picket fence, he picked his daughter up, spun her around.

"Dizzy girl, dizzy girl," he said and flung her into her bed.

It was not necessarily the most calming method for sending a child to bed, but for Caitlin, it worked. She overplayed the bed spinning and quickly got under the covers. Grabbing her favorite book that Melissa had given her, she pleaded for Curt to read it for what probably was the billionth time. Caitlin's original "Butterfly Kisses" book didn't survive the house fire. Thanks to Melissa, they were able to rekindle the tradition. By the time he got to the closing sentences, Caitlin had closed her eyes, and he was near tears. "I know I gotta let her go, but I'll always remember every hug in the morning and butterfly kisses." Somehow, the words that had so often applied to his daughter seemed to refer to his wife tonight.

"Calli, how can I let you go?" he whispered under his breath.

CHAPTER 4

From that fateful first night that started at Carter's and ended at Diamond Lake, Jackie and Stuart's relationship continued to blossom. Stu graduated from hanging out with his road crew at the bars Friday nights to going to the T-Rex Bar-B-Que with Jackie to listen to blues bands like The Nighthawks. The T-Rex Bar-B-Que was in a dingy part of downtown. What it lacked in location was more than made up for in personality, food, and fun. The moment you walked in, the smoky, tangy smell of barbecue hit your nose, eliciting a salivary response that would make Pavlov's dog proud. Posters, portraits of blue's guitarists, license plates, and large murals featuring a green T-Rex getting into all manner of mischief adorned every inch of the walls. Jackie and Stu liked to sit at the table right beside the Hostess Hut because it afforded the best views of the bands and avoided most of the crowd that generally packed the place.

On the weekends, they would take long walks or visit Stu's family for brunch after church on Sundays. Occasionally, they would take in a show at the Orpheum Theatre downtown. In the fall, during the volleyball season, Stu would attend Jackie's home games. They had an uncommonly harmonious relationship. Jackie's friends, witnessing this idyllic union, often engaged Jackie as their counselor when their relationships with young men suffered the more typical turbulence. These counseling sessions, which often extended into the wee hours of the morning, made Jackie appreciate Stu even more. She never had to concern herself with infidelity, jealousy, moodiness, drunkenness, insensitivity, or commitment issues. Stu never gave her a reason.

Stu was from Barron, a small town about 15 miles north of South Temple. Barron sat on the banks of the Macintosh River. Other than a small-town center, most of the area surrounding Barron was farmland. Raised on a dairy farm, Stu was used to hard work, long hours, and wholesome living. He had simple needs, and for what he may have lacked in brainpower, he made up in brawn. In High School, Stu was a standout football player. So good that many observers saw college football stardom in his future. While Stu liked football, he never saw it as his ticket out of Barron. He was not as disappointed as many, including his parents, when he did not receive any college scholarship offers. He had never considered himself college material, but he also did not intend to go into the family's dairy farming business. When he met Jackie, he was eight months into his Highway Maintenance Worker training program with the New York State Department of Transportation (NYSDOT). His job was not glamorous, but the pay and the benefits were better than working at the farm or flinging pizzas at Gino's in town. Stu's dream was to earn enough money to go back to school and get an Associate's degree in Automotive/Diesel Technology.

It wasn't a surprise to anyone when Stu and Jackie decided to get an apartment in South Temple at the start of her junior year. They had been constant companions for almost three years. If there was any surprise at all, it might have been that Stu had not already "popped the question." They certainly acted married. Stu had even carried Jackie across the threshold of the apartment, a move that Jackie had enjoyed. Their parents would have preferred marriage before living together. Still, Jackie and Stu had so endeared themselves to each other's parents that there was never any protest. Virtually everyone not only saw their unique compatibility but also, in some respects, envied it.

As Jackie's junior year at South Temple was winding down, she applied for a summer internship at AlzCura, a pharmaceutical company in Buffalo. AlzCura was developing a new drug, Recallamin, designed to treat Alzheimer's disease (AD). The drug was the brainchild of Dr. Asa Sheridan. As President and Chief Medical Officer of AlzCura, he was looking for an intern to help him navigate the Food and Drug Administration's (FDA) New Drug Application process. The drug had received its Investigational New Drug (IND) designation from the Food and Drug Administration (FDA). It was starting the most important and most expensive part of the drug approval process, Phase 3 Clinical Trials.

"Ms. Jacqueline Selaney," Dr. Sheridan pronounced.

"You can call me Jackie."

"Alright then, Jackie, why should I select you for this internship?" asked Dr. Sheridan, who was known for getting to the point and not being much for small talk or tact.

"I want to do something that has a higher purpose, not just something that will look good on my resume. My grandmother has Alzheimer's, as does my boyfriend's grandfather."

"So, how does that qualify you for this internship?" pried the doctor.

"Well, you might decide it doesn't, but if I were in your shoes, I'd want someone willing not only to put their brain into it but also their heart."

"Heart has little to do with the work of this internship. How does your heart help me navigate the bureaucracy of the FDA's drug approval process?" challenged Dr. Sheridan.

"I respectfully disagree. Heart has everything to do with this and any endeavor. If you don't have the heart for the work, why would you take the time and make an effort to learn how to navigate the FDA's bureaucracy? Besides, what's a little bureaucracy when 27 million people are diagnosed with Alzheimer's with no known cure?"

"I'll ask the questions if you don't mind, but I see your point." Dr. Sheridan softened.

Very few people could melt Dr. Sheridan's cold, clinical approach to most everything, but Jackie managed to that day. Dr. Sheridan knew he had his intern by the end of the interview. Despite his certainty, he told her that he would get in touch with her after interviewing all the candidates. She could not read Dr. Sheridan, and as she replayed the interview in her head while driving home, she feared she might have failed the interview. Arriving home, she gave Stu a blow-by-blow account of the interview with Dr. Sheridan. She thought the interview had gone well but worried that Dr. Sheridan might have thought some of her responses were challenging or even contrary. She feared that perhaps she had come on too strong and that Dr. Sheridan thought her more trouble than she was worth. Stu tried to counter her every fear and doubt with attempts to boost her confidence, to no avail. She stayed awake until the early morning hours. When she slept, she slept restlessly. By the time she received Dr. Sheridan's call later that morning, she was exhausted. He offered her the internship, and she happily accepted.

"I got the internship," Jackie said excitedly to Stu over the phone.

"Congratulations, Boo! See, didn't I tell you last night not to worry about it?"

"Yes, yes, you did, and I should have listened." Jackie conceded.

Two months later, her Junior year behind her, Jackie started her internship in Buffalo. She immersed herself in all the steps in the rigorous and expensive drug development and approval process. Although it meant that she had to be away from Stu, Jackie felt fortunate to have landed the internship and saw it as her first real step in her career. During the weekdays, Jackie would stay with her parents, and on the weekends, drive to the apartment in South Temple to be with Stu.

Jackie's parents lived in Nora, NY, a quaint and inviting village about 15 miles southeast of industrial Buffalo. The small downtown area was walkable and surrounded by middle-class neighborhoods punctuated by mature, majestic trees. Nora was a safe and comfortable community with little notoriety. Her parents lived on Clifton Street, a tree-lined street across from the park where Jackie had played as a child. As hard as her parents tried to make her comfortable in her old bedroom, living under her parents' roof was difficult. If not for being able to drive back to South Temple to be with Stu on the weekends, she wasn't sure she would have been able to endure the summer with her parents. She loved them dearly, but there comes a time when living with your parents doesn't work anymore.

Jackie loved the internship work, and after the first six weeks, Dr. Sheridan and other AlzCura executives spoke with her about her future. They encouraged her to consider a career in the Pharmaceutical industry. That weekend, excited that Dr. Sheridan had taken an interest in her future, she spoke to Stu.

"Hon, how would you feel if AlzCura offered me a job after college?" Jackie asked while she was preparing dinner.

"That'd be great," Stu replied, "I didn't think a college-educated beauty like you would stay put forever."

"What a charmer," Jackie sighed, "but what about your job, Hon?"

"If it happens, I can look into getting a transfer to Region 1," Stu replied while taking out the lettuce to make the salad.

"And you wouldn't mind leaving your family for Buffalo?"

"Listen, if I wanted to stay here," Stu replied, "I would be squeezing cow tits and trying to put the moves on Betty Sue at the local market in Barron."

Betty Sue was the fictionalized character that Stu had cooked up the first time he had met Jackie at Carter's bar. Since then, Betty Sue had become a running joke and a recurring character in their conversations. The name had also become playful code to signal a desire to get intimate. Stu's response had the intended effect.

"Wha Stuey, wha don't yew come ova heya to ma check-out counta. I'll let yew check out ma titties," Jackie responded in her best southern accent while cupping her breasts in her hands.

"Wha Betty Sue, I'm gonna bend yew ova dat counta ova dare and dew yew like yew nevah bin dun befora," twanged Stu as he reached to loosen his belt buckle.

Suffice to say, Jackie and Stu's relatively late-blossoming sex lives had advanced considerably from their first fumbling efforts. Now, armed with the intimate knowledge of each other, combined with their athletic bodies and stamina, their lovemaking sessions became epic. A potentially difficult discussion at dinner transformed into a hot bedroom marathon. They didn't return to the kitchen until the next light of day.

CHAPTER 5

The move to the Terrace Hill Apartments, a necessary interim step in Curt and the kids' recovery, was not the perfect environment by any means. On the first weekend there, Curt decided to investigate the shopping that the Terrace Hill Apartment ads claimed was "within walking distance." He learned that this was only true if you didn't mind navigating a windy, narrow, descending trail through a spooky tangle of bushes and trees. His journey down the path provided an education and risks to which he would rather not expose Caitlin and Cade. Discarded condoms, packs of cigarettes, and broken bottles littered the trail. Towards the end of the trail, he discovered an inebriated old geezer lolling in the underbrush amidst a couple of empty bottles of Thunderbird. Curt knew that Caitlin and Cade's natural curiosity would eventually cause them to explore the nether reaches of the property. He had to find a way to discourage such sightseeing.

"I had the biggest scare today," Curt said to the kids as he was making them lunch.

"What happened?" said Caitlin.

"I went down a trail that is supposed to lead to a shopping mall, but I never made it," Curt said for dramatic effect. Convinced that he now had drawn both kids' attention away from the TV, he continued.

"Not only is there a big drop off in one place, but I saw a

black bear." The kids' eyes widened, and both drew in a sharp breath. Curt knew this would be an effective deterrent. Children in Maine learn early to avoid black bears.

"What did you do, Daddy?" Caitlin questioned as Cade asked, "Are you OK?"

"Yes, I'm OK, but he was not very happy to see me. Luckily he was more interested in eating the plants. I backed away slowly, and when he couldn't see me anymore, I ran back up the trail. I don't want you," He didn't need to finish his sentence.

"I'm never going near there," cried Caitlin

"Me either," chimed Cade. "I don't want to get eaten. Maybe we should move, Daddy."

Curt didn't want to traumatize his kids, and he wondered if he had maybe oversold it with the black bear story.

"We'll be OK as long as we stay away from that trail, Cade. Black bears only eat plants and berries, but they don't like people near them. So stay off the trail."

Cade's face told the story. He was terrified. "I'm never going to the playground again."

"The playground is safe, Cade," Curt responded, "Bears sleep during the daytime and don't like to be in the open."

"But the bear you saw was awake," Caitlin reasoned unhelpfully.

"It was really early this morning, and it was still a little dark in the woods," fibbed Curt, who was trying hard to modulate Cade's reaction. He was only partially successful. The next few days, Cade was afraid to leave the apartment without getting his Dad's permission and then only if Caitlin or Curt were with him. Curt had the opportunity to regret the black bear story many times after that. The fire had been traumatic enough, and now he felt like he contributed further to his kids' fears and anxieties. Calli had always been so good at managing the kids. Now, as he struggled through his emotional nightmare, he felt like he was ill-equipped to address his children's emotional needs.

To most, Caitlin seemed to have managed the trauma best of the two kids. Other than keeping to herself more, her schoolwork, serial friendships, sleeping patterns, and appetite all seemed unaffected. Curt, however, felt like there was a storm brewing in Caitlin. She had his wife's temperament, and like Calli, Caitlin would go silent in the face of stress or difficulty. Rather than a constructive response to stress, this would often lock the pain away temporarily, only to come out later in an unexpected fashion in response to some seemingly minor stimulus. Caitlin was like a volcano, and Curt could see the puffs of smoke signaling a future eruption. Although Curt had tried on occasion to provide Caitlin with an outlet to express her feelings, she would dismiss his efforts in an unconvincing, Calli-like fashion.

Cade wore his anxiety on his sleeve, and the symptoms of the trauma he suffered were immediately apparent. The most striking thing was his need to know what "the plan" was for the days ahead.

"Daddy, what is going to happen tomorrow?" he would ask as Curt prepared him for bed.

"I'm going to wake you up, and then you'll go to school."

"What time will you wake me up?" demanded Cade.

"At 7:10, like always."

"When will the bus pick me up?"

"At 7:50, like always."

"After school, what will happen?"

"You'll come home, and I'll be here."

"Will you fix me a snack?"

"If you want, I can fix you a snack after school."

"And what's going to happen the tomorrow after that?"

asked Cade, who had not yet mastered the phrase "the day after tomorrow."

It was as if Cade needed predictability, the certainty that the day would hold no surprises. Unfortunately, Curt didn't have a crystal ball, and Cade could not tolerate the slightest variation between what was predicted to happen and what would actually occur. Curt learned that defining the coming day's events in too much detail only increased the chances of paralyzing Cade with anxiety due to some perceived variation. However, Cade was rarely satisfied with generalities, so these father and son conversations often turned into bedtime negotiations. In short, until Cade was satisfied with the level of detail, Curt could not sing Cade's lullaby - the National Anthem.

After Calli's murder, Curt rarely slept more than 3 hours a night. He would have trouble getting to sleep, and when he did sleep, he would often sit bolt upright in bed a couple of hours later, feeling terrified and drenched in sweat. His nightmares were sometimes thinly veiled symbolism. Like the night he dreamt about having Thanksgiving dinner with his family. It started as an enjoyable dream. Calli and the kids were there, and all were helping with the dinner preparations. As usual, Curt was responsible for the turkey.

"Curt, better check the turkey," said Calli in the dream.

"Thanks, sweetie," said Curt approaching the oven.

He turned the oven light on and saw the turkey done to perfection. He tried to open the oven door, but it was locked. He then tried to turn off the oven; it wouldn't turn off. He went to the breaker box, and flipping the switch failed to shut off the circuit. He returned to the oven, and he saw that the turkey was starting to burn. He woke up with a start after taking a hammer to the oven window failed, and the turkey started on fire. Other nightmares had little to no symbolism and were more like reliving the actual horror. Like the time he was a firefighter, and upon arriving at a house in flames, he recognized it as his home. Initially, he was magically successful. He was extinguishing fires throughout the house with ease. As he got closer to the bedroom where Calli was, he found it harder to move and the flames resistant to the water. Calli's screams were what usually woke him.

Curt was also not eating well and had lost 15 pounds in a week. He had difficulty concentrating, and more than once, as he was driving to work, he thought about veering into the oncoming path of an 18-wheeler. Each time, it was the thought of his kids that snapped him out of acting on that impulse. After two days at work, Curt, one of two managing partners at a small healthcare consulting company, decided to take an extended leave. He could not concentrate on the job.

Then there was Darius Scott. Darius Scott, the living nightmare that haunted Curt and the kids since that surreal moment when he came out of the flames through the front door proclaiming success. Although Curt would have rather forgotten all about Darius Scott, he couldn't insulate himself from the gnawing questions or those of Caitlin and Cade.

"Who was he?"

"Why did he do it?"

Although the media provided some information about Darius Scott in answer to the first question, no information was available to answer the second. Curt and the kids twisted in the wind trying to make sense of what was senseless. With the mystery of Darius Scott, the fragile state of his kids, and Curt's equally precarious emotional stability, Curt started to see a counselor.

CHAPTER 6

J ackie completed her summer internship at AlzCura, and company executives felt Jackie had shown great promise. They had eyes on grooming her to become a Pharmaceutical Representative after graduation. Even going so far as giving her financial support to pursue her certification through the National Association of Pharmaceutical Representatives during her senior year. In June 2006, with a degree in Communications and Rhetorical Studies from South Temple University and an NAPR certification in hand, AlzCura offered Jackie a job.

The FDA had approved Recallamin after several encouraging studies. AlzCura executives justifiably felt they were sitting on a gold mine. They were hiring as many bright and energetic people as they could to market what they thought was going to be a blockbuster vaccine. Unlike other Alzheimer drugs currently on the market, Recallamin, the company claimed, was the only vaccine that could protect against Alzheimer's. Not just reverse the atrophy of the temporal and parietal lobes of the brain thought to cause it

Magnetic Resonance Imaging studies of people with Alzheimer's, who had taken Recallamin, seemed to confirm the company's claims. In motor and memory tests, patients on Recallamin outperformed patients on the leading Alzheimer drug. Side effects were comparable to the leading drugs, with only a small percentage of patients experiencing nausea, vomiting, diarrhea, insomnia, or headaches. This seemed to be a small price to pay to restore or retain your memory. This meant that the market for Recallamin included not only those already diagnosed with Alzheimer's but also those who had the so-called Alzheimer's gene. While the gene was not reliably predictive of getting Alzheimer's, the company felt that some percentage of people with the gene would want to go on the drug for prevention purposes.

Stu and Jackie's lives suddenly went from predictable stability and routines to a whirlwind of change. In addition to Jackie's job, Stu applied for and received a transfer to NYSDOT Region 1. They moved from their apartment in South Temple to one in Nora. Except for Jackie's parents, who lived in Nora, all the people and places that had defined their lives changed almost overnight. The prospect of Jackie's frequent travel for her job was also looming. Some couples would have considered this period stressful. For Jackie and Stu, the changes were an exciting new chapter that they took on with enthusiasm.

They rented a second-floor unit at the Village Square Apartments, a modest 4-unit structure on Main Street. What it lacked in amenities was made up in proximity to Jackie's parents and downtown. Stu, according to a tradition, once again carried Jackie across the threshold.

On the evening after Jackie's first day at AlzCura, Stu took Jackie for a celebration dinner at the elegant Rue Franklin in Buffalo's theatre district.

"To the best and most beautiful Pharmaceutical Rep in the world," Stu toasted as they clinked their glasses of champagne.

"Thanks, Hon, this is the perfect ending to a perfect day," Jackie exclaimed at their intimate courtyard table.

"No, it isn't perfect, Boo," Stu argued.

"What?" Jackie looked surprised.

"This is the perfect ending to a perfect evening," said Stu as he produced a small box.

"Jackie, will you marry me?"

Jackie's eyes misted, her face flushed, and her hands trembled as she opened the box to reveal a small diamond engagement ring. To Jackie, it looked like the biggest diamond she had ever seen.

"Oh, Stu, yes," she gushed, "Yes, yes, yes, a million times, yes."

"I know it's not very big," Stu began but was cut off by Jackie.

"No, Stu, don't you dare. This is the most beautiful ring, and I am so happy right now." Jackie and Stu got up from the table and embraced, their lips meeting in a long, tender kiss.

"I love you, Jackie."

As Jackie and Stu held their embrace, the other guests in the courtyard recognized the moment, breaking into cheers and shouts of "Congratulations." Returning to their seats, Stu placed the ring on Jackie's trembling finger as the waiter arrived to decant the rest of the Moet Chandon into their glasses. Dinner was almost an after-thought, as they lost themselves in talk of their future as man and wife. They skipped dessert, anxious to get home to consummate their evening with a different kind of dessert.

Over the next few weeks, Jackie proved she was a quick study at AlzCura. While she would not have called herself a whiz in her biological science classes at South Temple, she did have the gift of being a convincing communicator. Given enough information about anything, Jackie could make a compelling case for it. One of her professors at South Temple once described Jackie as being able to "Convince people that red was blue, and blue was red." After shadowing a more seasoned Pharmaceutical Rep for three months, the company sent

Jackie on her first solo sales call to a local health system in the Buffalo area. Jackie spoke with passion about the benefits of Recallamin, and physicians sensed her authenticity and enthusiasm. She was an immediate success. Many doctors detest physician detailing, the one-on-one marketing technique that Pharmaceutical Reps use to influence physician medication choices. That said, physicians seemed to receive Jackie well. Impressed by her early success, the company expanded her territory and the number of accounts for which she was responsible. This meant travel outside the local area.

"Hon?" Jackie asked as she opened the front door of the apartment.

"In the kitchen, Boo."

"Hi, Hon," said Jackie giving Stu a peck on the cheek. "The company has given me a wider territory to cover. They want to send me to Boston next week."

"That's great, Boo. Way to go!" said Stu in his characteristic upbeat and supportive way.

"So, you won't miss me?"

"Nope, not in the least." joked Stu, "I was starting to feel a bit smothered."

Jackie dug her fingers into his ribs, tickling Stu, who almost knocked the pot of soup he was stirring off the stove.

"OK, OK, I'm kidding," said Stu as he rescued the pot of soup. "Boo, it will just be like your away games in volleyball. Except I hope you won't wear those skintight volleyball shorts when you visit the doctors."

"Oh, you liked my volleyball shorts, did you?" she teased, knowing full well how Stu loved the way they accentuated her butt and long legs.

"No, I liked what was in your volleyball shorts," Stu said as he hugged her and reached his hand down to squeeze her left buttock. "Why don't you go put them on, and I'll put dinner on the table."

"I think I'll put them on later," said Jackie, "Something tells me that if I put them on now, we'd never eat dinner."

"You college-educated girls are just too smart."

The next morning Jackie boarded a plane to Boston for her first client visit outside the Buffalo area.

CHAPTER 7

After August 20th, the media had a feeding frenzy trying to unearth information about the monster that allegedly torched a home in Campion and incinerated the mother of two children. To their chagrin, there was precious little known about Darius Dale Scott. He was a 48-year old electrician who lived with his mother in a doublewide trailer near Barry, Maine, about 18 miles from Dracut-Campion. Darius' mother, Elvira, was a former paper mill worker on disability. She spent her days knitting baby booties to sell at markets in and around Barry and occasionally at the Dracut-Campion Farmers Market. Darius' father, Dale, who also worked at the paper mill, had died when Darius was 18 when a 5,000-pound roll of paper fell and crushed him.

Darius' parents lived in Ramsey when he was younger, and he had attended Ramsey Elementary and Ramsey High School. His academic records, or those that remained, as Ramsey High School had closed, were unremarkable. Very few teachers that may have remembered teaching Darius were still around. Those who were could recall him only as "the boy whose father died in that paper mill accident." As is so often the case with people who snap and kill indiscriminately, people reported he was a "quiet boy who kept mostly to himself." Darius didn't play organized sports, he wasn't a cub scout or boy scout, and he didn't go to school functions. Darius' mother, due to failing health, went on disability, sold the house in Ramsey, and bought a trailer in Barry shortly after her husband's death. Elvira collected a small life insurance settlement, but the paper mill avoided her lawsuit claim of negligence when they proved that Dale had been in a restricted area when the accident occurred.

Darius professed to be an electrician, but there was no record of his licensure at the Office of Licensing and Registration in Harlow. His mother indicated that he had done some electrical work around Barry, but if he did, no one owned up to it.

The trailer where Darius lived was in a state of disrepair, and order and cleanliness were obviously not a priority. Pieces of the aluminum siding were pulling away, some of the windows had cracks, and the front screen door was absent a screen. Any steps leading to the front door were gone, replaced by a precarious assemblage of a plastic milk crate on top of a rotting wooden palate. The yard was mostly dirt with a small area of grass that hadn't seen a lawnmower anytime recently. There was a dilapidated Chevy pick-up truck along the side of the trailer that may have been Darius' father's at one time. Parts were missing, and reporters surmised that Darius might have been selling them. A prominent female TV reporter, Leslie Anderson, known for her brazenness, convinced Elvira to open her door one day, promising no cameras. The reporter entered the trailer, scanned the kitchen and living room, and Elvira suddenly realized that the cap the reporter was wearing contained a mini camera. Elvira physically threw the reporter out of the trailer, followed by some choice expletives. This didn't stop the reporter from dusting herself off, fixing her hair, and taping the voice-over and cutaways to accompany the video she had just shot in the trailer.

"The first thing you notice is the smell," said the blond, blue-eyed reporter crinkling her nose for effect.

"Cat urine mixed with overflowing garbage bags. Add to this stench, dirty dishes, and visible grease and grime in the kitchen." The voice-over for when she panned the trailer with her hidden camera.

Then came a journalistic leap and her usual flair for the dramatic.

"It makes one wonder if the neglect seen here extended beyond the household to how Darius Scott was raised and how he lived. The only signs of any connection to the outside world are an old TV, a small radio, and several overflowing stacks of weekly tabloids, a fire hazard amid this stench and squalor."

Leslie didn't care what it took to get a story. In most cases, the presence of a TV camera prevented people from acting out. Very few people want to risk having their bad behavior broadcast on TV. Leslie pushed people's buttons, and she had sent Elvira over the edge. Shortly after they wrapped the voice-overs on the scene, the trailer door slammed open.

"You fucking two-faced bitch, get off my property," Elvira screamed, wielding a shotgun.

Leslie and her crew didn't need any more encouragement. While Elvira was trying to navigate the rickety steps, they ran to their van.

"If you play any of that on the news, my attorney will file a lawsuit against your company and you personally," Elvira warned, taking a cautious step forward. "You'll never see your whoring ass in your fuck me pumps on the TV again. I'm warning you, you motherfu,"

Elvira's words cut off as the crew slammed the van's sliding door shut, and the driver goosed the accelerator sending a plume of dirt and gravel flying. When they looked in the rearview mirror, Elvira was standing in the middle of the road, waving her shotgun in one hand and wildly flipping them the bird with the other. While they could no longer hear her, her mouth was flapping a mile a minute.

"Jeez, that former paper mill worker could make a sailor blush," said the van driver.

Not only did they use the video and voice-overs, but they also embellished it. At the TV station, the production crew thought it would be good to patch in some banter between the reporter and the anchor. They recorded the following to put a bow on the story.

"Leslie," the anchor broke in, "Were you able to ask Ms. Scott about her son or see his room?"

"No, Jeff," recorded Leslie in a deflated manner, "Ms. Scott declined to answer any questions about her son, stating that to do so may compromise his pending trial."

"Thanks, Leslie. Great job as always," beamed Jeff as the camera caught a close-up of Leslie's best smoldering reporter look. The camera then slowly panned out to show Leslie's curves, short skirt, and legs that viewers often mentioned on the TV station's webpage. The nature of the comments revealed a significant difference of opinion about Leslie's appearance, but provocative worked in the TV business, and the ratings proved it. Men watched it and were thrilled, and women watched it and were incensed. Regardless of their reactions, they continued to watch it. Their reactions, often a topic of conversation around the office, just bred more viewers.

Additional information about Darius Scott was difficult, if not impossible, to find. Darius was a ghost. In an age of information overload, he was an anomaly. The only thing that popped up on an Internet search of Darius Dale Scott was his recent arrest in connection with the fire and alleged murder. There seemed to be no link between him and his victim, Calli Barnes.

CHAPTER 8

C urt had chosen his counselor through an Internet search. The name Timothy Darling, LCSW, had caught his eye because he had, on more than a few occasions, called his wife "Calli darling." The bio indicated that Timothy Darling was a former minister specializing in divorce, depression, and grief counseling.

Curt arrived at the two-story Victorian home whose first floor was converted to office space. The front hallway was the waiting room with a few chairs, a table with a lamp that made the area feel less hallway-like, and a small coffee station. On the wall hung a sign: "Please make yourself comfortable." On the floor next to the door marked "Office – Do Not Disturb" was a device that gave off a slight hissing sound, a sound masking device to protect the privacy of conversations in the office. Bare of any reading material, Curt was left to ponder the hissing device and try to figure out how he was going to greet the counselor. Reverend Darling? Mr. Darling? Counselor Darling? None of them seemed comfortable. Before he had a chance to solve this puzzle, the office door opened.

"Mr. Barnes? Come in, my name is Tim," said the counselor as if he had read Curt's mind and magically relieved this initial conflict. Curt, who had hesitated to seek help from a "mental health professional," began to wonder if maybe counselors did have certain mental powers.

"Thanks for seeing me. You can call me Curt," he responded as the two shook hands.

Tim Darling or his office did not fit the pictures Curt had in his head. He had expected an older man in priest-like garb in an office with a crucifix or at least some religious icons. While Tim was elderly, he dressed in beige Dockers, a sweater vest, and comfortable-looking suede Rockport shoes. He looked like someone's friendly grandfather, not a man of the cloth. One wall of the office contained all manner of books on counseling. Posted on another wall hung a graph titled "The Evolution of a Relationship" with a line that looked sort of like the letter S laid on its side across a horizontal plane. The x-axis was labeled "Time," and the y-axis was labeled "Happiness." On the opposite wall was a poster entitled "The Five Stages of Grief." Two comfortable chairs next to a small table with a lamp and a box of Kleenex tissues stood in one corner. Tim motioned for Curt to take a chair that happened to be closest to the Kleenex box.

"Curt, I know you called me about the loss of your wife. Before we begin talking about that, though, I would find it helpful to learn about you and your family before you met your wife. Can you tell me about your experiences growing up, your parents, your brothers, and your sisters?"

Curt was relieved, as just Tim's brief mention of the loss of his wife almost had him reaching for the Kleenex. He talked about how his family had their roots in Blackmore Vale in Dorset County, located in southwest England. The family always liked to say that Barnes meant "warrior," but Curt had dispelled that notion. When he looked into his ancestry, he learned that his forebears were dairy farmers, and his last name originated from "barn." This was not as noble or heroic as the family myth but certainly explained the wholesome and hardworking Barnes descendants. For 45 minutes, Curt was able to talk easily and happily about his childhood, his education, his parents and brother BB, and his career. Nothing about the trajectory of his life could have prepared him for the horror of how he lost

Calli. His upbringing and even his adolescence were surprisingly free of major conflict, loss, or trauma. He was a virgin when it came to emotional turmoil.

"You certainly sound as if you've lived a charmed life up until now. Has there ever been any difficult time before this? Arguments? Disappointments?" explored Tim.

"Not really. I mean, BB and I would get into typical brotherly fights occasionally. We wouldn't get into physical fights, just words. It was usually over something stupid."

"Let's stop here for now," Tim said in his warm manner, "thank you for sharing a part of your life story. I would like to see you twice a week unless you want to see me more frequently."

"No, that sounds fine."

"I know you mentioned not sleeping, losing weight, and not eating well. You must start taking care of yourself. You can't care for your children if you don't care for yourself. Do you have a primary care doctor?"

"Yes, I do."

"Then I would like you to make an appointment to see your doctor about a sleep aid. I think if you can get some good sleep, not only will it help your emotional health, but you may find your appetite returns. Will you do that?"

"Yes, I will."

"Today, OK?"

"Yes, today." Curt felt almost hypnotized as he responded to Tim's guidance. It felt good to have someone laying out a plan for him. He hadn't realized how dysfunctional he had become.

"I have Thursday at 3:30 p.m. open. Would that day and time work for you?"

"Actually, I need to be home then for the kids. Do you have

anything during school hours?"

"Well, not Thursday, but we could do 10:00a.m. on Friday."

"That will work great."

Curt left Tim's office with renewed energy and punched the number of his doctor's office as he walked to the car. His vigor would not last long as he started to realize that his counseling session hadn't even begun to address the demons that had been taunting him. He reached his doctor's office, and the receptionist connected him to his doctor's nurse.

"Hi Jenifer, this is Curt Barnes."

"Oh hi, Mr. Barnes, I'm so sorry for your loss. How can I help you?" Jenifer Henderson was the type of nurse who could almost heal a person by her sunny disposition, palpable compassion, and boundless optimism.

"Thanks, Jenifer. I haven't been able to sleep, and I was wondering if Dr. Huseby could prescribe something for me."

"Dr. Huseby is in with a patient right now, but I'd be happy to ask him the minute he steps out," Jenifer responded while pulling up Curt's record on the computer.

"That would be great, Jenifer. Do you think I need to come in?"

"No, I don't think that will be necessary as long as nothing has changed in your medical history. I'm pulling up your records now," Curt heard the clickety-clack of the keyboard, "It shows here that you're not on any medications now, is that correct?"

"Yes, that's right."

"I'll see if Dr. Huseby can prescribe you something. Our records show that you like to have your medications delivered to Shield's Pharmacy on Center Street. Is that still correct?"

"Yes, that would be great. Thanks, Jenifer."

"My pleasure Mr. Barnes. I or someone else from the office

will get back to you as soon as possible."

A health care management consultant, Curt was more familiar with the failures, inconsistencies, insensitivity, lack of coordination, extensive waits, and errors more the rule than the exception in healthcare. It was for this reason that he felt lucky that his contact with his counselor and his doctor's office seemed to go off without a hitch.

About 30 minutes later, Curt received a call at home from Jenifer, saying that Dr. Huseby had prescribed Ambien 5mg at bedtime as needed.

"And make sure you've got at least one leg in the bed before you take this, Mr. Barnes. Ambien is pretty potent. You don't want to be doing anything but trying to sleep after you take them, OK?

"Yes, thanks, Jenifer."

"Promise?" Jenifer said in a drawn-out sing-song way.

"I promise," said Curt, who suddenly pictured Jenifer, a petite, blue-eyed blond with ample breasts and a million-dollar smile.

"Good. If you run out, Dr. Huseby will probably want to see you. He doesn't like to prescribe Ambien for more than a week or two. Call me if you need anything else, OK?"

"OK, thanks again, Jenifer. You've been great," he said as the phone disconnected, and images of Jenifer continued to dance in his head. He put the phone down and started to cry. In moments, he was wailing. He missed Calli, and not having her around or feeling her body against his at night was causing not only emotional pain but physical pain. He ached for her, and he realized that his fantasies about Jenifer were withdrawal pains from a lack of Calli's touch and closeness. Slowly, his chest stopped heaving, and his tears subsided. He grabbed his keys, anxious to get the Ambien from the Pharmacy so that he could get a good night of sleep. Turning out of the pharmacy and accelerating, he saw an 18-wheeler approaching from the opposite direction.

CHAPTER 9

J ackie's visit to Boston was a success, and she exited the airport towards the passenger pick-up area, anxious to tell Stu all about it. Like clockwork, Stu was there waiting. She got into the car, kissed Stu, and talked about her trip all the way to their apartment.

"Wow, I haven't seen you this stoked about your job since your first day at work," Stu said.

"I feel like I'm helping to give people hope, Hon. Just think, maybe your grandpa and my grandma can be helped. It has been a while since we visited them. Let's go to see them soon, OK?"

"Sure, great idea," said Stu as they got out of the car.

"I'm famished," said Jackie, "those airplane snacks leave something to be desired. What should we make for dinner tonight?"

"I don't know. I'll have to see what we have left in the fridge." As Stu opened the apartment door for Jackie, she noticed the apartment was dark except for a flicker of light coming from the dining area.

Turning the corner, Jackie exclaimed, "A candlelit dinner for me?"

"Just for you," as he pulled her chair out.

"What's the occasion?" she said, stripping off her coat and handing it to Stu. She sat down at the table draped in white, with fine china, glassware, and silverware she didn't recognize, two candles, and a bucket of ice with champagne.

"Your success on the job, my promotion, and our wedding date," listed Stu.

Jackie was speechless as her mouth dropped open. Stu poured her a glass of champagne.

"Well, aren't you going to say something?"

"Ah, ah, I don't know where to begin. You got a promotion?"

"Yep, I'm now a Heavy Equipment Operator," he said while walking to the kitchen.

"That's great! When did that happen? Did you get a raise?"

"They told me yesterday, and yes, I'll make about $6,000 more a year," he said as he carefully pulled out several dishes from the oven.

"Hey, what did you do, toil all day in the kitchen making dinner for me?"

"Wish I could say I did, but it probably wouldn't have come out as nice as this."

"What is it?" said Jackie starting to get up from her chair.

"Ah, ah, ah...just sit that pretty little butt back in the chair. You'll find out soon enough."

"OK, so what's this about a wedding date?"

"I figured we'd celebrate and top off the evening by trying to decide our wedding and honeymoon plans. Or are you too tired from your trip?"

"Tired? With this treatment, I could go all night." Jackie blurted as Stu's raised eyebrows tipped her off to the double entendre, "I mean, stay up all night, Casanova!" she laughed.

"Well, if you can stay up all night, I'll try to stay up all night, too," Stu fired back with a double entendre of his own as he put two serving dishes down on the table.

"Stu, this food looks and smells awesome. Where did you get it?"

"At the Rue Franklin."

"They do take out?"

"No, but they remembered me from our engagement dinner. I asked them for a favor, and they obliged."

Jackie and Stu ate, drank some Champagne, and talked, and cuddled, and drank some more Champagne, and talked some more. The candles had nearly burned down to nubs when they finally completed their wedding and honeymoon plans.

"Do you want to go practice for our honeymoon, Betty Sue?" teased Stu.

"Well, I seem to remember you saying something about staying up all night. We better not waste that," she said, getting up from the couch. Jackie walked toward the bedroom, her hips swinging in an exaggerated runway model manner. Turning her head to flash Stu a wink, she unbuttoned her blouse, dropping it on the floor behind her. Stu, mesmerized by her raw sensuality, sprang up in more ways than one and followed her into the bedroom.

CHAPTER 10

After Darius' arrest, police officers took him to the Emergency Department at Alford County Hospital to treat the 3rd-degree burns on his leg and arms. His bizarre verbalizations and behavior continued in the ED, and the nurse repeatedly shot looks of concern towards the officers as she loosely wrapped his arm and legs with a dressing. Darius would not or could not respond to questions from the nurse or the doctor. He was in his own little world and seemed removed from his body, and the pain his burns would have caused any normal person. After consultation with the ED physician and the Sergeant on duty, police took him under protective custody to the Harlow Psychiatric Institute. There, a psychiatrist evaluated Darius and signed involuntarily commitment papers. Two days later, the psychiatrist filed a court order with the District Court for continued hospitalization beyond the 72-hour initial commitment period.

Darius' case was assigned to Attorney John Dryer, an inexperienced attorney who wasn't thrilled to have a high-profile media circus case. Dryer, however, didn't have a choice. Maine doesn't have a public defender system. Instead, a small cadre of private defense attorneys agree to take cases of indigent clients on a rotation, and it was Dryer's turn. Murder cases in Maine cause great attention, due in large part to their relative infrequency. Bizarre murder cases were even rarer, and this one certainly appeared to meet that criterion. Despite the legal presumption of innocence, in the court of public opinion, Darius was guilty and crazy until proven otherwise. Who hasn't seen the TV footage of witnesses shortly after the fire?

"Jeezum, he came chajin out da dohah somethin wicked," said a crusty old man, roots firmly planted in Maine, "Then he stahts to hollerin' that she wanted to die and that she toll 'im to kill ha."

No less than three witnesses appeared on TV in the first 24 hours following the fire. Each story had a general consistency but enough variation to cause some questions. This could work to his advantage, thought Attorney Dryer.

"I thought he said he wanted to die and that he had set her free. I couldn't figure out what he meant by that," said a stay-at-home Mom from across the street, clutching an infant in her arms.

Another witness said, "He screamed that she wanted to die, and he had set her on fire – simple as that. He had this crazy look sorta like Jack Nicholson in that movie where he sticks his head through the door."

Attorney Dryer and nearly every Mainer with a TV had undoubtedly seen these news clips. How could anyone draw any other conclusion than his client meant to do it and thought he was doing Calli Barnes a favor?

As he drove to the Harlow Psychiatric Institute, he held an internal debate in his head, trying to come up with some scenarios that explained something other than murder.

Maybe it was robbery, and he burned the house down to cover up the evidence? Then why had nothing been found in his possession except the kerosene and propane torch?

Maybe he had stashed the goods outside somewhere. Then why hadn't anything been found yet?

Maybe he just wanted to burn the house down. Then why

did he make all those statements that the neighbors attributed to him? There was also the police report of him saying, "Her fate is sealed. She is finally free." Then his saying "Yes" repeatedly. To Dryer, the phrase "Her fate is sealed" sounded almost biblical. Then the self-congratulatory and affirming "yeses." Maybe his client had some religious or grandiose delusions. Not guilty by reason of insanity?

Maybe he was provoked in some way to take these actions. Perhaps that provocation, whatever it was, could help to prove manslaughter rather than murder. It was doubtful that it could have been self-defense. And who uses kerosene and a torch as their weapon of choice? Usually, self-defense involves a gun or a knife, or a blunt object grabbed in the immediacy of the actual or perceived threat.

Maybe his client didn't start the fire or kill Calli at all. Perhaps she set the fire and, seeing the flames, ran into the house, heard her say she wanted to die, found the kerosene and torch, but couldn't get to Calli. Maybe he tried to save her. Maybe his ramblings were from the trauma of the event.

Dryer forced himself to stop all the questions in his head. He realized all this speculation, before he even had the opportunity to meet and talk with his client, was not helpful. Until additional evidence arrived during pre-trial discovery, he needed to withhold judgment. He needed to trust his legal training and not assume anything.

"Tabula Rasa," Dryer said to himself, "Tabula Rasa," he repeated, using the Latin phrase meaning blank slate to try to clear his mind. It was a technique he used when his mind became over-active and ran ahead of him as it just had.

Harlow Psychiatric Institute (HPI) stood on the banks of the Quantahella River in the shadow of the 150-year old Harlow Asylum for the Criminally Insane (HACI). HACI was an imposing, granite behemoth that had once housed as many as 1,600 patients with mental illness. HACI's storied history ended shortly after the new millennium. HPI was diminutive in comparison to the sprawling HACI facility and had just opened a few years before Darius darkened its doors.

Driving up Arnold Avenue, Dryer could not help but notice the stark contrast between the two facilities. Together they represented both ends of the history and spectrum of psychiatric hospitals in the United States. One building a cold dungeon, pre-dating Sigmund Freud, where slave labor was sold as "therapeutic work" in vast, bucolic fields that had once surrounded it. The other building, the diametric opposite. A small, modern structure, neatly landscaped, with a warm hotel-like lobby atrium, brightened using both natural and artificial lighting and artwork. While it lent a dignity in feel and appearance, it still housed people tortured by thoughts, feelings, and actions that were dark, stormy, and, in the case of Darius, dangerous. Dryer signed in, and a staff member led him through the secure facility to a room where Darius, his client, sat.

"Hello, Mr. Scott, I'm John Dryer," he said, extending his hand, "I'm the attorney assigned to your case."

Darius stared at Dryer's hand but didn't move to shake it. "Her fate is sealed," said Darius softly.

"Darius, may I call you Darius?" asked Dryer.

"Her fate is sealed," said Darius more loudly.

"I need to ask you a few questions, Mr. Scott."

"Her fate is sealed," Darius repeated.

"What do you mean her fate is sealed?"

"She is finally free," said Darius moving his eyes from the table and staring directly into Dryer's eyes for the first time.

Dryer couldn't help but notice the piercing nature of Darius' stare. It was unsettling. It was like there was a tempest brewing behind his eyes. As if he was trying to say more than just the two phrases but couldn't.

"She? Who is she?" probed Dryer.

Darius looked away and then looked back into Dryer's eyes. Darius' eyes had changed. Now a confused look came over him. Like he was searching for an answer to the question but couldn't find it. His lips trembled as if he was trying to say something, but no sound came out. He looked away again and then back. Now again, his unsettling piercing gaze returned.

"She is finally free."

Exasperated, Dryer tried a different tactic to get Darius to say more than his stock answers.

"Mr. Scott, if you don't answer my questions, I can't help you. And if I can't help you, you will be charged with the murder of Calli Barnes."

Darius' eyes lit up with recognition that gave Dryer hope that he was finally getting to his client.

"If you are charged with murder and are found guilty, you will be sentenced to life in prison. Do you understand?"

"I, I, I," stammered Darius. "Her fate is sealed."

"What did you try to say, Darius? Tell me. I what?"

Darius looked down, then away, and then back. Now his eyes seemed distant, like there was no more recognition. Like he didn't even see Dryer in front of him.

"She is finally free."

Dryer couldn't hide his frustration.

"Darius," he shouted while simultaneously slamming his hand down on the table. "If you don't talk with me, they are going to say you murdered Calli Barnes by setting a fire in her home."

Darius tensed in reaction to Dryer's aggressive action. Now his eyes blazed with anger that made Dryer fearful that he had unleashed some monster. Dryer started to look around for his exit strategy should Darius act on the violence that was in his eyes.

"I... will burn her with my fire," said Darius in a loud, angry, and punctuated manner that did nothing to ease Dryer's increasing fear.

He felt that he had pushed Darius too far, and while he had managed to drag new words from Darius' lips, he didn't dare push further.

"Thank you, Mr. Scott," Dryer said, his open hands, palms down moving in a manner meant to convey a request for Darius to calm down, "I think that's enough for today. I will leave my contact information with the staff if you want to get a hold of me, OK?"

Darius' expression changed again to the confused, distant gaze. He was gone, and Dryer had no interest in staying to see if the monster he had glimpsed would return. Dryer, shaken by the experience, wobbled a little as he stood up. His staff escort arrived and guided him back to the lobby, where he made an appointment to speak with Darius' psychiatrist the next day. As he drove away, Dryer couldn't help but think of the dissonance between the bright, sunny new psychiatric center and the gloominess he felt leaving it. As he drove by HACI, he realized that its external appearance better represented what he felt.

CHAPTER 11

C urt arrived home with Ambien in hand, having resisted once more the urge to kiss the grill of a 40-ton Kenworth that had barreled by him on his drive. He wished he could take a pill now, but Caitlin and Cade would be arriving home from school soon. Looking at the tablets, he couldn't imagine how such a tiny pill could induce sleep as quickly as Jenifer had suggested. His phone rang, interrupting a potential return daydream about the buxom blond nurse.

"Hello, this is the District Attorney's office in Campion," said the female caller, "Is this Mr. Curt Barnes?"

"Yes, it is," he responded, wondering why the DA's office was calling him.

"The DA would like to set up a time to meet with you regarding the Mr. Scott case."

"Mr. Scott?" said Curt momentarily, confused. He had blocked Darius Scott out of his mind and didn't at first recognize the caller's formal reference to him.

"Mr. Darius Scott," said the caller.

"Oh, yes, yes, I'm sorry, of course. When would he like to see me?"

"Tomorrow at either 1 p.m. or 3 p.m., he's in court in the morning."

"1 p.m. will be fine."

"Thank you, Mr. Barnes. We will see you tomorrow at 1 p.m. then. Do you know where our office is located?"

"Yes, I do. Thanks."

A shadow seemed to come over him as he ended the call. He felt like he was making strides all day to recover from the nightmare, but this call set him back a notch or two. He had completely blanked out that he might need to come face-to-face with his wife's killer. It was hard enough to bear the loss of his wife, manage the needs of his kids, and prepare to return to work. As he wrestled with the dark cloud that was Darius Scott, he heard the familiar squeal of brakes that signaled the arrival of Caitlin and Cade's school bus.

"Hi guys, how was your day?" said Curt trying to sound up-beat and interested.

"It was okay," said both kids in a less than convincing fashion. Caitlin turned into her room, and Cade flipped on the TV.

"Don't you want to go to the playground Cade?"

"No, I just want to watch TV."

Curt wondered if he was still suffering from the fear of the bear that he had planted in Cade's head.

"I'll go down there with you and spin you," trying to entice his son to take him up on the offer.

"No thanks," Cade replied, his eyes staring almost trance-like at the TV.

"How about a snack?"

Cade didn't reply.

"Cade?"

Cade was lost in the TV program and had tuned out his father. Curt walked to Caitlin's room and knocked on the door.

"Caitlin, do you want a snack?" he said, poking his head into her room.

"No thanks, Dad," replied Caitlin as she sat on the floor, playing with her Breyer horse set.

"Is everything okay?"

"Yep," she responded, again not as convincingly as Curt would have liked.

Caitlin tended to go to silence when she was angry or depressed – a trait that Calli had that drove Curt insane. Curt wanted to talk things out. His wife and daughter seemed to need to let things simmer or eventually boil over on their own schedule. This was something Curt could never get comfortable with, but he was determined not to push Caitlin as he used to push Calli. He had learned that doing so just made things worse. Curt couldn't help but realize that just as he was suffering and in need of help, his kids were too. He made a mental note to talk to Tim on Friday about finding support for the kids.

The kids picked disinterestedly at their dinner despite it being one of their favorites – macaroni and cheese with sliced-up hot dogs. He couldn't even interest them in Raspberry Rumble ice cream. When they had lived in their house, the kids loved to greet the food truck delivery man when he pulled into their driveway every other week. They would fight over the catalog and Curt, or Calli would frequently have to veto their extensive food choices. Then the kids would fight over who put the little orange reminder sticker on the calendar. Raspberry Rumble was the one sinful pleasure they always allowed. Perhaps more than anything, Curt knew, by their declining the ice cream, that there was something wrong with the kids. Shortly after dinner, both Caitlin and Cade went to their rooms. When Curt went to check on them, they were both sound asleep. He wished he could fall asleep so quickly, but this just heightened his concern for the kids. They had never gone to bed willingly or easily. He didn't need to be a psychiatrist to know they were depressed.

Although it was only 8 p.m., Curt got ready for bed. True to his promise to Jenifer, he took the little white pill after he got into bed. Resting his head on the pillow, he cracked open the latest issue of Healthcare Executive, determined to start preparing himself for his return to work. He started reading an article about leveraging innovations in technology.

Curt opened his eyes and had to shield them from the glare of the lamp on his nightstand. Something was poking him in the side, and he found a slightly bent issue of Healthcare Executive amidst the covers. As his eyes adjusted to the light, he glanced at his alarm clock. It read 6:14. Still a bit foggy from waking up in a lit room, he tried to determine if it was morning or night. He thumbed his cell phone, and the date and time sprang to life. It was morning, and he had slept 10 hours. If he had read anything in the magazine, he didn't recall it. Somewhat refreshed, he had slept more than he had in the previous three days. His sleep had also been free of nightmares. He was about to christen Ambien as the new wonder drug when he realized that the kids had to get ready for school. He went to the bathroom and splashed his face with cold water.

"Good morning beautiful, how was your night?" Curt sang the first few lines of Caitlin's favorite song by Steve Holy. It never failed to wake her and put a smile on her face. Thankfully, this morning was no different.

"Cade, time to get up for school," Curt called from the kitchen as he started to fix the kids' breakfast.

"Do you want scrambled eggs or chocolate chip waffles for breakfast?"

Surprisingly, they both selected chocolate chip waffles. It was a rare day when their choices were unanimous. Curt began to wonder if maybe he was just overreacting to the kids' behavior last night. Maybe they, like him, just needed a good night's sleep. The kids' early morning preparations were efficient, and without a hitch, they boarded the school bus at 7:15

a.m.

The District Attorney's office was in the Alford County Building, a red brick building with narrow circle top windows guarded by a Civil War memorial erected 125 years ago. A white clock-tower cupola with a copper dome topped with a weathervane was its distinguishing feature. As Curt climbed the stairs, his stomach did flip-flops, anxious that he would have to relive the horror of that day, now two weeks ago to the day. The receptionist who had presumably called him the previous day greeted him as he opened the office door.

"Hi, I'm Curt Barnes, here to see District Attorney Wydman."

"OK, Mr. Wydman will be with you shortly. Please have a seat," she said, gesturing to the waiting area.

District Attorney William Wydman had a reputation for being tough but fair. In grade school, kids used to tease him by purposely mispronouncing his name.

"Weed-Man, Weed-Man, Hey, got any Weed-Man?" they would chant.

The taunting went on for weeks. It scarred him so emotionally that whenever someone would mispronounce his name now, his eyes would flash, and with teeth gritted, he would correct them. Although he had been a gifted athlete in high school, the years had not been kind to him. Ironically, as if giving everyone a visual cue, his body now resembled the proper pronunciation of his last name – wide man.

"Mr. Barnes," called the receptionist, "Mr. Wydman will see you now."

DA Wydman stood up from his mammoth desk as Curt entered. After shaking hands, he directed Curt to a chair at a small table in the corner of the office. On the table lay a legal-size file.

"How are you doing, Mr. Barnes?" asked the DA

"Fine," said Curt out of habit, not expecting this would be the DA's first question.

"Fine, really, Mr. Barnes?" the DA questioned.

"Well, er, not really. I guess I say that because I don't want to go into how I really feel. And please, call me Curt."

"I can understand that, Curt. You've been through a very tough time."

Curt was beginning to wonder if the DA had forgotten that he was a legal counselor, not his mental health counselor.

"Are you doing things to take care of yourself?" the DA continued, "The legal process could take months, and I'm sure your children need you more than ever."

"Yes, I am," Curt said, still not sure where this was going, "I'm seeing a counselor, and I'm taking sleeping pills to help me sleep."

"Good," said Wydman, "and the kids?"

"I'm sorry, the kids?" Curt had expected to talk about Darius Scott, not his kids.

"How are your kids doing?" the DA amplified.

"Well, I'm going to talk with my counselor this Friday about what services might be available for them."

"You mean no one from County Social Services has contacted you yet?" Wydman bellowed.

"No, I didn't know they were supposed to."

"Jeezum crow, what the hell do we have a Grief Counseling program for, if they can't even deploy for one of the most heinous crimes in Central Maine in years, maybe decades." Wydman exploded.

Curt, not knowing what to say, sat silent while DA Wydman fumed.

"I'm sorry, I shouldn't get so worked up, but damn it, you and your kids should have had our support the minute after, not when I meet with you two frickin' weeks afterward."

Curt still didn't know what to say. Although he was pleasantly surprised that a State official had initially taken more interest in him and his kids than in prosecuting the case.

"Ok, Curt, I'm not going to make you wait for them to get their heads out of their asses," he said while walking to his desk and digging in one of the drawers.

"There's a grief support group for kids in Portland," he continued.

The DA found a dog-eared pamphlet and handed it to Curt.

"You can ask your counselor about it if you wish, but if they were my kids, I'd call them today and arrange for them to attend. I know it's a bit of a drive, but it's worth it. Besides, you can take the kids to Buckaroo Barn & Steakhouse near the Mall afterward. Have you ever been there?"

"Yes, we have. The kids love it."

"I love that talking moose. And the little raccoon with glowing red eyes that pokes his head out of the barrel. I was there once and almost had a heart attack when that li'l critter popped out," laughed the DA.

Curt was beginning to wonder if they would ever get to Darius Scott. He never thought the meeting with the DA would result in referrals to a support group and a restaurant.

"Okay, well, we better get down to business," said the DA as if reading Curt's mind.

For the next 30 minutes, the DA questioned Curt about his recollection of the events of August 20th. Whether he had any possible leads as to who Darius Scott was or why he would have acted as he did. The questions necessarily touched upon some sensitive topics, queries that had infuriated him previously when investigators and police had asked. Somehow, the strange preface to his meeting with the DA made it easier for Curt to answer the questions and maintain control. He even found himself laughing at DA Wydman's question about whether Calli might have been seeing Darius Scott secretly. There were no problems in the marriage. He didn't own a propane torch or a can of kerosene. The long and the short of it was that Curt had never seen Darius Scott before, didn't think Calli knew him, and didn't believe Calli had a death wish. In Curt's mind, Darius Scott was crazy and randomly chose his house to torch.

Curt left DA Wydman's office with no more answers about Darius Scott but unexpected help for Caitlin and Cade. He called the number on the pamphlet, and a pleasant voice greeted him.

"Children's Support Group of Portland, this is Kelly. May I help you?"

"Yes, my name is Curt Barnes. I was wondering what programs you might have for my two children."

"Oh, Mr. Barnes, I'm so sorry for your loss. We'd be happy to help Caitlin and Cade."

Curt was initially shocked when Kelly used his children's names. Then he realized that his family was the unfortunate victim of the media's blitzkrieg on "the bizarre and gruesome tragedy in Campion." You couldn't watch TV, listen to the radio, read a newspaper, or order a donut and coffee at the local coffee shop without hearing the phrase.

"Thank you, Kelly," Curt said, recovering from the surprise, "I just met with District Attorney Wydman, and he recommended I contact you."

"Oh, no problem, Mr. Barnes, how old are Caitlin and Cade?"

"Caitlin will turn 8 in two weeks, and Cade just turned 6."

"OK perfect," Kelly said, "We offer group counseling. Caitlin and Cade would be in the 6 to 9-year-old group. Groups are 2 hours and meet weekly for 12 weeks. The next group starts on Friday, November 7th."

"Oh, I was hoping for something sooner," Curt said dejectedly.

"I'm sorry, Mr. Barnes," Kelly said, "but it wouldn't be fair to Caitlin and Cade to start them in the middle of a group. If you think they need support sooner, perhaps your local Social Service agency can help you. I can get you their number if you'd like, Mr. Barnes," she said in her ever helpful and pleasant manner.

Curt was not excited about the proposition of having to call the agency that had their "heads up their asses," as DA Wydman had put it so graphically. His surprise at Kelly's early recognition had also transformed into admiration for how comforting, reassuring, and genuine she seemed. Having worked in healthcare for 15 years, he marveled at the wide variation in the interpersonal skills of people in the so-called "helping professions."

"No, no, I think my kids can wait until November, Kelly. Would they be in the same group?"

"Yes, unless there is a specific reason you think they can't be. We find it helpful for siblings to be together. Do you have any other questions?"

"Do you offer any individual counseling?"

"On an as-needed basis. We assess the children while they are in their group, and if we think they may benefit from individual sessions, we will let you know. Most of the time, children seem only to need group. Anything else?"

"No, Kelly, thanks, you've been great. What do I need to do to get them into the November 7th group?"

"I just need to take some basic information from you, and you will be all set."

Curt supplied the necessary information. As he turned into the driveway to the Terrace Hill apartments, he felt a sense of relief that he would soon be providing Caitlin and Cade with some professional support. As he climbed the three flights of stairs to the apartment, he also began to think that it was time for him to get back to work.

CHAPTER 12

When their friends and family heard that Jackie and Stu had set January 27 as their wedding date, they thought that they had lost their marbles.

"Only a heavy equipment operator," said one of Stu's friends, "would want his wedding limousine to be a snowplow!"

While most of their friends and family thought otherwise, their reasoning was quite practical.

"Mom," Jackie explained, "there are a ton of good reasons."

"Name one," Doris said with skepticism.

"I can do better than that; I'll name five. First, we won't have any problem getting the reception hall and caterer we want. Second, all the costs associated with the wedding are lower at that time of year. Not to mention, travel and lodging costs will be cheaper for our friends that need to come here. Third, it's the weekend before the Super Bowl, which is a slow sports weekend, so no one will have anything better to do. If the Bills get into the Super Bowl by some miracle, it would be a great pre-Super Bowl party. Fourth, we want to honeymoon in Arizona, where it's usually 70-degrees at that time of year. Fifth, fifth, well, okay, I can only name four."

"Impressive," exclaimed Doris, "you two really have thought about this. I just hope we don't have a blizzard that weekend."

The seven months leading up to their wedding date flew by. Stu's new job kept him busy, and it wasn't uncommon for him to work 10 to 12-hour days. He didn't mind the extra hours as it allowed him to squirrel away a little extra cash for the honeymoon. Jackie was no less busy, traveling every week to meet clients in the Northeast. They reserved weekends for making progress on the wedding and honeymoon arrangements. One of their first stops was Saint Paul Church, where Jackie introduced Stu to Father Woznewski.

"It's good to meet you, Stuart," said Father formally, "I have known Jacqueline since she was our star center on the Girls Basketball team. That would have been in..." he paused in thought.

"1996, Father," Jackie completed his sentence.

"Yes, yes, 1996, thank you, dear. You should have seen her take it to St. Bernadette's in the championship. You should take Stuart to the school and show him the team picture and trophy in the trophy case."

"I'd love to see that," Stu said with a hint of sarcasm that earned him a firm poke in the ribs from Jackie.

"Father, we were hoping that you would be able to marry us this coming January."

"It would be my honor, dear," Father replied, "Call Mary in the rectory on Monday and make sure the church and I'm available. You're a lucky man Stuart."

"Oh, I know that, Father. She's my dream come true," he said, earning back some points with his fiancé.

Father walked them from the twin-spired church to the simple rectangular red brick school built nearly 90 years earlier. He opened the door and invited Jackie and Stu to take their time down memory lane, asking that they make sure they pulled the door locked when they left.

"Jeez, this place hasn't changed a bit," said Jackie, "it's just like I left it 15 years ago."

"Is it me, or do all Catholic grade schools smell like this?" said Stu, "I wonder if heaven is going to smell like this?"

They walked down the long corridor as Jackie reminisced about some of her favorite and least favorite teachers. When they arrived at the trophy case, Jackie quizzed Stu.

"See if you can find me," she challenged.

"That's easy, there you are," pointing to a short, stocky girl with frizzy hair.

"I guess you didn't want to marry me after all," she said while simultaneously punching him in the shoulder, "That was the catcher on the softball team. Try again, and you better get it right or no Betty Sue for a month!"

"In that case, that's you right there," he said, pointing to the tallest girl in the basketball team photo, "I'd know those sexy legs anywhere."

"I was like 13!"

"Yes, and you were hot even then," to which Jackie checked him with her hip. He exaggeratingly flung himself into the lockers on the other side of the hall for effect. The crash echoed down the deserted corridor.

"I'm going to get Father, so you can confess to having impure thoughts about an underage girl."

"Bless me, father, for I have sinned," recited Stu, "it has been ten years since my last confession. Father, I had impure thoughts about Jackie Selaney. I couldn't help it; I mean, look at her. Wouldn't you like to tap that?"

"Stuart Thomas Deno, you're going straight to hell!"

"And you're the sexy little devil who is sending me there." He said, grabbing her and pulling her into him. "Ever think you'd make out with your future husband in this hallway?"

They kissed long and deep. They had been a couple for four years, and somehow, the playfulness and the romance never seemed to get old.

"Stop," she said, taking a deep breath and pushing him back, "I don't want Father to catch us. He'd excommunicate us before we even make it to the altar!"

They continued their tour, visiting the gym. Jackie couldn't believe how small the gym seemed. She remembered her first game there and how big and overwhelming the venue and the crowd had been. She picked up a stray basketball. Stu feigned defending her. She easily drove past him and completed the lay-up.

"We'd better hit the road if we're going to visit your Grandpa," Jackie said, tossing the ball to Stu.

"He shoots, he scor..." Stu said while missing the basket entirely.

"Airball, airball," Jackie taunted, "better stick to football."

They left Jackie's grade school memories and headed East towards Barron, two and a half hours away. They stopped outside Rochester for lunch and arrived at Meadow Ridge, an assisted living and memory care residence in Stu's hometown. The residence was in a planned community. Unlike the rest of Barron, which was small-town quaint, Meadow Ridge and the newly built executive style homes in the development nestled amongst acres of wooded area, expansive greenery, and miles of walking trails. It was remote, quiet, and safe.

Stu's grandpa, Ernest Deno, had come to Meadow Ridge's Assisted Living residence three years ago, shortly after his wife had died. The initial transition was rocky, but after about a month, he had made friends and adjusted well. One night, about a year ago, Grandpa Ernie decided to take a walk. While Assisted Living residents could take walks during the day, this walk occurred at 2:00 a.m. Grandpa Ernie somehow slipped out the front door and walked to Royal Road no more than

200 yards from the residence. Neighbors called the police as Grandpa Ernie was pounding on the door of a home that was unoccupied, screaming for Emma to let him in. The neighbors thought Emma must have been Grandpa Ernie's wife. When the family members heard about the episode, they knew it signaled the need to move Grandpa to the locked Memory Care residence. Grandma Shirl (short for Shirley) had been dead for almost five years, and no one in the family had any recollection of Grandpa ever knowing an Emma. It was fortunate that Grandpa hadn't walked across Williams Parkway and into the wooded area beyond. What had once seemed remote and safe now became remote and dangerous.

Jackie and Stu got out of the car and approached the new yellow with white trim facility. The receptionist let them into the locked Memory Care unit. "Hi Grandpa Ernie," Jackie said animatedly while bending to hug him as he sat in his wheelchair. Since Grandpa Ernie's "escape," his physical abilities had declined dramatically, to the point that he became wheelchairbound.

"Hi," he tried to respond with equal enthusiasm, his eyes betraying his voice as they searched for some hint of recognition.

"Hi," he tried again, once again failing to find a name.

"Hi, Grandpa," said Stu, also bending to hug him.

As his eyes slowly shifted away from Jackie to Stu, his eyes lit up.

"I know you, "Grandpa said, "Art, Art, how are you doing, son."

"I'm Stu, Grandpa," corrected Stu, "I'm Art's son."

"So, how's the dairy business?" said Grandpa, impervious to Stu's correction.

"All the cows are utterly fantastic," joked Stu knowing that Grandpa probably wouldn't get it.

"Good, good, good," Grandpa trailed off, distracted by the woman next to Stu.

"Who are you?" Grandpa asked, pointing at Jackie.

"I'm Jackie, Grandpa."

"She's my fiancé Grandpa," Stu added.

"You're getting married?" asked Grandpa.

"Yes, Grandpa, we're getting married," Stu said, finally glad that he understood something.

"Well, she's a beautiful girl Art. Does she know anything about the dairy business?"

When it was clear that Grandpa Ernie wasn't going to make the connections, Jackie and Stu tried to get him to talk about himself.

"Grandpa Ernie, what have you been doing today?"

"Well, I'm stuck here in this hospital. They won't let me go to work," he said, visibly upset.

"Grandpa, this is your home now, not a hospital," Stu tried to explain.

Grandpa shot Stu a look that could kill, eyes blazing. He huffed and then looked away. Then he turned back to look at Stu. All the anger had left his eyes, replaced with a blank stare.

"Who is she?" he repeated, pointing at Jackie.

"It's exercise time," announced a perky brunette dressed in a close-fitting jogging suit. "Come on, everyone, to the recreation room for exercises." Her name tag read "Elaine, Recreational Therapist."

Jackie and Stu wheeled Grandpa Ernie into the recreation room. Elaine asked the residents to stretch as she reached up into the air repeatedly with her right hand, then her left, each time her tee-shirt lifting to expose a trim, well-tanned midriff. Then Elaine led them in sitting exercises in time to such hits as "The Hokey Pokey" and "The Chicken Song." To Jackie

69

and Stu's surprise, Grandpa Ernie was quite attentive. He tried his best to lift his legs, clap his hands, and do whatever Elaine asked, especially when she'd bounce over near him.

"Come on, Ernie, show me how to do it. I know you can do it," Elaine said in such a way that Jackie and Stu looked at each other and simultaneously said under their breath, "Cheerleader."

In between exercise songs, Jackie and Stu said goodbye to Grandpa Ernie, who strained to look around them to catch Elaine bending over the Compact Disc player.

"Well, I guess he hasn't lost all of his faculties," said Stu as they exited.

"It's so sad, Stu. He doesn't even know us," Jackie said mournfully.

"Yeah, it's weird that he thinks I'm his son. I wonder what he'd think if Dad and I showed up together?"

"I should talk to his doctor about putting him on Recallamin," Jackie said.

"Does it work for someone that far gone?" Stu asked.

"I don't know. The studies said it worked with mild and moderate Alzheimer's, and to prevent Alzheimer's in those with the Alzheimer gene."

"The Alzheimer gene?" Stu looked at her quizzically.

"Yeah, there's a test now for whether you have a gene that could trigger Alzheimer's. If you have the gene, it doesn't mean you will necessarily get Alzheimer's, but your chances are better. Recallamin protects those parts of the brain that deteriorate, which eventually leads to Alzheimer's."

"Wow, I think we should buy stock," Stu said.

"Already done, Hon," said Jackie, "the company offers a stock purchase program, and I signed up." It was one of the few times Jackie "talked shop" with Stu. One of the great things about their relationship was that they rarely talked about their work. Sure, there were times, usually of great joy or great frustration, when they would talk about work. For the most part, however, their relationship was a haven away from their work. An oasis where the stresses of work melted away.

CHAPTER 13

Public defender Dryer was more optimistic on this, his second trip to the Harlow Psychiatric Institute. He had an appointment to meet with Dr. Sheldon Lang, the psychiatrist who was treating Darius Scott. He hoped that Dr. Lang had been more successful in extracting information from Darius. Otherwise, it was going to be very difficult to defend his client.

Dr. Sheldon Lang was a transplant from New York City who, ten years earlier, decided to escape the rat race of the big city for Maine, where he and his family had a summer home. While he was admittedly approaching the twilight of his professional career, Dr. Lang had seen it all. He was a respected psychiatrist with a gift of treatment success with some of the most challenging patients. He was easy to talk to and known informally amongst patients and staff as "Uncle Sheldon." Out of respect, none of the patients or staff would ever think to call him this to his face. Something about his communication style just extracted information and feelings that others could never tap.

"Come in," called Dr. Lang in response to the knock on his office door.

"Dr. Lang, I have Attorney Dryer here to see you about Mr. Scott," said his administrative assistant poking her head in the door.

"Please, Shelly, send him in," Dr. Lang responded as he pulled away from his desk.

"Mr. Dryer, the doctor will see you now," Shelly said in a practiced and inviting way.

"Mr. Dryer, welcome," said Dr. Lang closing the gap and shaking Dryer's hand as he entered the office.

"Good morning Dr. Lang."

"Can we offer you some coffee or tea, perhaps?" offered Dr. Lang.

"Thank you. Coffee would be great."

"How do you take your coffee, Mr. Dryer," asked Shelly from the door.

"Black, please," responded Dryer noticing how well Dr. Lang and Shelly seemed to choreograph this arrival process.

"Please make yourself comfortable, Mr. Dryer," Dr. Lang motioned to an inviting leather chair.

"Thank you," Dryer said as Dr. Lang stationed himself in the twin leather chair across from him.

"How can I help you today, Mr. Dryer?"

"I'm Darius Scott's attorney," said Dryer, "unfortunately, my first visit with Mr. Scott was not as productive as I would have liked."

"Tell me more," said Dr. Lang using a technique he frequently employed with his patients.

"Well, he just kept repeating the same two phrases," Dryer said, interrupted by a soft knock on the door.

Shelly announced herself and brought Dryer his coffee, exiting quickly and quietly.

"Continue, Mr. Dryer," prompted Dr. Lang.

"As I said, he just repeated the same two phrases: 'Her fate is sealed' and 'she is finally free.' When I pressed him, he said,

'I will burn her with my fire.'"

"Well, perhaps you have chosen the wrong career, Mr. Dryer," said Dr. Lang as Dryer took a sip of his coffee and looked up with a surprised, questioning look. "You got more out of him than I have," divulged Dr. Lang. "I hadn't heard the 'I will burn her with my fire' phrase and that he said 'I,' well that gives me some hope."

"Do you have any idea what's going on with Mr. Scott? I mean, is he insane?"

"Well, we prefer to say mentally ill, but without additional information, I can't say at this point. I'm going to have additional lab tests done, have our psychologist do some psychometric testing, and continue to meet with him."

"From the police report, it almost sounded like he thought he had been chosen to kill Calli Barnes, almost like some religious delusion," probed Dryer.

"Well, schizophrenia with religious delusions or hallucinations had crossed my mind. He does look at times like he may be seeing or hearing things. He turns his head, and his eyes get that vacant, far-away stare that sometimes is a telltale sign of visual or auditory hallucinations. The problem is that he has had no psychiatric history that I can find. Schizophrenia usually exhibits itself in adolescence or young adulthood. It would be exceedingly rare to have a first episode of schizophrenia in a 48-year old man."

"Well, what else could it be?" asked Dryer.

"That's hard to say. It could be something drug-induced, although the tox screen didn't reveal any of the typical drugs associated with such behavior. It could be a dissociative fugue. It could be any number of other psychiatric disorders. It could be something organic. We don't have enough information at this point."

Dryer left Dr. Lang's office once again, frustrated by the

mystery that was Darius Scott. He tried to find solace in the few facts that Dr. Lang was able to supply. Darius' actions weren't drug-induced, and he didn't have a psychiatric history. Dryer could also stop beating himself up about his first meeting with Darius, having extracted more information out of him than Dr. Lang had.

As Dryer got into his car, he committed to scheduling another meeting with Darius. His cell phone rang, and his assistant notified him that the pretrial discovery information had arrived. His hope reignited, he negotiated the chaotic traffic circles a little faster and recklessly than usual. Arriving at his office, he asked his assistant to schedule another meeting with Darius Scott. In return, she handed him a large envelope.

Attorney Dryer poured over the pretrial evidence gathered by investigators. The initial reports were witness statements and police reports that he had already received. Fire investigators had done their best to document the scene with photos, videos, and drawings. The gruesome images of Calli in a pugilistic pose were hard to look at and didn't seem to provide many clues to Dryer's untrained eye. He gained a newfound respect for fire investigators as he read the report. They provided more details than Dryer would have guessed possible.

The incinerated bedroom, Calli Barne's charred remains, as well as firefighter's efforts to suppress the fire, had destroyed some of the potential evidence. Although most of Calli's body was charred black, a bracelet-like pattern of tissue on her wrists and ankles and natural fibers different from her clothing led investigators to conclude that she was bound to the bed by her arms and legs in a spread-eagle fashion. Investigators determined from the delicate, feathery gray ashes that the rope used was made of cotton, linen, or sisal. Synthetic rope materials would have melted into a hard, black substance. The investigators believed that only the center of the mattress where Calli's back and buttocks made contact was doused with a line of kerosene. This was because the skin on her back and buttocks were as charred as the rest of her body. Typically, the tissue in contact with a surface, like a bed mattress, in this case, would not be as burned as severely as those parts of the body, not in touch with the surface. What police initially thought were lacerations on her body and blunt force trauma to her head turned out to be rupturing of the skin and fracturing of the skull due to heat. Burn patterns on Calli's arms suggested that Darius burned her several times with the torch before applying the accelerant. Darius had not just doused Calli with kerosene and then set her on fire. He had been purposeful and precise, using the accelerant and lighting it in three stages, splashing first her legs, then her arms, and finally, her torso and head. He made sure to soak the restraints, so they eventually released. Calli's death had not come quickly. The sequence of the fire setting guaranteed maximum pain. Investigators calculated that Calli had writhed in agony for 2 to 3 minutes until she succumbed to the flames that finally engulfed her head. Though impressed by the detail investigators had included in the report, it did little to illuminate anything except that Calli had died a horrible death. The nagging questions about why Darius had done it and what connection, if any, existed between Darius and Calli were unanswered. Feeling queasy from the graphic description of how Calli Barnes died, he set the fire investigation and the autopsy report aside in favor of something less descriptive - Darius' bank account information.

Dryer perused the 12-month checking account details. It didn't take long. Darius' checking account activity was extremely sparse. Dryer started to feel the frustration growing as he flipped through the first few pages finding nothing of interest from September 2007 through July 2008. He flipped the page to August 2008, the last page in the report, the month Calli Barnes died. Dryer noted that Darius had a balance of $126.43 on August 29, 2008. There were only two entries for August. The first charge was from the 15th for $8.67 to Harrington's Pizza in Barry. The next entry made Dryer feel like someone had punched him in the stomach – hard. A charge on August 19th, the day before Calli's death, for $39.09 at Lester's Home Improvement in Campion. Dryer's mind flipped through all the new questions this entry raised. Did Calli Barnes work on August 19th? If she did, did she have contact with Darius Scott? Could that contact have been the genesis of their fatal connection just 24 hours later? What did he buy? He needed to call Lester's. This was the first shred of evidence that potentially tied Darius to Calli in something other than random chance.

CHAPTER 14

With the help of Ambien, Curt strung together three consecutive nights of healthy sleep. It was not without one night of drama, however. Curt had made the mistake of answering his cell phone one evening when BB had called shortly after he had taken his Ambien.

"Hi, big brother," announced BB, "just callin' to see how you are doing?"

"Thanks, li'l brother, I think things are looking up.

"Sounds good. How are the kids?"

"They're doing OK. Going to school and hair is arguing like spaghetti." Curt said, his words beginning to slur.

"Curt? Are you alright?" BB said, concerned.

"Id's awwright, the angels think id's snowflakes."

"Curt? Are you drunk?" said BB. "Curt? Curt?"

Curt had fallen asleep and didn't realize the extent to which his nonsensical responses had sent BB into action. While Curt was in la-la land, BB had hopped in his car and drove to the apartment. When ringing the doorbell and pounding on the door didn't produce results, he knocked on the window to Caitlin's room. Initially startled and scared, she had considered crawling under her bed. When she realized that it was her Uncle BB, she went and opened the door for him.

Cade heard the commotion and came out of his room, rubbing his eyes and shielding them from the glow of the kitchen light. BB, as concerned as he was, didn't want to startle the kids anymore and calmly told them to go back to their bedrooms. However, they wouldn't go to their rooms without an explanation. Thinking fast, he said that their father had asked him to come over, but he must have fallen asleep. Satisfied, they trudged off to their rooms.

As BB approached Curt's bedroom, his fear was in full bloom. Barged into the room, he reached for the light switch, only to realize that Curt's bedside lamp was on. He called Curt's name in a loud, more panicked way than he intended. Curt didn't budge. His cellphone had fallen on the floor, and he was snoring up a storm. Still breathing was a good sign, thought BB. He shook Curt by the shoulders once, nothing. Then again. Still nothing. It stopped the snoring, but not the sleep. BB smelled for alcohol on Curt's breath and detected nothing except the faint hint of Italian spices mixed with a minty toothpaste smell. He then saw a prescription bottle on the nightstand and a half-empty glass of water. He picked up the prescription bottle and read, "Zolpidem, one 5mg pill as needed for sleep". The warning labels cautioned against operating heavy machinery and drinking alcohol. Another label recommended taking the medication after a meal.

Had it not been for the warning labels and Curt's breathing, BB would have probably called 911. As he sat at the bedside, he called Michelle and asked her to do an internet search on Zolpidem. When Michelle read that bizarre verbalizations were one of the side effects, BB grew less concerned. Had Michelle stopped there, BB probably would have left and gone home. Michelle continued to read the litany of side effects. When she learned about instances of sleep eating and sleep-driving, BB decided to stay the night. Ironically, while Curt got a good night's sleep, BB had a restless night on Curt's couch.

"What in the hell are you doing here, BB?" Curt said when

he sauntered into the kitchen at 6:00a.m. to make his morning coffee.

"Mornin'," said BB groggily, propping himself up on one elbow on the couch.

"What? Did you and Michelle have a fight or something?" asked Curt.

"No, you bonehead, you had us all scared to death last night."

Curt, who didn't even remember having taken BB's call, looked at BB as if he was crazy. "Why would you be scared to death about me?"

"You don't remember?" asked BB.

"Remember what?"

"Our phone call."

"What phone call?" thought Curt wondering if his brother had lost his mind.

"Jeezum Curt, we talked last night. You started mumbling something crazy about hair, arguing with spaghetti and angels with snowflakes. I thought you were having a stroke."

"Right li'l brother, nice try. What is this, some practical joke?" said Curt, still not believing anything BB was saying.

"I'm serious, Curt," he said with conviction. Curt, seeing tears welling up in his brother's eyes, finally convinced him.

"Really?"

"Yeah, really! Have you read about all the side effects of that stuff you're taking? Zol, Zolpa…"

"Ambien, it's called Ambien," said Curt helping BB spit the name of the drug out.

"Whatever it is," said BB dismissively, "You said those crazy things, and then you didn't respond to me. I thought you were drunk and passed out or were having a stroke."

BB went on to fill Curt in on all the details. Curt couldn't believe his ears. As it was almost time for the kids to get up, BB felt it best to leave so as not to have to field their questions.

"Oh, before I forget, the kids might ask you about my visit last night. So, don't be surprised."

"What should I tell them?" asked Curt.

"Tell them we had to talk about something. And you might want to call your doctor about those sleeping pills. I don't want you sleep-driving any time soon!"

"Thanks, BB. I'm sorry I scared you."

Curt got the kids up, and as his brother had predicted, they asked him about Uncle BB's visit. He successfully negotiated their questions and got them ready and out the door to catch the school bus. When they were safely on the bus, he went to prepare for the day. He was anxious for his second session with Counselor Tim at 10:00a.m. that morning. He also wanted to stop in at work and talk to his partner about coming back to work next week.

As he languished in the shower, feeling the hot stream of water massage his shoulders, he replayed BB's story of last night in his mind. He couldn't make sense of what he said and still couldn't believe it. He thought that maybe he should call Dr. Huseby's office. Then he remembered the words of Nurse Jenifer.

"You don't want to be doing anything but trying to sleep after you take them, OK?"

What he was remembering wasn't so much what she had said but how she said it. He heard her sweet, sexy, pouty question.

"Promise?"

His erection was almost instantaneous. Turning to let the hot water flow down his chest and onto his aching penis, he couldn't help but close his eyes and let his imagination go. Before he knew it, Jenifer was climbing into the shower with him. Her blond hair darkened by the water, clinging to her face as water coursed over her breasts. One of her hands was pulling him closer as the other hand guided him into her. Promise? Promise? Promise he heard her repeatedly saying, in time to his rhythmic thrusts. He almost fell out of the shower dizzy from the ecstasy of release combined with the hot water. His heart was pounding heavily, and his head was swimming. He had to sit down on the toilet and thought he might have a heart attack. As quickly as he had felt ecstasy, he now felt shame. He was hardly three weeks removed from being with his wife to fantasizing about his doctor's nurse. He didn't know anymore what was normal. Everything that had been normal was gone - his wife, his home, his kids' mother, their peace of mind. Curt decided it best not to call his doctor's office, sleep-driving side effects or not. In his mind, the side effects of Nurse Jenifer had become more dangerous.

With a couple of hours until his counseling session, Curt drove over to his office. As he walked into the modest offices of Jackson & Barnes Consulting for the first time in nearly three weeks, Loribeth Lacroix greeted him enthusiastically.

"Oh my god, it is so good to see you," Loribeth exclaimed, coming around her desk to give him a hug.

Loribeth had been Jackson & Barnes Consulting's administrative assistant since the day that Curt and his partner, Sam Jackson, had opened their consulting business. While Sam and Loribeth were colleagues, they were more like family.

"Where is Sam?" asked Curt.

"He's at Pen Bay today," said Loribeth referring to the picture-postcard peninsula on the mid-coast of Maine.

"Must be rough. I guess it will be a lobster salad for lunch and a round of golf at the Rockland Resort before he heads home."

"Worse," Loribeth said, "he took his family, and they're

spending the weekend there."

"Lucky dog, maybe I should take Caitlin and Cade down there. They could use a little fun."

"Great idea, Curt, you should do it," she encouraged. "What brings you in? Are you ready to get back to work?"

"You know me too well, Loribeth."

"Well, your timing is impeccable, Curt. Maine Employers Group on Healthcare has a Request for Proposals that Sam thinks may be a real opportunity for us."

"Great, I'll be in on Monday."

"Oh, don't forget the IRB meeting at Dracut Regional Monday morning at 7:30," Loribeth reminded him.

"Oh yeah, I would have forgotten about that. Thanks, LB, you're the best."

Curt had agreed to volunteer as a community member on the Dracut Regional Institutional Review Board, a committee that reviews, approves, and monitors clinical trials of investigational medications used in the hospital. Dracut-Campion Regional Medical Center had been a community fixture for over one hundred years. Despite marketing campaigns over the years, the legal name never caught on, and everyone in Dracut-Campion still referred to it as Dracut Regional.

Curt left the office anxious to get back into the swing of things. He arrived at Counselor Tim's office in high spirits, feeling that he had accomplished much in the last three days since his first session.

"Well, you certainly seem more upbeat since our first visit," exclaimed Tim.

While Curt ticked off all he had accomplished in the last few days, Tim sat listening quietly. Curt talked about the sleep he had been getting, the plans to have the kids start attending the Children's Support Group of Portland, and his plans to go back to work on Monday. Curt conveniently left out the episode when BB came to the house, the occasional thoughts of driving head-on into an 18-wheeler, and his shower fantasy with Nurse Jenifer. It took Tim precisely four words to knock the wind out of Curt's sails.

"Do you miss her?"

The words were like a kick in the groin, radiating up into his stomach, clenching his throat shut, and bringing tears to his eyes. He initially felt angry that Tim asked him such a question when he had been doing so well. He couldn't talk, and he reached for the tissues.

"Of course, I miss her," he sobbed.

"I'm glad you've done some things this week that show you want to take care of yourself and the kids," stated Tim. "Now, the hard work begins. I want you to tell me about the times that haven't been so good this week. What haven't you told me?"

"Why do you think I haven't told you everything? Curt said defiantly.

Tim turned and pointed at the Kubler-Ross poster of the five stages of grief.

"Denial?" asked Curt.

"Exactly," responded Tim.

Curt was beginning to feel again like Tim had some magical powers of perception. He told Tim about the Ambien episode.

"Ok, thanks for telling me about that. However, that's normal, and I'm sure it gave your brother a pretty good scare, but you're still avoiding something."

"I don't understand," Curt hedged.

"When was the last time you thought about Calli?"

Tim's question speared Curt.

"I think about her all the time," Curt said, defensively feeling his heart rate jump and his face beginning to flush.

"Prove it," Tim challenged.

"Prove it? You sonofabitch, how dare you ask me to prove it!" Curt erupted. "I loved Calli, and we were married for ten fucking years. I can't believe you'd be so fucking insensitive to ask that question. You're a god-damned quack if you ask me!"

"Who are you angry at?" Tim interjected.

"You. You asshole!" Curt screamed.

"Now, who are you really angry at?" Tim repeated.

The repeated question caught him by surprise. He had expected an apology and was about to jump across the table when the question hit him like a cold, wet blanket shocking him out of his misplaced anger.

"Darius fucking Scott," Curt erupted and broke down in a fit of tears. He could hardly catch his breath. Every time he went to take in a breath, it caught. He seemed locked in a perpetual effort to take in a breath, his efforts coming rapid-fire to the point that he wasn't really breathing in or out. When he was finally able to take a breath, his exhale was more of a wail. He dropped from the chair to his knees.

"Oh, God, Calli...I miss you." Curt cried now, doubled over his head nearly on the floor. He cried for a couple of minutes. At some point, he felt Tim's reassuring hand was on his shoulder. Regaining his composure, he accepted the wad of tissues Tim was holding for him. Sniffling and wiping his eyes and nose, he repositioned himself on the chair.

"I'm sorry," Curt said in a wavering tone, still an octave higher than his normal voice. He was on the verge of losing it again.

"There is nothing to be sorry about, Curt."

Tim spent the last 15 minutes of the session putting Curt back together. In the process, Curt realized that he had been avoiding feeling the hurt, the loneliness, and the anger. He admitted to his suicidal thoughts, his fantasy about Nurse Jenifer, and his subsequent shame. They reviewed Kubler-Ross's stages of grief. Tim warned Curt that he would not necessarily progress through the stages smoothly or sequentially. Curt gave Tim assurances that he was not going to act on his suicidal thoughts. Curt felt curiously exhausted but renewed by the end of the session.

"I'm sorry I called you all those names, Tim," Curt apologized.

"I've been called worse, Curt. See you next Tuesday."

That night, Curt fell asleep without the Ambien but woke up in the middle of the night, drenched in sweat and fear.

CHAPTER 15

With her angelic face framed in a white veil, she looked up at Stu and began. "I, Jacqueline Elizabeth Selaney, take you, Stuart Thomas Deno to be my husband. I promise to be true to you in good times and in bad, in sickness and in health. I will love and honor you all the days of my life."

Stu followed with his vow, and the rest of the ceremony was a blur. All Jackie and Stu heard after that was Father Woznewski saying: "I now pronounce you husband and wife. You may now kiss the bride."

Jackie and Stu's wedding embrace and kiss felt as natural and as exciting as the first day they met. Each knowing it was right.

"Ladies and Gentlemen, I now present to you, Mr. & Mrs. Deno," Father announced.

There was applause, but Jackie and Stu would later confess they didn't recall it. Although Saint Paul Church had 200 of their family and friends witnessing the blessed moment, they felt blissfully alone floating on some different plane. If not for the wedding pictures and video that seemed foreign when viewed a couple of weeks later, they probably would not have recalled half of the people or the events. Jackie and Stu had been there physically, but their minds so wrapped up in each other allowed them to retain only snippets of the ceremony and the reception.

The weather in Nora that January morning was a crisp 24 degrees that mercifully rose to just above freezing for the ceremony. Although it hadn't snowed the night before, a sparkling frost coated the trees. Jackie and Stu had fortuitously arranged to take their wedding pictures before the afternoon ceremony and caught the frost glinting like a million diamonds in several of the photos. Like so many things in Jackie and Stu's relationship, things just seemed to work out.

One thing Jackie and Stu would never forget was what greeted them as they emerged from the church following the ceremony. A group of loud friends and family, armed with Instant Snow Powder, covered them. Instead of the white stretch limousine waiting curbside stood a 28-ton, bright yellow International 4900 Snowplow. Trailing behind the truck were not the traditional tin cans but empty plastic containers of ice melt. Playing along, Jackie and Stu boarded their snow-removing limousine. They hammed it up for a few pictures, making a production out of Jackie's climb up into the cab. Friends got one picture of Stu playfully pushing Jackie up by her butt and her feigning a look of taking offense. Trying to get Jackie's gown and train all into the cab was a trick. Before she closed the door, Jackie took the opportunity to tease Stu and the audience by lifting her gown to show a little leg. This caused the females in the crowd to let out a high-pitched woo and the males to let out a lower-pitched whoa. Stu clutched at his heart and stumbled back into his best man's arms. Finally, Stu took his place beside Jackie in the cab, and firing up the engine and laying on the horn, they made their way to the reception hall. The sight of a caravan of cars following a behemoth snowplow all honking their horns was a unique wedding procession through Nora.

The reception hall continued the theme of the season, with the room decorated like a winter wonderland. The reception had the usual traditions, the toasts, the first dance, feeding each other the wedding cake, and tossing the bouquet. However, the groomsmen and bridesmaids had something unique planned. The best man announced that all the kids should follow him to another room for a special surprise. With great anticipation, the handful of kids followed the best man out of the reception hall and down to another large room. The groomsmen and bridesmaids then sprang into action. Lining up in a chorus line, in front of the happy couple, the groomsmen began to sing to the tune of Jingle Bells.

"Flashing through the snow," as the bridesmaids quickly lifted and dropped their skirts.

"Oh, if we weren't so gay."

"Under those skirts, we'd go."

"Exploring all the way, but we're gay, but we're gay."

Now the bridesmaids started to sing.

"Balls on boy's ding-a-ling," as the groomsmen dropped their pants.

"So big and such a fright," as the bridesmaids feigned surprise and made the five-dollar footlong sandwich gesture.

"What fun it would be to ride and sing."

"And hop on those tonight," as the bridesmaids bob up and down.

"Ohhhhh, dicks and balls, dicks and balls, too bad you are so gay."

"Oh, what fun to be inside" as the bridesmaids once again flash the groomsmen

"Too bad you go the other way, hey" As the groomsmen ignore the bridesmaids and start checking each other out.

They had to do an encore, after which thunderous applause and laughter caused some of the kids to come back to see what they missed. Fortunately, by that time, the performers had regained their composure and their clothes. Many of the kids stayed in the room, where a mini carnival had been set up with candy floss, snow cones, a bounce tent, and some arcade games.

They partied until well into the evening. When it was time for Jackie and Stu to leave, a white stretch limo replaced the bright yellow snowplow. Jackie and Stu had intended to stay at their apartment to save their honeymoon stash for their trip to Arizona. However, their families had other plans and arranged for them to stay at The Castle.

The Castle was an elegant hotel built in 1867. Recently renovated, it now seamlessly blended new world amenities with old-world architecture. In a nod to tradition, Stu carried Jackie across the threshold into a grand living room with a fireplace. On the table were a plate of chocolate-covered strawberries and a bottle of Moet Chandon on ice. Surveying the rest of their suite, they found a whirlpool bath and multi-head shower in the bathroom.

As they stood in the bathroom, their feet aching, they both had the same idea. Jackie removed her heels and started peeling off her wedding gown. Stu kicked off his shoes and went to get the strawberries and champagne. When he returned, the water was running, and Jackie had lit several scented tea candles rimming the bath. She stood there like a goddess as the candlelight flickered off her nakedness. Returning, Stu quickly set down what was in his hands and replaced them with generous handfuls of his wife's bare skin. As the bath was filling, they kissed and caressed. The sound of the flowing water, the emotion of the day, and Stu's persistent and effective touch made Jackie buckle at the knees. They were so enthralled in their honeymoon dance that the tub almost overflowed. Stepping into the bathtub, they fired up the jets. They cuddled, lounged, fed each other strawberries, and toasted their marriage as the barrage of bubbles drained any stress or pain from their bodies. Jackie, recovered from the pleasurable sensitivity of the pre-bath appetizer, straddled Stu as small waves mixed with the bubbles. It was their wedding night, but there was no awkwardness. They knew each other's bodies intimately. While they could make these sessions last hours, tonight, they moved with determination. Soon, the waves produced were too much for the tub to contain, and several crashed over the tub extinguishing tea candles and sending them and the water onto the floor. The couple choreographed their movements, their bodies tensing and shuddering as they met simultaneously at the end. Sapped from the emotions of the day and the physical release, they fell into bed, naked and wrapped in each other.

Despite their intentions to attend church the next morning, they slept until 10a.m. and realized that they only had 2 hours to get ready and get to the airport. Jackie and Stu showered together more out of necessity, given their lateness. They did make, however, a commitment that when they got their first home, they would install a multi-head shower.

It was a cold, windy day, and Jackie and Stu were happy to be leaving Buffalo. They arrived in Phoenix 5-hours later and had gained about 50-degrees. Stepping out of the airport into the bone-dry warmth, Jackie and Stu realized their clothing was better- suited for blustery Buffalo. Peeling off what clothes they could, they made their way to the rental car agency. Soon they were sitting in a brand-new Chevy Tahoe, cranking up the AC and punching in the address of the Oasis Hotel & Spa into the GPS.

"Exit right for Scottsdale Road in point 3 miles," said the insistent female GPS voice. Within minutes they were at the Oasis Hotel & Spa, but they thought they had arrived in heaven. The palm trees, the desert colors, 72 degrees, a luxury hotel surrounded by pools, and nothing on their agenda but relaxation. They checked in and had one thing on their mind – get into their swimsuits, order up a couple of drinks, and start soaking in some sun.

Their suite was almost as big as their apartment back in Nora. They were in their rooms just long enough to pull their suits out of their luggage and head out to the nearest pool. They navigated winding trails beautifully appointed with desert flora. Arriving at the first pool, they quickly vetoed it as it contained dozens of screaming kids sliding down the twin waterslides. A short distance away, they spied a perfect destination – a large pool drenched in sunshine with a cabana bar. Finding two lounge chairs, Jackie settled in while Stu went to the bar.

"The usual boo?" Stu asked.

"No, I feel like living dangerously," replied Jackie, "get me something with an umbrella in it."

Stepping out of the sunshine into the shade of the cabana, a petite blonde with a dark tan piped up before Stu saw her.

"Can I get ya something to drink?" said the enthusiastic young woman in a half t-shirt and short shorts.

"Yes, ma'am." Stu stammered, trying not to be too distracted by the buxom, nearly bare beauty approaching from the bar.

"Oh, now, if you're going to call me that, I may have to cut you off right now. I'm Sunny," she said. Sunny shot out her hand and followed it with a smile that only proved she was appropriately named.

"I'm Stu," taking her hand, "Sorry, I didn't mean to offend you."

"I'll forgive you this time. What brings you to Arizona?"

"How do you know I'm not from here?"

"Ahhh, let me think," Sunny paused while dramatically putting her index finger to her temple, "maybe because you and your wife look like you haven't seen the sun in 6 months?"

Sunny's use of the word "wife" in connection with Jackie caused Stu great joy. "Oh, yeah, I guess we look a little white."

"White? Ghosts is more like it, Stu," countered Sunny, "Now about those drinks?"

"I'll take a Jack and Coke, and my wife would like some kind of umbrella drink."

"I know just the thing. How about a Baja Pineapple Grenade?"

"Sounds exotic and dangerous."

"That's perfect then. That could describe your wife. She's beautiful."

"Thanks, I think so too," said Stu turning to watch Jackie as she was starting to rub suntan lotion on her long legs.

"Now let me give you some advice, Stu," Sunny said with seriousness as she splashed a healthy dose of Jack Daniels over ice. "Have you or your wife ever been to Arizona?"

"No."

"OK, here's rule number 1. Drink lots of water. You don't know how many people come here, and within hours they're dehydrated. I'm going to give you your drinks and two bottles of water. The water is on the house. If you're poolside for more than an hour, I'll bring you another couple of bottles of water."

"OK, thanks."

Sunny started coring a whole pineapple and into the vacant space started pouring the magical elixirs for Jackie's drink – melon liqueur, tequila, pineapple juice, Sprite, and grenadine.

"Rule number 2. I don't care what level of SPF that lotion is that your wife is using, but you'll burn if you stay in the sun for more than 30 minutes. There's a couple of lounges over there in the shade. Throw a couple of towels on them to reserve them and rotate from the sun to the shade. Spend most of your time today in the shade. And don't think you can't get burned when you're in the pool."

"Do you take care of all of your guests this way?

"No, just you and your wife, Stu," Sunny said sarcastically, "Of course, I do. How's a girl supposed to get tips if her customers are passing out from sunstroke or getting sunburned? College ain't cheap." Sunny put the finishing touches on the garnishes to Jackie's drink.

"Where do you go to college?"

"ASU."

"A Sun Devil."

"You betcha," Sunny said, handing Stu his drinks and moving towards a cooler to get the water bottles.

"What are you and your wife here for?"

"It's our honeymoon."

"Wow, congratulations. In that case, let this first round be on me."

"Thanks, Sunny, you've been very helpful."

"We aim to please! Let me give you a tray for those drinks."

Stu, balancing the tray of drinks, returned to Jackie. She was lying on her back, the straps of her top off her shoulders, and her bikini bottoms scrunched to reveal as much skin as dignity would allow. Sunny's words echoed in his head "exotic and dangerous" indeed.

"What were you doing over there? Putting the moves on that blonde?" Jackie said without opening her eyes.

"No, she was giving me tips about how to survive the Arizona sun."

"What? She offered to rub suntan lotion on your hard-to-reach places, or maybe just on your hard places?"

Stu took a piece of ice out of his drink and let a few drops of ice water hit Jackie's belly.

"Hey," Jackie shot up, almost losing her top and finally opening her eyes.

"You're the only one I will ever let rub lotion on my hard places."

They kissed, and Stu excused himself to take two towels to the shaded lounges on the other side of the pool.

"And you did that because?" Jackie asked.

"Because Sunny told me to."

"Oh, I see, you're on a first-name basis. Sunny? How appropriate," Jackie said, only half kidding.

Jackie's jealousy jag started to wane as Stu recounted the benign conversation he had regarding proper hydration and skin protection with Sunny.

"She also gave us these drinks for free in honor of our honeymoon."

"That was nice," Jackie said, softening, "what the heck is this anyway?" She drew a sip of her drink from the straw.

"It's a Baja Pineapple Grenade."

"Whoa," Jackie said, shuddering from the combination of the tang of the pineapple and the kick of the tequila. "That is strong and delicious."

"Oh, that reminds me. When Sunny recommended the drink, I said it sounded exotic and dangerous. She said that the drink was perfect then because she thought you looked beautiful, exotic, and dangerous."

"She did?" Jackie intoned, looking towards the cabana bar where Sunny was busy wiping down the bar, "maybe I'm going to like Sunny after all."

Jackie and Stu drank their drinks and took in the desert oasis so different from what they left just hours ago. Sunny started cleaning up pool-side and eventually made her way over to Jackie and Stu.

"Hi, I'm Sunny," stretching out her hand accompanied by her characteristic smile, "Has your husband told you all the rules I told him?"

Jackie took Sunny's hand. "Yes, he told me everything, thank you. I'm Jackie."

"Did he tell you how beautiful I think you are?"

"No, he didn't say that," Jackie said with feigned surprise.

"What? I did too," Stu protested.

"Yes, he did, and thank you. You're pretty awesome looking yourself."

"Thanks, but I wish I had those longs legs."

"I don't think you need to wish for anything. You're beautiful just the way you are." Jackie felt like she was back in college counseling her friends, who often felt self-conscious about their bodies.

To Stu, this conversation was starting to sound surreal or something from some men's fantasy magazine. Before he knew it, Jackie and Sunny were talking up a storm and acting as if they had known each other for years. Seeing he wasn't going to get a word in edgewise, he jumped into the pool, marveling at the scenery – the Arizona desert, his gorgeous wife, and Sunny.

They managed to avoid sunburns, but by dinnertime, their heads were swimming from the drinks Sunny had served them. Their Eastern Standard Time bodies were also getting the better of them, so instead of going out to dinner, they ordered off the room service menu. They had dinner on the balcony in their swimsuits, and that was the crowning blow. They both were ready to go to bed by 7:30 p.m. and willingly gave in to the Sandman.

Their week in Arizona was better than they could have imagined. They hiked several trails, took golfing lessons at the TPC, made a day trip to Sedona, shopped, dined at a different restaurant every night, and got plenty of pool and sun time. They even went clubbing with Sunny and some of her friends in Tempe one evening. By the end of the week, they had tans even some of the native Arizonans would envy. Reluctantly, they boarded their plane back to Buffalo, which had been blanketed by a foot of snow from the previous day.

CHAPTER 16

Armed with Darius' banking records and the possibility that there may have been a connection between Darius Scott and Calli Barnes, investigators revisited the Lester's where Calli had worked.

"Mr. Letourneau, I'm Investigator Adams from the Campion Police Department," he announced while producing his credentials.

"Please call me Reggie. Everyone else does," replied store Manager Reginald Letourneau. "How can I help you?"

"I'm here investigating Calli Barne's death. We have reason to believe that Darius Scott made a purchase here on August 19th." Reggie's face lost all color, and he had to steady himself.

"Why don't you come back to my office," motioned Reggie.

Reggie had trained Calli. She had only been in the position for six months but had learned her role quickly. His head swimming over the possibility that Darius Scott had been in the store, Reggie struggled to find his words, "Wha, what can I help you with?"

"First, I'd like to know if Calli worked on August 19th and, if so, when?"

Reggie wiggled the computer mouse, and the computer sprang to life. His hands were trembling, and he was having a hard time clicking on the right icons, "Damn, I'm sorry, I'm so nervous. I can't believe he was here."

After finally navigating to the computerized time records, Reggie said: "Yes, yes, it looks like she worked 3:30 p.m. to 11:00 p.m. that day." Reggie stared broodingly at Calli's time record. Investigator Adams asked him a question. He didn't hear it.

"Hey," shouted Adams.

"Oh, I'm sorry," Reggie said with a start, "I can't believe this."

"Is there any way of knowing when Darius Barnes made his purchase that day?" asked Adams.

"Sure, give me a minute," Reggie replied as he started tapping away on the computer.

"And while you're at it," the investigator added, "could you determine what he may have bought?"

After a minute, Reggie announced, "Here it is. It looks like the transaction occurred at 7:28 p.m."

"Was Calli the cashier?" asked Adams.

"No, Roberta was the cashier."

"What did he buy?"

Reggie gulped and stuttered, "k, k, kerosene, rope, and" the last item he voiced so softly Investigator Adams couldn't even make out.

"And what?" Adams prompted.

"A propane torch," blurted Reggie as tears started running down his face. Reggie was devastated as he wrestled with the knowledge that Darius Scott had been in his store and had purchased the kerosene and torch that he ultimately used on Calli.

"I'm going to have to speak with Roberta," Adams declared.

Reggie was in his own reverie, lost trying to remember the last interaction he had with Calli.

"Reggie?"

"What?" Reggie said, finally snapping out of his trance.

"I'm going to have to speak with Roberta."

"She's here. Let me get someone to cover for her so you can speak with her."

Reggie exited while Adams scanned the Employee of the Month photos that adorned the hallway leading to Reggie's office. Calli's picture hung over March 2008, the month she was promoted to Supervisor. He then noticed surveillance cameras and made a note to ask Reggie about them. Reggie approached, escorting a petite, almost fragile-looking middle-aged woman.

"Inspector Adams, this is Roberta Plante," Reggie introduced.

"Thanks, Reggie. Can we use your office for a few minutes?"

"Sure, take all the time you need," as Reggie left the office, swinging the door shut.

Turning to Roberta, who now seemed like a scared little bird, he began, "Ms. Plante, on August 19th at 7:28 p.m., Darius Scott came through your aisle. Do you remember him?" he asked while producing a photograph. Roberta stared at the photo and slowly looked up at Inspector Adams.

"I'm sorry, I wish I could remember, but I don't. I see so many people that they kind of blur together after a while."

"Please, take another look at the photograph," prompted Adams. "Take your time."

Roberta looked at the photograph again, and 15 seconds later raised her head and said, "I'm sorry, Inspector Adams, nothing."

Reaching into his pocket, he produced his business card. Thanking her for her time, he encouraged her to call him if she should recall anything in the future. Roberta left, and Reggie returned.

"Reggie, I see you have surveillance cameras in the store. Would you happen to have the tape from August 19th?"

"They're actually digital video cameras that store about six weeks of data. Then we download the data to CDs. So yes, we should have video from that day."

Before Adams could ask, Reggie was logging in to the security camera program and scrolling back to August 19th.

"How many cameras do you have?" asked Adams.

"Twenty," replied Reggie. "six for the doors, four for the cash registers, and ten in-store cameras." As Reggie scrolled through the split-screen showing cameras 1 through 4, the hulking figure of Darius Scott pushing a cart with three items appeared at Roberta's cash register at 19:27 on camera 1. Isolating camera 1, Roberta looked to be talking to a colleague at the next checkout lane, appearing not to even acknowledge or look at Darius.

"Who is she talking to?" asked Adams.

"That's Mindy," Reggie said with a fair amount of frustration in his voice. "I always have to break those two up because they forget that they're there for the customers, not for social hour!"

It was now clear why Roberta did not recall her interaction with Darius; she hadn't had one. She scanned the items and robotically put them in bags while carrying on a conversation with Mindy. Darius seemed content not to draw Roberta's attention. The only time it appeared that Roberta might have had eye contact is when she handed Darius the receipt. Reggie rolled his eyes and groaned.

"Can we scroll back and see if we can see if he had any contact with Calli Barnes?" Adams asked.

Reggie returned the monitor to the split-screen mode and scrolled back in time. Adams watched as Darius walked backward out of view of camera 1 and into view of camera 3 in the "Tool Town" section of the store, where he put back the propane torch. At the same time, Calli Barnes appeared on camera 6.

"That's Calli," pointed Reggie stopping the backward scroll. While the miniaturized frames of cameras 3 and 6 were in close proximity on the screen, Reggie announced that the locations were not nearby in the store.

They followed Darius' backward path to an aisle that contained ropes and chains by the foot as well as packaged rope. Darius put back a roll of sisal rope lingering for quite some time, avoiding the many varieties of rope made from synthetic. Inspector Adams found it interesting that Darius had taken so much time and given so much thought to the type of rope. Calli had moved to the lighting section, where she was conferring with an associate and a customer. While Darius and Calli had moved in closer proximity, they were still not within view of each other.

Tracing Darius' path back, with only the 1-gallon kerosene container left in his cart, he and Calli appeared to be on routes that would unite them. Calli was making her way towards the bathroom fixtures while Darius headed towards her. Reggie and Inspector Adams both took in an anticipatory breath and held it. Was this finally going to tell the story? They never saw each other. Darius was traveling the main horizontal row in the middle of the store. At the same time, Calli had suddenly elected to take a shortcut behind a row of appliances. Reggie ran the sequence back and forth several times, but it was clear, they had not seen each other. Both exhaled in a protracted and defeated manner. Darius arrived at an aisle with seasonal items. He put back the kerosene that sat next to several types of kerosene heaters that had recently gone on display in anticipation of the chilly autumn nights that would arrive within a month. From there, he returned his cart and left the store. The camera at the door recorded his entering the store at 19:19. He had been in the store for 9 minutes but had not had any contact with Calli Barnes.

Inspector Adams thought about interviewing Mindy, the cashier that Roberta was conversing with while Darius checked out. He also thought about questioning the associate who Calli was speaking to in the lighting section. Weighing these options in his mind, he almost decided not to do so. There had been no contact, so what would be the point. His training told him not to assume.

"I'd like to interview Mindy and that Associate that Calli had been talking with," asked Adams.

"OK, but both Mindy and Travis are off today."

"When do they work next?"

Reggie consulted the electronic work schedule.

"Both are on tomorrow. Mindy works 8 to 4:30, and Travis works 12 to 9. If you can come in tomorrow around noon, I can arrange for them to meet with you."

"That will work. Can we have the video available?"

"Sure," said Reggie.

Adams thanked Reggie for his assistance and exited the office. Before he left, he decided to retrace Darius' path through the store, walking it in sequence rather than in reverse order as they had watched it. Although he was a hardened investigator who had cultivated a cold and clinical distance from his cases, a shudder ran through him as he picked up a 50-foot roll of 3/8 inch sisal rope. Adams could see why it had taken Darius so long. The sisal rope occupied a small space, lost amongst the multiple types of nylon, polypropylene, and other synthetic ropes. Lingering in this aisle and selecting sisal rope had to be purposeful...premeditated. What Adams still couldn't reconcile was why Calli Barnes? Could it just have been a coincidence? Adams had come into the store ready to find the evidence that would finally explain the connection, but still, there was none.

The next afternoon Adams returned to Lester's, anxious to see if Mindy or Travis could shed any additional light on the mystery. The start was not very encouraging as Mindy walked in, exaggeratingly chewing gum. Only her bizarre appearance made the gum-chewing mundane. A shock of hot pink hair stood up straight from the center of her head in a seeming tribute to Dr. Seuss' Cindy Lou Hoo. Her eyeliner extended out to an unnatural length in a failed attempt to give her an Egyptian Queen's appearance. Purple lipstick completed the bizarre package. Before Adams even spoke, he just imagined how convincing anything Mindy could say would be to a jury.

After Adams introduced himself, he asked Mindy to watch the video of the time when Darius checked out.

"Mindy, do you remember anything about that person?"

"Roberta? Oh, sure…"

"No, the man Mindy," Adams rolled his eyes and couldn't conceal his frustration.

"Oh, can I watch it again?"

"Sure," Adams sighed and waited while she watched the video again. She looked like a clown, thought Adams. While he was trying to be patient and not to judge, he couldn't help but feel that Mindy was the epitome of the dumb blond.

"Anything?" Adams asked as Mindy continued to stare at the screen even though it had gone blank 10 seconds earlier.

"No, I guess not."

Adams couldn't imagine why he was handing her his card and asking her to contact him if she remembered anything, just protocol, he guessed. As Mindy bopped out of the office, Reggie called after her.

"Before you start work, go home and fix that hair and wipe that silly make-up off your face. This is your last warning. Next time, you can stay home for good."

"I can only hope Travis is a little more helpful," Adams remarked.

"Travis is a good kid. Good head on his shoulders and responsible. If anyone can help you, it's him."

"Good afternoon, Travis."

"Good afternoon, sir."

"I'd like you to watch a video and pay attention to the man who is checking out. Then I'd like you to watch some video of you meeting with Calli Barnes and a customer around the same time as that man was in the store."

Reggie rolled the video and showed Travis the two sequences.

"Do you remember that day?"

"Yeah, the customer had some questions about track lighting and Calli, and I were helping him."

"Have you ever seen this man with Calli?"

"No."

"Did Calli ever say anything to you that you thought was strange? Maybe a run-in she had with a customer, anything?" Adams was reaching now.

"Well, Calli never said anything to me, but Derek talked about some guy who used to hang out in the parking lot, claiming to be a mind-reader."

Adams' eyes widened. "Tell me more."

"Not much to tell. I never met him. Derek thought he was some crazy homeless guy."

"Who is this, Derek?"

"He's one of my warehouse guys," Reggie chimed in.

"Is Derek here today," Adams asked.

"He is. I'll get him."

A couple of minutes passed, and Derek walked in and gave

Travis a fist bump

"What's up, my whigga?"

Derek was tall and wiry with long pitch-black hair and bangs that he was forever trying to flip out of his eyes with a tick-like jerk of his head. He shuffled more than walked, dragging his feet as if the effort to pick them up was too great. Running up his right forearm was a tattoo that said, "Mother." Partially hidden by his t-shirt sleeve and running up his right bicep was "Fu." It didn't take much imagination to figure out what the rest said.

"Derek," Reggie interrupted, "this is Inspector Adams."

"Whassup?"

"Derek, Travis here mentioned that you met some guy in the parking lot that claimed he was a mind-reader. Do you remember that?"

"Yeah, I was just chillaxin, havin' a smoke when dis whacked out dude starts talkin' this crazy shit about knowin' what I'm thinkin'."

"Derek, cool it with the ghetto act," Reggie said pointedly. Derek worked in the warehouse, the only place someone with his vocabulary could work without offending the customers.

"All right, my man."

"Derek, I'm going to show you a video of a guy who was in the store a few weeks ago. Watch this and tell me if you think this is the same guy."

The video started to roll. "Holy shit, that's the dude. That's the guy who needs a check-up from the neck up."

"Are you sure?"

"Absofuckinglutely!"

"How often did you see him hanging around outside?"

"A few times."

"Can you remember what days?"

"You must be pullin' my dick? I can hardly remember the last time I took a shit."

"Was it a few times in the last month? A few times in the last six months? What?"

"A few times in the last month or two, probably."

"Did you ever see him in the store?"

"Nah, just by where I smoke my butts."

"What did you hear him say?"

"Same fuckin' thing over and over. I know what you're thinking. I know what you're thinking. That's it."

"Was he ever out there when Calli Barnes was working?"

"Shit, probably."

"Did you ever see her out in the parking lot when he was out there?"

"No man, are we about done with the 21 questions?" Derek was getting tired and needed a smoke.

"Almost. Can you show me the area where you smoked and saw him?"

"Sure, I need a butt anyways."

Derek led Adams and Reggie through the warehouse and out a side door to a picnic table chained to a post. A halo of cigarette butts surrounded the table forming a perimeter. To the side of the table stood a cigarette disposal container resembling the shape of a pawn piece in chess. It was either full or unused. Reggie was perturbed, but now was not the time to get after Derek and a handful of other employees that used this space to smoke. There was a small parking area, reserved mostly for staff.

"So, you were sitting here when you saw him?" asked Adams.

"Yeah," Derek replied, reaching for his smokes.

"Where was he?"

"Standing at that light post," pointing to a pole about 25 feet away from the picnic table.

"What was he doing there?"

"Like I said, bro, he was saying the same thing over and over."

"Was he doing anything else? Smoking? Anything?"

"No man, you wearin' me out here."

"Last question, did you say anything to him?"

"No man, I just gave him the finger and went on smokin'. Are we done?"

"Yeah, we're done, for now, Derek. Thanks. Here's my card. If you think of anything else, call."

Derek didn't say anything, but the look on his face shouted, "Don't hold your fucking breath."

If Derek recognized that he could have easily been Darius Scotts' target by giving him the finger, it didn't seem to register with him. Derek seemed stuck in his angry ghetto speak world. Something told Adams that Derek was almost as clueless as Mindy.

Adams and Reggie walked outside towards the front of the store.

"Does this area have cameras?

"No, we have some cameras in the delivery bays out back, but most of the outside cameras are in the front parking lot where all the action is. Customers don't generally park back here. That's why we set up this smoking area."

"Thanks for your help, Reggie. You have a pretty colorful crew."

"Tell me about it," Reggie strained to smile.

Adams got to his car, his spirit buoyed by the information

Derek had so uniquely conveyed. He didn't mind that Derek wasn't your typical poster boy witness. Or that the jury would probably need to consult the Urban Dictionary if he ever took the stand. He finally felt like he was making progress connecting Darius Scott with Calli Barnes. Excited to report the news, he called Attorney Dryer.

"John, I got a lead on a possible connection between Darius and Calli," Adams said excitedly.

"Darius is dead," said Dryer stopping Adams in his tracks.

"What?"

"He's dead."

"How?"

"Don't know. I called HPI to set up a time to interview him, and they told me he was dead. I asked some questions, but they wouldn't tell me anything. I guess there will be an investigation, but obviously his fate is sealed."

When he said those last three words, he shuddered, realizing that he had just uttered one of Darius' oft-repeated phrases. If Adams caught this, he hadn't said anything.

No sooner had Adams gotten off the phone with Dryer when his cell phone sprang to life. It was his Unit Supervisor informing him of Darius' death and asking him to go to HPI to meet with Dr. Lang. Although Harlow was not in his jurisdiction, the Campion and Harlow Police Departments recognized that Adams had been investigating the Calli Barnes case. Rather than bring in someone cold to the case, they had agreed to cooperate and have Adams continue his investigation. Now, however, the investigation had two unsolved questions: What was Darius' relationship, if any, to Calli Barnes? And how did Darius Scott die?

CHAPTER 17

His pillowcase soaked with sweat, Curt's heart pounded as if he had just run the 100-yard dash. His nightmare had been so vivid that he was certain Darius had taken Caitlin and Cade from him. It was 4:00 A.M. on Saturday, and not trusting it was just his unconscious mind torturing him, he padded down the hall and peeked into Caitlin and Cade's rooms. Although they were safe in their beds, he couldn't forget the violent inferno that had burned in his brain just minutes earlier. It was too real. Knowing he would never be able to go back to sleep, he went to the kitchen for the day's first cup of coffee.

Curt didn't take Caitlin and Cade to the luxurious Rockland Resort that weekend, as Loribeth had suggested. It wasn't because he didn't want to take them. He was fully prepared to do so. However, when the kids arrived home from school on Friday, Caitlin had run up the stairs and, in breathless urgency, pleaded for Curt's permission to allow Jordan to sleep over. It would have been hard to deny Caitlin, who was so clearly excited by just the prospect of having her BFF over. Caitlin was conniving enough to have Jordan in tow when she asked, an almost foolproof way to shield her from a dreaded "no" response from her father. Although Curt knew that he was being "played," he didn't mind accommodating Caitlin's plan. The girls shrieked with delight and ran out and seven doors down to accost Jordan's parents for permission.

Jordan was a couple of years older than Caitlin. In Curt's estimation, she had a positive influence on his daughter. She was also one of the few things, other than horses, that could put that radiant smile back on Caitlin's face. Caitlin's smile, in the last few weeks, had become as rare as seeing a shooting star. Cade, who had a habit of trying to adopt Caitlin's friends, to his sister's irritation, also liked Jordan. Curiously, Caitlin didn't have her customary hissy fit when Cade would ask to be included. Caitlin would even sometimes seek Cade out to join them. This was totally out of character for his daughter. Jordan represented a peace treaty that averted his kid's usual conflicts.

Hearing a commotion outside, Curt stepped out of his door and peered down the concrete walkway. Jordan had received permission and armed with a sleeping bag and seemingly, enough other stuff to allow Jordan to stay a week, the girls' excitement reached a crescendo. Only the tenants who were deaf didn't know the girls' plans. Curt didn't care, Caitlin's smile had returned, and the promise of a peaceful weekend was music to his ears.

Jordan ended up staying two nights, and while the kids occupied themselves, Curt spent most of the weekend plowing through the reams of research protocols and patient consent forms in anticipation of Monday's Institutional Review Board meeting. Sitting on an IRB is not scintillating work by anyone's definition. However, as he prepared, he felt a sense of purposefulness that had been absent in his life over the last three weeks.

Curt had joined the Institutional Review Board two years ago. When he joined the IRB, he had received extensive training on his role, responsibilities, and the regulations on human research studies. He had learned that Institutional Review Boards came about in the 1970s through regulations that sought to prevent research abuses. The two most egregious examples of those abuses were the Nazi experiments uncovered after World War II and the 40-year Tuskegee Syphilis Study conducted by the U.S. Public Health Service on black men in rural Alabama until 1972. Despite good intentions, Institutional Review Boards had recently come under considerable scrutiny. At their last meeting, members had reviewed a report that one-third of IRB's had members with industry financial ties, and another third of IRBs rarely, if ever, reported potential conflicts of interest.

In contrast, Dracut Regional IRB included diverse representation from within the organization as well as individuals, like Curt, from the community. Also, all members had to complete an extensive Disclosure of Potential Conflicts of Interest Form annually. This form required members to list organizations with which they or their family members had professional or financial dealings, as well as any investments they had in healthcare, medical device, or pharmaceutical companies. Dracut Regional IRB was squeaky clean and one of the few community, not-for-profit organizations that continued to maintain such a Board. Many organizations had abandoned IRBs, in favor of contracting with for-profit Regional or National IRBs.

Monday dawned, and Curt arrived at the meeting, where members greeted him warmly and expressed their condolences and support. Coffee and Danish in hand, Curt took his familiar seat at the table, and the IRB Chairperson called the meeting to order. For the first two-thirds of the 90-minute session, a parade of principal investigators and their research coordinators presented research protocols in fulfillment of the Board's primary purpose of assuring that clinical trials approved by the members met human rights, ethical, and regulatory standards. For the last 30 minutes of the meeting, one of the principal investigators would provide the results of a clinical trial that the Board had previously approved. To Curt, hearing about the benefits that accrued to patients in the community from the leading-edge research the Board had passed made the sometimes-mind-numbing review process all worth it.

Dr. Steven Caron, a young and ambitious neurologist, had come to the Dracut-Campion community several years ago. He quickly made a name for himself by not only having an office in Dracut-Campion but also opening outreach clinics in several surrounding communities. Dr. Caron recognized that to be successful in rural Maine, he would have to go to where the pockets of people were rather than expecting them to come to him. He also became the Medical Director of Dracut Regional Memory Care Unit. He had an interest in research and was a frequent guest at the IRB meetings presenting protocols for approval. Dr. Caron was respected by his medical staff colleagues and gifted with the ability to describe complex research protocols in a way that even a layperson could easily understand. Today, he was back to report on the Recallamin trial that the Board had approved about a year ago.

"Good morning. I'm excited to be able to report research results that will change the lives of millions of Alzheimer's sufferers for the better," he started tantalizingly.

"A little over a year ago, you approved the SMILE trial. Which stands for Stop Memory Impairment and Loss Evaluation. It involved a new drug that, unlike any other Alzheimer's drug, hoped not only to slow the Alzheimer's disease process but also to stop it. If this premise wasn't audacious enough, the manufacturer, AlzCura, hoped to prove with this study that Recallamin could not only stop it but reverse it. The SMILE2 trial, which you also approved last year, incredibly seeks to prove that Recallamin may also be able to prevent Alzheimer's for those with the so-called Alzheimer gene. If Recallamin proves any one of these things, either stops or reverses the advance of Alzheimer's or prevents it all together, it will be the most important medical discovery since Fleming discovered Penicillin 80 years ago."

Dr. Caron had a flair for the dramatic. In his 30-second opening statement, he had the Board's undivided attention.

"Last month, the FDA approved Recallamin for use in mild and moderate cases of Alzheimer's, finding enough evidence that in most cases, it does stop the progress of Alzheimer's. In some cases, there was a slight improvement in mental functioning. This is phenomenally great news. Studies on the preventive capabilities of Recallamin will necessarily take years to determine. While studies have not yet been done on patients with severe Alzheimer's, AlzCura is working on the SMILE3 protocol. I hope to bring that protocol here for your consideration in the next month or two."

"Dr. Caron, this is fantastic news," Curt piped up. "Can you tell us about our local experience with Recallamin? How many patients did you enroll, and how are they doing?"

"I thought you'd never ask," responded Dr. Caron cheerfully, eliciting chuckles from the Board members.

"This multi-center study enrolled about 3,000 patients nationally. We enrolled twelve patients for the SMILE trial. Eight patients had moderate Alzheimer's, and four had mild Alzheimer's. As the study was a randomized, double-blind controlled study, I cannot tell you who received the study drug versus the standard treatment or placebo. I can tell you that of the twelve patients, three showed definitive improvement."

"Can you refresh us on how improvement was assessed, Dr. Caron?" asked the Board Chairperson.

"Sure. We assessed improvement in three ways. Before and after Magnetic Resonance Imaging of the brain, before and after performance on a standardized memory test, and by surveying the study participant's family members on their perceptions of whether their loved one's memory or behavior had improved following treatment. This way, we were able to get anatomical, cognitive, perceptual, and behavioral data."

"In those three patients that improved, "asked a pharmacist, "did they improve in all areas?"

"No, only one improved in all three areas. All had brain changes on MRI, while two of the three showed improved performance on the memory test. One only had brain changes and favorable family survey results on memory and behavior change.

"We have a small number of patients," Curt stated, "what were the overall findings from the study?"

"Boy, I couldn't have planted a better person in the audience," joked Dr. Caron as he took a stack of reprints out of a manila folder.

"These are reprints of the article that appeared in Neurology," he said while handing the stack out for distribution.

"While I'm sure you can read the results for yourself, the study found that Recallamin was more effective than standard treatment or placebo in both brain changes and performance on the memory test. Results were somewhat better for mild versus moderate cases. The authors surmise that the family survey results may not have been statistically significant. Family members, who desperately want to believe that improvement is possible, may "see" it whether there is an actual improvement or not."

"What about SMILE2?" asked another physician on the Board. "Have you enrolled any patients in that trial, and have you seen any results?

"Yes, I have enrolled six patients so far. It is harder to recruit patients for SMILE2, as many people don't even want to have the genetic test to determine if they have the Alzheimer's gene. Those that do have the test and have the APOE-e4 gene also know that the jury is still out on the exact relationship. New information on a genetic component to Alzheimer's seems to come out every few months. Of the six I enrolled, four are still part of the study, and two have been lost to follow-up. Here again, because this is a random, double-blind, controlled trial, I don't know who is getting the study drug. All of the patients I have enrolled have been in their 40's to early 50's, so besides data on side effects, we won't likely have outcome results for some time."

"What do you mean 'lost to follow-up'?" asked one of the newer Board members.

"Lost to follow-up is the term we apply in research when a patient who was participating in the study gets lost, leaves the area, or leaves the study. Although we attempt to contact them by phone and by letter, if they don't respond or we can't reach them, they are called lost to follow-up."

"What are some of the side effects in study participants in both the SMILE and SMILE2 trials," asked Curt.

"In SMILE, as you can read in the article, I distributed, nausea, vomiting, diarrhea, insomnia, and headaches were the most commonly associated side effects. Dosing in SMILE2 is slightly lower, and while the national results are not available yet, only 1 of my 4 patients has complained of headaches."

"I seem to recall a few Adverse Event reports that we reviewed that involved patients that died who were on these SMILE protocols," stated Curt.

"Yes, but in each of those cases, it was determined that the death was unrelated to the drug. One of the difficulties in studying the effects of drugs in older populations is that many of them suffer from comorbid conditions like heart disease, heart failure, diabetes, and COPD. Some proportion of these patients are going to die from these conditions. For example, the average age of patients in the SMILE protocol is 70 years old. If we tried to eliminate these types of patients from the study, we wouldn't ever have enough patients to answer the research question. The raw mortality rate for SMILE patients that received the study drug was slightly higher than in the standard treatment or placebo arms of the study. However, the difference was deemed not to be statistically significant."

"OK, we're bumping up against our time to adjourn," announced the Board Chairperson. "I'd like to thank you, Dr. Caron, for taking time out of your busy schedule to tell us about these exciting results. It is days like today when each of us can be proud of the work that we are doing to reduce harm and save lives in our community. Thank you again, Dr. Caron, and thank you, Board members, for your continued dedication to the important work of this Board. See you next month."

Curt would have lingered after the meeting, as was customary, but was anxious to get back to the office to tackle the backlog of work that had accumulated after being out nearly a month. It was Caitlin's birthday tomorrow, and shopping for her present also had to be done. He also had a counseling session tomorrow. Things seemed to be on an upswing, but he was a bit apprehensive. If tomorrow's session was anything like the last one, it would put him through the emotional wringer again.

"Good morning LB," Curt said, setting a hot chocolate with whip cream on Loribeth's desk.

"Well, haven't I missed that greeting and this treatment?!"

"It's the least I could do."

"Great to have you back."

"Great to be back."

"Now, before you start in on those piles of work, the DA's office called. He wants to meet with you tomorrow. Do you have a time preference?"

"What does my schedule look like?"

"Clear. I knew you would need plenty of office time to play catch up."

"Well, I have an appointment at 10:00a.m. for an hour, and I need to be home tomorrow by 3:30 p.m.. It's Caitlin's birthday."

"Oh, how old will she be now 8?"

"Yep, growing up fast."

"How about I book you for a 2:00 p.m. meeting with the DA, and you can go home from there?"

"Sounds great," Curt said with false enthusiasm.

He was already starting to dread tomorrow. The counseling session followed by the visit with the DA could be a brutal one-two punch before Caitlin's birthday. The events of August 20th had caused him to miss celebrating Cade's birthday on August 22nd. He had promised Cade they would celebrate later, but that promised celebration had yet to occur. Now, the fallout from August 20th was threatening to disrupt Caitlin's birthday. He couldn't help but feel like he was falling behind. He had an acute sense that what Calli had managed so effectively was now disintegrating in his hands. As he sat down in his chair, scanning the neat piles of work that Loribeth had laid out for him, an unfamiliar feeling of incompetence washed over him. He got up, closed his door, and started to cry.

CHAPTER 18

J ackie and Stu stepped out into the frigid arctic blast that caused snow to swirl up like mini-tornadoes. This, and both of them going back to work within 12 hours, was a rude awakening.

They stepped into their apartment for the first time as Mr. & Mrs. Deno but had little time to enjoy it. They had picked up some Chinese take-out on their way home, knowing that the fridge was empty. They had become so used to eating out over the last week that the thought of shopping and cooking seemed too arduous a task. They ate in silence, lost in a reverie somewhere between the idyllic dreamland from which they had just come to the harsh reality in which they now found themselves. It was odd how one week away had converted the familiar into the foreign.

It was Super Bowl Sunday, and their beloved Bills had fallen woefully short of the playoffs. They turned on the game just in time to watch Hester's 92-yard opening kick-off return for a touchdown. After that, however, they paid more attention to the commercials than to the game. Despite a close game, they shut it off after Prince's halftime performance. Although their bodies were still operating on West Coast time, they forced themselves to go to bed, knowing that morning would come faster than they wished.

Jackie arrived at her office cubicle the next morning, dragging a bit. A post-it noted greeted her on top of a stack of papers that read simply: "See me, Dr. S." She took the elevator up to the top floor and walked down the hall to the double glass doors that led to Dr. Sheridan's office. His administrative assistant greeted her and asked her to take a seat.

"Mrs. Deno, I presume?" said Dr. Sheridan. "So nice to have you back."

Jackie smiled, not used to Dr. Sheridan sounding chipper. "Thanks, Dr. Sheridan. It's good to be back."

"Come into my office, young lady. We have much to discuss."

Dr. Sheridan's office was on the top floor with windows that looked out over Lake Erie. Buffalo couldn't boast the most stunning views, as a part of what caught your eye was the rusty and skeletal remains of the Bethlehem Steel Plant in nearby Lackawanna. Curious and somewhat controversial structures were now sprouting up from the once-proud steel mill – wind turbines. Eventually, they would distract the view of the steel mill, but you couldn't say it improved the view.

"Before we get started," said Dr. Sheridan handing an envelope to Jackie, "this is a little something from the leadership team in honor of your wedding."

"Thank you, Dr. Sheridan. I certainly didn't expect,"

"Oh, it's nothing really," Sheridan cut her off, "Just a little something. Now let's get down to business. There's been an explosion of interest in Recallamin, and we can't hire and train Pharmaceutical Reps fast enough. We want you to take the entire northern tier of the Northeast Region – Connecticut, Rhode Island, Massachusetts, Vermont, New Hampshire, and Maine."

"Really? But I..."

"Yes, really," he cut her off again. "You're one of our best and brightest, and we have to back up a great vaccine with great support. It will mean that you will be on the road more, but we're prepared to offer you a 10% increase in salary."

"Really? But I…"

"Yes, really," she was starting to wonder if he would ever let her finish a sentence. "We have outlined your schedule over the next six months. It's on your desk. Any questions?"

Finally, she thought but then realized that she was too shocked to remember what she may have wanted to ask.

"No, I guess not. Thank you, Dr. Sheridan."

"You're welcome. Now off to your desk. I think you have a flight out of here tonight." He whisked her out of the office by the elbow. Before she knew it, she was standing by the elevator, feeling as if a truck had just hit her.

Grabbing a coffee from the staff kitchen, several colleagues offered their congratulations as she navigated back to her cube. Thankfully, they all seemed too busy to engage her in conversation about the wedding and honeymoon. She had not yet recovered from the wham, bam, thank you ma'am meeting she just had with Dr. Sheridan. Sitting down at her desk and feeling like she had already worked a full day, she tried to collect her thoughts. Before she had a chance to even pick up the first packet of papers from the stack on her desk, Cheryl Baker, her boss, came up behind her.

"So, I hear you're going to DC tonight."

"Huh?" Jackie said, turning to face her boss. "DC? I thought Dr. Sheridan said I was covering the Northeast?"

"Yeah, Dracut-Campion, Maine, they call it DC up there. That threw me too the first time I heard it."

"They call it DC, really?"

"Yep. I remember listening to the radio driving from Portland, and the weatherman is talking about the forecast for DC. It was two days before I realized he had been talking about Dracut-Campion, not Washington DC. I mean, when he said the high was going to be 12 degrees, I thought, Wow, 12 degrees in DC. That IS news."

"Why DC?" asked Jackie, still trying to get her bearings.

"There's a doctor up there. His name is Caron. His practice participated in the Phase III trial. He is growing a large regional practice in Central Maine. Besides a booming outpatient practice, he's associated with the largest nursing home and memory care unit in the State. Strategically, if we keep him happy, he could single-handedly influence colleagues at Maine Med in Portland and Eastern Maine Medical in Bangor. The State would be ours."

During Jackie's internship, she had the naïve notion that the work of a Pharmaceutical Representative was purely educational. She had learned very quickly that education was window-dressing. The work of a Pharmaceutical Rep was sales. Influencing those that held the keys to the kingdom, that is, doctors, to use AlzCura products. The more Jackie learned about her relatively new profession, the more she realized it was like politics. You lobby key individuals in a market, and if successful, they use their local reputation to influence others to use AlzCura products.

A fair amount of work also went into market analytics. Researching the patient demographics of a city, region, or state and identifying the big-name physicians. Who were the movers and shakers? The stack of papers on her desk contained the results of this research so that she could better understand and talk knowledgeably about the market in which she was operating.

Finally, Jackie noticed that most Pharmaceutical Reps were unusually attractive young women with good heads on their shoulders and bubbly personalities. When education and market analytics weren't enough, and more often than pharmaceutical companies would like to admit, the attention and attraction of a well-dressed young lady could sway a doctor. The few male Pharmaceutical Reps were young, athletic GQ types who curiously seemed to get the lion's share of visits to the growing female physician population.

While all pharmaceutical companies used these techniques, the government had been cracking down on what companies and reps could and could not do to influence physician behavior. Also, many health systems started to shy away from or eliminate pharmaceutical-sponsored educational sessions. Gone were the free trips and generous honoraria for physician speakers. Gone were the extravagant meals delivered to educational session attendees, courtesy of the company.

In response to these growing restrictions, pharmaceutical companies started to market directly to potential customers through radio and TV advertising. If the company's ability to directly influence physician behavior was going to be limited, it would try to get patients themselves to change physician behavior. Get enough patients to ask a physician about a particular medication, and voila, the physician, whether they like it or not, starts to change their prescribing habits.

She was gone a week, and in less than 30 minutes, she could feel that the stakes and the pressure to perform were ratcheted up. Cheryl had handed her the e-tickets for her flights to Portland and had left. Her coffee had gone cold. Before she tackled the stacks of paper in front of her, she nuked her coffee. Sliding her finger under the flap of the envelope that Dr. Sheridan had given her, she removed a check. After picking herself off the floor, she called Stu.

"Honey, you won't believe it," she said breathlessly.

"What?"

"The company gave me a check for $5,000 for our wedding!"

"Wow, that's awesome! I knew I married into money."

"That's not all. They have given me the northern tier of the region and increased my salary by 10%."

"Jeez boo, go out and buy a lottery ticket. It's your lucky day! You've accomplished all that, and all I've done is snow-plow 25 miles of highway. Why am I so lucky to have you?"

"Well, you might not consider yourself so lucky after I tell you this."

"What's that?"

"I have to fly to Maine this afternoon."

"Well, you can buy a lot of lobster with that $5,000!"

"But I'm upset that I won't see you tonight. This is all so quick."

"It's quick because you're a superstar, boo. Enjoy it. We just had an awesome honeymoon, and you come back and get a gift, a promotion, and a raise. That's great!"

"That's what I love about you. You're always so upbeat and supportive."

"Damn, and I thought it was because of my superior love-making skills."

"Well, that too," she said, laughing.

"Love you, boo. Bring me back some lobster."

Jackie realized that she only had a few hours to get through the stack on her desk, go home, pack, and get to the airport. The first document was a calendar showing the next 60-days. After scanning it, she realized she would be on the road for the better part of 7 out of the next 8 weeks. Her travel itinerary had her traveling out on Sunday afternoons, visiting two cities, and returning home Thursday evenings, followed by a half-day in the office on Friday. The slate of locations for the first four weeks included Portland and Dracut-Campion, Boston and Providence, Manchester and Concord, and Hartford and Springfield, followed by a week off from travel. The remaining three weeks included trips to New Haven and

Waterbury, followed by shorter weeks with one week in Burlington and the other in Worcester. Ominous question marks followed these last two locations. Either this meant that these trips were tentative, or more likely, they hadn't identified the additional areas yet.

She picked up the folder for her Portland/Dracut-Champion trip containing advance information on Dr. Caron and the demographics of Central Maine. An hour later, she decided she could finish her reading on the plane and headed to the apartment to pack. She stopped at the bank to deposit the check. It was a welcome gift, replenishing their bank account after their honeymoon expenses.

If her dark tan body looked out of place in Buffalo, it was going to look even more out of place in wintery Maine. After she finished packing, she felt a little mischievous. She stripped from the waist down, removed her panties, spritzed them with her body spray, and left them on Stu's pillow. On a post-it note she wrote, "Betty Sue misses you! XO". Grabbing a fresh pair of panties, she put herself back together and headed out the door for Maine.

CHAPTER 19

Inspector Adams drove from Lester's in Campion to HPI in Harlow, anxious to learn the circumstances of Darius Scott's death. He was pleased that the Campion and Harlow PDs had elected to cooperate and have him investigate the case. Typically, police departments are ferociously territorial and cling tenaciously to retaining control over their jurisdictions. As he entered the main lobby, a commotion immediately caught his attention.

"You killed him. You killed my baby!" screamed a woman as police tried to restrain her.

"You locked him up and killed him. You fucking bastards!"

Based on her out-of-control behavior, Adams thought this was a patient in the process of admission. An HPI staff member met him by the door and led him safely around the chaotic scene and through the locked doors toward Dr. Lang's office.

"Jeez, it must be tough dealing with patients like that every day," exclaimed Adams.

"That's no patient. That's the mother of one of our patients."

"Elvira Scott?" asked Adams.

"Can't say, sir, confidentiality rules, but yes, it is sometimes tough dealing with the patients and their families."

Dr. Lang greets Adams as he entered the office waiting area.

"Inspector Adams, I'm Dr. Sheldon Lang. Please come in."

"Good morning Dr. Lang," Adams said, shaking his hand.

They sat down in the office, and Dr. Lang started to brief Adams.

"One of our nurses, Raylene Baudette, found Darius dead at 4a.m. checks. He had been sleeping at 3 a.m. check. It happened sometime in that hour."

"How was he found?"

"In bed. Raylene said it looked like he was sleeping. Staff is trained to check more closely if they don't see movement or signs of breathing. When it appeared as if he wasn't breathing, she shook his shoulder, and he was cold and didn't respond. She turned the lights on, called a Code Blue, and went back to Darius. It was then that she saw red blotches around his eyes and on his arms. The Code Team arrived, but Raylene had already determined that there had been no respirations, and she couldn't get a radial, brachial or carotid pulse. The overnight Nurse Practitioner, who responded to the Code, confirmed that Darius was dead."

"Could someone have done this, or could he have done this to himself?"

"No. There were no marks on his neck, and we examined the video from the hallway camera. No one entered his room except Raylene for her hourly checks and the Code team, of course."

"Is he still in the bed?"

"No, he's at the morgue."

"The morgue? Did you move the body?

"Well, yes, we called the Medical Examiner as required in such cases, and he had the body transported to the morgue. Since we don't have any facilities for keeping a dead body, we thought that was prudent advice."

"Did someone take pictures of him in the bed before removing him?"

"I don't know, perhaps the people who came to pick up the body. This is the first death we've had here since opening a few years ago. We don't have much experience in these matters."

"Can I see his room?"

"Certainly. The police have cordoned the room off. And the way Darius' mother is talking, it's good that you begin your investigation immediately."

"How's that?"

"Ms. Scott believes we killed him. She thinks we overdosed him with our "crazy drugs," as she calls them. I tried to talk with her this morning, but there was no reasoning with her. She's convinced we killed him and says she's going to sue."

"So that was Elvira Scott throwing a tantrum out in the lobby?"

"Huh?" Dr. Lang said, looking surprised.

"Oh, Security was restraining a woman in the lobby. I asked one of your staff if that was Elvira Scott, and he wouldn't tell me because of confidentiality rules."

"Oh, I see," said Dr. Lang. "Well, we do train our staff well here. As for confidentiality, that ended when Mr. Scott died. His being here and dying are now matters of public record."

"What drugs was he on that got his mother so incensed?"

"None, all he had ordered on his MAR were our standard meds for headaches, stomach discomfort, and constipation."

"MAR?"

"I'm sorry, Medication Administration Record. We tend to speak in acronyms around here."

They walked to the forensic unit, where a police officer was standing guard in front of a room that had yellow crime scene tape across the doorway. After Inspector Adams showed the officer his credentials, the officer removed the tape, allowing Adams entry. Dr. Lang stayed in the hallway. The room was nondescript, bearing no visible evidence that Adam's trained eye would call suspicious. Darius' body was gone, which removed the most crucial piece of evidence. If pictures weren't taken, and Elvira Scott did sue, and the case went to court, this would be one of the first breaks in protocol that she and her lawyer would hang their hat on. Adams hoped that the Medical Examiner had performed an adequate investigation.

"Officer, do you know if the Medical Examiner investigated before the body was removed," Adams asked.

"No, sir. The Medical Examiner asked our department to take photographs and bag any useful objects at the scene."

"And was that done?"

"Yes, sir. We delivered the photographs to the Medical Examiner's office. There were no items found at the scene that required bagging. A copy of the medical record was requested, and I believe that hospital personnel is working to satisfy that request."

"Yes, our Health Information Management Manager is working on that," Dr. Lang confirmed.

"Thank you, officer," Adams said with a sense of relief.

"You're welcome, sir."

"Can I see the hallway video?" Adams asked Dr. Lang.

"Sure, come on back to the staff lounge."

They watched the video, and as Dr. Lang had indicated earlier, there had been no traffic in and out of Darius' room except for Raylene. Her punctual rounds impressed Adams. She also made good use of her flashlight. At 4 a.m. checks, she went into the room. About 10 seconds later, she was seen turning on the light and speaking into the communication badge clipped to her pocket.

"What is that?" Adams asked.

"That's a wireless communication badge," Dr. Lang said, pulling his badge out of his jacket pocket to show Adams.

"All Raylene had to do was press this button and say, 'Code Blue' with the room number, and it broadcast to all available personnel in the hospital."

Indeed, shortly after Raylene was seen speaking into the badge, a team of individuals pushing a cart arrived at Darius' room.

"What is that?"

"It's a crash cart. It has resuscitation equipment and medications."

"Is Raylene still working?"

"No, she works the night shift. She was pretty upset, as you can imagine. After the police took her statement, one of her colleagues drove her home and made sure she was OK."

"I guess I can read the police report and meet with her later if need be. What was Darius' behavior like during the day?"

"His behavior was nothing out of the ordinary during the day. Same few sentences he has always said. 'She wanted to die. She told me to do it. I have set her free. Her fate is sealed.' But before he went to bed, Raylene heard him singing some different lines over and over.

"What were they?"

"I can't remember, but she documented it in the record. Let me pull that up on the computer."

Dr. Lang tapped away at the keyboard bringing up Raylene's note. Dr. Lang read:

"The patient had been repeating his usual sentences when I arrived tonight. As I was walking down the hall on midnight rounds, I heard him singing. He kept singing the same lines repeatedly. I was finally able to listen to the words and write them down.

I prayed and kneeled

She broke us apart

Her fate was sealed

She broke my heart

I will build a pyre

I will never be healed

I will burn her with fire

Her fate is sealed

When I arrived at his room, he stopped singing. He was holding the left side of his head. I asked him if he had a headache. He nodded. I then asked if he would like something for his headache. He nodded again. After I gave him his PRN, he went to bed and was asleep at 1 a.m. rounds."

"Sounds like a pretty thorough note, but what's a PRN?"

"That's that acronym thing again. Pro Re Nata, which is Latin for 'as needed.' In this case, his as-needed medication was Tylenol."

"Did he have frequent headaches?"

"No. When we looked at the MAR, he had received some Tylenol that morning and then again that night. Those were the only times we had given him Tylenol."

"Could his headache have been a symptom of something that would kill him?"

"I suppose, but that's not for me to say. The Medical Examiner's autopsy will confirm or rule that out."

Adams thanked Dr. Lang, who guided him from the Forensic Unit and back to the lobby and to freedom. There were no signs of Elvira Scott or the skirmish that had transpired earlier. Adams hoped that the Medical Examiner would have some answers.

It was a short drive to the Medical Examiner's office. The attendant at the front desk dashed any hopes to extract additional information out of the Medical Examiner.

"I'm sorry, the Medical Examiner is in court at the moment. I can take a message and have him get back to you."

"Is there anyone else here who can answer my questions? I'm Inspector Adams, and I am investigating the Darius Scott death," he said while flashing his credentials.

"I'm sorry, only the Medical Examiner is authorized to provide communication regarding Medical Examiner cases. May I take a message?"

Adams could tell that the attendant was well-practiced in her responses and realized that this conversation was going nowhere fast. He wondered if the Medical Examiner was in court or if this was just the usual protocol designed to screen and triage the requests for information. He imagined that the office probably received many requests from media types trolling for information and even misrepresenting who they were. Relenting, Adams gave the attendant his contact information and left frustrated.

CHAPTER 20

C urt managed to get through his first day at work even after the tearful beginning. He met with Sam, and after catching him up on where he was personally, they discussed the Maine Employers Group on Healthcare (MEGH) Request for Proposals. They agreed that it was right up their alley and divvied up the various sections of the proposal. Curt and Sam's skill sets were a perfect compliment. Sam was the financial wizard, and Curt was an expert in quality and safety assessment. The proposal called for the marriage of both. MEGH was a business alliance that had formed about 15 years earlier to try to address both the runaway cost of healthcare as well as the variable quality of services. Most of Maine's employers were small mom-and-pop operations with less than 50 employees. Only a few large employers had any leverage to influence the costs that employers bore for healthcare. The alliance grew, and in less than a decade, the employers the alliance represented included nearly one in every four lives in Maine. This made the fractured healthcare system sit up and take notice. When one of the major employers in the alliance threatened to send all their employees to Maine Med in Portland for their cardiac care, it sent a ripple through the major hospitals in central and eastern Maine. What had formerly been impossible for hospitals in terms of cost concessions in these regions magically became possible.

Jackson and Barnes had a good reputation and steady work, but landing this contract would certainly increase both. Curt knew the stakes and realized that he would have to be at his best over the next few weeks to prepare and present their proposal. Looking that far ahead was difficult. He had become almost like his son Cade, needing to know what was going to happen over the next 24 hours and then preparing himself.

One day of work under his belt, he went to pick up Caitlin's birthday present. As usual, she had her heart set on adding to her growing collection of Breyer horses. She had conveniently left him a list a few days ago that filled almost an entire 8.5 by 11-inch sheet of paper. She had starred the ones she wanted most. It would have been easier for her to star the ones she didn't want. He went to the hobby store by the mall and picked up two Breyer horses. There was no way two horses were going to satisfy Caitlin's expectations, but Curt had a surprise in store. Curt had Loribeth to thank for the idea. The minute she had suggested it earlier that day, he knew it was the perfect gift. He made a phone call and set the plan in motion.

Curt also knew that Cade would be none too happy if Caitlin was able to have her birthday celebrated before his postponed one. He decided that Cade would have his birthday party tonight. Shopping for Cade and Caitlin was easy. They both were master communicators when they wanted something. Cade's latest desire was to have a battery-powered scooter. He had seen a couple of older kids at the apartment riding them. Curt had initially dismissed his pleas, thinking 6 too young to zip around on a motorized scooter. Then one day, Caitlin overheard them debating the matter.

She walked in and said, "I don't know what the big deal is Cade, they don't go any faster than your bike, and it's lower to the ground."

Unwittingly, in trying to dissuade Cade from wanting a scooter, she had managed to support his argument for having one. Caitlin, who frequently impressed Curt as being brilliant beyond her years, stopped the debate cold. Cade, aided by his sister's incisive rationale, looked up questioningly at his father, who had grown suddenly quiet.

"Dad?"

After a long pause, he said, "I'll think about it."

To which Cade shot up like a rocket.

"I can't wait to get it," as he ran out of the room excitedly. "I'm going to go tell Jordan and the kids at the playground."

Curt hollered unconvincingly, "I didn't say I'd get it. I said I would think about it."

"Thanks, Dad," Cade called back as the front door slammed.

With Caitlin and Cade, anything that was not a "no" repeated multiple times was as good as a yes.

Curt stopped at the sporting goods store that Cade had said carried the scooters. He got the last blue scooter available and added a new pair of hockey skates for the upcoming season. On the way home, he picked up Orange Chicken from Panda Gardens and stopped at Shield's Market for Cade's favorite ice cream cake.

Curt wasn't used to having everything kid-related fall on his shoulders. As he drove home, he realized how much easier life had been with Calli as a partner in this adventure called parenthood.

"I wish you could be here, Calli," he said aloud as tears welled up in his eyes.

He quickly stopped the one-sided conversation, realizing that if he continued, he would likely need to pull over. Although he stopped talking, a voice in his head remained.

"I wish you could have helped me shop for them. Cade and Caitlin are going to be so happy. It won't be the same without you there."

It didn't matter that the voice was silently in his head, the tears began to flow, and he pulled off the road. For the second time that day, he wept.

After a couple of minutes, he gathered himself and continued his trek home. He had arranged to have Jordan's mother watch Caitlin and Cade after school. He originally had planned to bring them to after-school daycare, but the kids had strenuously vetoed this plan. They brought up examples of kids that weren't considered cool because they had to go to daycare after school. Curt found it surprising that this kind of social pressure already existed in grade school. In his day, only High School exerted this kind of peer pressure. It had been Caitlin's suggestion that rescued them from certain damnation by their school bus peers.

"Dad, Jordan's Mom can watch us."

"No, I wouldn't want to impose on Jordan's Mom."

"Why not? Jordan's home-schooled, so her Mom's always there."

"I don't want her to have to deal with you and Cade fighting."

"We don't fight when we're over there. We get along."

She had a point, and he started to feel himself cracking. "I will have to ask her."

"She already said we could stay with her after school."

"Caitlin, you had no business asking her."

"I didn't. She suggested it."

Curt ultimately walked the 150 or so feet to Jordan's apartment. Jordan's mother indeed had suggested it and said to Curt how good it was for Jordan to have some friends. Jordan was something of a loner, and Caitlin and Cade were the only kids around which she felt comfortable. Curt offered to pay her, but she refused.

"Jordan is always at your place for sleepovers, two hours a day is nothing."

He had to admit that this after-school arrangement seemed better and more convenient than his original plan. Driving home that evening, he hoped that he would be able to sneak into the apartment to arrange Cade's surprise. Luckily, Caitlin and Cade were nowhere in sight. He huffed up and down the stairs twice, hid Caitlin and Cade's presents, set the table, and strung up a Happy Birthday banner. Standing there examining his quick work, the fourth table setting haunted him. He had set it for Jordan, but Calli was on his mind. He had to remain resolute and upbeat. There was no time for tears now.

He walked down to Jordan's apartment, and Caitlin and Cade greeted him with enthusiasm. Seeing them so happy was a relief. As the kids said their goodbyes, Curt asked if Jordan would like to join them for dinner.

"Really, Dad?" asked Caitlin.

"Sure, we'd love to have Jordan join us."

"Come on, Jordan," pleaded Caitlin.

"OK," Jordan said as her eyes lit up. This brought a round of enthusiastic cheers from Caitlin and Cade, and they raced down the walkway. Curt couldn't have choreographed things better. They raced into the apartment, and Curt, still 50 feet from the door, heard their chorus of "Whoas." Caitlin poked her head back out the door.

"But Dad, my birthday isn't until tomorrow."

Entering the apartment, Cade was sitting on the couch, looking sullen.

"It's not for you, Caitlin; it's for Cade."

Magically, Cade's grumpy face transformed into a beaming smile, the likes of which Curt had not seen since before August 20th. Once Curt had assured Caitlin that she would get her birthday celebration the next day, the kids devoured the Orange Chicken, fried rice, and fortune cookies. The doorbell rang, and Curt asked Cade to answer it.

"Happy Birthday!" greeted Uncle BB and Aunt Michelle.

Cade hugged them and gladly accepted the present that no amount of wrapping paper could adequately conceal.

"Thanks for the hockey stick. Dad, look at my new hockey stick," as he started to rip away at the paper.

"It's not time to open presents yet — time for cake," as he brought out the ice cream cake complete with lit candles.

"Oh boy, my favorite," said Cade dropping the hockey stick and charging to the table.

The group that had grown to six huddled around the table for four. They sang Happy Birthday, after which Cade made his wish and blew out the candles. Cade was the first to finish, knowing that the cake was the only thing standing in the way of presents. He suffered for a minute or two until the rest of the group had finished their cake.

Curt brought out a box, and Cade clawed at the wrapping paper revealing his new skates. Happy but not delighted, he hugged his father. Cade didn't have to say anything; his eyes were saying, "Is there anything else?"

"Oh, Cade, I think I may have forgotten a gift for you in my closet. Could you go get it?"

Cade didn't need to ask. He ran to his father's room, opened the sliding closet door, and there stood his shiny new, blue Razor Scooter. All the group heard from the living room was Cade's exclamations.

"Alright! Wow, this is so cool!"

He came out rolling the scooter into the living room. His face told Curt the birthday party was a success. The rest of the evening consisted of watching Cade ride his scooter in the parking lot. As it was growing dark, he had to confine his riding to a small, lit area. Curt realized that this was the first time he had seen Cade outside after dark since his unfortunate bear story. Everything wasn't perfect, however, as when Caitlin asked to try the scooter. It took some convincing, but Cade finally let her ride it, albeit only briefly. He had less difficulty letting Jordan take a spin. Had the battery not worn down, Curt probably would have had trouble getting Cade back into the apartment. Cade took the scooter to his room while Caitlin asked if Jordan could come for her birthday tomorrow.

"Sure, if Jordan's mom lets her."

"Can we go ask her?"

"Sure."

The girls ran off. Curt checked on Cade, who was wiping down his scooter with a damp hand towel.

"You have to keep it clean. Otherwise, it won't run so good," professed Cade, who had become a scooter expert in the last hour. Curt left him to practice the art of scooter maintenance and went to clean up the wrapping paper strewn across the living room and the dishes from dinner. From the kitchen, he heard Cade talking.

"I wish you could see this, Mom; it is so cool."

For the third time that day, Curt wept.

CHAPTER 21

S he finished the portfolio of information on Dr. Caron and Central Maine shortly before landing in Portland. This was Jackie's first visit to Vacationland. She had pictured her drive from Portland to Dracut-Champion, filled with views of the ocean crashing into a rocky coast dotted with lighthouses. What she found was a strip of concrete and asphalt winding through a tight corridor of trees. Endless trees.

She checked into the hotel, and the lead into Kylie Minogue's "Can't Get You Out of My Head" rang on her cell phone. She had picked this as her ringtone for Stu years ago. Not only did it fit her near-obsession with him, but it was also popular when they first met in 2002 when she was a freshman at South Temple.

"Hi, Hon," she answered.

"Well, Betty Sue, I do believe you may have forgotten some dainties here on my bed," said Stu in his best southern accent.

"Oh my, what pray tell, could that have been?"

"I love the smell of your perfume, and your body spray isn't too bad either."

"I thought you might like that."

"I did. How was your flight?"

"Fine."

"What's Maine like?"

"Cold and full of trees. How was work?"

"Not bad. "

"Hey, I deposited the $5,000 check."

"Super, our account was looking a little sad before that, I'm sure."

"Stu, I'm thinking about that check and the increase in my salary. Maybe we should think about buying a house?"

"That would be nice. But wouldn't you miss our downstairs neighbor blaring his rap music and the old lady across the hall hollering for her damn cat all the time?"

"No, I wouldn't. Let's go look at some houses this weekend."

"It's a date."

After they hung up, Jackie prepared for bed and turned on the TV to watch some news. Sure enough, when they got to the weatherman, he said, "The forecast for DC tomorrow morning will be a cold and crisp 14 degrees rising to a balmy 21 by midday." She woke up around 2:00a.m. with the lights and the TV still on. She found the TV remote and clicked the off button. She could not get herself to reach the lamp and fell back to sleep.

Jackie couldn't believe how young Dr. Caron looked. While she knew that he had only completed his medical training four years ago, most of the doctors she had met with were more her father's age. It was amazing to her that someone this young and so recently transplanted to Maine could be so influential to the medical community in Central Maine. She quickly learned why.

Dr. Caron was charming and energetic with a business sense beyond his years. He had declined Dracut Regional's offer of employment, recognizing that accepting could potentially limit his acceptance by the medical community at Alford

County Hospital. By staying independent, he felt he could have the best of both worlds. He was also not afraid of striking out into the smaller communities in the region. By doing so, he hoped to attract more business to his practice and more potential subjects for his aggressive research agenda. He had leased space in Ramsey, Namahoe, and Farrisport. While his main office was in Campion, where he customarily saw patients 4 days a week, he held regular clinics in these outlying areas. To avoid getting a reputation as an intruder who was trying to steal patients, he applied for and gained membership and consulting privileges on the medical staffs at the hospitals in these communities. One thing was evident; he was not afraid to work long and hard.

To Jackie's surprise, Dr. Caron had blocked off the last three hours of his day for her. As well-received as she usually was, it was rare for a physician to give her more than 15 minutes of their time. Dr. Caron was excited to show Jackie his outlying offices and had planned a dinner that evening in Farrisport with a few other physicians from the Central Maine area. Jackie, accustomed to arranging such gatherings on her own, found that Dr. Caron was doing her work for her. He opened the passenger side door of his BMW for Jackie, an act of chivalry that was rare in men under 50. Even his choice of classical music, which emanated from the satellite radio, clashed with the usual tastes of a man his age. As they drove the 120-mile circuit from Campion to Ramsey, then on to Namahoe, and finally to Farrisport, he dominated the conversation. While Jackie appreciated the dedicated time and the orientation to Central Maine, she began to get the sense that for Dr. Caron, it was all about him. It was not rare for a physician to have a big ego, but Dr. Caron seemed to have an extra helping. Dr. Caron, in small doses, was endearing. Dr. Caron, for 3 hours, was getting painful.

Jackie was more than looking forward to the opportunity to meet other physicians as Dr. Caron pulled his Beemer into the parking lot of the Farrisport Inn. He had reserved a small private dining area and introduced Jackie to several physician colleagues. Thankfully, Jackie got somewhat of a reprieve from Caron, who had moved on to schmooze with a colleague, allowing her to converse with an internal medicine physician from Farrisport. The dinner was spectacular, and the break from Caron's loquaciousness was just enough to prepare her for the 20-minute drive back to Campion with Dr. Aren't I Wonderful. He seemed more reserved as they began the trip back to Campion. He surprised her when he finally said something.

"Are you from the Buffalo area originally?" It was his first question directed to elicit information about Jackie.

"Yes, Nora actually," she said, grateful that the conversation would shift to something other than Dr. Caron. "It's a small town south of Buffalo."

"So, the name Deno, is that German?"

"I'm not sure, actually. My maiden name is French."

"My mother was German. Ingeborg Schwartz. Can't get more German than that."

Jackie sighed. He proceeded to regale her on his ancestry. How his German mother had met his French father. How he drew from them only the best qualities of their German and French cultures, which apparently didn't include humility.

Finally arriving at her car, she put on her best face as he opened her door and thanked him effusively for his time and generosity. Shaking hands, she detected a slight pull. She resisted it. Then a more purposeful pull and realized that he was coming in for a hug and maybe more. Her phone rescued her from the awkward moment when Kylie Minogue struck up her la, la, la, la, la, la, la, la.

"Oh, that's my husband calling," she announced, gracefully dropping his hand, turning her back and reaching for her purse. "Thanks again, Dr. Caron," she said over her shoulder as she walked towards her car.

His aggressive move to become more familiar with her was unnerving. Sure, other physicians had made suggestive remarks and flirtatious comments to her in the past, but this had been bold. She tried to settle herself before answering the call from Stu.

"Hi, Hon," she said in as bright a tone as possible.

"How you doin' boo?"

"Just got back from dinner," she said as she slammed her car door. She noticed Dr. Caron looking towards her, still where he had been standing when she left him. She waved and started the car.

"Is everything all right?"

"Yes, I was just getting into my car. Can I call you back when I get to the hotel?"

"Sure, talk to you then, love you."

"Love you too," she said, hitting the "end" button and driving out of the parking lot.

When she looked in her rearview mirror, Dr. Caron was still standing there as if he expected her to come back and finish the evening as he had wished. She was happy to have a 5-minute drive to the hotel to clear her mind of what just happened. By the time she reached the hotel, she had written it off to the wine, perhaps loosening up his inhibitions.

Kicking off her shoes and oozing onto the bed, she called Stu back.

"Hi, Boo," Stu answered.

"Hi Hon, I'm sorry I had to cut our last conversation short. I didn't want to talk and drive."

"It sounded like you were upset."

"Well, the doctor I was with was an egotistical boor who

thought the world revolved around him. I was just a bit tired from listening to him rattle on and on." This was the truth, but not the whole truth.

"Did it go well today, otherwise?"

"Yes, he may be full of himself, but he certainly is an asset when it comes to selling Recallamin. So, I guess I better learn to hear more about the great and wonderful Dr. Caron. How was your day?"

"It sucked, frankly. I was out in East Bumfuck, and my plow blade hydraulics went out. I couldn't fix it there on the side of the road, so I had to come back and pick up another plow truck."

"Sorry, hon, that must have made for a long day."

"No shit, I just got home when I called you."

"Have a beer. That will make things better."

"Too late. I'm already on my second."

"And?"

"And that and talking to you have made the end of my day, the best part of the day."

"Well, I can say the same thing, even without the beers."

Jackie spent the next day visiting Internal Medicine physicians in the Dracut-Campion area who had mature practices and many patients who were potential candidates for Recallamin. Most of these visits lasted only 15 to 30 minutes but were promising, nonetheless. On her way to Portland that evening, she decided to stop in Farrisport to visit Farrisport Outfitters, where she bought Stu a Storm Chaser jacket and a pullover fleece. She bought a pair of Wicked Good Slippers for herself. Sexy, they were not, but so incredibly soft and warm that she couldn't resist. She decided to stop at the Farrisport Inn, but this time ate in the warm and cozy Tomahawk Tavern. She ordered a bowl of lobster stew and the grilled salmon salad with a glass of Chardonnay. While she was waiting for her order, she called Stu.

"Hi, Hon."

"Hi Boo, where are you? Oh, I'm a poet and didn't know it," Stu laughed.

"I'm at the Tomahawk Tavern in Farrisport."

"What, your first business trip, and you're already trolling for action at the bar?"

"Aren't you funny? But it is a great place. Let's come up here sometime when it's not February. You'd love it."

"OK. It sounds like you had a better day today?"

"Absolutely. I'm just grabbing a bite to eat here, and then I'm going to Portland for the next two days. How was your day? Better?"

"Can't complain, no breakdowns and smooth sailing all day. I miss you like crazy, though."

"I hear ya. Thursday night can't come soon enough. Oh hon, my food is on its way."

"Ok, enjoy your dinner. I'll talk to you later."

"Love you, hon."

"Love you too, boo."

Stu's parting rhyme put a smile on her face as the waitress set the generous bowl of lobster stew on the table. After her second delicious meal in as many nights in Farrisport, she shoved off for Portland. On her way, an ad on the radio caught her ear. The voice sounded familiar, and then she felt her stomach lurch. It was Dr. Caron.

"Do you or a loved one tend to forget things? Do you misplace your car keys? Forget the names of people you meet? Has anyone in your family ever been diagnosed with Alzheimer's disease or dementia? If so, now there is help. I'm Dr. Steven Caron, a board-certified Neurologist specifically trained to treat these conditions. I offer the most effective treatments and participate in leading-edge research that may be the answer to your problems. You may even qualify for a research study, be paid to participate, and get free medication. If you or a loved one are forgetful, or you've had a family history of Alzheimer's or dementia, I offer free screenings at any one of my four convenient locations in Dracut-Campion, Ramsey, Namahoe, and Farrisport. Call 1-555-4Memory and start getting your memory and your life back today."

She couldn't believe what she just heard. Dr. Caron wasn't only full of himself; he was entrepreneurial to the extreme – dangerously entrepreneurial in her estimation. Who hasn't forgotten where they put their keys or the name of a person you just met? Who hasn't had a family member with Alzheimer's? He was casting a wide net and reeling them in with offers of free screenings, paid participation in research, and free medication. This couldn't be proper. She jotted down the radio station call letters and the day and time she heard the ad in the hopes of getting a recording or a transcript to share with Cheryl and Dr. Sheldon when she returned to Buffalo.

She had a productive day and a half of meetings with physicians in Portland. All had been professional, even Wednesday's dinner with adult beverages at Harbor Street, a unique restaurant just a block from Portland's Old Port district.

"Table for four?" asked the hostess.

"Yes, please," said one of the three physicians joining Jackie for dinner.

Jackie loved the brick interior, and the wood-burning oven and grill were visible from their table. They watched their meals being prepared, and the fire gave off a cozy warmth and a comforting woodsy aroma. The dinner conversation was light, pleasant, and balanced, unlike the discussion that more resembled a monologue Monday evening. She had a salad with a delicious plate of grilled scallops and vegetables and a glass of wine. They all decided to splurge and share a decadent pastry dessert with ice cream and chocolate and caramel drizzle. The physicians, the conversation, and the dinner had been the perfect antidote to Monday's unpleasantness.

Before boarding her plane on Thursday afternoon, she picked up a couple of lobsters to bring home for Stu. Although Jackie didn't know the first thing about cooking a lobster, or for that matter, disassembling and eating one, she thought it would be fun for them to learn. She arrived home at 8:30 p.m. The lobster cooking experiment would have to wait until the next day. After four days apart, Jackie and Stu wasted little time getting reacquainted.

CHAPTER 22

D r. Louie Corpisen was Maine's Chief Medical Examiner. In his many years of service, he had never experienced the feeding frenzy that Darius Scott's death caused his office. The Maine media had been voracious enough, but even media outlets from as far as Boston and New Hampshire had taken an interest in the case. In addition, after Darius' mother left HPI under police escort, she drove to the Medical Examiner's Office, stormed through the doors, and terrorized the front desk attendant. Fortunately, the police had tailed her and once again restrained her at the Medical Examiner's Office. Before they could remove her, she spewed allegations of the ME's involvement in the cover-up and how he would destroy any evidence of HPI's culpability for her son's death. Had she not calmed down and left the office when she did, the police were prepared to arrest her. The police left an officer at the Medical Examiner's office until they confirmed that she had left the area, presumably on her way back to her double-wide in Barry.

It never ceased to amaze Dr. Corpisen how the media expected immediate autopsy results. Darius Scott's body had not been in the Medical Examiner's custody for more than 2 hours, and the calls and visits had started. He had released the standard statement that the autopsy results would not be available for 4 to 6 weeks. This did little to help quell the level of interest.

Of course, Elvira Scott was a willing media star, fueling the media fires by tossing allegations left and right to anyone that would listen to her rants. Anyone that is, but the notorious TV reporter Leslie Anderson, whose previous attempt to capture Elvira's colorful tirades with a hidden camera had backfired. One afternoon, Elvira was holding court for a gaggle of local media reports outside her trailer in Barry. She had started to happily answer Leslie's question when she recognized her as the reporter who had previously tried to pull a fast on her. As Leslie held the microphone out, Elvira snapped a surprisingly fast straight left jab and scored a direct hit to Leslie's nose. Blood erupted from the reporter's nose in a stream. Try as she might, Leslie could not prevent the blood from splattering her scoop-cut white t-shirt. What had been designed to expose her considerable cleavage now just formed a perfect funnel, directing the blood flow between her breasts.

As Leslie tried to staunch the flow, Elvira punctuated the moment, "There you go, you fuckin' bitch. You didn't listen, did ya? I told you no cameras when you visited me the other day. You illegally filmed and interviewed me, you little cunt."

Leslie turned and bent over at the waist, making gurgling sounds while trying to move away from her attacker. This only gave Elvira another target. Before Leslie could navigate down the trailer steps or her colleagues could assist her, Elvira kicked Leslie in the ass, causing her to pitch forward and sprawl to the ground. Outlined on Leslie's backside was Elvira's muddy boot print.

"Now, get off my fucking property, or this boot will have to be surgically removed from that whoring ass of yours."

Happy with her handiwork, Elvira started laughing, which continued until it sounded like some demonically possessed screech.

The incident had been caught on camera by all the media

outlets present, and it made for great fodder on the evening news. Within hours, clips of the event had gone viral on You-Tube.

Leslie and the TV station could have pressed charges but declined to do so in hopes of avoiding becoming the next target of Elvira's wrath and litigious threats. Instead, the TV station sent Leslie to see a plastic surgeon and then on a two-week vacation to recover from her broken nose and black eyes.

Ironically, like most things in the media, any publicity, regardless of whether favorable or not, only fueled Leslie's and the station's popularity. After Leslie's vacation and return to the airwaves, her reputation and the station's market share had grown. They capitalized on this by flaunting Leslie's notoriety in ads for their news program. They would show a clip of Leslie full cleavage reporting and then show her walking away with the focus clearly on her swaying derriere to the following voice-over:

"With TV 6 news super reporter Leslie Anderson, keeping you abreast of breaking news and bringing you the truth to boot."

As the voice-over says, "to boot," an image of a boot print appears on Leslie's swaying tush. That advertisement, not surprisingly, also ended up going viral on YouTube.

Leslie Anderson had single-handedly caused the usually reserved and proper Maine media to become venomous and backbiting. They had first ignored her offensive tactics and painfully obvious use of sexuality, hoping that the sensibilities of Mainers would be insulted and reject her. Competing stations took the strategy of increasing their marketing to portray themselves as "serious and professional news stations" to no avail. As the ratings for her news station grew, they finally gave in and tried to adopt similar tactics. She was making a mockery of news programs, but competing stations felt there was little choice.

The Maine media was becoming more like a soft porn circus as one station after another hired nubile reporters and encouraged them to emulate the surprisingly successful Anderson. Most news stations failed, but at the height of this trend, one station started to make inroads into Anderson's market share. A competing station had hired weather girl April Titkowski. April was neither a meteorologist nor was Titkowski her real surname. She did have physical attributes that, you might say, were befitting such a name. Predictably, male viewers nicknamed her "Titillating Titkowski." April's claim to fame was a wardrobe that graphically let the audience know the forecast. It had male viewers praying for rain, 90-degree weather, or lots of snow. When rain was in the forecast, April would don a tight white t-shirt with two strategically placed umbrella decals. As she reported the forecast, her t-shirt would be doused with water making her report look like some Spring Break wet t-shirt contest. On those rare 90-degree days in Maine, she would wear a bikini and slather suntan lotion on her body. Her signature move came at the end of her report when she would turn her back to the camera, hold out the lotion to the anchorman, and ask him if he would "do her back." Over Maine's long, cold winters, April would appear dressed appropriately in winter wear. Sequentially, as the camera would cut back and forth from April to the weather map, she would remove pieces of clothing until, in the end, she would just be wearing form-fitting long underwear. The coup de grâce, however, was the suggestively titled "Getting Slammed by Twelve Inches" feature when winter storm warnings were forecast. April would appear in a fur bikini and shovel imitation snow. She would end by trading her shovel for an icebreaker tool, which she would grab with both hands and piston up and down on imaginary ice. The imagery and the physical reaction of her ample bosom when the tool hit the ground repeatedly had the intended effect. Suffice to say, April's act outraged women viewers and made Leslie Anderson's shtick look like child's play in comparison. A few passionate conservatives picketed the station for weeks. Their banners read, "Out with Tits Out ski," and "April showers bring Devil's Powers," and "Boycott Weather Porn." The station, in response, laughed all the way to the bank.

CHAPTER 23

C urt woke up Tuesday morning knowing that a couple of emotional hurdles stood between him and celebrating Caitlin's birthday that evening. He woke her with his usual rendition of "Good Morning Beautiful," staving off her attempts to have him tell her what presents she was getting. Having avoided the onslaught, he put the kids on the bus and prepared for the day.

Although, in many ways, yesterday had been a success, breaking down and crying three times concerned him. He hoped he could be more resolute in the face of inevitable emotional stress today. Counselor Tim was sure to try to excavate his feelings during their session like an archeologist of emotions. And preparing for Darius Scott's trial with District Attorney Wydman was undoubtedly not going to be a party.

He drove to work in silence. He had turned off his radio a month ago and didn't dare turn it on today. While he customarily had listened to a country station, he found that since August 20th, nearly every song reminded him of Calli or the pain he felt. He thought it was odd because, before the loss, he didn't recall country songs being that heart-wrenching. Now, every song was torture.

"Good morning, LB."

"Well, you must be pretty happy today."

"I am. Cade's birthday party went off without a hitch last night, thanks to your suggestion."

"Thanks, but I didn't mean that. I meant about Darius Scott."

Her mention of his name hit him like a bucket of ice water. Why was she bringing him up? He stood in stunned silence.

"Oh, Curt, I'm sorry. I thought you would have heard. They found him dead yesterday morning."

"Dead?" Curt struggled to wrap his head around this lightning bolt of information.

"Yes, it's been all over the news this morning and on the front page," she said, holding up the morning issue of the Dracut-Campion Star Ledger.

The headline, "Alleged Murderer Found Dead," and the side-by-side photos of Darius Scott and Calli hit him like a ton of bricks. He collapsed into a chair next to Loribeth's desk, usually reserved for waiting clients.

"Oh my god, Curt, I am so sorry," she rushed over to him and put her hand on his shoulder.

Collecting himself, he tried to talk.

"That's OK, LB. How would you know?"

"Can I get you something?" she said and then felt stupid for asking because she didn't know what, other than a coffee or a Midol she could give him if he responded.

"No, no, I'll be OK. Just let me sit here a minute."

Loribeth, usually the picture of composure, started to cry and wring her hands. She wanted to take back the words she had said. Her tears helped Curt snap out of his catatonic state, and he went over to LB's desk and hugged her. She shook in his arms, burying her head in his shoulder, repeating, "I'm sorry" over and over. He shushed her and told her everything was all right, although tears started to fall down his cheeks. When her apologies turned to apologies for crying on his suit jacket, she straightened up, and Curt released her. She grabbed a wad of tissues and started to dab at Curt's jacket and his face.

"Well, this is a hell of a way to start a day," Curt said, which struck both as funny.

They started to chuckle, even though they were both still wiping away tears.

"Can I get you a coffee?" she asked after regaining her composure.

"Sure, and I'll take it with two shots of whiskey," he replied, spurring another round of laughter.

He took the coffee and the newspaper into his office. Sipping his coffee, he debated whether he wanted to read the newspaper article. The pictures disturbed him. Why did they have to put those pictures together? He wanted to know how he died, but he didn't want to have to read a recap of the whole event or any conjecture or sensationalism that the media often brought to their reporting. Just putting those pictures together was bad enough. He walked out to LB's desk with the paper.

"Here, I don't want to read this. But can you do me a favor?"

"Anything, boss, I think I owe you."

"I can't read this, and the pictures disturb me. I want to know how he died, but I don't want to read or hear about anything else. Does it say how he died?"

"No. It says they found him dead in his bed in the early morning yesterday, and the cause of death is pending investigation by the Medical Examiner."

"OK, thanks LB. You can hold the shots of whiskey."

They smiled at one another, and Curt turned back into his office to start work on the Request for Proposal. He would read a paragraph about the requirements for the RFP but then realize that thoughts about the death of Darius Scott distracted him, and he needed to re-read the section. It was slow going, and retaining anything was difficult. Other than a preliminary outline for his part of the RFP, it had been a rather unproductive morning. At 9:45, he left for his appointment with Counselor Tim.

"How are you doing today?" asked Counselor Tim. For Tim, this was not just one of those throwaway greetings, and Curt knew by now that "Fine" was not an acceptable answer.

"I had a pretty rough start today, and yesterday was pretty emotional, but I'm also making progress with the kids and in my job."

"What was pretty rough today?"

Over the next 50 minutes, Curt filled Tim in on the shock of finding out about Darius Scott, the episodes of crying the previous day, his attending the IRB meeting and going back to work, the success of Cade's birthday party, and his excitement for Caitlin's party tonight.

"And how are you sleeping? Are you still taking Ambien?"

"I've been sleeping without the Ambien. Some nights are better than others. I usually sleep through the night."

"Have you had any dreams?"

"Most of the time, if I dream, I don't recall them. I did have one nightmare a few nights ago."

He told Tim about the nightmare in which Darius had come to the apartment and set Caitlin and Cade's rooms on fire and his inability to save them. When Tim asked Curt about how he felt about raising Caitlin and Cade as a single parent, a lump swelled in his throat, and the tears that had been all too frequent lately revisited him. With Tim's help, Curt realized that the nightmare related to his fears and insecurities about being able to take care of Caitlin and Cade on his own. Before the session ended, they identified all the examples over the past week in which Curt had proven he was an able parent and some ways he could improve. They spent very little time talking about Darius' death, and he left not entirely sure of his feelings around it. Perhaps by Friday's session, it would become more evident.

Arriving back at work, LB informed him that the DA's office had called to cancel his meeting. She confirmed that the meeting had been to prepare him for the trial now rendered unnecessary by Darius' death. Curt was one part relieved, another part perturbed, but determined to put in a few good hours on the RFP. He was marginally successful, putting down some of his thoughts for his sections of the proposal. Fortunately, he was able to use previous proposals he had produced and retrofitted them to meet the specific expectations of the Maine Employers Group on Healthcare's needs.

What kept gnawing at him, however, was that he might never know why Darius had done it. While most people thought that Darius' death would bring him relief, it hadn't. He needed and wanted proof that it was either just a random act of violence or something more to put his heart, mind, and soul at peace. Now, with Darius gone, the State had no reason to continue the investigation that had begun. Apparently, the authorities also didn't feel any compulsion to brief him on what they had found to date. This wasn't right. He wasn't just some man on the street. He and his kids were victims, and they deserved answers. He picked up the phone, called DA Wydman's office, and asked to keep the original appointment for 2:00 p.m. with the DA.

"I'm sorry," said the DA's secretary, "he has scheduled another appointment at that time."

"Well then, I suggest that he unschedule it and see me," Curt said in an angry tone that surprised even him.

"Ah, ah, I'll see what I can do, Mr. Barnes. I'll speak to him when he's back from lunch and call you back. Would that be OK?"

"Yes, thank you," he softened, realizing that his angry tone had made the secretary nervous. "I'm sorry for snapping at you. I would just like to see Attorney Wydman today if possible."

"I have a 4:00 p.m. time available. Would that work for you?"

"I'm sorry, no. It's my daughter's birthday, and we have plans. It would need to be 2:00 or no later than 3:00."

"Ok, I will call you back when I have a chance to speak with him."

"Thank you."

He felt upset for barking at the DA's secretary. Counselor Tim had warned that his anger would take over at odd and sometimes unexplainable times. This had been one of those times. He tried to regain his composure and concentrate on the RFP. Fifteen minutes later, he was still staring at his computer screen, not having progressed on the proposal. The phone rang. LB answered it and called Curt.

"Curt, I have the DA's office on the line for you."

"Thanks, send it in LB."

"Mr. Barnes?"

"Yes."

"Unfortunately, Attorney General Lewis Talcott has asked the DA to come to Harlow for a meeting, so I will not be able to reschedule you. For that matter, even if we had kept your 2 p.m. appointment, I would have to be calling now to cancel it. I'm sorry." She was taking great pains to avoid an angry response from him.

"Ok, I understand. Can I connect you to my assistant and have her find an alternate day and time for me to meet with the DA?

"Sure thing Mr. Barnes."

He transferred the call to LB and hung up the phone. He had handled that call more diplomatically, but inside he was boiling. Between now and this evening, he would have to find a way to dispense with his anger. He had the perfect birthday planned for Caitlin, and he didn't want to ruin it by being surly. As it was almost lunchtime, he told LB he was going to the gym and would be back by 1:30. LB took a double-take when he said this.

"I know, I know, I hardly ever use my gym membership, but I need to work off some stress," Curt answered, in response to her look of disbelief.

"Well, good then. You do that, but don't overdo it."

"I won't."

He got to the gym, changed, and had a plan to warm up with a jog on the treadmill and then do the weightlifting machine circuit. He hit the start button on the treadmill and, after 3 minutes, still felt tight. He hadn't stretched. He could have stopped and stretched, but he decided to run through it. His motivation to run through it grew when a young, shapely brunette hopped on the treadmill beside him. He threw his towel over the display screen and committed himself to run as fast and as long as possible. Try as he might to focus, the brunette's womanly curves entered and exited his peripheral vision as she ran beside him. She plugged into music instead of plugging into the bank of elevated TVs in front of the treadmills. She was setting a surprisingly fast pace. He figured that she was either doing interval training and would slow down or was doing a short, fast-paced run. He was wrong. After 10 more minutes, he was loose, had worked up a good sweat, and beginning to worry about keeping up his pace. After another 5 minutes, his stride was a bit ragged while hers looked fresh and strong. As motivating as her speed and her attractive features were, he was beginning to doubt his ability to continue. That's when he saw Calli and Darius staring at him from one of the TVs. Although there was no sound, there they were again, side-by-side as he had seen them in the paper that morning. This time it enraged him. The anger fueled a burst of energy.

Suddenly, Curt's imaginary running partner spoke.

"I'm so glad that crazy pyro died. What a nightmare for her kids and her husband."

Curt looked over and met the young women's eyes. Something in his look must have concerned her.

"I'm sorry, are you OK?"

"I'm her husband," Curt blurted, not knowing what else to say.

She almost fell off the treadmill and hit the pause button on her machine.

"No, keep running," Curt urged. "I need to run, and your pace is helping to motivate me."

"Oh my god, I'm so sorry. I didn't know," she said as her treadmill got back up to speed.

"Don't worry. How could you know?"

"I feel awful."

"Don't. Your running beside me the last 15 minutes has helped me."

They continued to run, talking little but pushing each other physically. Curt would increase the pace, and then she would. He learned her name was Chelsea, and she was a senior at Boone College. Curt didn't know if it was the endorphins, his anger, or Chelsea's athletic body running next to him, but he felt as if he could run a marathon. Fifteen minutes later, they agreed to stop. Stepping off the treadmill, they both commented on that weird sensation when your feet suddenly touch a surface that isn't moving.

"Can I buy you a drink," Curt joked, pointing towards the cooler that contained complimentary bottles of water.

"I'd love one."

He pulled two bottles of water out of the cooler and handed one to her.

"Thanks," she said.

"No, thank you. You don't know how therapeutic this has been for me," he responded.

"Even with me and my big mouth?"

"Probably because of you and your big mouth. Really, this has been one of the best things I've done for myself since that day."

Curt still stumbled over how to refer to the day of Calli's murder. He usually would say, "that day." He couldn't say when Calli died or when Calli was murdered. Those were too graphic, too real.

"I have to hit the shower and get back to work. Maybe we can run together again sometime."

"I'd like that. I'm usually here at lunchtime on Tuesdays and Thursdays. I hope everything works out for you and your kids."

"Thanks, Chelsea, and I hope everything works out with your studies."

Curt took a shower and went back to work, where he put in a very productive afternoon. Even LB noticed the change. Chelsea had been an angel that excised his demons that day, and he left work in a great mood, ready to surprise his daughter for her birthday.

CHAPTER 24

J ackie woke up and was happy to see she was in her bed with Stu instead of a hotel room. She leaned over, kissed Stu, and walked to the bathroom to prepare for her half-day at work. It was the lobster dinner and house hunting this weekend that danced in her head, however. She stepped into the shower and was joined shortly after by Stu. It wasn't anything like the multi-head shower experience they had on their honeymoon, nor did what transpired focus much on hygiene, but it certainly was hot.

They left the apartment together, kissed, and got into their respective vehicles. When Jackie arrived, Cheryl greeted her.

"So, how was Lobster Land?"

"Interesting."

"As I gathered from your email," she said. "Why don't you settle in, get some coffee, and we can talk in my office in, say, 15 minutes?"

"Sounds good."

Cheryl Baker was a Pharmaceutical Rep veteran. She had all the goods it took to be successful in the business – gregarious, organized, and well-schooled in salesmanship. Her youthful good looks had evolved to sophisticated elegance. She had a colorful vocabulary and a way of getting straight to the point that Jackie admired. Her incisive perspective on things could be wildly entertaining and humorous or painfully blunt and hurtful. Most people in the company felt she had reached her Director position through hard work and getting results. There were a few, however, who believed she held the job because she serviced more than just Dr. Sheridan's professional needs. Although Jackie was still relatively new, she had seen no evidence of this and thought it was probably just sour grapes from a few malcontents. Jackie pulled out all her Maine-related materials from her bag and placed them next to the stack of documents that had grown in her office over the last few days.

"Hey, Jackie," said a colleague passing her cubicle. "You know that transcript of Dr. Caron's ad you wanted me to research?"

"Yeah?"

"I did you one better. Dr. Caron has a website, and there's a link to his ads."

"Really?"

"Oh yeah, take your pick. I sent you the link to the site. Piece of work that guy."

"You're telling me. Thanks."

She fired up her laptop, anxious to show Cheryl how Dr. Caron was marketing his services. While her computer was booting up, she picked up her schedule for the next week - Boston and Providence. Her heart leaped for joy when she saw she would not have to fly out on Sunday night. There was a direct flight from Buffalo to Boston at 7:00a.m. on Monday. This gave her and Stu more house hunting time and an extra night together. She went to get a cup of coffee. When she returned, she logged in and opened the email with the link to Dr. Caron's site. Jackie was sure that the pose that Dr. Caron had struck for his website meant to convey confidence and competence, but all she saw was a smug, self-absorbed jerk. She clicked on the "Watch My TV Ads" link, and thumbnails of four videos popped up. Two were 30-second spots and the other two 1-minute ads. As she viewed them, the coffee started to churn in her stomach. She thought it was probably due to her failure to eat breakfast, but it might also have been due to seeing and hearing Dr. Caron. The videos were all pretty much the same. She grabbed her coffee in one hand and her laptop in the other and made her way to Cheryl's office.

"From your report, it sounds like your visit to Maine was a huge success other than your concerns about Dr. Caron."

"Yes, but I guess his ad and his behavior, which I didn't put in my report, kind of over-shadowed my visit."

"Well, let's take a look at the ad, and then we can talk about his behavior."

Jackie clicked on the video. To Jackie, the radio ad had been egregious enough. The video seemed to make it even more outrageous.

"Do you or a loved one tend to forget things? Do you misplace your car keys? Forget the names of people you meet? Has anyone in your family ever been diagnosed with Alzheimer's disease or dementia? If so, now there is help. I'm Dr. Steven Caron, a board-certified Neurologist specifically trained to treat these conditions. I offer the most effective treatments and participate in leading-edge research that may be the answer to your problems. You may even qualify for a research study, be paid to participate, and get free medication. If you or a loved one are forgetful, or you've had a family history of Alzheimer's or dementia, I offer free screenings at any one of my four convenient locations in Dracut-Campion, Ramsey, Namahoe, and Farrisport. Call 1-555-4Memory and start getting your memory and your life back today."

Jackie had expected Cheryl to react with at least some concern, if not outrage. When the ad ended, and she didn't say anything, Jackie was confused.

"Don't you think that's irresponsible, unethical, potentially damaging to our reputation?"

"Jackie, he doesn't mention our company or our drug."

"Yeah, but how can he make those claims?"

"We're not the regulators here. He could be involved in dozens of other clinical trials and performing voodoo for all we know. We can't concern ourselves with this. If we did, we'd probably do nothing else but investigate physicians' marketing campaigns. Now, if he had mentioned our company or our drug, then I might be concerned."

Jackie was shocked but recognized that what Cheryl was saying was the unfortunate truth. AlzCura was in the business of manufacturing and selling drugs, not regulating physician's marketing campaigns.

"So, what did Dr. Caron do that upset you?" her supervisor transitioned.

"After dinner, he drove me to my car. When I shook his hand, he tried to pull me towards him. I resisted, and he pulled harder. If my husband hadn't called at that moment, I don't know what he would have done."

"What did you think he wanted?"

"I think he wanted to hug and kiss me."

"Did he have any drinks at dinner?"

"Yes, a couple, I think."

"Listen, I know this upset you, but let me tell you about your job. I used to be a sexy young lady selling pharmaceuticals just like you. I don't have enough fingers and toes to count how many times a physician wanted to get cozy with me. Hell, I even had a female physician proposition me once."

"Really?"

"You betcha. I didn't think anything when she gave me a friendly hug, but when one of her hands grabbed my ass, and the other started to squeeze my boob, I realized it was more than just a friendly hug."

"What should I do about Dr. Caron?"

"Nothing," Cheryl stated bluntly.

"Nothing?"

"Nothing. He probably has forgotten it or wants to forget it, and you need to continue to make sales calls. He pulled your arm. That's it. It's not like he threw you up against the hood, ripped your clothes off, and fucked you up the ass...excuse my French. Physicians are just like anyone else; they're human. Even if they think they're not. You're a gorgeous young woman, and you're going to get hit on. You're going to have to deal with it. Think of it like high school when the pimply, sweaty kid asks you to the dance. Your job is to let him down easy, so you don't go to the dance with him, but he still worships the ground you walk on."

"So, I'm curious, what did you say to that woman physician?"

"I said I had a headache, that it was company policy not to mix business with pleasure, and I couldn't afford to lose my job."

"And what did she do?"

"She stopped, apologized, and offered me some Tylenol. I went home to bed, and she went home and probably wore out her vibrator!"

They both laughed.

"It worked," said Jackie.

"It worked, and she's still prescribing medications manufactured by that company."

"Wow, I guess I have a lot to learn."

"You're doing great, Jackie. Just don't get yourself roped into fighting a crusade to cure the ills of the U.S. healthcare industry. As I like to say, it's fucked, and it's going to stay fucked.

You're also not going to change the animal instincts of men or women. Behind all the posturing we humans do to appear to be fine, upstanding citizens lies a basic itch, and everyone wants to have it scratched. If you know what I mean. I know that may not sound very proper or delicate to your virgin ears, but the sooner you realize that you're in a sick system filled with little fuckers, the better."

If Jackie had come into Cheryl's office with an ounce of youthful idealism, she was leaving with a ton of stark reality.

"Sell the drug, nothing else," Jackie said.

"Exactly! See, that's not so hard. The beauty of it is that despite our sick healthcare system and some of the unbecoming jerks in it if we sell the drug, people get better. That's what's important, making people better."

"Thanks, Cheryl, this helped."

"That's what I'm here for, kid! Have a great weekend and knock 'em out in Bahstin next week. Don't forget where you pahk ya cah," Cheryl said, adopting a Boston accent.

"I will, and I won't," Jackie said with a smile on her way out of Cheryl's office.

When Jackie got back to her desk, she couldn't believe the transformation in her perspective. In less than 10 minutes, Cheryl had taken her from roiling indignation to purposeful focus. Sell Recallamin and make people better despite the flaws in the system and the people in it. She spent the rest of the morning completing the work on her Maine trip and preparing for her Boston trip. She left shortly after noon optimistic about the job and excited about her more immediate weekend plans.

She stopped at the grocery store on her way home. Stu had pretty much cleaned out the cabinets and frig during the week, and they needed some accompaniments for this evening's lobster fest. She picked up some potato salad and coleslaw. Had she thought ahead, she would have asked her mother to make the potato salad. Doris Salaney's potato salad was a family favorite, but it took several hours to make. While many had asked for the recipe, Doris kept the recipe a secret almost as tenaciously as Kentucky Fried Chicken weaseled away its secret formula. She often said in response to requests, "I'll give you the recipe before I die." Jackie also picked up some cornmeal, flour, vegetable oil, and eggs to make cornbread. She was heading to the checkout counter when she realized she had forgotten the butter and maple syrup. Then she realized she had also wanted to get a nice bottle of white wine. Jackie recognized her mind had been elsewhere. Lost somewhere between house hunting and her meeting with Cheryl that morning. "Just sell the drug," she repeated to herself, trying to fight off the discomfort that returned every time she thought about Dr. Caron.

Coming up the walkway when she arrived home, a large grey squirrel clattered from their balcony and skillfully traversed the red bricks to the neighbors' balcony. Jackie had an "ah-ha" moment, knowing now why things on the balcony seemed to disappear or moved from their rightful place. She had always blamed Stu, and he had always vehemently denied any culpability. As much as she loved him, he was a typical guy who didn't pay much attention to how things in the apartment were organized. Now she realized that she had wrongfully accused him. She watched the squirrel as it started to dine on the cat chow in a dish on the neighbors' balcony. No wonder the squirrel looked like it weighed 6 pounds! No wonder the neighbor lady was always calling for her cat. It probably saw that gargantuan squirrel and ran away! She owed Stu an apology. She owed Stu lots of apologies.

With a couple of hours to spare before Stu came home, Jackie explored Home.com to research homes for sale in Nora. She had grown up on Clifton Street across from Oak Grove Park and remembered with fondness the days she would walk across the street to play with friends. Her parents still lived in the same house. Her grandmother, who had Alzheimer's disease, was at the Spring Creek Memory Care unit on Buffalo Street, not far from her parents. Jackie hoped they could find a home close to both. She didn't get very far in her search before she found herself reminiscing about her childhood and daydreaming about the future. She had visions of her and Stu living in a house, having a baby, taking the baby to the park, and visiting Grandma and Grandpa, and hopefully, Great Grandma. She found a few homes and printed out the listings. She called a Realtor and gave her some idea of the type, price, and location of homes in which she and Stu were interested. The realtor agreed to pick them up Saturday morning to begin their house hunting. Satisfied with her progress, she powered down her computer and prepared for Stu's arrival.

Stu walked in and found their dining table decked out in a tablecloth and set elegantly with wine glasses and candles not yet lit.

"Honey, I'm home," he called, reprising a phrase that husbands have used since time immemorial.

"Well, hello there, handsome," said Jackie stepping out from the kitchen. She was dressed in a form-fitting orange t-shirt with a blue "S" and her blue, equally form-fitting, volleyball shorts.

"Oh, you are in trouble," Stu crooned.

"Not so fast, lover boy. Why don't you go take a shower and get into something comfortable? I have a feeling this lobster dinner could get messy."

"Yes, ma'am. Cold shower. Comfortable clothes," he said, kissing her on the cheek as he marched past her towards the bathroom. He couldn't resist squeezing her shapely ass on the way by.

"You'll pay for that," she said.

"Oh baby, punish me," he pleaded as he disappeared into the bathroom.

Jackie couldn't help but reflect on Cheryl's story about the female physician who grabbed her ass. She smiled, remembering the ingenious way Cheryl had avoided the situation and kept the physician in her good graces. She hoped, no, she needed to develop this skill.

Stu emerged in the t-shirt and jeans he had worn at Carter's when he had first met Jackie. He was no fool. Just as Jackie's volleyball shorts turned him on, his simple ensemble turned Jackie on.

"Oh, I see you're fighting fire with fire," said Jackie.

"Only fair," he said, walking past her without paying her much notice. She grabbed his ass as he passed.

"You'll pay for that," he said.

"Oh baby, punish me," she said in a voice that almost caused him to turn and take her to the kitchen floor.

"Where do we start?" he said in a matter-of-fact tone, resisting the urge.

"Oh, I know you better than that," she said, coming up from behind him and reaching around and grabbing the front of his jeans. "I knew it. I still got it."

"So, the pretty volleyball player can get the football player excited, big deal," he said while reaching down to the front of her volleyball shorts. "I knew it. I still got it," he mocked, dancing around the kitchen. They kissed and went to work on preparing dinner. It had been the appetizer before the real feast they would undoubtedly have later. Dinner was just the interlude.

"What? I thought lobsters were red," exclaimed Stu as he opened the box and pulled out instructions and plastic bibs that had been included.

"Oh, it says here that they turn red when they're done

cooking. How convenient, an automatic signal of doneness."

Jackie put a large pot of water on the stove and poured a couple of glasses of wine while Stu oriented himself to the cooking of lobsters.

"Let's have a lobster race," Stu said as they waited for the water to boil. "Which one do you want to bet on?"

"That one," said Jackie pointing to the slightly smaller one.

"OK, here we go," he said as Stu placed them on the counter.

After a minute, they still hadn't moved.

"Do you think they're dead?"

"The guy said they would live 24 to 36 hours."

They left the lobsters, picked up their wine glasses, and toasted to house hunting. Jackie showed Stu the listings she had printed off and told him about tomorrow's appointment with the realtor. She also told him about the squirrel and apologized for indicting him for lost or misplaced items in the past. She promised she had plans to make it up to him later. When they went to check the water, they noticed that the lobsters had moved a few inches.

"I guess lobster racing will never be a spectator sport," Stu joked.

"Yes, but I think my lobster has a slight lead," said Jackie crouching down to eye who was winning.

"Now that's a spectator sport," said Stu pointing to Jackie's backside.

"I guess more than just the water's boiling, huh, big boy?" she said as she grabbed the lobsters. "I can't do it. You do it," she said, handing Stu the lobsters.

"Ok, let the pro do it," grabbing the lobsters and dropping them headfirst into the boiling water. Before he had a chance to put the cover on the pot, a lobster flipped its tail, splashing Stu's arm with hot water.

"Way to go, pro," Jackie said as Stu howled and went to the sink to run cold water on his forearm.

"I guess that was its parting shot."

They completed the lobster preparation process without further incident. Sitting across from one another with reddish-orange crustaceans looking up at them, the traditional fork, knife, and spoon set up looked inadequate to the task. They consulted the plastic bibs and realized that nutcrackers, skinny metal picks, and wooden mallets were things that would have come in handy. They would have to improvise. With fondue forks, slip-joint pliers, and the plastic handle of a screwdriver, they fought their way to the succulent lobster meat. While it was delicious, they both agreed that it was too much work, particularly without the proper tools. They left the shattered remains on the table and retired to the bedroom to finish what they had started in the kitchen earlier.

Jackie woke up to rattling and banging sounds. She looked over and realized that Stu was not in bed beside her. She trudged to the source of the clattering and found Stu cleaning up from last night's dinner.

"What's gotten into you?" she said.

"Just cleaning up before house hunting," he said as he wiped down the counter.

"Well, hon, I appreciate that, but isn't you cleaning the kitchen a little out of character?"

"Maybe, I just wanted to see how the other half lives," he joked. "Besides, I figured that maybe we could make a day of it today – house hunting, maybe visit your grandma, dinner, and a movie?"

"My, aren't you ambitious? What's playing at the Palace?"

"That chick flick you want to see, 'Catch and Release,' starring your uglier older sister."

Stu had once told Jackie that she looked like a younger,

prettier Jennifer Garner. She had been flattered. There was a very definite resemblance.

"Sounds like a plan," she said, kissing him and then trudging towards the bathroom to get ready for the day.

They saw four houses by noon, and while the realtor had a few more on her list, they had seen enough. After the realtor dropped them off at the apartment, they got in their car and drove to Isabella's Deli to pick up a couple of sandwiches. From there, they drove back to Clifton Street and parked in front of the house they had liked best to eat their lunch. Between bites, they discussed the pros and cons of the homes they had seen. After lunch, they drove past the other three houses just to be sure. By mid-afternoon, they stopped by the realtor's office to make an offer on the house on Clifton Street, just a block and a half from Jackie's parents.

They had intended to visit Jackie's grandma, but when they had called, the staff had said that she was not feeling well and was in bed sleeping. Anxious to tell someone the news, they stopped at her parents' house. Although Jackie and Stu already lived close to them, you would have thought this move was coming home from having lived across the country. The foursome decided to brave the brisk February weather and walked the block and a half to see the house. On their way back, Jackie received a call from the realtor. The owner had counteroffered. Jackie conferred with Stu briefly.

"We'll take it," said Jackie as her parents and Stu formed a chorus of cheers in the background.

When they arrived back at her parent's house, Jackie's father suggested a celebration.

"How about we take you kids out to Danielle's Restaurant tonight?"

"That would be great, thanks," said Jackie.

There were hugs all around as Jackie and Stu left. Filled

with the joy of first-time homeownership, they stopped the car in front of the house again and kissed.

Dinner was set for 6:30 p.m., giving them a couple of hours to get ready. Arriving back at the apartment, they couldn't stop talking about what they planned to do once in the house. The 3-bedroom home built in 1900 preserved some of its old-world charms while tastefully updating key areas, like the kitchen and bathrooms. The living areas, however, had stunning hardwood floors and the original oak woodwork. Although the fenced-in backyard was small, it had a decorative stamped concrete patio and a majestic white birch that was unique to the neighborhood. It had a small garage, handy in wintertime, and a large front porch for outdoor lounging in the summertime.

They met at Danielle's Restaurant, and the conversation about the house continued between Jackie and her mother. Jackie's father told Stu about a breakthrough his company had made on the design of an artificial heart valve. Jack Selaney was the shop foreman of a medical device company. It was mainly due to his ingenuity and work ethic that the heart valve innovation came to pass. Stu was happy to be talking about something other than the house. Although he was certainly excited about it, lingering on every little detail and talking about decorating ideas were not his thing. They had a leisurely dinner that was, as always, spectacular. Jackie and Stu invited Doris and Jack to come to the movies with them, but they begged off.

After an exceptional day, the movie had been a bit of a disappointment. The storyline of a young woman's fiancé dying just days before their wedding was not particularly uplifting, especially for newlyweds like Jackie and Stu. Billed as a romantic, comedy, drama, they both found it lacking in each genre. Perhaps the best they could say about the movie was that Jennifer Garner and Timothy Olyphant were easy on the eyes, and it had a good soundtrack. In fairness, it would have been difficult for any movie to rise to the level of joy they had experienced earlier that day.

Their house-hunting behind them, they went to early mass on Sunday, followed by gorging themselves on carrot cake pancakes at Momma's Diner for brunch. They were looking forward to relaxing at the apartment for the rest of the day when Jackie's phone rang.

"Grandma died," Jackie's mother sobbed into the phone.

"What?" Jackie said as tears came to her eyes.

"She died. I can't talk about it right now. We have to go see her."

Their idyllic weekend shattered by the news, Jackie and Stu drove to the memory care unit.

CHAPTER 25

District Attorney Wydman arrived at Attorney General Lewis Talcott's office anxious to learn what had caused him to have to clear his afternoon schedule. When he walked into Talcott's office, Dr. Corpisen, the Chief Medical Examiner, was also there.

"The Medical Examiner's preliminary findings show some anomalies," said AG Talcott.

"Anomalies? What kind of anomalies?"

"Tell him, Louie," directed the AG.

"It looks like his brain had swelled, and he also had a major bleeding event."

"What caused those?" asked Wydman.

"Many things can cause brain bleeds, a ruptured aneurysm, high blood pressure, blood vessel anomalies, a tumor, but," said Dr. Corpisen pausing.

"But what?" urged Wydman.

"But the extent of the swelling and the number of the ruptured blood vessels is something I have never seen before."

"Never?"

"Never."

"So, do you have any ideas what could cause this?"

"Hard to say. Super-Giant aneurysms are possible but extremely rare. There didn't appear to be any head trauma that could have caused it, and I didn't see any tumors. Perhaps he had a congenital defect. He also had some evidence of liver failure, but that is not what killed him. We're flying blind to some degree because there are no previous medical records."

"No medical records?"

"No, he apparently hadn't been seen by a doctor or been hospitalized in at least the last ten years."

"As I'm sure you know," interjected AG Talcott, "it only adds fuel to Elvira Scott's allegations if we are unable to explain the cause of his death with certainty."

"The toxicology results may give us additional clues, but this is far from your usual case," responded Dr. Corpisen.

"Did they give him any medications at HPI that could have had this effect?" asked Wydman.

"No. The record says he only received Tylenol."

"Are there any medications that could cause this?"

"Aspirin and warfarin and other blood thinners can cause bleeding, but that doesn't account for the massive swelling. Until we get the toxicology results, there isn't any reason to conjecture further," said Dr. Corpisen.

"OK, well, couldn't you have called me about this?" asked Wydman irritated that his afternoon had been wasted because of this 15-minute meeting.

"We're sorry we had to bring you here, but given the sensitive nature of this case, we thought it best for you to hear it in person," said the AG. "We also need you to step up Investigator Adams' investigation of Darius Scott. We need him to concentrate on Darius' medical history. Did he visit any free clinics? Make any pharmacy purchases? Did he use illegal drugs? We need something, anything that might give us a clue. If he needs more resources, give them to him. We need answers, quick."

DA Wydman left the office and drove back to Campion. On his way there, he called Inspector Adams and briefed him on what he had learned at the AG's office. Inspector Adams was grateful for the information that now helped focus his investigation. One thing Wydman had asked him to do was not on his Top 10 list of things to do, meet with Elvira Scott and try to get information out of her. He had to find a way to make her feel he was an ally. The simple fact was that there was precious little information about Darius, and she was the only person who may be able to shed some light on matters. In some respects, the interests of Elvira Scott and the State were aligned – they both wanted to know what killed Darius Scott. On the other hand, she had already convicted the HPI staff and the Medical Examiner's Office. She was unlikely to harbor anything but mistrust and suspicion for anyone associated with the State.

Before Inspector Adams took on the challenge of Elvira Scott, he could do a few things beforehand. He requested additional bank records and needed to go back to the original documents he had reviewed to look for anything that could explain the anomalous brain findings. Although hospitals in the area had claimed they had no medical records on Darius, he knew that hospitals were sort of like calling airlines for ticket prices. Call one day and get one answer. Call another day and get a different answer. He could also check with some of the local mental health agencies that weren't any more reliable than hospitals regarding providing reliable information. He would also check with all the local pharmacies to see if he had filled any prescriptions. With any luck, the toxicology results from the Medical Examiner would come back before he had to meet with Elvira. Perhaps he wouldn't have to meet with her at all.

There were no pharmacies in Barry, but at least 30 pharmacies within a 20-mile radius. Hoping to avoid having to visit the six different pharmaceutical companies that represented these 30 pharmacies, Adams first checked the Maine Prescription Monitoring Program. Not only would this online service list any scheduled medications ever prescribed for Darius Scott, but it would also link him to a physician or physicians. Unfortunately, Darius Scott did not appear in the database. Inspector Adams would have to visit at least one of each of the six pharmacy companies. Perhaps more if they didn't have integrated information management systems to see purchases at their other stores in the area.

Inspector Adams spent the next day driving the pharmacy circuit. After striking out at the first three pharmacies, the Shield's Pharmacy offered some promise. Adams showed the pharmacist his credentials and the subpoena. The pharmacist instructed Lillian, the pharmacy clerk, that she could help access the records Inspector Adams was requesting.

"Could you please check if you have a record of any prescriptions ever filled for Darius Scott here or at any other Shield's Pharmacy?" Adams asked.

"I'd be happy too," said Lillian, who looked like everyone's favorite grandmother. She tapped away at the computer.

"Yes, we do have records for Mr. Scott," exclaimed Lillian taking Adams by surprise.

"Could you print those records for me?"

"Sure thing."

After a minute, Lillian took five pages of records off the printer and handed them to Adams.

"Thank you very much, Lillian; you've been a great help."

"My pleasure, Inspector Adams."

Adams turned to leave but then thought of another question.

"I'm sorry, Lillian. Is what you printed for just this store or all the Shield's Pharmacy stores?"

"Well, it would print for all of them, but Mr. Scott always picked up his medications here."

"You can see that on the records you printed?"

"Well, yes, but I know Mr. Scott. He is in here quite often."

Shocked, Inspector Adams knew he should have reviewed Darius' bank records first. He would likely have seen Shield's Pharmacy charges that could have prevented him from the wild goose chase he felt he was on.

"So, you knew Mr. Scott?"

"Oh, I still know him. He was just in here a few days ago."

Confused, he looked down at the report Lillian had given him. Under the customer name, it read "Harris Scott."

"Lillian, I think we've had a miscommunication. I asked for Darius Scott's records, not Harris Scott," he said as he handed back the records.

"Oh my, I guess I heard you say, Harris Scott. What a nice man. He is always so pleasant and courteous. He never fails to ask, please and say thank you, just as you did. Not like the younger folks today. No one ever says please or thank you anymore. Have you noticed that? And opening doors for your elders, forget it. It never happens anymore. I couldn't understand what Mr. Scott could have done to cause someone to subpoena his medication records."

Lillian probably would have gone on and on if Inspector Adams hadn't finally found a way to nudge her gently back to the reason he was here.

"I'm sure Mr. Harris Scott is a fine man, but about Darius Scott?"

"Oh, there I go, rambling again. I'm sorry, let's make sure I get it right this time. That first name is spelled?"

"D-A-R-I-U-S" Adams spelled out for her.

"I'm sorry. It says no records."

"Thank you, Lillian," Adams said as he turned to go.

"You're so welcome, Inspector Adams. By the way," Lillian said, causing Adams to stop and turn back to her. "Are you married?"

"Yes, I am," lied Adams, suspecting Lillian's question had an ulterior motive.

"I knew it. All the good men are taken. My granddaughter is just the loveliest young lady, but do you think she can find a proper gentleman? "

"Thanks again Lillian, I've got to run. Duty calls." Adams responded, trying to break away.

"And so responsible too. All the best to you, Inspector Adams," she called after him. "Oh, I forgot one thing."

Adams turned again but felt like he was going to regret doing so.

"What's that, Lillian?"

"You open the car door for your wife, don't you?"

"Yes, Lillian, I do," he said, exasperated.

"I knew it. You can tell a gentleman from a mile away. Come back and visit Inspector Adams."

Finally escaping the pharmacy that fronted for Lillian's social club and dating service for her granddaughter, Adams continued to Namahoe and the final Pharmacy of the day. As he was pulling into the parking lot of the pharmacy, an ad came on the radio.

"Do you or a loved one tend to forget things? Do you misplace your car keys? Forget the names of people you meet? Has anyone in your family ever been diagnosed with Alzheimer's disease or dementia? If so, now there is help. I'm Dr. Steven Caron, a board-certified Neurologist specifically trained to treat these conditions. I offer the most effective treatments and participate in leading-edge research that may be the answer to your problems. You may even qualify for a research study, be paid to participate, and get free medication. If you or a loved one are forgetful, or you've had a family history of Alzheimer's or dementia, I offer free screenings at any one of my four convenient locations in Dracut-Campion, Ramsey, Namahoe, and Farrisport. Call 1-555-4Memory and start getting your memory and your life back today."

Inspector Adams wrote down Dr. Caron's name and number. He entered the Namahoe pharmacy and struck out. Six pharmacies and no luck. He then realized that perhaps his luck had been in meeting talkative, error-prone, Lillian who had detained him. Had she not done so, he would have missed the radio ad that now serendipitously seemed like the best lead he had. It was still a long shot, but it seemed more promising than visiting Elvira Scott and trying to win her over.

CHAPTER 26

Caitlin was standing with Jordan on the landing of their apartment when Curt drove into the parking lot. She bounced up and down and waved. Curt was glad he had something special planned to meet the high expectations that she had for her birthday. Cade rolled up on his scooter as Curt stepped out of the car.

"Hi, Dad. This is so awesome. Thanks again."

"Yeah, but that helmet won't do you any good if you don't fasten that chin strap."

"But all the other kids don't fasten theirs."

"Fasten it, or I take the scooter away. I don't want you to crack your head open when you fall."

"OK," he said grudgingly and fumbled with the chinstrap until it snapped.

"We're going to leave soon, so wrap it up with the scooter, OK?"

"Where are we going?"

"You'll see," as he strode past the soda machine that stood next to the center cement staircase that bisected the 3-level apartment building. Caitlin met him breathless on the first landing.

"Can I open my presents now?"

"And hi to you too. It's so good to see you," he said sarcastically. Curt's parents had always insisted on proper greetings and farewells, and now, raising his kids, he found himself passing it down. Like Curt, when he was young, Caitlin and Cade felt it was a useless formality.

"Hi, Dad," Caitlin said, rolling her eyes. "Now, can I open my presents?" Patience was not one of Caitlin's virtues.

"I'll let you open one when we get upstairs, and" she turned and bounded up the stairs before he had even finished the sentence. She even ran past Jordan, who was just now reaching the landing to join them.

"Hi, Mr. Barnes," Jordan said pleasantly as they started walking up the steps.

"Hi, Jordan. I guess she's kind of excited about her birthday."

"Yeah, she hasn't stopped talking about it."

"When is your birthday?"

"In two weeks," she said with no sense of excitement or anticipation in her voice.

"Really? In two weeks?"

"Yeah, September 30th."

"Well, we'll have to celebrate."

Jordan's eyes lit up, and something almost resembling a smile crossed her face. She didn't say anything, but Curt sensed that he had struck some chord.

"Thanks, Mr. Barnes. I'm going to catch up to her," she replied as Jordan bounded up the stairs like a shot.

Curt knew very little about Jordan's home life. He knew that her mother was disabled, and she spent the day homeschooling Jordan. Her father always seemed to be "away on business." Curt had lived at the apartments for almost a month now and had never met or seen Jordan's father. Jordan was a bright and well-behaved, soon-to-be 11-year old who was reserved when compared to Caitlin and Cade. She wasn't depressed, but her affect was generally very flat. She never seemed to get too high or too low.

Curt finally caught up to Caitlin and Jordan in the apartment, only to find Caitlin scouring the cabinets in search of presents.

"Hey, get over here, you little rascal."

"Where did you hide them?"

"Who said I bought more than one?"

"Daaad," she said, rolling her eyes. "I gave you a list."

"Yes, but you would have to be Bill Gates's daughter to get all the presents on that list," he said.

"Who's he?"

"He invented computers. He is one of the richest people in the world," said Jordan.

"Good Jordan, you're pretty sharp," congratulated Curt. She almost smiled again.

"Here," Curt pulled a wrapped present out of his briefcase.

"Why did you have it in your briefcase?" asked Caitlin starting to rip at the paper.

"Because I knew that if I tried to hide it here, you'd find it."

"Awww," was Caitlin's predictable response when she saw a Breyer Appaloosa and foal combo. "They're so cute. Thanks, Dad," she said, hugging him quickly and opening the box to free the horses from their cardboard corral.

"Jordan, are you going to be able to join us tonight for Caitlin's party?"

"Yes."

"Well, then why don't you girls get ready and hop in the car."

Curt called to Cade, who reluctantly put his scooter into the first-floor storage area. For once, the kids didn't fight over who got the shotgun seat. Caitlin and Jordan were content to play in the backseat with the mare and foal. While the girls filled the car with horse sounds, Cade began his 21 questions.

"Where are we going?"

"You'll see."

"Can't I just stay at home and ride my scooter?"

"No."

"Why not?"

"Because it's your sister's birthday, and she came to your celebration last night."

"Yeah, but I didn't get to have a friend over."

"Jordan's your friend too. Was there someone else you would have wanted there?"

"No. Are we going to eat? I'm getting hungry."

"Yes, we will eat."

"Where?"

"You'll see."

Cade didn't like to be left out of the loop, and while Curt had planned this evening out, he had not briefed Cade. This made Cade feel anxious. When Cade was troubled, he asked endless questions. While he had always been curious, this went beyond curious. This was something new since that day. He needed and demanded predictability. He needed to feel in control of what was going to happen. Curt hoped that the Support Group, which didn't start for another six weeks, might be able to help Cade. Getting through life meant being able to deal with uncertainty, disappointments, and change. Cade had become less resilient to these realities, and it worried Curt.

As Curt pulled into the Morgan Farm Riding Stables, an excited and deafening screech sprang from Caitlin's mouth.

Looking in the rearview mirror, Caitlin was bouncing like a ping-pong ball around the back seat. As they passed a pasture with several horses, Caitlin screeched again. Her excitement was infectious, and even Cade and Jordan were smiling.

Stepping out of the car felt like stepping into the Old West. The unmistakable smell of horses, hay, wood chips, dust, and leather, mingled into a cocktail that some people, including Caitlin, found irresistible. Joanie, the owner, met them as they entered the barn. Her weathered face told the story of many years in the wind and sun taking care of horses. She was short, stocky, and muscular but walked with a slight limp, obtained after a rambunctious gelding kicked her in the knee years ago. Her short blond hair almost looked like a horse's mane. She looked like a horsewoman - boots, jeans, and a long-sleeved flannel shirt. When Curt shook her hand, her grip was firm and her hands hard.

"You must be Mr. Barnes."

"Hi Joanie, call me Curt."

"And which one of you is Caitlin?" asked Joanie.

Caitlin raised her hand.

"Well, I understand that Happy Birthday is in order. Happy Birthday, Caitlin! I understand you like horses."

"I love horses," Caitlin emphasized.

"Well, what you are doing standing there then. Let's go pick out a horse for you to ride."

Caitlin's eyes grew wide. "Really?"

"Why, yes, really. Would you rather just muck out the stalls because I could use another hand."

"I'd like to ride."

"And who are these other buckaroos?"

"I'm Cade."

"I'm Jordan. I'm Caitlin's friend."

"Are they going to ride today?" asked Joanie.

"No, it will only be Caitlin today," said Curt. Jordan and Cade didn't look disappointed. They seemed happy enough, just to be there.

"Caitlin, have you ever ridden a horse?"

"A pony once when I was little." Curt and Calli had rented a pony for Caitlin's 5th birthday.

"Well, now that you're a big girl, we need to find you a big horse. How's this one look?" she pointed to a chestnut horse with a white blaze and four white socks.

"What's his name?"

"Freckles. And he's the best horse I got."

"Why is he called Freckles?"

"Well, that's a secret, but if you're really good, I'll tell you the secret later."

"Can I pet him?"

"Better yet, why don't you help me saddle him up, so you can ride him."

"OK"

"Dad, you'll have to fill out some paperwork before she rides. Can you go to the office and ask Chantel for the release form?"

"Sure," Curt said and headed for the office.

"Now, Cade and Jordan, I have one rule, no horseplay around the horses. These horses love people, but they can get spooked if you move suddenly or make loud noises. You can pet all the horses in this stable except for one. Spirit, he's down in the last stall, tends to bite. So, stay away from him."

"Can we feed them?" Cade asked.

"Nope, they already had their dinner. If you're good while sister's riding, maybe I'll let you feed them an apple or some peppermints later."

"Peppermint?" asked Cade.

"Oh yes, they love hard peppermint candies. And it makes their breath smell fresh too."

That made all three kids laugh. While Joanie and Caitlin went off to the tack room, Cade and Jordan went from stall to stall, visiting all the horses except Spirit. Even as they approached the end of the aisle, they heard Spirit's distressed whinny and his hooves hammer against the wooden stall. The top edge of the top board of his stall was ragged, where he was trying to chew his way out.

Curt returned just as Caitlin was brushing Freckles before applying the saddle pad and saddle. She needed to stand on a stool to reach. Dust and wood chips flew, and amidst it all was a little girl with a smile that would not leave her face. Curt pulled out his phone and took a picture. Joanie explained every step in the process to Caitlin, who eagerly drank in every word she said. Where she could help, she did. Joanie showed her how to hold the lead rope to guide Freckles to the indoor arena. The sight of his 65-pound daughter leading a 1,000-pound horse was exhilarating and frightening all at the same time. He took another picture and another. Caitlin led Freckles to the right of a wooden platform. While Joanie held the horse in place, Caitlin climbed up the platform, her smile growing with each step. She put her left foot in the stirrup and tried to swing her right leg over the saddle and broad back of the horse. Her heel caught the first time. Joanie encouraged her. She tried again. Success! She was on top of the horse and on top of the world. More pictures.

Joanie adjusted the saddle, stirrups, and reins. She instructed Caitlin on how to hold the reins and explained to her how to turn, stop, and start Freckles. For the next first 15 minutes, Caitlin practiced what Joanie had told her. She would try to kick Freckles and make the clicking noise with her mouth as Joanie had done it. Her little heels hardly extended down below the saddle pad, and her first attempts to click her mouth sounded more like little kisses. Finally, she kicked with all her might and made a passable clicking noise, and Freckles started to walk forward. Caitlin laughed and was beaming ear-to-ear. Stopping Freckles was easier. Caitlin often just needed to say, whoa. When he needed more encouragement to stop, she would say whoa and pull lightly on the reins. She learned quickly how to make Freckles turn. For the last 30 minutes, she made big circles around the arena, and on Joanie's command, would turn Freckles and head in the opposite direction. Joanie introduced a couple of jump poles laid on the arena floor and first had Caitlin negotiate around them in an S-shaped pattern. Before long, she had Caitlin take Freckles over them.

"Good, Caitlin! You're a natural," shouted Joanie. "Keep that back straight. Hands in riding position and heels down. Good! Now give Freckles a nice pat on the neck. Tell him you love him."

Caitlin would make a couple more circles, and Joanie would correct her posture and give her positive feedback. She asked Caitlin if she wanted to go a little faster. There was no fear and no hesitation.

"OK, give him a little kick and a couple of clicks."

Caitlin followed Joanie's instructions, and Freckles picked up the pace to a trot. His silky-smooth carriage transitioned to a bumpy, staccato-like ride, bouncing Caitlin up and down. She couldn't stop laughing. When she did stop and tried to talk, her voice sounded like she was talking through a fan. After a minute, Joanie directed her to slow Freckle's pace. As if letting up on the accelerator of a car, he obeyed Caitlin's soft command.

"Alright!" Joanie said excitedly. "Wow!"

Caitlin led Freckles around for a few more circles. Curt took a few more pictures. Jordan and Cade pet a few more horses.

Then the riding lesson ended, and the lessons for taking care of a horse and the tack began. Joanie had Caitlin lead Freckles back to the aisle near his stall and clipped his halter to ropes on either side of the aisle. The horse secured, they removed the saddle and pad. Beneath was a dark sweat mark punctuated by even darker marks that looked like big freckles. The secret revealed, Caitlin giggled.

"Just wait until we wash him," Joanie said. Then she produced a metal hook on a plastic handle that looked like a question mark.

"This is a hoof pick. We just call it a pick. Do you wash your feet every day?"

Caitlin nodded.

"Well, horses' feet need to be washed too," she tapped Freckles' front hoof with the pick and said, "Foot," and Freckles shifted his weight to the opposite side and magically lifted his hoof. Grabbing his ankle and holding his hoof up, she expertly started picking out the compacted dirt. When she finished with one, she handed the pick to Caitlin.

"Your turn."

Caitlin went to the other front hoof and tapped it. Once again, Freckles shifted his weight and slightly lifted his hoof. Caitlin struggled some trying to find the best way to stand but got to a comfortable position and started to remove the dirt. Freckles exhaled loudly, his lips flapping. This momentarily startled Caitlin, but then it struck her as funny, and she began to laugh. Cade and Jordan, who had come over to watch, laughed too. She finished the hoof picking, and Joanie disconnected the ropes from Freckles' halter. She had Caitlin lead Freckles to the wash bay.

"Now I'm going to wash Freckles this time. You watch and learn."

All of Freckles spots came into view as Joanie wet his entire coat, giving him a polka dot appearance. Joanie let Caitlin hold the hose once to allow Freckles to drink from it. The way he held his lips and wiggled them while drinking made her laugh, and she ended up with a fair share of water on herself. She didn't care. Nobody cared. She was the happiest little girl, and Curt, determined to capture the moment, kept snapping pictures.

After Freckles was clean, they brought him back to his stall, and Joanie pulled a handful of peppermints out of her pocket. Freckles flapped his lips in response, once again causing everyone to laugh. Joanie showed the kids how to offer the mints to the horse by holding their hands flat. Caitlin fed Freckles, and the crunching and his lip twisting just continued her delight. Cade and Jordan ran off with mints in hand to feed other horses.

"Yuck," said Cade as he came back, wiping his hand on his pants after a horse had drooled on his hand. Everything seemed like cause for laughter by this point. Curt thanked Joanie, and the kids chimed in as a chorus.

"You, my little lady, are a natural. You handled Freckles like a pro, and I can tell he loves you."

"Well, I love him."

"It showed."

Caitlin gave Freckles a final pat and one more mint and caught up to the group making their way out of the barn. She jumped up and wrapped her arms around Curt's neck.

"Thank you, thank you, thank you," she said, squeezing his neck hard. "This is the best birthday I've ever had."

"You're welcome, sweetie. I'm glad you enjoyed it. Who's up for pizza?"

"Me, me, me," their answers rained down.

On the way to the restaurant, the kids recounted their experiences at the stable. The Breyer horses that had consumed the girls' attention on the trip there left neglected on the seat between Caitlin and Jordan. They could now talk about real horses.

"Dad, could we go to Joanie's again sometime?"

"No, honey, I mean, you didn't look like you liked it. So, I told Joanie we would never come back."

"DAAAAD!"

"Yes, as a matter of fact, if you want to go there every Saturday morning and Tuesday night, they have a walk, trot, canter class for kids your age."

"Really?"

"Yep."

She leaned over the front seat and tried to hug him, but it became more of a modified chokehold.

"OK, OK," he coughed out. "If you choke me to death, I won't be able to bring you."

"Can Jordan come and ride too?"

"Well, if Jordan wants to ride, she will have to ask her mother and have her fill out some paperwork. It also costs money."

The girls started plotting their strategy for asking Jordan's mom.

"How about you Cade, do you think you'd like to ride horses?"

"Nah, I just like petting them and feeding them candies."

"OK, well, you let me know if you change your mind."

"I will."

It was 7:30 p.m., and they were famished. They wolfed down a large pizza, and then the staff came out with a cake and sang Caitlin the Happy Birthday song. On the cake was inscribed "Happy Birthday Cowgirl" with three toy horses grazing on the green frosting pasture.

"How did they know?" Caitlin asked, initially confused.

"I have no idea," Curt said sarcastically.

Caitlin smiled, recognizing now that her Dad had choreographed this part of the evening. She thought about asking what he would have done if they had said they didn't want pizza, but now the cake lay in front of her, its candles beckoning her to make a wish and be extinguished. She stopped to wish, but instead of blowing out the candles, she got up and buried her head in her father's shoulder. At first, he thought she was doing this to thank him again until he felt her little body trembling and felt warm tears wet his shoulder. Her stoicism replaced by shattering grief. The whole evening had so delighted and occupied her that it wasn't until the few seconds pause to make a wish, and the flames, caused her to think of her mother. Then her absence became all too real. She wasn't there to share in her previous joy. Now she was staring at the thing that had killed her mother – fire. Her childhood innocence and belief in wishes coming true crushed. Blowing out the candles could not make her wish come true. Now she felt as helpless and hopeless as she had on August 20th.

"Do you just want to go home?" Curt asked, recognizing what was likely causing her sudden anguish.

She nodded her head up and down, buried in his shoulder.

"Cade and Jordan, can you blow out the candles and bring the cake?"

They were confused but nodded and complied. Curt threw $40 on the table, picked Caitlin up, and brought her to the car. She wanted to be in the front seat and turned her face into the upholstery, which now absorbed her tears.

"What's the matter?" Cade finally had to ask as he and Jordan got into the backseat.

"Cade, I think your sister misses Mom."

This brought a sob from Caitlin, confirming Curt's suspicion and effectively ending any further conversation for the ride home. When they arrived, Caitlin had recovered enough to get out of the car but held Curt's hand as they mounted the steps. She couldn't talk, and her eyes were red and puffy.

"Jordan, thank you for joining us tonight," Curt said.

"Thank you for bringing me. It was fun."

"Talk to your mother about joining us on Saturday if you want to."

"I will."

"And if Caitlin is up to it, maybe you can sleep over this Friday night."

"OK. Goodnight, Mr. Barnes. Goodnight, Caitlin."

Caitlin waved her hand, buried her head into Curt's side, and renewed her tears. The mention of Jordan's mother was like salt in her wound. Curt picked her up at the apartment door and carried her into her room. He laid his broken daughter on the bed and sat down beside her. She reached for him, and they hugged. She wouldn't let him go, and he was content to let her hold him. No more than a minute passed, and her arms fell off his neck, and she was asleep. He pulled the covers over her and shut out the light. It was a painful end to an emotional roller-coaster day.

CHAPTER 27

J ackie's grandmother was only 72 years old when she died, but she had never been the healthiest of physical specimens. Living with diabetes most of her life, battling obesity mostly unsuccessfully, and high blood pressure all combined with her progressing dementia. She had lived in the Spring Creek Assisted Living facility for the last four years, moving there shortly after lung cancer had claimed her husband. Ironically, they both died at the age of 72.

Jackie and Stu arrived at Spring Creek Assisted Living and met Doris and Jack in the lobby. After consoling one another, the Director of the Assisted Living program met them and led them to a private family room where she recounted Grandma's last 24 hours. The previous day, Grandma had gone to bed early, saying she didn't "feel well." They couldn't get any specific symptoms out of her as she had never been one to complain. They had taken her temperature, which had been normal. She had waved staff away, indicating that she was just tired and needed to rest. The next morning, when the nurse made rounds to administer morning medications, she found her. She had passed away sometime during the night. The Medical Director had been called, and he suspected a heart attack. He indicated that she probably didn't suffer much as they found her in a peaceful position in the bed. The Director asked them delicately if there was anything more the family would like for them to do to determine how she passed, avoiding words like death, investigation, and autopsy. Doris declined to have more done. Expressing relief that her passing had been quick and without pain. The Director confirmed their wishes concerning the Funeral home. When they had no more questions, the Director indicated that they could see her. Doris thanked the Director for taking care of her mother.

"It was our honor, Mrs. Selaney. If there is anything more we can do for you or your family, please don't hesitate to call me," said the Director as she quietly exited the room and closed the door.

They all hesitated, seemingly stuck to their chairs. Jackie mentioned how this was just like four years earlier when they convened for Jackie's grandfather. Except at that time, her grandmother had been present. Jackie could not get herself to stand and go to her grandmother's bedside. Her grandfather's appearance in death had haunted her for weeks, and she did not want the picture she had of her grandmother spoiled by the pall of death. The pale bluish color, the cold skin, the sickening feeling that the presence of death brought that seemed to suck the life out of the living. Then there was the inevitable pain, tears, and choking loss that they would feel as they left her side. What to say? What to do? There was nothing natural or easy about saying goodbye. Reluctantly, they made their way to her room, and shortly after that, they left.

They went to Doris and Jack's house and sat in silence for a time until Jack could not stand it anymore. He went to the cabinet where he stored the liquor, pulled out a bottle of single malt scotch that had languished in the cabinet for several years, and poured each of them a glass. They toasted Grandma, and after their first glass, they each had another and toasted her again. The alcohol unlocked their grief and their lips. For two hours, they each recounted their experiences with Grandma.

Jackie and Stu both woke up the next day a little hungover from the scotch and a lot drained from the emotional roller coaster weekend. Nonetheless, they made it out the door in time for Jackie to catch her plane to Boston. She was happy that she didn't have to go to work. She knew that if she had, all her colleagues would be asking her about her house hunting, and she would have to relive the weekend. Instead, she focused on the folder of information that prepped her for the next four days.

After Jackie's successful visit to Boston, she came home to almost an emotional replay of the previous weekend. Stu and Jackie excitedly went to the bank and realtor Saturday morning to complete paperwork in service to the purchase of their home, followed by the somber ceremony of Grandma's funeral in the afternoon. They held a small reception at Jackie's parents' home afterward. Just as the week prior, the foursome found solace in the bottle of scotch that they had used to dull last week's pain. While none of them had ever drunk scotch beforehand, something about its mossy, smoky bite and warmth going down anesthetized them. They would forever after that associate scotch with Grandma. Each year, Jack would buy a bottle of the single malt scotch, and they would come together and toast Grandma on both her birthday and on the anniversary of her death. The rest of the year, they never touched the stuff.

Jackie and Stu closed on their new home just as spring was arriving in Nora. The buds on the trees and the early flowers were beginning to bloom, and the dull gray of winter transformed into the rich greens and vibrant colors of the new season. The closing occurred on a week when Jackie was only out of town on Monday and Tuesday. After a short day on Wednesday, she met Stu at the bank, and by 5 p.m., they were officially the proud owners of their first home on Clifton Street.

Although they had scheduled the move for the following day, their first stop was their new home. Jackie opened the front door and walked in.

"Hey, get back here," commanded Stu.

"What?" said Jackie as she strode into the living room.

"You didn't let me carry you across the threshold."

"Oh ya, I'm sorry," Jackie said, reversing her steps so Stu could reprise the tradition that they had followed at every previous abode they called home.

"You have a great ass, Mrs. Deno," said Stu setting her down and letting his hand slide up to her rounded bottom nicely contained in snug blue jeans.

"Why Mr. Delivery Boy, I am a happily married woman," Jackie said indignantly in a southern twang. "If you don't behave yourself, I may not give you your tip."

"That's okay, ma'am," Stu said, adopting a delivery boy persona, "I have a big tip for you."

"Oh my, you do seem to be carrying a nice package there," she said. "Why don't we find a place to put that. Now, where would be a good place?" she said, putting her hand to her chin in thought and shifting her hip out, accentuating the curve of her ass.

"I hear they should be stored in warm, moist environments, ma'am."

"Oh, in that case, I know the perfect spot."

Locking the front door, they went upstairs to play out their housewife/delivery boy fantasy in the empty, carpeted space of the master bedroom. It was a unique way to christen their new home, but not necessarily unusual for Jackie and Stu. Their passions continued to fire their 5-year relationship that showed no signs of being quenched. With a couple of hours of daylight yet remaining, they decided to start the move-in process early. While the U-Haul was not fully packed, they wanted that night to be their first night in the house. They went back to their apartment, grabbed some essentials, and threw their mattress in the U-Haul. After an hour, they had unloaded the bed and most of the boxes they had brought over. With darkness setting in and famished, they ordered pizza. Stu went and bought a six-pack of beer. They sat on the mattress in the room they had previously christened and ate pizza, drank beer, and talked about the future. It wasn't elegant, but it was pure bliss.

Over the next few days, Jackie and Stu completed their move. Doris and Jack came over and dropped off a barbecue grill as a housewarming present. They made quick use of it, inviting them over that same evening for steak, corn on the cob, and baked potatoes. Absent patio furniture, they resorted to their kitchen table and chairs.

Over the following few months, they added more furniture and other household items that they never needed previously. On the weekends, Jackie and Stu got into the new routines of homeownership, including mowing, trimming, weeding, and watering the grass, tending the garden, and making household repairs. Cleaning a space that was three times as large as anything they had lived in previously took more time and effort. Many would have seen this as drudgery, but to Jackie and Stu, it was just part of their exciting and magical adventure. Throughout the summer, they made good use of their front porch and back patio. They would have friends and family over for barbecues and parties. Stu's parents even came to stay for a weekend, making use of one of the spare bedrooms that Jackie had taken great pride in furnishing and decorating.

Just as their new home was coming together, so were their careers. Stu never found the time or the money to go back and get his Automotive and Diesel Technology degree. Yet, he had completed all the training offered by the Department of Transportation. This and exceptional performance on the job earned him a promotion that summer to Maintenance Supervisor. Not only did this result in a healthy raise, but he was given a heavy-duty NYSDOT pick-up truck to use. Jackie continued her success on the road and at AlzCura. Ever humble, she wrote it off as the success of the vaccine more than her skills. They gave her the Newcomer Award and a big bonus that summer for outperforming the cadre of reps that had less than two years of experience. She began to realize that perhaps she had a knack for the business.

Jackie had grown in the job, and what used to disturb her became child's play. On the road at least 12 days a month, she became accustomed to the occasional advances of married, middle-aged physicians asking to sample more than just her company's pharmaceuticals. She deftly deflected these advances by putting on just enough charm to make the sale but retain her dignity. She was a success and no longer suffered the disillusionment and revulsion that Dr. Caron's aggressive advances had heaped on her. She recognized that sometimes her client's attraction to her physical attributes would win out over the scientific merits of the randomized, double-blind studies, but so be it. She easily distinguished between the physicians who were scientists deeply devoted to the Hippocratic Oath from those few who were base animals more interested in using her as their seminal receptacle. There was no need for judgment, as her supervisor, Cheryl, had put it, just sell the drug, and she did.

CHAPTER 28

"Neurology Consultants of Maine, may I help you," answered the polished and pleasant female voice. "Yes, this is Inspector Adams with the Alford District Attorney's office. Is Dr. Caron available to speak with me?"

"I'm sorry, Inspector Adams, Dr. Caron is on his way to Paris, France, to make a presentation at the International Conference on Alzheimer's Disease. He won't be back until late next week. May I take your number and have Dr. Caron contact you when he returns?"

"Is there anyone else who might be able to help me? I am investigating a case and need to know if the person I'm investigating was a patient of Dr. Caron's."

"Our Office Manager may be able to help you. Would you like to speak with her?"

"Yes, please."

"Please hold." Ten seconds elapsed, and then she was back on the line. "Inspector Adams, the Office Manager's name is Rebecca. I will connect you now."

"Thank you."

"This is Rebecca. May I help you, Inspector Adams?"

"Yes, Rebecca, I'm investigating a case and need to know if

Darius Scott was a patient of Dr. Caron's."

"I'd like to help you, Inspector Adams, but I cannot provide you any patient information over the phone. You would need to come to the office, provide two forms of identification and a legal document showing permission to access such information. Our office policy also requires that we inform Dr. Caron of any requests and that he be present before any release of information is made. "

"So, I'm confused. Does that mean Darius Scott was a patient there?"

"No, Inspector Adams, it does not. I'm just informing you of the process we require for you to obtain information on any patient here. I do not know if Mr. Scott is or was a patient and couldn't release that information even if I did know. I'm not trying to be difficult; we just are obligated to protect the confidentiality of our patients. You understand I'm sure."

"Yes, I do. So, when will Dr. Caron be back in the office?"

"Next Thursday, but he has a full clinic schedule that day. Could you come by the office next Friday?"

"Sure. What time?"

"Why don't you come around 12:30."

"Thank you, Rebecca."

"My pleasure, Inspector Adams."

He could not sit on this case until next Friday and contemplated his next steps. He couldn't avoid it any longer. He had to go and visit Elvira Scott. She was his last remaining hope, and putting this off would only get him into hot water with DA Wydman, who was anxious for some answers.

Begrudgingly, he got into his car and started the 40-minute trek from Campion to Barry. He rehearsed his lines, trying to find a symphony of sentences that would gain Elvira's trust and get her to open up to him. As he passed the Barry cemetery and turned onto the Paris Hill Road, he almost felt confident.

Turning left, he followed the dirt road to the infamous trailer that had most recently been the scene of Leslie Anderson's bloody nose and literal ass-kicking. The confidence that he found a minute before left him. Replaced by a gnawing feeling in his gut, similar to how he felt last summer after eating a bucket of clams that had tasted slightly off. Unlike the spoiled clams, he hoped meeting Elvira would not result in the violent gastrointestinal fireworks that had him worshipping the porcelain god for two days.

He got out of his car and approached the trailer cautiously. Stepping up onto the makeshift stairs, he knocked on the wooden door through the screenless aluminum frame door. Receiving no response, he knocked again, this time a bit louder. The only sounds he heard were the irksome cries of a band of grackles that had liberated some trash at the side of the trailer. They competed with a black cloud of flies buzzing from the garbage and through a broken window on the trailer. The birds' iridescent bodies flashed in the sun, and their cries sounded like a dozen rusty gates opening at one time. He smelled the trash, and it renewed the disgust he had for blackbirds in general. The smell seemed to be getting more intense. He peered into the window and discovered the real source of the stench. Elvira's bloated, fly-infested body filled the living room chair. He fell backward off the milk crate step catching himself just before falling. He was a hardened investigator who had seen many dead bodies before. This time, however, his memory of the tainted clams and the sight and smell of her bloated, decaying body were too much to handle. The contents of his stomach exploded up and out with force and in seemingly endless waves. When he finally recovered, he called the police and the Medical Examiner. He couldn't help but wonder how long she had been dead. Had he visited her two days ago, would she have still been alive? What secrets about her son died with her? How did she die?

CHAPTER 29

C urt walked in with a flower bouquet and set them on
Loribeth's desk.

"Ah, Curt, it's not Christmas for another three months, and my birthday isn't until next August. What's the occasion?"

"The occasion is your bright idea and for making my daughter the happiest little girl on the planet."

"The horseback riding?"

"Yes, the horseback riding. It was a big hit," he said, showing her a few pictures of Caitlin on Freckles.

"Aw, how sweet. She does look pretty happy."

"You win the understatement of the year award. Cade and her friend Jordan also had a blast. If not for you, I probably would not have thought of it. Thanks, LB, you're the best."

He conveniently left out the part of the evening when the birthday candles brought on Caitlin's grief. He had rationalized that she was probably just tired from all the excitement and would be better in the morning. It helped that when he started singing her wake-up song, she smiled, hugged him, and thanked him again for the riding lessons. It was almost as if the last part of the evening hadn't happened, and Curt certainly wasn't going to raise the issue that morning. Breakfast was a Freckles-fest with both Caitlin and Cade recounting their experiences from the previous night and talking about going again on Saturday. He got them out the door and to the school bus, thankful that the broken little girl from last night had apparently healed overnight.

"Oh Curt," Loribeth called after him as he was about to enter his office, "I've scheduled you to meet with DA Wydman at 3 p.m. today. Is that OK?"

"Sounds fine, LB, thanks," he said while closing his office door.

Curt didn't emerge from his office until 2:30 that afternoon, working straight through lunch. Up until that day in August, his laser focus and hyper-productivity at work were legendary. Today, for the first time in a long time, he felt he was back in the zone.

"Well, I was wondering if you were ever going to emerge again?" said Loribeth as Curt walked out of his office.

"Yeah, I guess I was a little engrossed in my work today."

"I guess I have to give my understatement of the year award to you now!"

He smiled.

"I sent you an email with a draft of my section of the proposal. Could you proofread it, please?"

"You finished it?"

"Well, I have a few things left to do, but the bulk of it's there, I think."

"You're amazing."

"When you've worked in healthcare for nearly 20 years, nothing is particularly new," he intellectualized. "It's mostly just recycling and repackaging previous strategies and ideas. Technology allows us to recycle and repackage faster."

"Quit being so damn humble, and thank me for the compliment."

"Thank you, LB," he said obediently.

"Now make me believe it," she prodded.

"Thank you, LB, so nice of you to say," he said with a sarcastic and false cheerfulness. "Maybe I'll win the Employee of the Month certificate this month, oh boy!"

They both laughed. It was a well-known fact that for Curt, the work was its own reward. He was quick to deflect any compliments and detested anything that smacked of those disingenuous recognition programs that organizations so often used to try to give the illusion of having a positive work culture. He thanked LB again, this time genuinely, for the birthday idea for Caitlin and left for his appointment with DA Wydman.

"Mr. Barnes, I was so sorry for the cancellation yesterday," said Wydman, obviously prepped by his receptionist.

"I understand," Curt strained to sound believable.

"Now, how can I help you?"

"What? How can you help me? Are you fucking kidding me?"

Wydman visibly moved back from his desk, and his friendly face turned to a look of pure shock.

"Whoa, whoa, whoa, Mr. Barnes," said the DA causing Curt to flashback to the stables last night and his daughter's horseback riding. "What is the problem?"

"The problem is that I had to learn about Darius Scott's death from my administrative assistant. The problem is that no one from your office or otherwise has been keeping me in the loop. The problem is that everyone else seems to know more about this case than me, and I'm the fucking victim here."

"Okay, Mr. Barnes, what about the County Social Services Victim's Advocate. I called them after our last meeting and told them to contact you."

"I haven't heard jack shit from anyone," Curt spat, feeling himself rolling downhill fast and hoping that he could eventually get control of himself.

"I understand your anger and frustration, Mr. Barnes. I would be angry too. Hell, I am angry," bellowed DA Wydman as his face turned a blistering shade of red. "This is why the government gets a bad name," he said as his arms started to gesticulate wildly. "How could anyone see this as anything but ineptitude? It's a fucking wonder anything gets done."

Seeing that Wydman was now as angry as he felt, Curt was able to corral his anger. Now he worried that he might have to rescue Wydman from going downhill.

"I want some answers. I have nothing but questions," Curt said, feeling his anger quickly transitioning to pain. He could feel the precursors to tears coming on and fought hard not to fall apart in front of the DA.

"I understand, Mr. Barnes."

"Curt."

"What?"

"Call me, Curt."

"Okay, Curt. I wish I could give you some answers, but we still have more questions ourselves and precious few answers. Let's get a cup of coffee and talk."

He strolled over to a coffee maker and poured a couple of cups.

"How do you take it?" asked Wydman.

"Black."

Handing him a cup, they both seemed to regain their composure.

"Let me tell you what I know, Curt, and if you have any questions afterward, I will try to answer them."

Wydman brought out the file that Inspector Adams and

others had assembled since August 20th.

"Curt, some of this information is very disturbing, and there are pictures. You will have to tell me what you're comfortable with hearing and seeing."

"I'm not comfortable with any of it, but I want to know and see it all."

"Are you sure?"

"Absolutely. The questions are haunting me, and I'd rather know some of the facts than none."

For the next 45 minutes, they went through the file in detail. At times, they would have to stop, and Curt would have to shore up his crumbling courage to continue. Other sections were almost incomprehensible in their complexity or too gruesome in detail, like the medical examiner's autopsy report and the fire investigator's report. Reading about the appearance, smell, color, and texture of Calli's cooked internal organs was more than Curt had bargained for. He wondered as he read the reports if he was doing more harm than good to the wounds August 20th had created. Some of the file contents seemed helpful, like the fact that Darius had been in Lester's the day before. However, each bit of information just seemed to raise more questions. Other than the medical examiner's preliminary report on Darius' autopsy, which was not yet in the file, Curt saw and read it all.

"Any questions?" asked Wydman.

Curt looked up shell-shocked and struggled to find his voice.

"I still don't know why he did it and if Calli had ever met him before."

"And we don't know how he died either. Nothing but questions," responded Wydman. "I'm sorry that it's taken this long for someone to meet with you about this."

"I don't suppose you're going to continue investigating if

he had a connection to my wife?"

"No. I know that's an important question to you, that's perfectly understandable. It's just not a question the State needs to answer anymore. I'm sorry. We are investigating Darius' death, and if anything in that investigation is pertinent to the questions you're wrestling with Curt, I will be certain to call you."

"Thanks, Mr. Wydman."

"Will."

"What?"

"Call me, Will. It's actually William, but my friends call me Will."

"Thanks, Will," Curt said, shaking the DA's hand, feeling a sense of camaraderie replacing the venom that he had walked in with just an hour earlier.

That night, Curt struggled to find sleep. Eventually, he gave in and took an Ambien. The next morning, when he walked out of his room, he found BB on the couch again.

"Good morning, little brother. What are you doing here?" Curt asked, gently shaking his shoulder.

"You must have had one of your sleeping pill episodes again," BB said, stretching and rubbing the sleep from his eyes.

"You're kidding."

"Wish I was, but Caitlin called me at 2a.m. You were hollering to beat the band and not making any sense. She was afraid and called me."

"Jeez, I don't even remember anything. What was I saying?"

"I could hear you over the phone. I couldn't catch everything, but you were hollering about cooking the liver and kidneys on the barbecue. Remind me never to come to one of your cook-outs," BB joked, but it hit Curt like a hammer - the autopsy report. This was his reward for insisting on knowing the details. He walked away from BB.

"Where are you going?"

"I'm going to throw those damn pills away."

"Well, if you ask me, that's a great idea."

When Curt came back from flushing the rest of the sleeping pills down the toilet, Caitlin had emerged from her room.

"Are you okay, Daddy?"

"Oh yes, honey," he said, picking her up and hugging her. "I'm sorry if I scared you last night. Daddy couldn't sleep, so I took a sleeping pill, and it made me say stupid things. I won't take those pills anymore."

"Good," said Caitlin hugging him tightly. "Who is Chelsea?" she asked out of the blue.

"Huh?"

"Chelsea. You said her name last night. You said she was coming to the barbecue."

Rather than complicate anything further, he decided to play dumb.

"I have no idea, honey. Boy, those pills are really bad."

His dumb act worked on Caitlin, but BB knew when his brother was hiding something. After Caitlin went to take a shower, the inquisition began.

"So, who is Chelsea?"

"She's a young lady I met at the gym the other day," Curt responded, knowing he could not fool his brother.

"And?"

"And nothing. She's a college student who just happened to be on the treadmill next to me when the news of Darius' death came on the news. She said something about being happy he was dead, and eventually, I told her who I was."

"And invited her to a barbecue. Is she cute?"

"No. Listen, BB, yes, she's cute, but that's not the point. I met with the DA yesterday and went through all the files on their investigation. It was awful, especially the autopsy report and pictures. I don't want to go into it, but obviously, what I saw and read yesterday had everything to do with what I may have been babbling about last night."

"Wow. You read the autopsy report and looked at the pictures?"

"Yeah. Can we talk about this some other time over a beer or 6?"

"Sure thing, big brother, I'm glad you're alright, and I'm glad you won't be taking any more of those pills."

"And I'm glad you're my brother and came over to take care of Caitlin. Sorry for causing so much trouble," he said and hugged BB.

BB left, and Curt got the kids ready for school. In the back of his mind, he was wrestling with why a cute college coed had invaded his late-night sleeping sermon. It was easy enough to explain where the cooked organ references came from, but Chelsea? It was Thursday. Didn't she say she usually went to the gym on Thursdays? He got the kids on the bus, packed his gym bag, and left for work.

At noon, after pitiful productivity at work that morning, he left for the gym. He boarded the same treadmill and started running and wondering if the college co-ed would make an appearance. Ten minutes later, just as he was working up a sweat, he saw someone climbing up on the neighboring treadmill. It was an older woman whose pear-shaped body was the polar opposite of Chelsea's supple and perfectly proportioned figure. A minute later, his motivation to continue was gone. He climbed down off the treadmill, took a quick shower, and went back to work. His laser-like focus of yesterday was replaced with scatter-shot thoughts that invaded his mind every time he tried to concentrate on something work-related. He was losing his mind, he thought. He picked up the phone.

"Tim? This is Curt. Can you see me today?" he said, clearly in distress.

"I can see you after my last appointment. How does 5:00 p.m. work for you?"

There was a long pause.

"Curt, if anyone cancels this afternoon, I will call you. Will you be okay until 5?"

"Yes, I will," he replied, not entirely sure he actually believed that himself.

He couldn't for the life of him figure out what he would do for the next three and a half hours. He was beginning to think that he should have never reviewed that file. Maybe he would have been better off not knowing all those details. The idiom "better the devil you know than the devil you don't" kept running through his head. Perhaps all the questions he had beforehand were better than all the questions he now had. Now it wasn't so much the questions but the pictures and thoughts in his head. Why did the medical examiner have to describe things in such detail? The smell of her organs, really?

With the last shred of sanity left in him, he called Jordan's mother and asked if she could watch the kids until 6:30 p.m. No problem, she had said. She had even suggested that he could stay out later if he wished. He found that thought to be somewhat enticing and thanked her, not indicating whether he was going to take her up on the offer.

"LB, I'm going out and won't be back today. If you or Sam need me, you know how to reach me."

"Is everything okay?"

"Yeah, I'm just a bit preoccupied. I'm seeing the Counselor tonight."

"Okay, you take care. Let me know if you need anything,"

she said, eyeing him with concern.

"I will," he said, leaving with a sense of relief. LB was just as astute as Curt's brother, and he hoped he hadn't conveyed to her just how screwed up he felt. He needed to get away and organize his thoughts. His choice of environment for doing this was not entirely intuitive.

The Lost Loon Tavern on Sydney Street in Dracut was the last place anyone would think Curt would go to find his sanity. It was a small bar, painted black and white like a wart attached to the seafoam green, multi-unit mill house from the 1870s. What it lacked in size and appearance, it made up in anonymity and friendliness. The drinks were cheap, which made it a favorite of college kids on evenings and weekends. Suffice to say, Thursday afternoons were not The Lost Loon's busy time. Except for two grizzled old guys playing cards in the corner, Curt had the place to himself. He ordered up a beer and made himself at home. After his second beer, he realized that he hadn't eaten and ordered up a late lunch. Or was it an early dinner? A third beer had him feeling better, and a few more people straggled in, presumably after working the 7 to 3 shift. Before he knew it, he had lost track of time and the beers. He was flying high. While he had not talked to anyone, either the alcohol or the kinship in the bar brightened his mood. He had left his phone in his car, so he missed Counselor Tim's multiple calls and messages between 4:00 and 5:30 p.m. He also missed a call and a message from Caitlin at 6:15 p.m. At 7:00 p.m., a trio of college coeds came in. One of them approached Curt.

"Curt?" she said.

"Yours truly," Curt slurred.

"It's me, Chelsea, from the gym."

"Oh, Chelsea, I didn't recognize you in clothes," he laughed. "That didn't come out right."

She laughed with him, "I know what you meant. Are you drunk?"

"Probably."

"Can I sit with you?"

"Sure, I could use the company."

"Are you okay?"

"No, frankly. I miss my wife, and my kids miss their mother, and I have no fucking answers why he did what he did."

"I'm so sorry, Curt. I wish I could help."

"You have."

"Huh, I don't understand."

"You did. Remember? You ran with me. You were like an angel that rescued me that day. And now you're here again."

"How can I help you now?"

"I need to get home. I don't know what I did with my phone."

Chelsea's appearance had sobered him up enough to realize that he had missed his counseling appointment and was late in getting home to the kids.

"I can help you. Did you drive here?"

"Yes."

"Well, if you'll let me, I can drive you home in your car, and my friends can follow me."

"You don't have to do that. I can call my brother."

"I want to do it for you, Curt," she said with resolve as her beautiful eyes met his.

"Okay," he relented, mesmerized by her eyes.

"I'm going to get you a cup of coffee and tell my friends the plan, okay?" she smiled

"Thanks, Chelsea."

She got up, and the scent of her perfume wafted his way

as she walked by. She was an alluring angel, even more beautiful than he remembered. He couldn't believe his good fortune to have her appear and rescue him twice. She came back, commanded him to drink the coffee, and he obediently drank. After he drained his cup, she asked for his keys and helped him up and out of the tavern.

"Where's your car?"

"Over there," he pointed. "The black Maxima."

"Nice."

"Oh, I forgot to pay," he said, trying to turn and go back into the bar.

"Don't worry, I took care of it," she said, continuing to direct him forward.

He started rummaging in his pockets to pay her back.

"Don't worry about it, Curt. Remember, you bought me a drink at the gym."

They laughed as she opened the passenger door and poured him into the seat. He put his seatbelt on but felt out of place. He couldn't remember ever sitting in the passenger seat before, and it felt foreign. She stepped into the driver's side and turned the key in the ignition. The glow of the dashboard light illuminated her face. She was even more beautiful in the dim, eerie glow. He was now certain she was an angel.

"You're beautiful, Calli," he said softly.

"You're drunk, and I'm Chelsea."

"What? Didn't I call you, Chelsea?"

"No, you called me Calli," she said. "That's okay, Curt; I know you miss her."

He started crying and turned his head so she wouldn't see him.

"I'm going to need to know where you live, Curt."

"The Terrace Hill Apartments," he said as his voice broke,

giving away his emotional state. She reached across and put her hand reassuringly on his shoulder.

"Relax, baby, I will get you home, and everything will be alright," she said, stroking his hair.

He woke up, and Chelsea's face was just inches from his.

"Well, there you are," she said. "Not very gentlemanly falling asleep while I was talking to you on the ride home." Her scent was intoxicating, and her lips were so close to his.

"I'm sorry, Chelsea. I meant to say you're beautiful."

"I know that, don't worry," she said lightly, stroking his cheek with one hand. "Let's get you out of the car and to your apartment."

"What time is it?"

"8:30."

"Jeez, I have to pick up my kids," he said as she helped him out of the car.

"Where are they?"

"Oh, they stay with someone here in the apartments."

"Okay, well, are you sober enough to get them? If not, I could go and get them."

"No, no, I can get them."

"Okay, well here, I found your phone," she said, handing him his phone. "And here's a breath mint, so you don't knock your kids over with your breath."

"Chelsea, how can I ever repay you?"

"It will be tough, but I'll think of something," she said as she hugged him and kissed him on the cheek. Before he could catch his breath, she was off to join her friends. As she was getting into their car, she called back to Curt. "Oh, I put my number in your cellphone if you need anything."

He looked down at his phone and saw that he had 6 missed

calls. As he turned to climb the steps, he could still smell her perfume now on him from her hug. He checked his contact list, and she had added a photo and her phone number. He paused at the landing trying to will himself into some sense of sobriety.

"Daddy?" Caitlin called down from the third floor. "Is that you?"

"Yes, honey, I'll be right up," he hoped that she hadn't seen Chelsea but couldn't be sure.

"Why are you home so late?"

"I had a dinner meeting, sweetie," he said as he approached the 2nd-floor landing.

"Why didn't you answer when I called you?"

"I'm sorry, baby, I left my phone in the car by accident," he realized he had just used the same term of endearment that Chelsea had called him earlier. He had to keep her out of his mind, but it was difficult. When he got to the 3rd floor, Caitlin hugged him.

"I smell something," she said.

"What's that, honey?" Anxious that she might smell Chelsea's perfume or the beer.

"It's mint. Do you have one for me?"

"Nope, I'm sorry, it's my last one," he said with some relief. "I guess I smell like Freckles then," he managed to joke.

She laughed and offered to get Cade. He unlocked the apartment door and flicked on the lights. He went to the medicine cabinet in the bathroom, dispensed a couple of Tylenol into his hand, and downed them, cupping his hand under the faucet to form a cup. Fortunately, the kids were as tired as he was, and after they gave him an abbreviated version of their day, they both went to their rooms without him having to ask.

He was too tired to take a shower and laid down on his

bed without taking his clothes off. He thought how lucky he had been to run into Chelsea. What would he have done if she hadn't come to the bar? Call BB? Drive home drunk? Before he could answer his own questions, he was asleep.

CHAPTER 30

With Stu's promotion and Jackie's Newcomer bonus, they were able to accelerate their home decorating plans. They replaced their old kitchen table, bought a new living room set, and splurged on a big screen TV, primarily for Stu to watch his sports programs. They converted one of the bedrooms into an office for Jackie. True to the promise they made one another on their wedding night, they went to considerable expense to install a multi-head shower in the Master bathroom. In anticipation of winter, Stu held a series of weekend home improvement events with friends. Jackie helped by staffing the barbecue and making sure there was always a plentiful supply of beer on ice. One weekend they built a shed for their outdoor furniture, barbecue, and lawn equipment. Another weekend Stu and friends installed an automatic garage door opener. Every weekend seemed to hold some new household event or construction project that Jackie and Stu could share. By fall, they accomplished most of the improvements they had initially set out to complete.

For Jackie's birthday in November that year, Stu went to great lengths to make it unique. She arrived home from her road trip on Thursday night, as usual. Stu hinted that he had special plans for her birthday that weekend. Jackie went into work on Friday morning, and Cheryl called her into the office.

"Jackie, I'm sorry to do this to you, but I need you to go to

Boston today and meet with a few doctors."

"What? Today?"

"Yes, I know, this is unusual, but we have been trying to get these doctors onboard for ages. They have a huge practice, and their office manager called me yesterday to say they would meet with us, but we need to do it this weekend."

"I'm not even prepared."

"Not to worry. All you need to do is go home, pack, and get to the airport by 11 a.m. I have tickets waiting for you at the airport. I will send you an email with all the research and particulars about the docs and their practice. You'll be home by Sunday, and you can take Monday and Tuesday off."

"Okay," she said, trying to hide her disappointment. Stu was going to be upset. She called him with the bad news.

"Hon, I've got bad news."

"What?"

"Cheryl is sending me on a trip to Boston this weekend."

"WHAT? You never go on trips on weekends. Why this weekend? That fucking bitch just ruined my plans for your birthday."

Jackie was taken aback by Stu's swearing. He must really be upset because he rarely swore. She tried to smooth the waters.

"I know, I'm sorry. But I have Monday and Tuesday off. We can celebrate then."

"Oh yeah, sure, celebrate when I have to work those days. I can't believe she did this. I'm going to call her."

"No, Stu, you will NOT call her. I know you're upset, but it's only two days. I'll be back on Sunday. Honey, please, don't blow this out of proportion."

Silence.

"Stu?"

"Alright," he said dejectedly. "When will you be back on Sunday?"

"I don't know yet. The tickets are waiting for me at the airport. Once I find out, I will call you."

"Okay, I'm not happy."

"I know, I'm not happy either, but I love you."

"Love you too. Have a safe trip."

"I will."

She arrived home, packed, and left Stu a perfumed love note on the bed. She had just enough time to get to the airport at the prescribed time. At the ticket counter, she handed her driver's license to the agent and told her that her company had left tickets for her flight to Boston. The agent tapped on the computer.

"I'm sorry, Mrs. Deno, your flight has been canceled."

"Canceled?"

"Yes, it appears you're booked on another flight."

"At what time?"

"At 12:10."

"Oh, okay. I was worried it was going to be later."

"Yes, but it says you're going to Arizona."

"Arizona? No, I need to go to Boston."

"No, you don't," said Stu from behind her.

"What are you doing here?"

"We're going to Arizona."

It took Stu and the agent a little while to convince Jackie that she was going to Phoenix and that Stu's elaborate scheme had worked to perfection.

"But I packed for Boston. I have no clothes for Arizona."

"That's fine; I packed a few of your summer things in my

bag. Besides, I'm hoping you'll spend more time out of your clothes than in them."

At the gate, while they were waiting to get on the plane, Jackie checked her email. She opened an email from Cheryl with a subject line that read "Boston Itinerary." It read, "Happy Birthday, Jackie! Have fun in the sun in Arizona. See you Wednesday. Cheryl"

"I'm impressed," said Jackie turning to Stu. "You planned this surprise out well."

"Thanks, Boo, anything for your special day."

Jackie didn't know it, but Stu's surprises were just beginning. They arrived in Phoenix, rented a Chevy Tahoe again, and drove to The Oasis Hotel & Spa in Scottsdale.

"This is like déjà vu all over again," Jackie joked.

"Did you want to stay somewhere else?"

"No, no, this is great. I am going to love reliving our honeymoon. Something tells me you're going to love reliving it too," she said, leaning over and kissing his neck and running her hand up his thigh.

"Hey, hey whoa, slow down there, little filly. I got some trail left to blaze here before you start grabbing the wood and ask me to stoke your campfire," he said, running his hand up her thigh.

"Alrighty, partner. Just let me know when it's time to cook."

When they got to the check-in counter, the registration clerk greeted them.

"Welcome back, Mr. & Mrs. Deno. So good to have you back at the Oasis Hotel & Spa. Mrs. Deno, we're honored that you will be spending your birthday with us. We hope you will enjoy a free 3-hour spa visit on us at your convenience."

She looked at Stu, who was grinning ear-to-ear.

"How nice and thank you, I can't wait to enjoy it," she said to the clerk. "You are incredible, Mr. Deno," she said to her husband.

"Oh, you haven't seen anything yet."

They went to their room, which was the same room they had stayed in for their honeymoon. There was about an hour left of sunshine, and Stu suggested they hit the pool before going to dinner. Jackie didn't want to get her hair wet and countered with a suggestion they go to the restaurant. He finally convinced her to catch some rays at the pool and then go to dinner.

As they approached the pool, a small group of people at the Cabana Bar started to sing.

"Happy Birthday to you. Happy Birthday to you. Happy Birthday, dear Jackie. Happy Birthday to you."

As they clapped and cheered, Sunny emerged from behind the bar with a Baja Pineapple Grenade for Jackie and a Jack and Coke for Stu.

"Hi y'all!" she said, giving them her best Sunny smile.

"Oh my god, Sunny, it is so good to see you," said Jackie grabbing the drink with one hand and hugging her with the other.

"Here, let me take that other drink out of your hand, Sunny," said Stu.

"Not before I get a hug from you too," piped Sunny. He obliged.

"Stu, I can't believe you arranged all this."

"I didn't. I had a lot of help from Cheryl and Sunny. You know behind every successful man,"

"is a woman," Sunny and Jackie chimed, laughing at how in unison they were.

"Let me introduce you to some of my friends," said Sunny.

Within 15 minutes, Jackie and Stu felt like they had never left Arizona. Stu had even planned for dinner poolside. As the sun was setting, waiters delivered an array of southwestern dishes that they had missed since returning to Buffalo. Sunny also kept everyone well lubricated with her creative and powerful beverages. As darkness enveloped the bar, kerosene torches were lit, and electric ceiling heaters clicked on, keeping the area a comfortable 70 degrees. They partied until the drinks, the flight, and the time change all hit Jackie and Stu like a ton of bricks. They thanked Sunny and her friends for a great time. Jackie asked Sunny if they would see her again during their visit. Sunny said she was getting off early tomorrow, and maybe they could grab a bite in North Scottsdale. After hugs and kisses all around, Jackie and Stu propped each other up as they steered their way along the winding paths back to their suite.

"Ride em cowboy," Jackie commanded as she fell backward onto the bed.

"Yee-haw," Stu replied.

It was the perfect ending to a perfect day. After playing cowboy meets cowgirl, they fell asleep in each other's arms and didn't wake up until mid-morning the next day.

Jackie opened Stu's suitcase and looked down at what he had packed for her.

"Honey, I love you, and this is the best birthday present I have ever had, but remind me never to let you pack for me again!"

"What do you mean? I think I did a great job."

"You've got to be kidding," as she held up some shorts and a top that did not match.

"Well, you haven't looked hard enough then," said Stu. "Dig deeper."

Under the next set of unmatched clothes was an envelope. She opened it and looked at the card that read, "The most beautiful woman in the world deserves to be dressed in the most beautiful clothes in the world. Enjoy! Love Stu." A $500.00 gift card to the Fashion Square Mall fell to the floor.

"How in the world did you get a Fashion Square Mall gift card in Buffalo?"

"The wonders of online purchasing over the Internet."

"Stu, you realize that you're setting a pretty high bar for yourself for future anniversaries and birthdays."

"Yes, I guess I should probably tone it down some. How about we go to McDonald's for breakfast and stay at Motel 6 tonight?"

They drove down Scottsdale Boulevard until they arrived at the Mall. They had half the day to shop before they planned to meet Sunny for drinks and dinner. Stu hated shopping but was on his best behavior as they wandered in and out and around the dozens of stores that caught Jackie's attention. He knew she loved to shop and held off, giving voice to his growing boredom, knowing it would spoil her fun. Jackie, knowing this was probably killing Stu, would occasionally flash him while trying on clothes. He appreciated her attempts to distract him. He kept telling himself that it was only a few hours out of an otherwise idyllic four days.

Armed with a more appropriate wardrobe for Jackie, they left the mall with just enough time to freshen up at the hotel and leave again to meet Sunny in North Scottsdale. As Jackie and Stu made their way, the Sonoran Desert and sky lit up with the most brilliant colors either had ever experienced.

"God's artwork," Stu said, breaking their silent wonder.

"Wow, Stu, that's so perfect. I was trying to find a way to describe this, but it almost defies description. You nailed it."

"Thanks. You want to hear something else?"

"What?"

"You make God's artwork even more beautiful."

Jackie loved that her big, brawny husband could occasionally slip into a kind of poetic, romantic sensitivity. Something about what he had just said caught her in an emotionally vulnerable place. She looked over at him as tears began to well up in her eyes.

"Oh, Stu, I am so happy."

He looked over just as the first tear dropped and coursed a trail down her cheek.

"Well, you have a funny way of showing it," he said, reaching over and softly wiping the tear with his hand. She leaned into his hand and eventually grabbed his right arm and placed her head on his muscular bicep. She would occasionally wipe her face on his shirtsleeve as tears continued to fall. They continued through the heavenly artwork, the enormity of the rainbow-colored sky, rendering them once again silent. Despite the silence, they felt even more connected than ever.

Sunny was sitting at a high-hat table outside a bistro, sipping a drink as they approached.

"I hope you don't mind. I saved us a table outside."

"No, great, we're glad you did," Jackie said, giving Sunny a hug and a peck on the cheek.

"I love your outfit," said Sunny as the ladies quickly transition into comments about each other's clothes and appearance as Stu stood at the table.

"Stu? Get over here and give me some sugar," Sunny said, finally interrupting girl talk.

Stu sauntered over and hugged Sunny while she planted a kiss on his cheek. Before he could move away from her, she wiped a smudge of lipstick off his cheek with her hand.

"Sorry, Stu. That color doesn't look good on you, and your

wife would kill me," she said as both Jackie and Sunny laughed.

Stu couldn't help but remember Jackie's first jealous reaction to Sunny, but now they were like old friends.

"Oh, you have to order one of these," Sunny said, pushing her drink towards Jackie. "Try it. It's called a Lemon Drop."

Jackie took a sip of the candy-coated rim of the martini glass, and her eyes told the story before her lips did.

"Oh my god, that is delicious. It tastes just like a Lemon Drop. Stu try this," Jackie said, passing the drink to Stu.

"Wow, that is good."

As if on cue, an attractive female server appeared at their table.

"Can I get you anything?" said the server as she caught a stray strand of her long blond hair and tucked it back into its prescribed place.

"Oh, I want one of these," Jackie raved as she pointed to Sunny's drink. "Love your long hair," she added.

"Thanks, sometimes it's more trouble than it's worth, though," said the server as she ran her hand down one of her long tresses.

Stu marveled at the trio silhouetted against the brilliant sky. With so much beauty in one place, he was almost certain this must be a preview of heaven.

"And what can I get you," the server asked, interrupting Stu's reverie.

"Ah, I don't know, I don't usually drink martini's," Stu said, grabbing the list on the table.

Sunny and Jackie laughed and asked the server if she had any suggestions.

"The Vampire Kiss is popular right now. It's a special we only make around Halloween."

She described what it contained, and before Stu could cast

a vote, Sunny and Jackie had ordered it for him.

"Ah, I think I'll have the Vampire Kiss, I guess," Stu said sarcastically after the server had left.

Sunny and Jackie laughed and commented that he had better get used to them controlling the evening. Frankly, that suited him just fine. As Jackie caught Sunny up on her shopping spree that afternoon, he watched the brilliant sky slowly dwindle like someone turning a dimmer switch. Pinks darkened to purples. Yellows turned to gold as the kaleidoscope of colors made its way towards darkness. Stu had only one sip of the Vampire Kiss made with Chambord and champagne with a blood-red sugared rim. After Jackie took a sip, she traded him for her Lemon Drop. Sunny, having drained her drink and having sampled Stu's, now Jackie's drink, also ordered a Vampire Kiss. The conversation between Jackie and Sunny grew more animated as it turned towards the subject of Sunny's love life.

By this time, Stu's attention had shifted to conducting an informal survey in his head of people who walked by who may have had plastic surgery. It struck him, as people walked by, just how many "beautiful people" there were in Scottsdale. Contrary to the rising obesity rates everywhere else, almost everyone in Scottsdale seemed to have walked off the pages of Shape or Glamour magazine. As the soap opera-ish story of Sunny's most recent failed relationship wound down, they dismissed the server's offer of another drink in favor of their dinner options. After a short debate between a steak place and a pizzeria, they opted for the latter.

As they walked into the quaint, river-stone building with the red tile roof of Papa's Brick Oven Pizzeria, Jackie and Stu felt transported back to New York. The Brooklyn-themed interior clashed with the desert oasis they had just walked in from, but the aroma beckoned to them. Stu was happy to order a beer after his brief run-in with martinis. The ladies ordered wine. They decided to share a large pizza that was set on a raised metal platform on their table. The crisp, uniquely flavored crust was an outstanding accompaniment to the fresh garlic, tomatoes, basil, and mozzarella cheese that topped the tangy sauce. They also shared a piece of New York Cheesecake and a cannoli. The conversation turned predictably to New York. While Buffalo and Nora weren't on most people's lists of places to visit, Jackie and Stu had Sunny convinced that she needed to visit.

After dinner, they stepped out into the darkness, and the temperature had dropped perceptively. Waling back to their cars, Jackie and Sunny complained about the cold and leaned into Stu, who wrapped his arms around them to give them some measure of warmth. They passed an old couple who eyed the trio with suspicion. Jackie and Sunny burst into laughter and thought about making some suggestive comments but decided they didn't want to be responsible for any heart attacks. They parted ways at Sunny's car, arranging to see her when she next worked the hotel's Cabana bar.

When Jackie and Stu arrived at the hotel, they took a long, luxurious soak in the oversized, jetted tub. Although they had just settled into their first home, they talked for over an hour about whether they could ever see themselves living in Arizona. They realized that they had been there twice in the last ten months, and both times, they had avoided the intense heat of summer. Having their family all in western New York also made a move to Arizona difficult. They settled that Arizona wasn't in the cards any time soon, but they were quickly making it their winter haven. They went to sleep, and overnight, Jackie turned 24.

Jackie woke up to breakfast in bed. Stu walked in singing the birthday song while setting a tray of eggs benedict, pastries, coffee, a mimosa, and a red rose on the bed. She smiled, rubbing the sleep from her eyes.

"Your special day of experiences begins," said Stu after

singing.

"Thanks, hon," Jackie said, stretching her arms out and drawing her South Temple t-shirt tight against her breasts.

"No, thank you,' said Stu cupping her left breast in his hand while leaning over to kiss her.

"I'm going to take a shower experience, Boo. You enjoy your breakfast experience. Don't forget your spa experiences start in an hour."

"You're not eating?"

"Nope, I'm going to have a football and brunch experience while you're being tuned up," he called as he entered the bathroom.

Stu had upgraded the hotel's generous 3-hour spa offer to the deluxe package of services from the dizzying array of "experiences." Jackie and Stu had spent nearly an hour trying to sort through all the various "experiences" to come up with the perfect package. Afterward, nearly everything became an "experience" joke. While Jackie rejuvenated, Stu intended to do his favorite Sunday guy-spa experience – watch the Buffalo Bills. Stu had spied a Sports Bar on his way to the mall the previous day and planned to go there, have brunch, and watch his Bills win hopefully. The Bills' season started dismally, but they had won their last few games. If they could pull out a victory over the Dolphins today, they would be right in the thick of things. After their respective "spa" experiences, they intended to walk around Old Town Scottsdale, taking in the shops and art galleries before a fine dining experience at Socrates.

As Stu stepped into the shower, Jackie began to uncover her breakfast plates. To her surprise, under a small plate cover was a small, wrapped box. She smiled and shook her head in disbelief, as Stu's surprises seemed to be endless. She unwrapped the box, opened it, and revealed a pair of diamond earrings. She put in the earrings, jumped out of bed, and went to the dressing room mirror to inspect how they looked. Even with her bed hair and sans make-up, Jackie and the earrings sparkled. She took off her t-shirt and panties and opened the bathroom door.

"Hey, what are you doing here?" Stu said in mock surprise.

"I'm going to give you a shower experience you won't forget," she said, pulling him in and kissing him deeply.

Little did they know, but that shower experience would change their lives.

CHAPTER 31

The police arrived and cordoned off the area around Elvira's trailer. Inspector Adams reported to the police, indicating that he had vomited but had not otherwise disturbed the scene or gone in. Extra officers arrived to protect the scene. The media, which had featured Elvira's conspiracy claims against HPI and the Medical Examiner's office prominently over the last few weeks, was undoubtedly anxious to scoop this new twist to the story. Her death would add more intrigue and fuel to the fire of conspiracy theorists, of which Maine had more than its fair share. Inspector Adams, however, was not eager to stick around for the gruesome work ahead or the inevitable media circus. He left to clean himself up and take stock of his floundering investigation into Darius' death.

The Medical Examiner, Dr. Corpisen, arrived shortly after the police. They found the door to her trailer unlocked. Upon opening the door, no amount of Vick's Vaporub under their noses was enough to mask the stench. Flies were everywhere. Dr. Corpisen examined the body, being careful not to touch or disturb it. There were no visible injuries except for some petechial hemorrhaging in the eyes and on her skin. He didn't say anything at that time, but he had found similar hemorrhaging on Darius Scott. Photographs were taken, and before moving Elvira's body, Dr. Corpisen did an abdomen stab to help determine the time of death. Her core temperature indicated that she had been dead for over 24 hours. He suspected the time of death to be between 1 and 3 days, just from the presence of the flies and the absence of rigor.

Determining the time of death was far from an exact science. In the first 24 hours, the core temperature probe and stage of rigor mortis were helpful. Afterward, the body starts to decompose, and rigor mortis evolves to secondary muscular flaccidity. Then the medical examiner's primary tool becomes the type of insects present, known as forensic entomology. They moved Elvira to examine the other side of her body, finding marked lividity from blood pooling in her lower back and lap area caused by dying in a seated position. There were no visible signs of the cause of death, and she hadn't been moved. Police had searched the home, and while it was a disheveled mess, there were no signs of a break-in or burglary. Dr. Corpisen would have to reserve judgment on the cause of death until completing an autopsy. At this point, it appeared eerily similar to her son's death.

As the police and Dr. Corpisen concluded their work, and Elvira was placed in a body bag for transport to the morgue, the media arrived on the scene. The irrepressible Leslie Anderson also arrived, knowing that Elvira could no longer keep her away, bloody her nose, or kick her ass. A cadre of reporters and camera operators moved like an undulating amoeba, jockeying for the best position to film the scene. Getting shots of the body bag and speaking to any official within earshot was the prize. Leslie pushed past the yellow tape to the protests of other reporters to shove her microphone in the face of the medical examiner.

"Dr. Corpisen, can you give us a cause of death?" she shouted as an officer started to move in her direction. She continued her march towards the medical examiner.

"Was there evidence of foul play? Was she killed to shut her up and stop the embarrassment she has caused HPI and your office?"

She was an expert at coming up with outrageous and provocative questions. While they usually elicited a response, Dr. Corpisen kept his cool.

"There will be no statements until we have completed the autopsy."

"Aren't you concerned that this looks like a cover-up, a way to sweep her allegations against you under the rug?"

Dr. Corpisen did not dignify this with a response, and the police officer who had tried to shield her from advancing further finally intervened.

"Ms. Anderson, get behind the tape, or I will be forced to arrest you," he said, sticking his thick, muscular arm between the reporter and her path towards the medical examiner. Seeing she was getting nowhere with Dr. Corpisen, she turned her ire on the police officer. She purposely ran into his arm with her ample breasts and then tried to slap his arm away as if he had initiated the contact.

"Don't you dare touch me unless you want a sexual assault charge on your record," she shrieked.

"Ma'am, you ran into me. Please get behind the tape, or I will restrain you and place you in my cruiser."

"Oh, I'm sure you'd love to put those cuffs on me, wouldn't you, Officer Beefcake? Perhaps get your picture on the evening news? What are you going to do with me in your cruiser? Show me your tiny nightstick?"

This last salvo drew laughter and jeers from the media mob. As she so often did, Leslie Anderson was becoming the story rather than reporting the story.

"No, ma'am, I'm just protecting the crime scene," the officer said, biting the inside of his lip to keep from laughing himself.

"Jeez, Leslie, give it up," yelled one exasperated camera operator from a competing station. He thus became her next target.

"Shove that camera up your ass, camera jockey."

"Sorry, I'll leave that to you. You're the only one who likes a camera up their ass," said the camera operator drawing laughter and applause from the mob.

Several police officers now made their way over, and most of the media group started to leave the scene. Leslie was given a final warning to get behind the tape. She left in a huff but not before the camera operator got in one last dig.

"There's that camera-loving ass. Shake it, Leslie. I'll put it on the 10 o'clock news. Or would you rather I put it on your porn site?"

Leslie kept marching away but shot back a finger as she boarded the news van. Cheers and laughter erupted again as the van started to leave.

Dr. Corpisen returned to his office, happy to have avoided a scene with Leslie Anderson and becoming the next victim of her overly dramatic reporting.

"Dr. Corpisen," said one of his assistants, "we have the toxicology results back on Darius Scott."

Handing the report to Dr. Corpisen, he started to scan it as he made his way to his office. While his lab could do some of the basic testing, they relied heavily on a more sophisticated regional crime lab. Unlike TV crime shows, which gave the impression that toxicology results were almost instantaneous, they often took 4-6 weeks. The basic tests done at Corpisen's lab had been inconclusive. As he read the report, nothing caught his eye until the toxicologist's remarks regarding Darius Scott's tissue samples. It was common practice with autopsies not only to send bodily fluids but samples of tissues from all body organs. The report commented that an unidentified substance was found in varying concentrations in Darius' heart, liver, and brain. This substance wasn't any of the usual suspects, like opiates, amphetamines, or barbiturates. The regional lab had checked with other regional toxicology labs. None of the labs were able to match the substance they had found. The toxicity of the substance was unknown, and the Chief Toxicologist concluded the tissue section of his report as "suspicious but inconclusive."

Dr. Corpisen didn't know whether to be excited or disturbed by the finding. On the one hand, it might explain Darius' sudden death. On the other, the inability to identify the substance, or how it got into Darius' body, was damning. He picked up the phone to notify AG Talcott.

CHAPTER 32

C urt woke up with a start and peered over at the digital alarm clock on his dresser. 3:14 a.m. He had fallen asleep in his clothes and his shirt, now drenched in sweat along with his pillow. His hair was matted; his heart felt like it was going to pound out of his chest. The remnants of the terror he had experienced in the nightmare were still fresh.

The nightmare felt like it had gone on for hours and had started pleasantly enough. Unlike many dreams that seem disconnected from any stream of reality, this one started as if Chelsea had accompanied Curt after driving him home instead of driving off with her friends. The kids had not been present, which hadn't seemed odd at the time, but did as he now recollected the scenes. They entered Curt and Calli's house, which also seemed natural at the time but disturbing now as he remembered it. Chelsea had draped her arms around Curt's neck, pressed her body into him, and kissed him deeply. He pulled her in even closer and tighter. They didn't bother to turn the lights on in the house, and after the kiss, they struggled to keep their hands off each other as they made their way in darkness. Disrobing piece-by-piece, leaving a trail of clothes in the hall and up the stairs didn't seem as cliché as it did now to Curt. They fell into bed, and their bodies came together in a perfect union. Magically, their bodies moved, stretched, and arched in concert as if they had perfected this dance over years of practice. Despite their experienced moves, it somehow felt like the first time - new, fresh, and exciting. They brought each other to the edge of release, backing off at just the right time to maximize the experience and turn this moment into a marathon. Curt remembered it feeling like the day they ran side-by-side on the treadmills, each pushing the pace and each pushing the other to a new level. Curt rolled, and Chelsea was now on top like a rodeo rider. She drove into him, beckoning him deeper. His hands shifted alternately from her hips to her breasts as her back arched. Curt had closed his eyes, trying to control himself, listening for the telltale sounds that would tell him she was going over the edge.

"Relax, baby, I will bring you home," she kept repeating between her moans that were becoming louder, longer, and deeper. Wasn't that what she had said to him last night?

Their bodies started to move with increased speed and abandon. They were running for the finish line, and they were not going to stop the sprint. Her words turned from "Relax baby" to "Oh baby" and "Yes baby" as if permitting him to let go. He didn't need the encouragement. Her moans turned to screams. He opened his eyes, wanting to watch her in the throes of her ecstasy. When he did, a flicker of light from behind her head illuminated the darkened room. He didn't remember her lighting a candle. The light continued to flicker and grow more intense. Then Chelsea's hair erupted in flames, and her screams of ecstasy turned to screams of pain. She started to fall forward toward Curt, who was still lying between her legs. She seemed to be falling in slow motion. Curt was caught in a weird bodily experience between ecstasy and fear. Chelsea continued to fall towards him slowly, her face and shoulders now engulfed in flames. Her body was writhing from the pain, and he was trapped inside and under her. As beautiful Chelsea turned into a raging fireball slowly approaching him and threatening to consume him, he saw a figure emerge from behind her. He couldn't make the ominous figure out. Just as Chelsea's blistering and burning body was about to land on him, he woke up.

As he lay in bed, wiping the sweat from his forehead and removing his cold, damp shirt, he tried to relax and slow his heart rate. He felt like he was going to have a heart attack. While a morning erection wouldn't be odd any other day, today, it blurred his sense of what was real and what had been a dream. He tried to stop thinking about it but couldn't. It consumed him as effectively and as devastatingly as the flames had consumed Chelsea. He tried to remember what Counselor Tim had asked him after his last nightmare to help him interpret his dream. He had asked him how he felt during the dream. He had asked what meaning certain things in the dream held for him. Since he couldn't stop thinking about it, he tried his hand at self-analysis.

How had he felt? Well, curiously comfortable and ecstatic during their incredible lovemaking, but then horrified and scared when she erupted into flames. What meaning did making love hold for him? Closeness, intimacy, mutual fulfillment, knowing someone at the deepest and most basic level. What did flames mean to him? Destruction, loss, anger, fear, pain. What about being back in his house? What about no kids? Why did this all seem so normal in the dream and so horrifying now? Now he only felt guilt, shame, and helplessness. He gave up on his self-help session and got up to get a drink of water in the kitchen. He flicked on the TV in the living room and mindlessly watched fast-talking Vince show him the wonders of a super absorbent towel. When the next infomercial started to try to sell him on a versatile mini blender, he felt sufficiently distracted from the dream to shut off the TV and try to go back to bed. He had to get a dry pillowcase for his pillow before lying down. Sleep would not come. While he didn't sleep, his mind felt like it had shifted into neutral. He didn't remember thinking of anything, just lying there and being. It was an odd sensation but probably self-preserving. His mind had just worked overtime, and the respite was welcome.

The alarm rang, and he had fallen asleep at some point in the early morning. He was dead tired. Whatever sleep he got was not enough to restore him to any cognitive functioning. He was too tired to get up, and before he knew it, tiny hands were pushing on his shoulder.

"Dad. DAD," Caitlin shouted. "Are you taking those pills? Aren't you going to make us breakfast?"

He opened his eyes, and she was a blur. He rubbed at his eyes, and she came into focus. Caitlin had a genuine look of concern on her face. Yesterday he had scared her by his incoherent babbling in the middle of the night; now, he wasn't waking up. He realized that he had to get his act together before she and Cade lost faith in him. He struggled to his feet.

"No, honey, I didn't take any pills. I threw them away. I didn't sleep well last night, and now I'm tired. I'll make you breakfast. What do you want?"

"Chocolate Chip Waffles," responded Caitlin.

"Me too," Cade hollered from the hall.

He fought through his exhaustion and resolved to make some coffee as the waffles cooked in the toaster. He could do this, he thought. As he trudged into the kitchen, Cade approached him.

"Dad, I didn't do my homework. Could you help me with my math?"

"Now?"

"Yeah, I have to have it for today."

He was about to launch into Cade for not doing it the night before, but he was too tired and, to some degree, felt responsible for not being there for him last night.

"Okay, but just this once," he said in a semi-scolding tone. "Next time, you better do your homework the night before, you hear?"

"Yeah, Dad, I'm sorry."

Fortunately, 2nd-grade math was something even a hungover, bleary-eyed, sleepless person could help a 6-year-old complete in a matter of minutes. He started to feel better as the coffee began to work its magic. By the time the kids were out the door to school, he had canceled his original plan to go back to bed and, instead, got ready for work. As he was dressing, he realized that he had some explaining to do to Counselor Tim for his missed appointment.

He walked into work, and Loribeth greeted him and eyed him suspiciously.

"And good morning to you, LB. Why the evil eye?"

"Oh, just concerned about my boss, who I couldn't reach yesterday afternoon when your Counselor called saying he couldn't reach you."

He then realized that one of the missed calls had been from LB. He was caught. He knew better than to try to pull something over on LB. She knew him too well.

"I'm sorry, LB. Yesterday afternoon was pretty bad."

"I could tell when you walked out. Where did you go?"

"I went out. I left my cell in the car. Met a friend, and before I knew it, I had missed his calls, your calls, and my appointment," he hoped she wouldn't press him further.

"I arranged for the woman who looks after them to keep them late," he added, hoping to make it sound like he had been more responsible than he had actually been.

"Okay, well, are you feeling better today because you look a little green around the gills."

"I didn't sleep well. I had a nightmare that woke me up, and I couldn't get back to sleep. I need some more coffee."

"Well, let me get you a cup while you get reacquainted with

your office. The Maine Coalition proposal is due Monday, and I left your draft on your desk to review."

"Thanks, LB," he said. If she still harbored suspicions about his lost afternoon and evening, she didn't let it show. He picked up the proposal and started to review it. LB had made some helpful notations in the margins of some pages.

"Here's your coffee," she said, placing his cup on the desk.

"Thanks for this," he said, raising the proposal up. "I like your ideas."

"We're a team," she said.

"That we are," he acknowledged. "Thanks, LB, for everything."

She looked at him, and he could tell that she knew that there was more to yesterday than Curt had shared. She knew that he was fragile and didn't want to push him.

"You have a meeting with your Counselor this afternoon at 2 p.m. Otherwise, I've cleared your calendar so you can complete the proposal."

He looked up at her, and he could see the pain in her eyes. He got up, walked around the desk, and hugged her.

"Thanks, LB. I'll be okay. This is a tough time, and I appreciate your support."

He released her, and she wiped a couple of tears that were threatening to overflow their banks.

"I worry about you," she said with a sniffle.

"I know, but you have your own challenges. Don't try to take on mine too."

She smiled, and everything seemed back to normal. She left the office, and he settled in, hoping that he would be able to complete the proposal before his counseling session. After he drained the cup of coffee LB had made him, he went out and got another. Before working on the proposal, he thought about Chelsea and how fortunate he had been to run into her. He got out his cell phone and looked at her picture and contact information. In addition to her cell phone number, she had supplied her dorm - Milton House. He then got an idea and called a local florist. After he hung up, he got back to work on the proposal. It was 12:30 when LB stuck her head in his office door.

"Are you skipping lunch today?"

"No, I'm just putting the finishing touches on the proposal. I wanted to get it done before my session this afternoon. I have a feeling it's going to be a doozy."

"So, I shouldn't expect you back afterward?"

"No, probably not."

He returned to the proposal, but thoughts about what he would tell Counselor Tim started to leak in. He pushed them away, hoping that he could complete the proposal and get his thoughts together over a late lunch. When he finally clicked on the save icon and sent the file to LB for final proofing, it was already 1:45. There was no time for lunch and only just enough time to gather his thoughts on the drive to Counselor Tim's office. He gave LB a quick hug, wished her a great weekend, and zipped out of the office. He quickly dismissed developing an elaborate story and decided that he would go with the truth. Besides, he thought, don't they say that the truth will set you free?

Curt was surprised when Tim greeted him as if nothing had happened. He couldn't get used to his non-judgmental approach.

"I'm sorry, Tim," he said when Tim failed to ask what had happened. "I should have called you."

"I'm sure you had your reasons. Do you want to talk about it?"

"Yeah, I do. I want to tell you everything."

He proceeded to unpackaged it all, from reviewing the gory details of Calli's murder to his inability to concentrate at work. Followed by drinking himself drunk at the Lost Loon and needing Chelsea to drive him home. And finally, her kiss and his subsequent nightmare. He spoke for 40 minutes straight while Tim listened. When he finally stopped, Tim said, "So what do you think it all means?"

"I don't know. I thought you'd help me understand it."

"Okay, we have 10 minutes, but there's a lot of ground to cover. Let's see what we can accomplish. Let's start at the end. Your nightmare."

Tim led Curt through the dream analysis that he had failed to accomplish earlier that day. They explored Curt's anger over Calli's death, his guilt over his thoughts about Chelsea, how he was trying to replace Calli with Chelsea, and his fear of losing everyone and everything he held dear. While he could put his finger on all these emotions, he couldn't put his finger on a solution.

"So, what should I do?" he asked Tim as the session was ending.

"What do you mean? What should you do?"

"I mean, what stage am I in," he said, pointing to the Kubler-Ross poster, "and what do I do to get to acceptance?"

"I'd say you're bouncing between anger, bargaining, and depression. Getting to acceptance isn't a straight path for most, and there are no magic bullets. I think your best bet is to continue to meet with me twice a week. Oh, and take it easy on the alcohol."

He left feeling better for having leveled with Counselor Tim but still unsettled about his erratic behavior and emotions over the last 24 hours. He hoped that a weekend with the kids and bringing them horseback riding Saturday would introduce some measure of peace and sanity.

There was a knock, and Chelsea opened her door to find a delivery boy with a half-dozen deep pink roses. He handed them to her, and she excitedly brought them into her single-unit dorm and opened the card.

"Chelsea, Thank you for rescuing me again. You are my guardian angel. Curt"

The florist must have thought Curt was crazy. He had to consult the florist on every aspect of his purchase. When he was married to Calli, it was easy for him to order a dozen red roses and have them sent to her. Now, he wanted to show his thanks but didn't wish Chelsea to get the wrong idea. The florist had suggested deep pink, which he said, represented gratitude. He also suggested six roses as anything more would be perceived as over the top. Finally, he stumbled with how to end the card. Certainly, not "love." Probably not "fondly." "Thanks," sounded redundant. And settled on just his name, thinking that the guardian angel line conveyed a friendly tone without sounding as if he wanted to ravish her like in his dream turned nightmare.

He had just pulled into his parking space at his apartment complex when his phone rang. A picture of Chelsea popped up on this phone.

"Hi Chels," he said, wondering why he suddenly shortened her name.

"Thank you, Curt. They're beautiful."

"Well, so are you," he said, unraveling his carefully selected roses and card salutations meant to convey friendship.

"And I thought it was the alcohol talking last night."

He realized that he needed to turn this conversation around because it was heading toward more complexity than he was prepared for after having wrung himself out emotionally at the counseling session.

"I just wanted to give you a token of my thanks, Chels. I

was a mess, and you were kind enough to help me."

"Well, you've been through hell, Curt, and it was the least I could do."

"Well, thanks again. Listen, the kid's school bus is just pulling up. Have a good weekend, and maybe I'll see you at the gym next week?"

"Okay, it's a date. Tuesday at noon. Better be ready, cuz I'm going to make you sweat!"

"Bye, Angel," he said, wondering why he kept digging himself in deeper.

"Bye, Baby," she returned, followed by an audible smooch.

He hung up, and images of their sweaty bodies locked in the torrid lovemaking of his dream returned. Who was he kidding? He was lonely, and he wanted her.

As Caitlin and Cade were making a beeline for his car, he reluctantly let go of the fantasy.

CHAPTER 33

J ackie and Stu were ill-prepared for the blast of arctic air that hit them when their tanned bodies, still in Arizona attire, stepped out of the airport into the mid-November evening. Their time together in Scottsdale had so cemented their love that having to drive home separately was a disappointment. If they both didn't need to work the next morning, they would have probably left a car there so that they could ride home together.

The start of the holiday season was upon them, and Jackie and Stu hosted their first Thanksgiving dinner. They invited their parents, and while Jackie had visions of cooking the dinner herself, both mothers brought dishes. While this upset Jackie at first, she ultimately was grateful as all the planning, cleaning, and cooking had left her near exhaustion. They had strategically scheduled dinner for 3:15 p.m. so that guys wouldn't miss the end of the Lions-Packers game or the start of the Cowboy-Jets game. Dinner was a hit, and by 5:30 p.m., the two fathers were asleep on the couch in front of the big screen TV. Stu looked like he was about to join them. Jackie couldn't resist taking a picture.

The month between Thanksgiving and Christmas was a slow travel month for Jackie. Conversely, it was Stu's busy time as the DOT made preparations before winter struck in earnest. Jackie was happy with the reprieve from non-stop travel as ever since Thanksgiving. She had been feeling a bit sluggish. At first, she wrote it off as just the remnants of her hectic travel schedule over the last few months and the stress of the holiday season. She had missed her period, which didn't concern her too much as they were occasionally irregular.

A few days before Christmas, she bought a home pregnancy test. Shocked by the results, she went in to see her doctor, who confirmed the news. She was pregnant. She didn't need to worry anymore about what she was going to give Stu for Christmas. She was excited and scared at the same time. They had discussed having children someday and usually took precautions. She thought back and realized that their "shower experience" on her birthday must have been the time. She had joined Stu in the shower wearing only her diamond earrings. She had stepped into the shower with a gift and stepped out with another. She had the perfect idea of how to break the news and stopped at the store on her way home.

They had promised not to buy presents for each other for Christmas as their trip to Arizona for her birthday had depleted their savings. Stu reacted poorly when Jackie handed him a wrapped box on Christmas morning.

"I thought we said no gifts," he protested.

"I couldn't resist."

"Well, I didn't get you anything," he said in an exasperated tone.

"That's okay. I didn't expect anything."

"I wish you hadn't done this," he said as he slowly unwrapped the box.

When he opened the box, he found a shower cap and a diaper. Struggling to make sense of it, he looked at Jackie, who wore a radiant smile. The diaper he could associate with a baby, but the shower cap threw him.

"Ah, I'm confused," he said. "Is this one of your kinky ideas for fun in the shower?"

"No, silly, think a little harder."

"We're going to a baby shower?"

She laughed. "You're getting warmer."

"You're going to have a baby?"

"You got it, daddy."

"Oh my god," he said as he hugged Jackie. "That's great news, Boo. I only have one question."

"What's that, hon."

"What's the shower cap for?"

She looked at him, exasperated. "You mean you don't remember?"

"Remember what?"

"When was the last time we were in the shower together?"

"In Arizona," it then finally dawned on him. "That's when you got pregnant? On your birthday?"

"Had to be."

"Wow, a birthday baby."

Although they didn't need an additional reason to feel joy for the new life growing in Jackie's belly, conceiving on her birthday made it all the more special. They spent the rest of the day delivering gifts and the good news to their families.

With the New Year came morning sickness and an ambitious travel schedule as AlzCura ramped up their marketing efforts after the holiday swoon. Jackie did not tell Cheryl immediately about her pregnancy, anxious about how the news might be received. Besides, she hadn't started to show yet, and other than the inconvenience of morning sickness, she managed her travel schedule just fine. She was still well received by her clients, and sales were as brisk as they had ever been. Her condition did change one thing, her tolerance for her male client's flirtations and occasional improprieties. Whereas she had formerly been able to look past them, they now disgusted her. She found it harder and harder to hide her disgust, and she seemed incapable of the graceful way she used to deflect this behavior. Her job was starting to feel like a reverse car wash. She went in clean and fresh and came out feeling used and dirty. She kept telling herself, just sell the drug, but it was losing its strength as her maternal condition began to take over. When she unceremoniously slapped a physician's hand from her ass and glared at him, she knew she was losing her touch and her patience. Usually, she would have taken such liberties in stride and scolded him with a diplomatic response and a smile. She walked into Cheryl's office the next day and told her about her pregnancy.

To say Cheryl was not pleased to hear the news was an understatement. As usual, she didn't pull any punches.

"Well, that might be wonderful for you and Stu, but it's the death knell for sales. The only good thing is that your boobs will get bigger before your belly shows. In a couple of months, you'll be welcomed by the physicians like you're a skunk who just walked backward into their office."

"I'm sorry," she said, although she didn't mean it. "What should I do?"

"Well, make wise wardrobe choices to show off those mommy boobs and hide that belly for the next few weeks. I'm going to find someone you can train to manage your clients after you hit your 3rd trimester. By that time, you'll look like you swallowed a basketball. The company doesn't want the liability of having you flying around. We'll find you some office work, and you can call your clients."

Jackie left Cheryl's office, resentful that Cheryl had not said congratulations or exhibited any happiness for her. Rather than helping her, this had only elevated Jackie's growing disgust. Now she would have to train someone, undoubtedly some young, nubile rep, to be her temporary replacement. She began to wonder how brief, temporary would be and whether motherhood would spell the end to her pharmaceutical rep days. She came home to Stu devastated. After he was able to calm her down, he assured her that she would have a job and the company was protecting their assets. However, he had abbreviated the word assets. The baby was due in August, and they started to calculate the 12-week leave she was hoping to take. This brought on a new anxiety attack.

"Stu, the 12 weeks will end around Thanksgiving right at the start of the slow season. I won't be able to get back on the road until after the New Year."

"Relax. That's perfect. You won't want to be on the road right away."

"Relax? How can I relax when someone is replacing me? What if she's better than me?"

The hormones of motherhood had started to course through her body, and Stu was getting his first orientation to their powerful influence.

"No one can be better than you, Boo. Everything will be alright," he said as he hugged her.

"Stop, I don't want you to hug me," she said, pushing him away and storming out of the room to the bathroom.

Curt's quiet confidence and reassuring hugs had worked in the past but were powerless over whatever was tweaking her now. He decided not to pursue her, hoping that whatever antidote there was for her present condition resided in the bathroom. He went to the kitchen, grabbed a beer, and flipped on the TV. When she emerged, Jackie joined him on the couch.

"I'm sorry," she said as she placed her head on his shoulder. "I'm just not myself these days."

"Maybe we're going to have a devil child."

"I hope not," she laughed.

Jackie found a flower bouquet on her desk with a congratulatory note from Cheryl the next time she was in the office. Over the following months, Jackie weathered her hormonal storms, her clients' fascination with her mommy boobs, and her replacement, who was cute but not particularly bright. Relegated to her desk, she started to see the wisdom in the company's policy. Her past resentment and anger were steadily replaced with a maternal instinct that appreciated staying close to home. There were also no signs that her absence on the road was harming her sales significantly. Cheryl reassured Jackie that she would have her job back 100% when she returned from leave, showing her a stack of emails.

"These, mommy dearest, are from your clients. They adore you and have told me in no uncertain terms that they want you back."

"Did you get one from Dr. Caron?"

"I did. Do you want me to read it to you?"

"No, the thought of him still makes my skin crawl. I don't want his words to hurt the baby."

They laughed, and Jackie eased toward her due date, reassured that her standing in the company was safe.

Stu accompanied Jackie to her ultrasound appointment, and after they learned the fetus was healthy, they toiled over the decision of whether to be told the gender. They finally agreed, reasoning that they wanted to prepare for and decorate the baby's room.

"It's a girl," said the Obstetrician.

Delighted by the news, Jackie and Stu went home and began planning to convert the spare bedroom into the baby's room. The months flew by as Jackie trained her replacement, Stu worked on renovating the spare bedroom under Jackie's guidance, and the couple considered baby names.

Jackie woke up on her due date and started to get ready for

work just like any other day. She just stepped out of the shower when her water broke. Stu grabbed the overnight bag they obediently packed at the suggestion of their birthing class instructor. He helped Jackie into some clothes and the car. They were on their way to the hospital when Jackie gasped, startling Stu.

"What, Boo, is everything all right?"

"No, we haven't decided on her name yet."

Stu relaxed. "Jeez, I thought the baby was arriving on the front seat. Don't scare me like that."

"So, what's it going to be? Ashley or Caitlin?"

They had gone back and forth on these two names for the better part of the last two months. They had always ended their debate saying that it would eventually come to them before the baby arrived. Now the baby was arriving, and they were no closer to a choice. It was a helpful diversion to Jackie's intermittent contractions. As they pulled into the hospital parking lot, they finally agreed on Ashley. The argument that clinched it was that they both liked "Ash" as a shortened form of Ashley, but both didn't care for "Cate" as a shortened form of Caitlin. They called Jackie's parents as they were entering the hospital.

Ashley Lynn Deno was born at 3:16 p.m. after 6 hours of labor. Stu cut the umbilical cord, and Ashley was placed in Jackie's arms. Exhausted but elated, she managed a smile as Stu took pictures. After Jackie held her for a few minutes, Stu and the Nurse finished cleaning up Ashley, and Stu posed for his first picture with his daughter. Stu was surprised when the nurse told him to place his pinky in Ashley's mouth, but he did so.

"Now, pull your finger out," said the nurse.

When he did, an audible pop like a cork from a bottle of champagne emanated from Ashley's mouth. Stu and Jackie both laughed as the nurse indicated that it was time for Ashley's first feeding. Stu placed Ashley in Jackie's arms, and as if on a swivel, Ashley's head turned into her mother's breast. Jackie looked down at her daughter. When she looked up, a tear rolled down her cheek.

"Rooting reflex, check," said the nurse. "So far, so good Mom and Dad. Now, Dad, it's time to hit the button."

"Huh?"

"Come with me and leave the girls to their business."

Stu followed the nurse out into the hall. They walked halfway down the corridor when they came to a receptacle on the wall with a label that read, "Press after delivery."

"Go ahead, young man. Mom did all the hard work. Now you get to do the easy part."

He pushed the button, and Brahms lullaby began to play through the paging system speakers throughout the hospital. When he returned to the room, Ashley had finished her first meal. Stu looked down at them. The feeling was indescribable.

CHAPTER 34

The Scott family of Barry, Maine, having moved on to places beyond, left Inspector Adams with little to go on. The tantalizing news of Darius' tissue samples made him even more anxious to speak to Dr. Caron. It would be a few more weeks before Elvira's autopsy results were available.

The Friday of his appointment with Dr. Caron finally arrived. He made sure he had a copy of Darius' toxicology report for Dr. Caron's information. Adams had met with Dr. Corpisen to understand the tissue findings, but the pathologist's explanation was way over his head. He hoped that Dr. Caron would be able to derive enough information from the report to be of assistance. If not, he would arrange for Dr. Caron to meet with Dr. Corpisen.

He walked into Dr. Caron's Campion office, and the receptionist had him take a seat in the waiting area. In a few minutes, the Office Manager, Rebecca, with whom he had spoken previously, introduced herself and brought him back to Dr. Caron's office. Adams handed her the subpoena necessary to gain access to any information they may have. Rebecca thanked him and said that Dr. Caron would be in in a few minutes. Fifteen minutes later, Adams was still sitting in the office, having perused all the diplomas on the wall. Adams was amazed at all the disheveled stacks of journals, books, and papers strewn on his desk and on the floor. The piles looked like they were multiplying and threatening to take over all the available space in the office. Finally, Dr. Caron breezed into the office and offered a half-hearted apology for his lateness and the appearance of his office.

"What can I do for you, Inspector Adams?"

"I'm investigating the death of Darius Scott and was hoping you might have some information on him."

"And why do you think I may know something about him?"

"I don't know. I'm just following a hunch. I heard your radio ad. Your office in Ramsey is close to where he lived, and your offer of getting paid to participate in a study may have attracted someone like Darius, who was unemployed as far as I could tell."

"Okay, that does sound like a stretch."

"Well, your office manager indicated that you might be able to look up whether Darius had ever participated in any of your studies."

"Sure, I can do that. Do you have the paperwork to allow me to share any information I may find?"

"Yeah, I gave it to Rebecca."

"Okay, well, excuse me then. I believe you, but I can't be too careful. I want to see it for myself and see what exactly I can share with you." He stepped out of his office and was back a few minutes later.

"Alright, everything looks in order," he said as he started to tap away at his computer. "There he is, Darius Scott of Barry."

"You treated him?" asked Adams excitedly.

"Nope. He attended one of my free clinics in Ramsey. He signed up for one of my clinical trials about two years ago, but he was lost to follow-up."

"Lost to what?"

"Lost to follow-up. It means he started the trial and then didn't comply with the protocol. In this case, he didn't come back to the office for follow-up visits as prescribed. We tried to reach him by phone, by letter and consulted the SSDI per the study protocol, but we never heard from him. So, he was dropped from the study."

"SSDI?"

"Social Security Death Index. He wasn't on it at the time."

"Did he receive any medications?"

"Don't know."

"How can you not know?"

"Double-blind study," he said matter-of-factly.

"Double…"

"Double-blind study," Dr. Caron said, a bit exasperated. "It means that the study subject and the study investigator don't know whether the subject receives the medication or not. That's important not to bias the research."

"Well, can you find out whether he received the study drug?"

"No."

"Why not?"

"The pharmaceutical company's protocol requires that we send all litfoo data to them. All we have in the record is the contact information, the consent form, and the litfoo event report form."

"I'm sorry, litfoo?" said Adams, getting irritated.

"LTFU…Lost to Follow-Up. We do tend to speak in acronyms around here."

"So, you have no way to determine whether someone that died may have received the drug?"

"Well, yes, I can if the participant stays in the trial. Because this is a long-term study, the pharmaceutical company is better equipped to follow up and track litfoos. I track the active participants through regular exams and consulting SSDI. The company is responsible for those that drop out?"

"So, how do you know that the pharmaceutical company is tracking litfoos?"

"Well, I don't. That's their job. The FDA regulates them. For all the regulations around clinical research, how pharmaceutical companies handle litfoos is still poorly defined. Some pharmaceutical companies have us keep the data; some don't. Some use litfoo data in their study, and some don't. This is one area of clinical research where there isn't a standard approach. The research field is wrestling with this issue, but as of today, how litfoo data is handled is entirely up to the pharmaceutical company."

"But, someone died."

"Yes, but I don't make the rules. I just follow them. Besides, Inspector Adams, people die of all sorts of things. What gives you a reason to believe it might be some medication Mr. Scott took?"

Adams handed over the toxicology report for Dr. Caron's review. He studied it for a couple of minutes.

"Again, people take a lot of things. Mr. Scott died almost two years after potentially getting a study medication. Without ongoing assessment that he would have received had he stayed in the study, it would be hard to link those two events up. You'd have to account for everything else that might have killed him since potentially taking the study drug. I had a patient once who was drinking a cocktail of motor oil and brake fluid. He thought the oil would cure his arthritis, and the brake fluid would help him stop smoking."

"What happened to him?"

"It worked?"

"Really?"

"Yep, he died. No more arthritis or smoking!" said Dr. Caron deadpan.

Adams started to chuckle but stopped abruptly when Dr. Caron's face failed to register any emotion. He certainly was an odd duck, thought Adams.

"Is there anything else I can help you with," said Dr. Caron while glancing at his watch.

Trying not to sound irritated by his blatant attempt to shoo him out of the office, Adams continued his questioning.

"I would like to know a bit more about the clinical trial Mr. Scott was involved in. What can you tell me about it?"

"It's the second phase of the Recallamin trial that is seeking to prove that the vaccine can prevent Alzheimer's. The first phase of this trial has been approved, and Recallamin is now becoming a standard treatment for the reversal of Alzheimer's disease."

"So, what criteria did Mr. Scott have to meet to make him a candidate for this study?"

"He had the Alzheimer's gene and was in the study age range between 40 and 60 with no signs of memory loss."

"Are there results from the second phase of this study?"

"No. The second phase for the prevention of Alzheimer's is still underway. That phase will likely take 10-15 years before we have enough evidence. There may be interim reports, but at this point, it is too early to tell."

Dr. Caron was growing more fidgety in his chair, but Adams was determined not to leave empty-handed.

"For the first phase of this study, what was the mortality rate for patients that got the vaccine?"

"It was not statistically different than the placebo or standard treatment protocols."

"I see. What about other complications?"

"Same deal. Not statistically different. Please understand, Inspector Adams, Alzheimer's is a devastating disease that affects 27 million people in the U.S. and millions of others who are probably ticking time bombs for the disease. Virtually everyone either has a family member or knows someone with the disease. With one shot of the Recallamin vaccine, millions are recovering from the ravages of the disease, and millions will never get it. I hate to sound insensitive, but the death of one criminal in central Maine who MAY have had the vaccine and died from it doesn't stack up against the weight of evidence for this vaccine."

Now Inspector Adams knew Dr. Caron was trying in earnest to end this conversation, but he pressed on.

"OK, I'm almost done here, but I have a few more questions. Did Elvira Scott participate in any of your research studies?"

"Your subpoena is limited to information on Darius Scott, Inspector Adams. I can't give you any information on that person even if she was in one of our studies."

"Sorry, you're right. Can you give me the name of the pharmaceutical company and any contacts there that might be willing to speak with me?"

"Sure. The company is AlzCura out of Buffalo. Dr. Asa Sheridan is the Medical Director, and Jackie Deno is our representative. Nice gal, she probably can't give you specifics, but I'm sure she would be happy to try to connect you to the right people. I may have her card here," he said, rummaging through one of his desk drawers. Organization was obviously not one of Dr. Caron's strong suits.

"That's fine, doctor; I'm sure I can look up the number. I know you're busy, and I'll get out of your hair," he said while getting up from his chair.

"No, no, wait. Here it is," he said as he handed Jackie's business card to Adams.

"Thanks, Dr. Caron," he said, sticking out his hand.

"You're welcome," Dr. Caron returned, giving Adam's hand a firm shake.

Adams turned to leave, but just as he reached the door, he turned back.

"I don't suspect you could tell me whether it's worth my time to get a subpoena for Elvira Scott?"

"No, you're right, I can't tell you," he said, cracking a hint of a smile.

CHAPTER 35

"**D**addy, can Jordan stay over tonight? Her Mom said it would be alright," Caitlin asked as Curt stepped out of the car.

"Well, hello to you too, Caitlin!" Curt responded.

"Hi, Dad. Can she? Can she please?" she pleaded.

"Yes, she can stay overnight," he said. No sooner had he uttered his response, and she bounded up the steps like some gazelle singing thank you to her father.

Curt shook his head and smiled as he reminisced about how, at one time, he had had the same youthful energy and enthusiasm. He ordered a pizza and delivered it to Caitlin's room, where she found Jordan on all fours pressed into service as Caitlin's horse. Cade was sitting on the bed, awaiting his turn. Caitlin had wrapped one of her belts around Jordan's neck.

"Why don't you wait until tomorrow when you can ride a real horse?" he said upon entering the room.

"Pizza!" the kids yelled, and magically Jordan transformed back into a 10, soon-to-be, 11-year old girl.

Curt had hoped that concentrating on the kids would be a useful diversion to the turbulent thoughts, dreams, and events of the previous week, but such was not the case. As soon as he occupied the kid's time, he had peace and quiet. Unfortunately, peace and quiet were not something Curt valued right now.

It only allowed him to think, and thinking these days often ended in some torturous or painful way. He was getting good at occupying the kids' time, but he was incapable of filling in the gaps in his own free time. These were the times in the past when Calli or her "honey-do" list, or some social event she would arrange, had filled in Curt's schedule. Without these, he found himself sitting or pacing, trying to figure out what to do with himself. He slowly realized that Calli had defined much of his life and his time. Her absence left a hole in not only his heart but also a chasm where marital and homeowner activities used to reside. Any hobbies or interests he had before Calli were no longer of interest to him. Her friends had been his friends, but seeing those friends had been purely based on her initiative. Although he could be gregarious and social, he didn't have an affinity for their friends or a need or desire to continue the friendship after Calli's murder. This seemed to be mutual. While some of their friends had come around shortly after that day, over time, the calls and visits dwindled. Curt sat on the couch, staring blankly in the general direction of the TV, which was more background noise than anything to which he was paying attention. Searching his mind for something to grab on to, something to occupy his time, he failed repeatedly. He was just a bundle of restless energy with no outlet for expression. This nervous energy probably fueled his nightmares and fantasies. If he wasn't going to dictate the agenda of his life, his emotional turmoil would.

"You kids want to go out for ice cream?" he said, poking his head into Caitlin's room.

"No, we're full," Caitlin had said.

Even his attempt to occupy his time by suggesting the almost sure-fire ice cream run had failed. He went back to the couch and searched the emptiness. After another hour of fake TV watching, he got up and went to his bedroom. He didn't want to go to bed, but he didn't want to be sitting on the couch. He didn't know what he wanted. He went to the bathroom and stared into the mirror.

"You're depressed. Stage 4," he said to himself, but naming it offered no comfort. He trudged back to his room, lay on his bed, and continued scanning his brain for something, anything to provide some hope of emerging from this deep, dark hole. He even tried to reawaken his Chelsea fantasy. While it had been so vivid earlier, right now, it couldn't pierce the darkness. He closed his eyes, apprehensive about what might visit him in the night. He had failed to climb out of the gloom.

He woke up the next morning and was initially thankful for a good night of sleep without any horrific nightmares. As he walked through his morning routines, he began to realize that his mind was as blank now as it had been when he had gone to sleep. Taking the kids to the riding stables was still 3 hours away. After his coffee brewed and he had cleaned up the mess from the kids' sleepover, he had absolutely nothing to do.

He began to realize that his newest nightmare was not some scary images that sparked emotions. Instead, it was the absence of images and a void, a void so stark and consuming, that he no longer had an identity, a purpose. Work and kids, work and kids, these were the only thing that held him on earth, and their grip seemed so tentative. He sat on the couch, staring blankly at the TV, immune to anything it might have been trying to communicate to him. He sat there until he heard the rustling of children. Now he had something to do, something to live for.

He knocked on the door and poked his head into Caitlin's room. They had built a tent with blankets under which they had slept. It hid all but Jordan's feet. The place looked like a bomb had gone off with toys, plates of uneaten pizza, and bowls with Goldfish crackers strewn about. Some Goldfish had leaped from their containers and met a crumbly demise on the carpet. Virtually every horse in Caitlin's closet stable had gotten loose and was grazing across the vast prairie of her room.

He felt an urge to say something like, "What the heck has gone on here?" followed by something equally inane like, "You clean up this mess or no horseback riding," but he swallowed the clichés. He knew full well what had gone on – fun. He wished he could find some fun as they had.

"Time to get up, corral your horses, and clean up the pasture," he called to the occupants of the make-shift tent.

A whinny arose from under the tent, and Caitlin pranced out on all fours.

"Okay, little filly, time to get the herd together and move on out."

He closed the door, happy that his kids would give him a chance to escape the nothingness that had enveloped him over the last 12 hours.

The kids emerged from Caitlin's room a few minutes later. Curt couldn't believe that they had cleaned up the room in that amount of time but was surprised to find that they had. It was amazing how motivated they could be when something they wanted was on the line. They piled into the car for their trek to the stables. Chantel, who had helped Curt complete paperwork on their first visit, greeted them when they arrived. Chantel was a high school senior who, when not at school, was a fixture at the stables. She had started riding at the stables when she was about Caitlin's age and, over the years, had grown to be a decorated rider. Over the last two years, Joanie employed her. Chantel was a cute girl, distinguishable from all the other girls at the stable by her black cowboy hat. She was still a bit self-conscious about her braces, and only those things that struck her as hugely hilarious would get her to bare her braces in a full smile. Unlike Joanie, who struck most people as a bit hard and demanding, Chantel exuded gentleness even when she was disciplining a horse or a student rider. It was her gift, and it drew many of the younger student riders to her. Nothing about her gentleness, however, made her look weak or timid. Watching Chantel with the horses and the students just screamed of quiet strength, determination, confidence, and discipline.

By the end of the morning, Caitlin had formed a bond with Chantel that was palpable. She followed Chantel around like a little puppy dog. After they left the stables and headed to lunch, Caitlin, as she was prone to do when she was excited about something, talked non-stop about Chantel. Everything was Chantel this, Chantel that. This habit could be irritating at times, but Curt was quite pleased that Caitlin looked up to Chantel in this manner. While Caitlin was riding, he and Joanie had a long discussion about the virtues of horseback riding. She had mentioned how therapeutic it was, especially for young girls. Her premise was that learning to master riding a horse taught all the lessons one needed to master life. While some may have construed this as a sales pitch, Curt only had to look at Caitlin's face and Chantel's mature and strong carriage to believe Joanie's philosophy. Joanie also indicated that for high school girls, spending all their time at the stables also kept them out of the backseat of high school boys' cars. Although Joanie had used far more colorful language to get this point across. Although Curt didn't want to think about Caitlin as a teenager, this was useful information that appealed to him.

"Where are we going, Dad?" Caitlin finally stopped her Chantel-fest to ask.

"You'll see."

Ten minutes later, the kids cheered when they realized that he was on the way to the Chubby's in Belton. It was a bit of a drive, but it was always worth it. They pulled in and turned on their headlights for service. Chubby's was one of the few remaining vestiges of 1950's drive-up dining. While the nostalgia was lost on the kids, it brought back memories of when Curt's parents used to bring him there. His parents had had their first date at Chubby's. They used to tell Curt that this was because their parents wouldn't permit them to go to the Belton Drive-In Theatre, where they might be tempted to "neck." Curt remembered his discomfort when his parents first told him the story. Today he was glad they did, but he wasn't going to subject Caitlin and Cade to that story just yet. The Belton Drive-In Theatre didn't survive into the current modern age as Chubby's had. The kids did their best to gobble up the juicy burgers, fries, and tasty milkshakes. Curt had learned from previous visits not to order anything for himself, as eating the kid's leftovers made for a tidy meal. On the drive home, Caitlin's reverence for Chantel continued.

Jordan ended up staying over Saturday night as well. While the kids occupied themselves with more camping and horsey games in Caitlin's room, Curt was thrown back into his cell of nothingness. He tried to do some work but couldn't. He tried to inspire the kids to go to church on Sunday morning and failed. He had cleaned the apartment, even going so far as to clean the shelves in the refrigerator that scarcely needed it. The rest of the weekend dragged on, and while he anxiously awaited the beginning of the workweek, he realized that besides running with Chelsea on Tuesday and the start of the kid's support group on Friday, he had precious little upon which to look forward. He went to the only thing that seemed to occupy his time and give him some pleasure.

"Hey, kids," he said, opening Caitlin's door. "What do you say we have a birthday party for Jordan next weekend?"

Jordan's eyes lit up, and Caitlin and Cade's unanimous cheers were enough of an answer. He told them to make a plan and let him know how they would be celebrating. He realized that he should have asked Jordan's mother first, so after the kids went back to playing, he went to visit Jordan's mother. She was delighted at his suggestion, indicating that she didn't have any special plans, and Jordan's father wouldn't be in town.

"Jordan will be delighted," said her mother. "We haven't properly celebrated it in quite some time on account of my disability and my husband's work schedule."

"Good then. I will ask the kids what they would like to do. Would you like to join us?"

"Oh no, no, I really can't go out anymore. I will be happy that Jordan can have a real birthday celebration. Can I give you something for it?" she said, reaching for her purse.

"No, it's our gift. You hold on to your money."

Having received the permission he should have sought beforehand, he made his way back to the apartment. As he opened his apartment door, he sighed with relief. It was a brief reprieve from his emptiness and at least made the thought of next weekend tolerable.

Although most people delight in uneventful days, for Curt, they were beginning to be like torture. When he returned to work that Monday, he put the final touches on his part of the proposal. Loribeth had blocked the entire day weeks ago, in case finishing the proposal went down to the last hour. By 10:00 A.M., he was done and stared at the blank calendar.

"LB, any chance we can shuffle some of my appointments later this week to this afternoon?" he asked, poking his head out of his office.

"I'll see what I can do, boss."

He went back to his desk, shuffled some papers around, and threw away a few conference announcements that he had once thought about attending but didn't. When he started to think about how he could rearrange his office, he realized that he was in trouble. He customarily enjoyed gaps in his schedule. In the past, these were the times where he would get his best ideas. He would develop a business plan for a new service or come up with a strategy to expand their client base. Now the yawning gap in his schedule was painful. Thirty minutes later, LB called into his office and told him that she had been unsuccessful in rescheduling any of his appointments to the afternoon.

"OK, thanks LB. I'm going to lunch then."

"Everything okay?" she said as if she had a radar for Curt's mental state.

"Yeah, I was just hoping to decompress my schedule later in the week."

"Got plans?"

"Yeah, the kids and I are throwing a birthday party for one of their friends."

"You're becoming quite the expert at this birthday party thing since Caitlin's party two weeks ago!"

"Only because of you, LB. Only because of you. See you after lunch."

He left the office hoping that in that hour, he would find something to occupy the following 3 or 4 hours. To his chagrin, lunch did not fuel any brainstorms, and he returned to his office, not sure what he would do. After staring blankly at his computer screen for a long time, he resorted to the only constructive activity he could think of – organizing his office. LB, hearing drawers opening and closing and the shredder humming intermittently, knocked on his door.

"Everything okay in there?"

"Yep, just doing some Fall cleaning," Curt responded. "Do you need any 3-ring binders? I have about 10 empty ones here."

"Sure," she said, entering his office, "I can never have enough 3-ring binders. What's gotten into you?"

"Just felt the need to get organized and jettison some stuff I don't need anymore."

"Okay, but you know it's a bit out of character. You usually wait for me to tell you it's time to get organized."

"Turning over a new leaf," he shouted above the crunching

sound of the shredder.

"Okay, I will leave you to your fun. Call me if you need me," she said, shaking her head in wonderment as she left.

Curt emerged from his office 2 hours later with a few more binders, two dozen empty manila folders, and two bags of shredded documents.

"Need any confetti?" he asked LB.

"I think you're the one hosting all the parties. You feel better now?"

"Yes, but please tell me my schedule is a bit more challenging tomorrow."

"Yep, you and Sam are meeting for a couple of hours in the morning to prep for the MEGH presentation. Then you've blocked off 90 minutes for lunch. At 2:00 p.m., you give your presentation to MEGH, and then you have your counseling session at 4."

"Sounds delightful."

"Free time bothering you?"

"You're not kidding."

"I'll try to keep you busy at work. After work, you're on your own."

"Deal."

"Here's the proposal for tomorrow's meeting and your calendar. You have an hour in the morning before your meeting with Sam if you don't want to review it now."

"Thanks, I think I'll take you up on that offer. I'm out of here."

He headed home for at least a couple of hours filled with parental duties – dinner, kitchen clean-up, homework, and bedtime routines. By 8:30 p.m., the structured part of his evening was complete, and the kids were tucked away in their beds. He sat on the couch, not even bothering to turn on the TV. Tomorrow was a big day for the company, and he wanted to be at his best. He wondered if going to the gym with Chelsea before the presentation to MEGH was a good idea. He held an internal debate. He would be relaxed for the presentation if he burned off some energy – pro. She might be a distraction to him and throw him off his game – con. He really could use more exercise – pro. He worried that he was perhaps getting in too deep too soon – con. What's the big deal? She's a nice young lady who has been supportive in his times of need – pro. How would the kids react if they ended up being more than acquaintances? He didn't know the answer to this one but suspected that it was way too early for Caitlin and Cade to see their father with another woman. Counselor Tim hadn't said anything against it. Tim always told Curt that he had to take care of himself if he was going to be able to take care of the kids. Wasn't forming a friendship with another woman healthy? One thing was for sure; he wasn't going into tomorrow entirely comfortable. It was not enough to dissuade him from keeping the "date," as she had put it.

Tuesday morning's session with Sam went like clockwork. They had done many presentations before, and this one was right in their wheelhouse. Curt would address how they would be able to assist MEGH measure and improve quality while Sam would state the financial case. In addition to the proposal, they had created presentation slides that were animated. They had timed their presentations and choreographed things to such a degree that they had the confidence to have the slides advance themselves. For others, this may have been a risky move. Nothing looked more minor league than having to fumble for the mouse to stop the timed presentation and reverse the slides. They were confident they had a winning performance and broke just before lunch.

Curt arrived at the gym, and Chelsea was already walking on a treadmill. The treadmill beside her looked occupied as a towel hung over the handrail, and the track was moving slowly. She looked as delicious as he had imagined in the dream, maybe even more delicious. There was a treadmill open directly behind her, and he would have no difficulty "taking up the rear," so to speak.

"I guess you found another running partner," Curt said, pointing to the treadmill beside Chelsea.

"Hi handsome, don't be silly, that's my towel, and I started it running so no one else would take it. Now get out of those clothes and join me."

He entered the locker room and quickly had to check his straying mind. There was nothing more out of place in the men's locker room as being a little too pumped up! Finally attired in his running shorts, t-shirt, and running shoes, he exited the locker room and stepped onto the treadmill next to Chelsea.

"Here's your towel," he said, holding it out to her.

"Keep it. I think you're going to need it."

He shrugged and put the towel back on the handrail and cranked up the treadmill speed to match Chelsea's pace.

"You're looking awesome today, Chels."

"You're looking pretty good yourself, Curt. Better than the last time I saw you."

"That's not saying much."

"Okay, well, then I think you look hot. Wanna play a game?" she asked.

"A game?"

"Yeah. Whoever runs the farthest in 30 minutes gets to ask the other for anything they want."

"Sounds dangerous."

"Only if you lose. Now here are the rules. We clear our odometer and set the timer for 30 minutes. Then we both start walking at 2.5 miles per hour until the timer reads 29 minutes left. After that, you can set whatever pace you want. When the timer shuts off, we see who ran the furthest."

They stopped their treadmills, restarted them, and set their timers for 30 minutes. They began to walk at the prescribed pace, and Curt realized that his eyes were locked on Chelsea's eyes as they walked. He was getting lost in them when she said, "Oh my god, look at that," pointing across the gym. Curt turned to see what she was pointing at and didn't see anything particularly interesting. All he heard was the increased whir of a treadmill speeding up. When he turned back to Chelsea, she was almost in a full sprint.

"Hey, that's cheating."

"No, it's not. Look at your timer." It read 28:52.

"But you distracted me," he said as he pressed on the arrow to increase his speed.

"Not my fault. You knew the rules," she huffed as her pace must have been near 10 miles per hour.

Curt knew that he could not sustain a 10 miles per hour pace for 30 minutes and was determined not to try to match that pace. He set his pace at 9 miles per hour, hoping that he might have enough in his tank to run her down at the end. She kept taunting him as her stride looked quick but relaxed.

"Come on, old man, catch the college girl. I know you want to."

Although she was right about that, Curt didn't fall for the bait.

"Slow and steady wins the race, bunny rabbit."

Curt had not yet found his stride, and he hoped that that running on air feeling would come over him soon. He felt a slight twinge in his side. He could not afford a side stitch. He looked over at Chelsea, and her stride was as smooth as ever. He gazed a little too long at her features and stumbled as his foot hit halfway off the tread.

"I suppose you're going to say I distracted you again," she teased.

"Shut up. I was looking at the lady beside you."

She glanced over to see a woman who was walking, or more like waddling. Suffice to say, she was not a svelte, athletic type. While Chelsea was looking over at the woman, Curt increased his speed to 10 miles per hour. The timer read 23:00 minutes. By his calculations, he was almost a quarter of a mile behind her. He couldn't afford to fall behind much further.

"Naughty boy, now look who's doing the distracting. It looks like you're going a bit faster there."

"Just your imagination."

"Pardon my choice of words, but do you think you'll be able to keep it up?"

"It's never been a problem before," he said as he grabbed the towel to wipe his face.

When he wiped it across his face, her perfume hit him full force. It was intoxicating and blatantly unfair.

"Now, I see why you wanted me to use your towel."

"Like it?"

"Dumb question," he panted as the pace was getting to him.

She increased her pace, and Curt knew he was in trouble. The timer read 19:00 minutes. She couldn't keep up that pace, could she? She would have to slow down, and then he'd catch her.

"I'm at 2 miles, Curt. Where are you?"

He looked down and saw he was at 1.6 miles. He couldn't believe he was that far behind. He did some quick math in his head.

"No wonder you're still in college."

"Why do you say that?"

"You don't know how to count yet. At most, you're at 1.8 miles."

"Believe what you'd like, but I'm kicking your butt."

"We'll see whose butt gets kicked," he said as he increased his pace. The timer hit 15 minutes. If she didn't slow down by 10 minutes, he doubted he would have the time or the stamina to catch her.

Magically, she started to slow her pace.

"Did the bunny go out a little too fast?" Curt taunted as he continued his torrid pace. Now he was running faster than she was. He was gaining ground.

"No, just feeling sorry for the tortoise."

She slowed again, and Curt didn't need to over-extend himself. He dropped his speed and still was going considerably faster than Chelsea. As the timer hit 10 minutes, he sensed he had closed the gap and would be able to run her down by the 5-minute mark if they kept the same pace.

"I'm catching up to you, college girl. I can see your cute little caboose just up ahead."

"Is it motivating for you? I'm going to let you get just within reach, and then I'm going to take it away from you."

At the 7-minute mark, she increased her speed in time to Curt's pace.

"I thought it would be nice for us to move together at the same pace. Is it good for you?"

"Heavenly," was all he could manage. His lungs were bursting, and his legs were in pain. He waited for a second wind. He had to be close, but he would have to outpace her for the last 5 minutes.

As the timer hit 5:00, they both reached for the increase speed arrow. Curt fixed his eyes ahead, knowing that he could not afford a misstep or distraction now. He could see Chelsea's pace in his peripheral vision and tried to keep just ahead of it. At 4:00, he was beginning to think he wasn't going to be able to make it. She increased her speed. He had no choice; he had to increase his. At 3:00, he knew he wasn't going to be able to sustain the pace. She raised her speed, but he was spent. At 2:00, he decreased his rate, knowing he was beaten. She increased her pace for the final 30 seconds to a full sprint. He could only watch in amazement. Their timers hit 0:00.

"I think you have to grant me one wish. How far did you go?"

"4.0 miles," he panted, bent over at the waist, trying to catch his breath.

"Not bad, I'm impressed."

"Give me the bad news. What did you run?"

"4.3 miles."

"Youth wins out over beauty."

When he straightened up, she was standing beside him. Before he knew it, she hugged him and planted a kiss on his cheek.

"Was that your wish?" Curt asked.

"Oh, you're not getting off the hook that easy."

They walked to the water cooler, her right shoulder leaning against his left bicep. Their sweat formed a lubricant that made her shoulder slide back and forth on his arm. How such a little thing could be exhilarating, Curt didn't know, but the skin-to-skin connection was electric. They grabbed icy bottles of water and cracked them open, and let a fan waft over their sweat-soaked bodies. The physiologic reaction of the cold air on Chelsea's wet nylon top had a predictable effect.

"You keep saluting me like that, and soon my flag won't be flying at half-mast," Curt said only partially in jest.

"Wanna go to my place?"

"Huh?"

"Let's go to my place. Now."

"I can't."

"Why not?"

"I have a presentation in about an hour?"

"Then, after your presentation."

"I have a counseling session after the presentation."

"What's more therapeutic talking to your counselor or being with me?"

She certainly wasn't shy. He found her aggressiveness exciting.

"Well…"

"Well, nothing. Call your counselor and tell him something has come up. You won't be lying."

"Okay," he heard himself reply.

She brushed past him furtively, letting her hand slide over his running shorts, "And you think you're exhausted now."

Once again, he had to stave off an inappropriate state of arousal before heading to the Men's Locker room. He glanced at the clock and realized that he only had 45 minutes to get showered, dressed, and over to the offices of MEGH for the presentation. As he drove over to the office, he called Counselor Tim and told him he would have to reschedule. He promised to have his assistant call in the morning to find a mutually convenient day and time. He made it to the MEGH office with 3 minutes to spare.

"Had me nervous, buddy," Sam breathed a sigh of relief as Curt walked in.

"Just my flare for the dramatic," Curt replied, trying to sound nonchalant.

"Ready?"

"Like the Ever-Ready Bunny," he said inadvertently, causing him to think of Chelsea. He hoped he could block her and the activities planned afterward out of his mind.

They entered the Conference Room, and after introductions, Sam and Curt started their presentation. Their performance was flawless. Although rehearsed, they had a gift for making it sound natural and spontaneous. Sam and Curt even deftly managed one MEGH member who kept on interrupting their presentation to make a comment or question, potentially disrupting the timing. A few well-placed responses managed to hold off the questioner.

"That's a great question," Curt had said on one occasion. "I have a slide coming up that focuses on just that question."

"I couldn't have paid you for a better segue," Sam had replied. "I will be addressing that shortly."

When they finished, a few members applauded, breaking a cardinal rule these types of presentations usually operated under. Curt and Sam knew that it was always a good sign when an objective audience couldn't restrain themselves from reacting favorably. They left the conference room on a cloud.

"Let's go have a drink," Sam said, giving Curt a high five as they left the building.

"I'm sorry, I have plans. How about a rain check?"

"Okay, buddy. Great job today."

"You too, Sam. It was a pleasure dancing with ya."

Curt stepped into his car and turned the key. The engine fired to life. He sat there for a moment, wondering what in the hell he was doing. He shifted the car into gear and pulled out of the parking lot.

CHAPTER 36

Jackie successfully transferred her strong work ethic and productivity at work into her new role as a mother. Stu had successfully converted the spare bedroom into a pink palace for Ashley. Jackie, who had originally thought she might do some work from home, had neither the time nor the urge to do so. She quickly fell into the routines of motherhood while Stu suffered some of the typical afflictions that new fathers bear. Abbreviated sleep, Jackie's hypersensitivity about what was good or not good for the baby, and disinterest in anything remotely sexual. Jackie's moods the first few weeks home vacillated, sometimes wildly, but never debilitating or long-lived as to cause her or Stu concern. They were thankful that they had learned about the distinction between baby blues and postpartum depression during their prenatal class. They mistakenly had the notion before the course that the glow of having the child would automatically result in a prolonged period of bliss. Such was not the case, although they both experienced high "highs" during their first few weeks of parenthood.

Ironically, the last day of Jackie's family leave was her birthday. She had been dreading the day, not because she would become a year older, but that it signaled the end of her dedicated time with Ashley and her return to work. Stu did his best to blunt this feeling of dread. On the weekend before her birthday, he took Jackie and Ashley for a drive.

"Time for you to get out," he told Jackie as he stopped the car in front of a local Day Spa.

"What? No. I thought we were going for a drive."

"Change of plans," he said as Jackie's door opened suddenly.

Jackie, startled by the door opening behind her, looked up to see Sunny.

"Happy Birthday, girlfriend," she said as Jackie screamed with delight, startling Ashley awake.

"What are you doing here?" Jackie said, getting out of the car and hugging Sunny.

"Celebrating you. Now show me that baby before we go on our girl's day out."

Jackie picked Ashley up out of her car seat and handed her to Sunny. They both cooed with delight as Sunny snuggled Ashley to her chest.

"I need me one of these," Sunny said.

"Well, I can give you the recipe for how to make one," Jackie said, causing the women to laugh, startling Ashley enough to make her whimper. Sunny quickly gave Ashley a reassuring squeeze and a kiss on the forehead that immediately calmed Ashley.

"You're a natural," said Stu from the car. "Now hand over that baby so you girls can get pampered and primped."

"It's about time someone other than the baby gets pampered," joked Jackie causing another round of laughter.

While Jackie and Sunny spent the day at the spa, Stu brought Ashley over to Doris and Jack's house. He had arranged for his in-laws to keep Ashley for the weekend. Doris would begin serving as Ashley's daycare when Jackie went back to work in a few days. There was little concern about this transition, as Nana Doris and Ashley were well acquainted with one another. That evening, after the women got their buff and shine, Stu took them to Danielle's for dinner. Except for a small glitch in the distribution of the desserts, the dinner was flawless. Stu had arranged for Jackie's dessert to include a present he had bought for her. When the waiter came to deliver the desserts, he mistakenly gave the dessert ringed by a diamond necklace to Sunny instead of Jackie.

"Ah, I think this dessert is yours, Jackie," Sunny said, handing the dessert to her. "Of course, if you don't want it, I'll gladly take it."

"Oh my god," Jackie exclaimed as she looked down upon the necklace that matched the earrings Stu had given her in Arizona the previous year. As luck would have it, she was wearing the diamond studs, and Stu moved to place the necklace around Jackie's neck.

"Happy Birthday Boo. You're the most beautiful woman in the world," he said, kissing her.

"Thanks, Hon. And I thought you'd never be able to outdo last year's surprises."

"You guys need to stop this right now. I'm jealous," Sunny broke in. "Don't you have a brother Stu?"

"Yeah, but he's only 16."

"Perfect, then I can still train him before it's too late."

"I'm sure your brother wouldn't mind," Jackie said.

"I'm sure you're right," agreed Stu. "What 16-year old boy wouldn't?"

"What's a little robbing the cradle between friends?" Sunny laughed.

The trio spent the rest of the weekend together as Jackie and Stu introduced Sunny to their favorite haunts. They even took a road trip to South Temple and ate at the T-Rex Bar-B-Cue for old time's sake. Sunny's visit and Stu's penchant for surprises had their intended effect. Not only did Stu get lucky

Saturday evening, but Jackie's outlook on her last day of family leave improved significantly.

CHAPTER 37

D r. Corpisen called AG Lewis Talcott's office.

"Yeah, Doc, what you got?" AG Talcott said into the phone as he was about to exit his office.

"I've got the same results on Elvira's preliminary autopsy that I had on her son's."

"And that is?"

"To put it in layman terms, exploded brain. I'm sending the tissue samples out, but if I were a betting man, I'd say we're going to get the same results we got on Darius."

"Maybe it's hereditary, then?"

"Maybe, but we'll have to wait and see. She also had evidence of liver failure, which is consistent with her son's autopsy."

"Thanks, Doc; call me when you get the report."

Talcott exited his office and told his assistant to get DA Wydman on the line.

"Will," the AG said, "Looks like Elvira Scott may have died from the same cause as her son."

"Well, I'll be damned," DA Wydman sighed. "I'll get a subpoena and have Adams revisit Dr. Caron."

"And I will send a letter of request for information from the drug company."

"Sounds like a plan, Lew."

DA Wydman had briefed Talcott previously about Darius' involvement in a clinical trial. At the time, they decided not to pursue a subpoena of the drug manufacturer. Instead, they had Adams make a call to the contact Dr. Caron had given him. Adams had called the pharmaceutical company but had failed to reach Jackie Deno or Dr. Sheridan. Both were purportedly out of the office. Adams had then spoken with Cheryl Baker, who quickly referred him to the company's legal department. When he called the legal department, they stymied him, refusing to discuss the matter. They had indicated that they would not release any information unless there were written, legal authorization to do so.

Talcott now questioned the wisdom of their previous decision to call rather than subpoena the pharmaceutical company. The call had failed, and now the pharmaceutical company had been put on notice. AG Talcott feared that this notice had tipped the company off, making discovering the truth, if there was truth to be found, difficult, if not impossible. Pharmaceutical companies not only had big bucks and big legal departments but many friends in high places. He didn't relish the thought of waging a legal battle for information. Although the evidence from the autopsies was tantalizing, it was still weak from a legal perspective. It was doubtful, even given a written request for information, that the company would be forthcoming. Without a sense of excitement or optimism, he scheduled time on his calendar to draft a letter.

Wydman called Adams and conveyed the news that another subpoena and visit to Dr. Caron's was in his future. It struck Adams as strange that the State continued to investigate Darius and now Elvira's death. When Elvira was alive and threatening to bring a lawsuit, he could understand. Now that she was dead, there was presumably no one making the wild allegations she had been making.

"No disrespect, sir, but why are we continuing to pursue these cases?"

"First, if their deaths are linked to some drug, then we have a legal and ethical duty to report it and hopefully protect others. Second, the State Office of Advocacy and the National Alliance on Mental Illness both have formal complaints from Elvira. They won't drop the complaints unless we can provide information that refutes the allegations."

"Alright, that makes sense, thanks. Do you want me to do anything other than meet with Dr. Caron again?"

"Yes, I want you to go over the inventory of things the forensic team cataloged from Elvira's trailer. They didn't find anything suspicious related to her death, but there may be something that could give us clues about Darius and his actions."

"I'm on it," Adams replied.

"Not so fast, cowboy," DA Wydman said. "We are sending a subpoena for information from the drug company. We're requesting that they send information directly to you. If they're not forthcoming, I may need you to visit Buffalo."

"Okay, you sure they don't have an office in Key West?" he joked.

"Well, hopefully, they will just send you the information, and you can stay put in balmy mid-Maine in November!" he retaliated.

Adams' first call was to Rebecca, the Office Manager at Dr. Caron's office.

"Rebecca, this is Inspector Adams. I'm going to need another meeting with Dr. Caron."

"May I ask what the meeting pertains to?"

"I need to speak with him about whether Elvira Scott was a patient or ever participated in any of his clinical trials."

"Okay, you know the drill concerning supplying the legal request."

"I do."

"Dr. Caron's can meet with you this Thursday at 4:30 p.m. in our Campion office."

"That will be great. Thanks."

Adams hung up and went to the Evidence Room to review the inventory of items from Elvira's trailer taken by the forensic team. The inventory included an itemized list and photos. The inventory listed some items that were boxed and sent to storage. The list was notable more for what it didn't contain than what it did. Except for an expired bottle of Extra Strength Tylenol and a container of Tums, the inventory listed no other medications. It was the rare American home that wasn't well equipped with an assortment of pills and topicals for the usual maladies. The list for Darius' room was even more impressive in its brevity. A Compact Disc player, one Compact Disc, and a Bible. The CD was by Sorbitol Nightmare, a band with which Adams was not familiar. The list indicated that the Compact Disc had been stored in an evidence box. Adams made a note to retrieve the CD. He would not normally do so, but since Darius' belongings were so sparse, it made him curious about why this was his only CD. He also wanted to see the Bible. While he knew its contents, he was interested in whether Darius had made any notations in the Bible or highlighted any passages. Both might give him some clues into his mental state. The rest of the inventory didn't strike him as containing anything of value. From the pictures, it looked like the trailer included more trash than actual belongings. He jotted down the reference number of the evidence box and committed to going to the evidence warehouse the first thing in the morning.

Adams arrived at the warehouse, where forensic evidence was stored. Most criminal cases generate boxes of evidence, so it was odd for him to receive only one partially filled box.

Opening Darius' Bible first, he was rewarded with multiple underlined passages, some in pencil, some in pen. At first, the underlined passages seemed random: Genesis 15:17, Genesis 22:6, Genesis 22:7, Exodus 3:2, Exodus 12:8. On closer examination, Adams realized that every underlined passage had the word "fire" in it. He shuddered when he read Exodus 12:9, "Do not eat the meat raw or boiled in water but roast it over a fire— with the head, legs, and internal organs."

Although the evidence box contained only three items, his examination of them took all day. All in all, Darius had underlined 364 passages containing the word "fire" from Genesis 15:17 to Revelation 20:15. He had not made any notations in the Bible, but the underlined passages were ominous enough. Adams was amazed at how many passages spoke of fire, most in a negative and punitive way. On rare occasions, the Bible referenced fire in a positive sense, like its ability to give light or warmth. The Book of Amos Chapter 1 read like the journal of a pyromaniac. There were so many references to setting fire to the walls and houses and consuming the fortresses of families that Adams could almost sense Darius' delight in underlining the passages. That there were no underlined passages without the word "fire" was revealing. The overall impact of reading the passages left Adams exhausted. It was mid-afternoon before he broke for lunch. When he returned, he plugged in the CD player and inserted the Sorbitol Nightmare disc. If he had found the underlined Bible passages depressing and ominous, the CD just contributed to his unease. He advanced the CD immediately to the third track, "Her Fate Is Sealed," and was met with a stark, slow, dark musical track accompanied by a deep voice. He immediately recognized the words that Darius had sung, and Raylene, the nurse at Harlow Psychiatric Institute, had recorded on the night of his death.

I prayed and kneeled

She broke us apart

Her fate was sealed

She broke my heart

I will build a pyre

I will never be healed

I will burn her with fire

Her fate is sealed

He listened to the other tracks, most in the same dark, slow meter that reminded Adams of when he would play records at his grandparent's home as a boy. They had an old Blaupunkt Cabinet Stereo that played records at four speeds: $16\frac{2}{3}$, $33\frac{1}{3}$, 45, and 78 rpm. Sorbitol Nightmare sounded like when Adams would switch the stereo to the ultra-slow $16\frac{2}{3}$ rpm when playing one of his 45 rpm records.

The contents of the box confirmed his obsession with fire and a source for his verbalizations while in custody. It did not, however, provide any further clues as to why Calli Barnes had been his target. After burying himself amidst the gloom of Darius Scott's minimal belongings, he felt exhausted. He drove home, skipped dinner, and went to bed.

In the morning, DA Wydman called Adams and reported that AG Talcott had mailed a certified letter to AlzCura's legal department. Adams found a copy of the letter lying on his desk when he arrived at his office. He reviewed the "any and all" letter and found the "any and all" phrase a bit overdone. He understood that this was lawyer-speak meant to convey things in clear and absolute terms. All he could think was how Ms. Rudolph, his high school English teacher, would have beat the letter's author about the head with her copy of Strunk and White's Elements of Style!

Inspector Adams reviewed the cold case records of house fires in Maine again, even though investigators had previously done so after Darius was taken into custody. Given Darius' obsession with fire, he found it difficult to believe that this fire had been his one and only. When one unsolved house fire popped up on his search of cold cases within 10 miles of Barry, he felt sudden optimism. The fire had been in Bakersdale, just 7 miles from Barry, and had killed a family of four. His confidence flagged some when he saw it had happened 34 years earlier. He did the math and realized that Darius would have been 14. It was a long shot, but not entirely out of the question. Then it occurred to him that Darius had spent his first 18 years in Ramsey, not Barry. His optimism turned to despair. Seven miles for a 14-year-old was possible. Thirty-six miles was highly unlikely. The few remaining cold cases were all over 100 miles from where Darius had spent his 48 years on earth. Not surprisingly, he had hit another dead end.

Like most industries, the ability of investigators to do sophisticated research on individuals had grown immeasurably since the advent of the Internet. In addition, a concerted effort by the field to link disparate databases to allow investigators to research across regional or national levels had also helped. It was rare now not to find hundreds, if not thousands, of "hits" regarding someone during a computer search. Somehow, Darius had escaped such discovery. Elvira, on the other hand, had made a name for herself with frequent mentions in the media about her various exploits and crusades. Despite this notoriety, there was precious little personal information to glean. Although she was on disability, there were no recent records of a doctor-patient relationship. Like her son, none of the local hospitals had any recent records on her. Her life seemed to revolve around reading entertainment magazines and sitting in the chair where Adams had found her. Apart from her disability and social security checks, there was no other income.

As Adams drove to Dr. Caron's office that afternoon, he realized that Dr. Caron might hold the last hope of explaining the mysterious deaths of Elvira and her son. He started to wonder what he would do next if, after his first question, Dr. Caron told him that he hadn't seen or treated Elvira.

Rebecca saw Adams arrive and ushered him back to her office, where he handed her the necessary paperwork. He was anxious to get some answers but knew better than to ask Rebecca any questions. She had made it very clear before that only Dr. Caron could address patient inquiries. She perused the paperwork, seemed satisfied, and escorted him to the same chair in Dr. Caron's office where he had waited before. She gave what must have been her standard line about Dr. Caron would be in in a few minutes, and he settled in for what he knew might be a 20-minute wait. To his surprise, Dr. Caron bounced into the office within minutes.

"Inspector Adams, good to see you again."

"Dr. Caron, thank you for seeing me again," Adams said, shaking the doctor's hand.

"Rebecca showed me the subpoena. Elvira attended a clinic of mine," he said before Adams even had a chance to ask any questions. "She attended the same free clinic her son did and entered into the same clinical trial."

"Let me guess, she was lost in follow-up," said Adams trying to anticipate the doctor's response.

"No, actually not. And that's 'lost to follow-up' not 'lost in follow-up.' She didn't keep her follow-up appointment, but she had called my Research Coordinator and gave her follow-up information over the phone. The only thing pending was some lab work which she promised to have done."

"So, she was an active participant in the trial?"

"Well, no. She never came in to do the lab work as promised."

"What do you do in those cases."

"In those cases, we attempt to get the lab work within the specified timeframe. If not, I report a protocol deviation."

"What's that?"

"It's a break with the required steps in the study. For the

first deviation for lab work, I must report it to the study sponsor. If the participant misses a second lab draw, then I notify the study sponsor and the Institutional Review Board. A third miss and the participant is considered lost to follow-up and excluded from the study. Elvira was on that path."

"You didn't see her at any time after her visit to the free clinic?"

"Actually, I never met her. My research coordinator and a phlebotomist staffed the free clinic."

"So, you took blood at the free clinic?"

"Yes, to rule out any anomalous conditions or conditions that might prevent them from being in the study."

"Do you have Elvira's lab work?"

"No, the study sponsor had us send the specimens to a regional lab and then notified us which participants could be included in the study."

"Is that common practice?"

"It's getting more common. It has several benefits, including reducing variation in results when sending specimens to multiple labs, it reduces the cost to the sponsor, and it simplifies things for us investigators."

"Do you know what the sponsor does with the blood specimens?"

"No."

"Do you think they would store it?"

"I don't know Inspector Adams. You'd have to ask them," he said, glancing at his watch, which Adams knew meant he was about to bolt.

"Okay, one last question, doctor. Elvira and Darius Scott died from similar causes within weeks of each other. Do you think it's possible that Darius and Elvira Scott both could have received the study drug and that they both died due to an adverse effect of the drug?"

"Anything is possible, Inspector Adams, but it's highly improbable. First off, the study participants are randomized, so the chances that they both received the study drug are reduced. Second, if that were the case, I would think that the sponsor would have discovered this danger in earlier studies of the drug. What similar causes are you talking about?"

"They both had brain bleeds. Their brains had swelled, and an explosion went off in their heads. I think the Medical Examiner called it an aneur," Adams paused, trying to find the medical term.

"An aneurysm," Dr. Caron finished his sentence.

"Yes, that's it, but huge ones."

"Well, Super-Giant aneurysms are quite rare, so if both Elvira and Darius died from ruptured aneurysms, that would be rare indeed. However, I would first suspect a genetic link before anything else. Again, if the drug caused an increased incidence of ruptured aneurysms, I think the sponsor would have discovered this long ago and halted the study. Have you consulted Elvira and Darius' primary care physicians? Perhaps they know more about the family's medical history."

"They didn't have a regular doctor."

"Hmmm, well, then you have a mystery that will be pretty hard to solve."

"You don't have to tell me. This has been one dead end after another."

"I'm sorry I can't help you further," he said, standing up from his desk and extending his hand.

Adams stood and reached for the doctor's hand reluctantly. He felt like he was either missing something or that this was the unceremonious end of his investigation. Unless the pharmaceutical company could supply additional information, his investigation would end with a dissatisfying and unlikely explanation. A fire-obsessed man with no prior criminal history ironically purchases items for his crime from the store where the victim works and inexplicably sets her on fire, with no evidence that he knew or bore any animosity towards her. Then, he and his mother, who were both involved in some research study, would both die within weeks of each other from mysteriously similar and unexplained conditions. He hoped that the pharmaceutical company would see fit to respond favorably to the subpoena sent earlier that day.

CHAPTER 38

C urt fell back on Chelsea's bed. A sheen of sweat covered both their bodies. His heart felt as if it was going to explode. Their feverish session had started the moment Chelsea had opened her front door. Their workout at the gym earlier in the day had only served as foreplay.

She opened the door wearing only an oversized t-shirt and pulled him into her apartment, kicking the door shut. Their hands quickly occupied, Curt's clothes fell in a clichéd path to the bedroom. Despite this first encounter, their moves were surprisingly smooth and choreographed. They moved and matched each other's pace, almost as if they were still running on their treadmills. Aiding the moment was all that led up to it - his dream, her playful teasing, his loneliness, her youth, and three months since he last made love to Calli.

Like her running, she was relentless in her pace. He wanted to please her but knew there was no distraction strong enough to make this anything but a sprint. As if she could sense his thoughts, she left little doubt she was quickly moving towards her finish line. Coincident with the feeling that he was beyond the point of no return, she urged him on. He didn't need the encouragement, but it certainly didn't hurt.

When they recovered, he was surprised to find her face transformed from a rapturous glow to indifference. Her body moved and fell away. The temperature in the room dropped.

He rolled towards her to reclaim their union.

"What's the matter?" he asked, reaching for her.

"My name is Chelsea."

"I know that, Chels," he had said, wondering what had brought her obvious statement on.

"You called me Calli."

"What? No."

"Yes."

"I can't believe that. Really?"

She turned away and didn't respond.

"Chels. I'm sorry. I don't even remember saying that."

She didn't respond. He reached over to touch her shoulder.

"Don't touch me," she snapped and slid further away as if repulsed by his touch.

"Chels, I'm sorry. Please, if I said that, I didn't mean it."

"There's no if. You said it," she snapped and retreated further from him in the bed.

"Chels, I'm sorry. I must have said it out of habit," he said as a feeling of guilt was starting to sweep over him. Suddenly, he couldn't stop thinking that he had just cheated on Calli. When Chelsea didn't respond, he once again reached out to touch her but stopped short.

"Chels, I don't know what to say or do. I didn't mean it."

"Just leave," she sobbed as it was now clear that she had been quietly crying.

"I can't, Chels, not after what we just shared," he said as he slid up closer to her. He heard himself say three words that magically healed Chelsea but fatally wounded him the moment he said them. She had turned to him, and he had kissed her tears. She had embraced and kissed him back, and before he knew it, despite being an emotional wreck, he was making love to her again. If he hadn't looked at the clock, they might have continued indefinitely. It took him thirty minutes to get out the door, even though he was already hopelessly late in picking up Caitlin and Cade. Each time he tried to leave, they would lock in an embrace that would threaten to start another torrid session. Whatever harm he may have caused her earlier was gone, but the smile on his face as he finally left hid a raging turmoil.

As he drove home, he vacillated between feeling powerful guilt to a formidable desire to turn around. Her scent on his skin triggered more back-and-forth feelings. When he arrived home, he wanted to take a shower but didn't want to take a shower. He had been thrown into a topsy-turvy world where he was damned if he did and damned if he didn't. He had never felt so lost and so found at the same time. Although he felt protected in the cocoon of Chelsea's apartment, he now felt exposed and vulnerable. Everyone who looked at him seemed to know what he had done, and he could swear everyone was giving him disapproving looks. Even Caitlin and Cade seemed to be distant and cold to him. The objective observer would have seen two kids hopelessly excited and happy to see their father. The fury of his sexual encounter with Chelsea had blinded him. It had colored his every experience with shame and guilt. Their initial union had felt as though he was entering the gates of heaven. Now the consummation of that union felt like a hell from which he was uncertain he could recover. He tried to calm his mind by concentrating on his parental duties. He was hopelessly distracted, and Caitlin and Cade got their homework and bedtime routines accomplished largely without his full attention.

He woke up the next day with something resembling a hangover. Although he had avoided the torture of disturbing dreams, he was in a deep funk. His faculties could not deal with or fully comprehend the vibrant brightness of the day or the responsibilities that lay in front of him. Instead of waking the kids for school, he went back to bed. He lay there sure now of the answer to a question that Chelsea had asked him after running. "What's more therapeutic talking to your counselor or being with me?" The answer to that question had seemed so painfully obvious at the time. Now he knew better, and the only thing that got him out of bed that morning was his need to see Tim.

He got through the workday on automatic pilot. Physic-ally, he made all the usual and necessary moves but internally brewed a storm of disturbing thoughts and feelings. He knew that if he could hold it together until 4:00 p.m., he would be at Tim's, ready to fight off the demons that now possessed him. His cellphone had sprung to life twice during the day, each time Chelsea's picture had popped up. He had initially reached for the phone and then thought better of it. She had left mes-sages, and as he shuffled papers on his desk in a desperate attempt to look productive, he weighed whether to listen to them. His curiosity eventually got the better of him, and after listening to the messages, he wished he hadn't. There was now no hope that he would be able to focus his mind on anything resembling work. Her impassioned words played almost like those suggestive 1-900 phone sex numbers that guaranteed a cure for your loneliness. Unlike those numbers, however, he knew that a short 5-minute drive could make her spoken words come true. Although disturbed by what he heard, it hadn't failed to arouse him. He got in his car at lunchtime and had gone two blocks in the direction of her apartment, only to detour to a sandwich shop instead. If Chelsea's face had been the model for contentment, Curt's behavior was the model for conflict as he ping-ponged in a perpetual pattern of actions without direction and thoughts without conclusions. He chauffeured his sandwich back to the office but left it in the car. He had no appetite.

Finally, his torturous workday ended. As he made his way over to Tim's office, he saw an 18-wheeler barreling down the road in the opposite lane. He felt his hands move the steering wheel ever so slightly to the left. It felt like he was watching himself, not really directing his actions. Someone else was driving. He was watching. If not for the startling blare of the semi's air horn and his reflexive adjustment to the right, the outcome would certainly not have favored his survival. He wasn't even wearing his seatbelt. Over the last 24 hours, he had uncharacteristically failed to wear it. Had he not avoided the crash, the only thing the paramedics would have found was an impression of "Peterbilt" on his forehead. It was as if in making love to Chelsea, he had jettisoned every habit of self-preservation and sensibility.

He sat in the chair across from Tim but could not shake the feeling that he was just a spectator watching two people talking. He heard himself telling Tim about the events of the last few days. Still, when Tim asked him questions about his feelings, he was utterly incapable of answering. The dichotomous feelings of exhilarating sex followed by his cloying guilt transformed into a series of "I don't know" answers. It was as if he had no feelings. He was watching a man speak to his counselor, but he only saw the shell of the man. He had no sense of how the man felt. Suddenly, a bomb exploded.

"How do Caitlin and Cade feel about Chelsea?"

"They haven't met her yet."

"Do you intend to introduce them to her?"

"No, not yet."

"Why not?"

"It's too soon. Too soon after..." he couldn't even say it. Instead, the floodgates opened.

Tim waited in silence for a couple of minutes as Curt sobbed and tried several times unsuccessfully to shore up his composure. He wished Tim would say something. When Tim finally did, Curt wished he hadn't.

"After what?" Tim asked.

The two-word question threw Curt back into the despair he had just struggled to rise above. He disintegrated again into tears. After a minute, he attempted to answer.

"Calli's" was all he could manage before breaking down again.

Tim waited silently, expectantly. Curt was starting to hate Tim's non-judgmental, non-directive approach. He just wanted Tim, someone, to fix things.

"I can't do this," Curt finally said as he wiped his eyes.

"Can't do what?"

"Can't do this," Curt said, gesturing to the room.

"But you are."

"No, I'm not. This isn't helping."

"So, you don't think you've made progress?"

"Are you fucking kidding me? I'm a wreck. I just about bought it on my way over here. I didn't even know I was doing it, but I almost succeeded in kissing an 18-wheeler."

"So, you feel what?"

"Depressed. My life's a mess, and I can't concentrate at work. I can't handle the kids by myself. I'm fucking a college kid, and I can't believe my wife is dead."

"So, you still feel married?"

"Yes. I mean, I was married to her for ten years. It's not as if we got divorced. She was taken from me. You don't automatically feel unmarried after the way she was taken from me."

"So, if you still feel married, what are you doing with Chelsea?"

"I was lonely. She was so nice to me. But now I feel like I'm cheating," as tears erupted again.

"How do you think Calli wants you to feel?"

The question threw Curt. He was talking about Calli as if she could communicate something from the beyond. He allowed himself to explore the question after his initial shock.

"Happy?" was all he could manage.

"Is that a question or a statement?"

"Happy. I think she wants me to be happy."

"Why?"

"Because that's how she always wanted me to be. That's how we were when we were together. She'd want me to be happy for the kids."

"So, if she wants you to be happy, why aren't you?"

At first, he thought this was a stupid question. He had just remarked how much of a mess his life was, and now he was asking him why he wasn't happy? He turned the question over in his head a few times.

"Because I haven't let her go," he said in a flash of recognition that seemed so obvious but so elusive. The tears flowed again.

"And you haven't let her go because?"

"Because I loved her, and she loved me. Because we were so happy together and had so many plans and dreams for the future."

"Because you LOVED her?"

Tim's repeating his use of the past tense shot him like an arrow through his heart.

"Because I LOVE her."

"But you used the word 'loved.'"

"Because she's gone. Because it's over."

"Is it?"

Startled as much by what he had just said as by Tim's question, he tried to keep his composure.

"No, it's not over. I haven't let her go."

In that instant, he looked up at the Kubler-Ross poster and focused on the fourth stage – depression. So, this is depression. His eyes moved to "acceptance" and then to the earlier stages. He realized that as painful as this was, he was making progress. He realized that Tim hadn't responded to his answer. This usually meant he was waiting for more.

"I have to let her go," Curt said bluntly.

"Why?"

"Because I can't be happy holding on anymore. I have to move on. She'd want me to move on."

"Does that mean you don't love Calli anymore?"

There was another stupid-sounding question designed to generate insight.

"No, I will always love her, but she's gone."

"She's gone?"

"She's dead."

The words arrived with a thud of finality that he had never allowed himself to say.

He left Tim's office with a burden lifted. The otherworldliness feeling was gone. He wasn't naïve enough to believe he was totally out of Stage Four, but he could see the glimmer of acceptance up ahead. He was letting go of Calli. On the drive home, he realized that he had to curb or end his relationship with Chelsea. If it was too soon to introduce her to the kids, it was too soon for him to continue the intense relationship they had. Although it felt good coming to this realization, he had no idea how to go about backing off the relationship accelerator, hitting the brakes, or getting out of the car altogether. He drove past half a dozen 18-wheelers on his way home without incident and looked forward to a quiet night being Dad to Caitlin and Cade.

The next morning Curt felt as back to normal as he ever had over the last three months. This feeling was shattered mid-morning by two calls - the first from Chelsea.

"I'm sorry, Chels," he said when he answered the call.

"Well, you better be," she said in a good-natured tone.

"I've been swamped at work, and I'm planning a weekend getaway with the kids."

"Oh, where you going?"

"Well, the kids have horseback riding Saturday morning, but I'm thinking of taking them to the Rockland Resort afterward."

"Sweet. Can I come along?"

He wasn't sure if she was asking this for real or in jest. He decided he better assume it was for real.

"You know, that would be fun, but I'm a little worried about how ready the kids are to meet another woman in their Dad's life. I'd rather introduce you to them when I think they're ready. They have their first support group meeting this Friday."

"Okay," she responded dejectedly. "So, when can we get together?"

"It looks like it won't be until next week."

"How about the gym today at noon?"

"Sorry, I have a meeting then," he lied.

"Well, I'm going out to the Lost Loon with a couple of friends tonight. You could join us if you'd like."

"Thanks. I'll see how the day goes and whether I can find someone to watch the kids."

"Okay, we'll be there around 7:30. Hope to see ya."

"Okay, have a good day."

Just as he hit the "End Call" button, he heard her say, "Love you." He raised the phone to his ear, but the call had disconnected. It was a good thing because he wasn't even sure what he would have said in response. He had successfully navigated a couple of potentially sticky moments on the call, optimistic that he might be able to cool down this relationship. His work and his kids provided useful insulation from availability.

No sooner had he ended his call with Chelsea when Loribeth knocked on his door and poked her head in.

"Curt, the DA's office called. He wants to meet with you. I booked you for 2:30 this afternoon. I hope that's okay."

"That's fine, LB. Thanks."

He wondered what the DA wanted. The last time they had met, Curt felt as if it would probably be the last time they would meet. He struggled to remember their previous conversation. What circumstances would have prompted this meeting? He knew they were investigating Darius' death. He also knew that Darius' mother had recently died after creating quite a stir in the media. Could they have possibly discovered something related to why Darius had killed his wife? If this was the case, would knowing it give him any peace of mind? He remembered his emotional state after his last visit and how the gruesome details had haunted him. He didn't want anything disrupting the feeling of normalcy that he had at the start of his day. Despite his best effort, his mind started to roll through the questions that his scheduled meeting with the DA created.

"Mr. Barnes. Nice to see you again. How are you doing?" said DA Wydman, welcoming Curt into his office.

"Fine, I guess."

"Listen, I know you're probably still searching for answers, and I don't want to mislead you. We are investigating some things that may be related to Darius' behavior. It doesn't fully answer your questions, but I thought it would be important for you to know that we haven't entirely stopped trying to find answers."

"I appreciate that. What have you learned?"

"Darius' toxicology report mentions an unidentifiable substance in his system that was classified as "suspicious but inconclusive.""

"So, what does that mean?"

"It means that we are not exactly sure whether that substance could have contributed to his bizarre behavior or his death."

"That's it?"

"Well, no. It turns out that his mother died of very similar causes, and we are just waiting on the Regional Lab to let us know if she had the same substance in her system."

"And if she does?"

"Then we may have a lead because both Darius and his mother were enrolled in a research study. It's a long shot, but I just wanted you to know that we hadn't forgotten about you."

"Thanks, but I guess I can't make the connection. What does their involvement in a research study have to do with answering why Darius killed my wife?"

"Well, if there is a connection to the research study, perhaps it helps explains the bizarre and aggressive behaviors that we saw in Darius and his mother. As I said, it's a long shot."

Curt left DA Wydman's office disappointed. He had hoped to hear something more definitive than some sketchy connection to a research study. He knew DA Wydman was well-meaning, but this information just confirmed that he probably would never know why Darius had killed his wife.

Friday arrived, and Curt picked the kids up after school to drive them to their first Support Group meeting in Portland. After meeting the staff and filling out some paperwork, he had two hours to kill. Although mid-November in Maine can be inclement, it was rather mild, and Curt chose to drive to the Back Bay Cove for a stroll. He found that he was not the only one who wanted to take advantage of the unseasonably mild weather conditions. He found the 4-mile first lap so therapeutic that he decided to do another. He would have to pick up the pace, though, so as not to be late in picking up the kids.

He arrived back at the Support Group with minutes to spare. A counselor's assurance and the kids' excited pleas for him to look at their artwork announced that their first Support Group meeting had been a success. They chatted excitedly on their way to Buckaroo Barn & Steakhouse for dinner. There, as DA Wydman had predicted, the kids ate up not only the food but also the animated, talking animals that intermittently sprang to life. On the way home, they made plans for the weekend.

Curt awoke from a steamy dream of Chelsea writhing deliciously on top of him only to discover that the bouncing of the bed was Caitlin jostling his shoulder.

"Dad, wake up!"

"What, honey?" Curt responded, feeling embarrassed as if his daughter had caught him in bed with Chelsea.

"It's time to pick up Jordan and go horseback riding."

He looked at the clock on his nightstand and realized that he had uncharacteristically slept nearly 10 hours. Instead of feeling refreshed, however, he felt sluggish. He instructed Caitlin to get Cade ready and pick up Jordan while he quickly showered.

Despite the late start, they made it to the stables on time. Two horses stood at attention in the arena as today, both girls would be riding in honor of Jordan's birthday. An assistant named Melody accompanied Chantel for today's riding session. Melody would instruct Jordan while Caitlin, who was the more accomplished rider, worked with Chantel. Melody and Chantel formed a duo that visually could have passed for the female version of Oliver Hardy and Stan Laurel. Chantel was slender, tall, and shy. Melody was short, stocky, and gregarious. Unlike the bumbling antics of Laurel & Hardy, however, both were supremely confident and adept when it came to rider training and horse management. As had been the case in previous visits, a perpetual smile was pasted on Caitlin's face the moment she stepped into the stables. Even Jordan's usual flat affect was replaced by a slight smile, which for her represented a degree of delight that she rarely felt or expressed. Cade busied himself, visiting the other horses in the stable and feeding them stray strands of hay. Towards the end of their riding, Melody brought out Waffles, an immense Belgian Draft horse who was a favorite to all who visited the stables for her size and gentle demeanor. All three kids fit easily on Waffle's bare back as she sauntered around the arena. To dismount, Melody caught the kids as they slid off the back of Waffles, whose hindquarters formed a kind of equine slide. It was a great start to the weekend.

After riding, they grabbed burgers and fries at a fast-food place to sustain them for the hour and a half drive to the Rockland Resort. Curt and Calli had brought the kids to the Rockland Resort at least a few times a year, usually during the off-season when tourist volume was low. The Rockland Resort offered plenty of supervised kid activities that would allow Curt and Calli some adult downtime. The Sunday Brunch, the pool, the video arcade, movie night, and walking on the breakwater to the lighthouse were all family favorites. For Jordan, who had never been to the Rockland Resort, it was decidedly the most extravagant location she had ever been to for her birthday or otherwise. After checking in and settling into their Oceanside suite, Caitlin and Cade escorted Jordan around the resort, showing her all their favorite places. After taking in a few minutes of the brisk ocean breeze from the balcony, Curt retired to the lobby, where he flipped through a couple issues of Downeast magazine in a comfortable chair next to the fireplace.

Before long, the kids arrived in the lobby, breathless from a whirlwind tour of the property. They had chosen the pool and hot tubs for their first activity. This suited Curt just fine as the sluggishness that he had awoken with had carried on through the day.

Curt stepped into one of the two hot tubs and found a place where he could keep an eye on the kids who had grabbed foam tubes and jumped into the pool. As usual, during this time of year, the pool area was not overly crowded. Curt let the bubbles bombard his body as the kids jousted with their foam tubes. Their laughter and smiles were all he needed to see to feel content. A few other kids at the pool with their parents started to make their way towards Caitlin, Cade, and Jordan. As the band of kids started up a game of Marco Polo, Curt spied a shapely figure emerging from the far end of the pool. As she squeezed out the water from her hair, he admired how her bikini bottom had ridden up, forming a thong-like effect. As if she felt his eyes on her over-exposed backside, she expertly pulled the clingy material back to its proper place. Even with her wardrobe adjustment and the substantial distance, he felt a twinge of desire. As she bent over to towel off her legs, he caught a glimpse of her silhouette. As she started to walk from the end of the pool around towards Curt, he realized that it was Chelsea. Her eyes met his just as he reached this realization, and he couldn't tear his eyes off her body, moving sensually towards him. He glanced at the pool in a quick kid check, and they were still engrossed in their games. She took the steps up to his hot tub, and as she dipped her toe in the spa, she said, "Like what you see?"

"Love what I see," he heard himself reply, mesmerized by her body.

Before he knew it, she was sitting next to him. Before he knew it, her right hand found its way into his swim shorts. He was in her grip in more ways than one, and he nervously shot a glance at the pool.

"Don't worry, they can't see a thing," she said with a smoldering smile. "I just had to see you. I hope you don't mind."

"I..." he couldn't find any words. As he struggled to find some, her left hand pulled his left hand between her legs.

"Now, this is getting to be a real hot tub," she cooed.

He was about to give in when it all became too real, too fast, and potentially too damaging. His G-rated weekend was quickly becoming X-rated, and he couldn't let that happen. He pulled his hand away and removed hers.

"Chelsea, we can't do this," he said in as firm a tone as he could muster.

"Oh, don't be shy," she said, reaching for him again underwater.

"NO!" he said louder than he had intended. It echoed off the tile and momentarily stopped everyone in the pool. If Chelsea hadn't received the message the first time, this time, she had, she retreated, and her face twisted in a picture of shock, dismay, and rejection. Tears came to her eyes, and while her lips quivered as if trying to find words, she could not speak. Curt spoke for her.

"We have to stop Chelsea. I'm not ready for this. Please leave."

He could tell that his words had wounded her, and she quietly left the hot tub without a word. No sooner had she left the hot tub when the kids and their newfound friends piled in.

"Daddy, who was that lady?"

"I don't know, sweetheart."

"Then why did you yell at her?"

"I didn't yell at her, she told me a story about seeing a big whale out beyond the breakwater, and I didn't believe her."

"Oh, it sounded like you were mad."

"No, honey, I wasn't mad at her."

"Can we go see the whale?"

"Maybe tomorrow. It's too late now."

Seemingly satisfied, Caitlin went back to her friends, who had already exited the hot tub for another round of Marco Polo in the pool.

The rest of the weekend was a huge success with the kids, even though Curt felt a wave of rising anger that had not visited him in weeks. He tried to relax by the fireplace in the lobby as he had done when he had first arrived, but suddenly, being close to fire made him uncomfortable.

After the weekend, his dreamless nights were replaced once again by nightmarish visits from Darius Scott that would awaken him in the middle of the night. He felt as if he was back peddling. It had only been last week when he had left Tim's office, thinking that he was on the precipice of the acceptance phase. Thrust back into the anger phase, it gripped him, unlike any anger he had ever experienced. Over the next few weeks, he was short with almost everyone, and eventually, his rage seemed to spill over to Caitlin and Cade. Suddenly, they were back to the bickering and arguing that had so characterized their behavior before Calli's death. They couldn't agree on anything, and Jordan, who originally had a calming and unifying influence on his kids, became the object of jealousy and division. The three could no longer be in one room together without Caitlin or Cade crying foul. Curt was even short with Loribeth, and when Sam finally sat Curt down to address his behavior in the office, Curt felt like he had lost control.

Curt agreed to take some time off to try to pull things together. The simple fact was that he had not taken time off in nearly six months. Despite his counseling and the kid's Support Group meetings, the Thanksgiving, Christmas, and New Year holiday season had been disastrous. No amount of family or the best intentions or kindness of friends could replace the chasm that Calli's absence left. Everything seemed hollow and meaningless. Curt's 18-wheeler impulses returned. Caitlin became mute and emotionless. Cade became obsessively concerned with schedules and would howl if something occurred that wasn't on the schedule or didn't happen as planned. Everything seemed to be unraveling, and Curt felt like he was moments from going over an emotional cliff.

CHAPTER 39

Whe Jackie arrived for her first day of work in 3 months, she found her office cubicle filled with gifts. Many of the gifts were from clients. Before she could open and enjoy them, however, there was a conspicuous note on her desk from Cheryl. She knocked on Cheryl's door and entered her office.

"Welcome back, Mama! How is motherhood?" Cheryl said, uncharacteristically departing from her usual all-business, direct communications. After Jackie gushed about Ashley and showed her a few pictures, Cheryl got to the real point of her note.

"I asked you in here because we received a call for you while you were out from an Investigator Adams."

"I don't understand. I've never heard of him. What did he want?"

"Dr. Caron had given him your name. When he couldn't reach you, he was transferred to me."

This did nothing to clear up her confusion. If anything, it confused her even more.

"Why would..." she began but was cut off by Cheryl.

"Inspector Adams is investigating the death of some guy who torched a home and killed some woman in Maine. It sounds like they're trying to pin this guy's mental state and his death to his participation in the Recallamin trial."

"That sounds pretty bizarre," Jackie said, about to ask questions when Cheryl continued.

"I have referred it to legal. The guy's mother is creating a stink and thinks someone in the looney bin killed her son. The autopsy apparently uncovered some curious tissue samples they can't explain. The guy had been lost to follow-up, and Adams wants us to unblind the data to determine if he received the vaccine or not. Also, the guy's mother died shortly afterward, and they are getting a subpoena to investigate her death and whether she too was involved in the trial."

"Was she?"

"I don't know. To me, this sounds like a fucking wild goose chase. We don't just go releasing information to some backwoods investigator from lobsterland who has a wild hair up his ass."

"So, what do you want me to do?"

"Nothing. We'll let legal handle this. Don't breathe a word of this to anyone. Just refer any calls or questions you receive to me or legal. We can't be side-tracked by this nonsense. Don't give it another thought. Hopefully, by the next time you go to Maine, this will have blown over."

"When am I scheduled to go back to Maine?"

"Not for another three months. Mid-February."

"Okay," Jackie said uneasily. This was not the reception she had expected on her first day back to work. She had wanted to ask more questions, but Cheryl's message had been crystal clear – don't give it another thought. Unfortunately, Jackie found it impossible to turn off the information Cheryl had just shared. The combination of Dr. Caron referring the investigator to her, a murder, and the death of two people potentially involved in their clinical trials was more than alarming. Lost in her thoughts, she didn't even notice when her perky replacement, Margo, popped her head into her cube.

"Thinking about your baby?" Margo's salutation incorrectly guessed but served to startle Jackie out of her reverie.

"Oh hi, I'm sorry, I was just trying to organize my thoughts," replied Jackie trying to fast forward her mind back to the here and now.

"I'm sure you have lots to catch up on. I was going to brief you, ya know, on your clients. Do you have time?"

"Sure," Jackie said with false enthusiasm while adjusting her chair to face Margo, who pulled a chair over to the entrance of Jackie's cubicle making for an impromptu 2-person meeting space.

She found it difficult to concentrate as Margo briefed her. The cute girl had an irritating habit of punctuating many of her sentences with "ya know." That, and Jackie's desire to focus her attention on the news Cheryl had given her, made her antsy.

"Is this a bad time, cuz, ya know, we could meet some other time," Margo intoned.

"No, I'm sorry. Go ahead."

"Then I went to Boston, ya know, and met with the doctors there. They had some questions I couldn't answer. I told them, ya know, that you would be back in a couple of weeks and could call them. They said that was fine."

If she said "ya know" one more time, Jackie felt like she was going to explode.

"Ya know," Jackie started, realizing that Margo's language tic was contagious, "let's schedule another time to talk. I have something I need to do right now."

"Okay, that's okay, ya know. I know you're busy."

It took all of Jackie's fortitude not to go off on her so-called replacement. She just hoped that Margo had not irritated or ostracized her clients to the degree that she would need to spend the first few weeks back in service recovery mode.

Mercifully, Margo left, allowing Jackie the opportunity to investigate the shocking news that Cheryl had just shared with her. Cheryl had not given Jackie any names other than Inspector Adams. Through the wonders of the Internet, her search on "fires in Maine" produced multiple links to the case. Once she had the names Darius and Elvira Scott, she accessed the research database that she had become so familiar with during her internship. To her chagrin, she was unable to access the records of Darius and Elvira Scott. A notice appeared on her monitor, "Record quarantined by Legal Services," when she clicked on either file. She went back to reading the information she could access via the Internet.

"I didn't know that motherhood had such an ill-effect on hearing," said Cheryl from behind Jackie. Startled for the second time in the hour, she turned to see her supervisor standing with arms crossed at the entrance of her cubicle.

"Get your ass in my office...NOW," she commanded before Jackie could say anything in her defense.

Cheryl marched, and Jackie slunk behind her to the office. No sooner had Jackie entered when the door slammed, causing Jackie to jump. Unconcerned, Cheryl lit into Jackie.

"What the hell did I just tell you? Didn't I say don't give it another thought? Maybe you'd like a permanent leave so you can spend ALL your time with your baby?

Jackie opened her mouth to try to respond, but nothing came out, but a stammered "I, I," as Cheryl's tirade continued.

"This nonsense in Maine is none of your business, so don't go all CSI on me, or I'll be forced to fire your ass. So that you know, the IT department can tell me where you've been and what you've tried to access on your computer. The moment you tried to open those records, it raised red flags pointing directly to you. You're lucky you're still here. Legal just called me and told me to dismiss you. If it weren't for my assurances that it wouldn't happen again, you'd be in the unemployment line right now. Understand?"

Jackie felt like a beaten puppy. All she could manage was a meek "Yes, I'm sorry."

"Now get back to work," her boss said sharply. Jackie skulked out of her office and back to her cubicle. She hadn't been back for more than an hour, and she had almost lost her job. She closed her Internet browser and focused on the stacks of files on her desk. She was so fearful for her job that she worked through lunch. If not for Cheryl finding her still at her desk an hour past her usual quitting time, she may have worked through the evening.

"What the hell are you still doing here?" Cheryl had said when finding Jackie's nose still buried in the paperwork on her desk.

"Just working," Jackie said sheepishly.

"Get home to your baby. I'm sure she's screaming to suck on your titties by now," Cheryl blurted in her characteristic blunt and colorful way.

"Okay," Jackie responded, clearly still rattled by the tongue-lashing she had taken earlier.

"Hey, kid. I'm sorry I had to scold you today. Now get over it. I need my dynamic, sexy, super saleswoman back. So, give me that confident look and quit the hangdog expression."

Jackie forced a smile that, while strained, still flashed with the radiance that put people under her spell.

"Better. If I weren't a woman, I'd want to suck on those titties myself. You still got it. Now get out of here."

As much as Jackie appreciated Cheryl's attempt to buoy her spirits, she couldn't shake the weight of the news she had received that morning or the severity of Cheryl's scolding. As she drove home, she realized that it must be serious if it had engendered such security measures and such an aggressive and immediate response. The reaction just didn't fit Cheryl's characterization that this was just some wild goose chase. That Dr. Caron was somehow involved didn't surprise Jackie at all. She couldn't wait to get home where the tentacles of AlzCura's Information Technology couldn't reach and track her every move on the Internet.

When she arrived home, however, Cheryl had been right. Ashley was screaming. Both Nana Doris and Stu were trying their best to feed her a bottle, but she wouldn't have it. As soon as Jackie put her in her arms and offered her breast, Ashley settled.

"Jeez, we thought you'd never get here," Stu exclaimed. "What took you so long?"

"I just had a lot of work, and the time got away from me. I'm sorry, I should have called."

"A call wouldn't have helped," said Jackie's mother. "Neither Stu nor I have the proper equipment."

Jackie laughed. It was the first time that day that she felt content.

"How was work Boo?" Stu asked.

Jackie's sour expression told a story, and Stu quickly added, "Okay, I guess we'll move on to other topics. Great to see you, hon. Can I rub your feet? Massage your shoulders? Win the lottery, so you don't have to work anymore?"

She appreciated Stu's sense of humor and brightened. "No, I'm just fine," as she looked adoringly at Ashley, whose little hand rested on her breast, and her dark eyes looked up to her mothers' face. Once Ashley was fed and content, Jackie put her down in her crib. Stu had cooked dinner, but Jackie didn't have an appetite and only picked at her salad. She retreated to her office and fired up her computer to resume her search for information on the case that had concerned her company. She read with horror the events of August 20, 2008, shuddering when subsequent stories included photos of the burned-out house and side-by-side photos of the victim and the man who set her on fire. While the events read like some horror story, Jackie could not quite make out how there might be a connection to her company. The news media had speculated that Darius had either committed suicide or had been the victim of a serious medication error. The press was clearly frustrated by the Chief Medical Examiner, who put them and the declaration of Darius' death off until all testing was complete. After a couple of hours scanning what she could, she was exhausted and gave up. Maybe Cheryl was right. Perhaps it was just a wild goose chase.

As she trudged to bed, she heard Ashley fussing. Instead of turning into her bedroom, she went to console Ashley. The action of picking fussy Ash up and settling into the rocker caused Jackie to leak milk before she could even nestle Ash to her breast. The moment Ash rooted at her breast and looked up into Jackie's eyes was magical, and the worries of the day quickly faded away. When she opened her eyes, Stu was rousting her awake. She had fallen asleep in the rocking chair while feeding Ashley. Stu carefully put Ashley in her crib and helped his exhausted wife to bed. It had been a long day, and she was asleep again as soon as her head hit the pillow.

CHAPTER 40

D
r. Sheridan, Cheryl Baker, and Chief Counsel Chet Humphreys hovered over Dr. Sheridan's desk, looking down at the letter from Maine's Attorney General like it was an uninvited guest to a party.

"Bury it," shouted Dr. Sheridan, visibly irritated.

"Asa," Cheryl demurred, "we can't just ignore it. We signed for it. If we ignore it, it will just raise suspicions. It was reasonable for us to deny producing information when Inspector Adams called and was nosing around. A certified, written request from the Maine Attorney General is another matter altogether."

"Cheryl's right, Asa," Humphreys added. "I recommend we respond. We can cooperate, still protect our information, and drag this out for years. This is only a request. While it's from Maine's AG, it's weak. There is no reference to a lawsuit, no copy to the FDA, no threat to go to the FDA if we don't cooperate, and no compelling evidence as to why we should divulge this information. It's lame. I can draft something for your review."

"I don't like it," Sheridan puffed.

"None of us do, Asa," Cheryl reached and touched his arm. "We can handle this. Some AG from East Bumblefuck, Maine can't just ask for information because of a problem in his backyard."

"The AG's request has the legal weight of 'pretty please' Asa," added Humphreys.

"Ok, draft the letter, and let's review it. I don't want to send it until the last possible date."

Humphreys left Dr. Sheridan's office, but Cheryl stayed behind.

"What are we going to do about Jackie?" Cheryl asked Dr. Sheridan.

"Good question. We need to keep her focused on her job and prevent her from digging into this mess. Maybe we should reassign her?"

"No, I think that would just pique her interest further. She's too smart for her own good," Cheryl replied.

"Too bad she's not more like Margo. No brains, no conscience, and thinks her job is to fuck every doctor into using Recallamin."

"Yeah, she's a real gem...ya know?"

Dr. Sheridan erupted into laughter when Cheryl employed Margo's incessant verbal tic.

"I think the way to keep Jackie in the game is to do just the opposite of what you suggested," said Cheryl.

"How's that?" asked Sheridan.

"Remember when Jackie was all gung-ho about Caron's radio ads and lack of ethics?"

"Yeah."

"Well, she was surprised that we didn't pursue that more aggressively. If we now admit that she was right and we were wrong, we can get her to go on her crusade."

"That's fucking brilliant."

"She continues to believe he's the one with something to

hide, not us."

"But what if Caron spills the beans?"

"I don't think that would happen," Cheryl countered.

"Why not?"

"He passed the Margo test. He absolutely wore out every orifice that ditzy girl possesses and didn't say peep."

Sheridan erupted in laughter again, amused by her graphic description. When he finally regained his composure, he asked Cheryl if she wanted to have dinner later.

"Sounds good. Dinner at the usual place at the usual time?" Cheryl asked.

"I'll be there with bells on."

"Leave the bells, bring the Kielbasa," as she grabbed his crotch on her way out the door.

CHAPTER 41

I t was the slow holiday season at AlzCura, which relegated Jackie to making phone calls to her clients – all her clients except Dr. Caron. While Jackie didn't mind not having to contact the puffed-up and grabby Dr. Caron, that she was forbidden from contacting him just fueled her suspicions. That and a series of "training sessions" that the legal department had held for company representatives regarding what may and may not be discussed during sales calls.

Training sessions during this time of year weren't unusual. It was the over-emphasis on information sharing that piqued everyone's curiosity in the office. At first, Jackie thought it was just her hyper-sensitivity since being scolded by Cheryl. Until one of her colleagues expressed her own frustration.

"Jeez, if I hear 'failure to observe our information sharing policy will result in discipline up to and including termination' one more time, I think I'll scream."

That phrase had become such a staple at these training sessions that many of Jackie's colleagues would employ it in jest during their conversations with one another. Jackie found this less humorous than others, but it certainly supported her feeling that the company was over-compensating for the so-called "wild goose chase." If the training wasn't a tip-off that something was amiss, then the "attestation forms" they were all required to sign were. One full page of legalese virtually no one read, but everyone signed. In essence, they were designed to be proof that you understood what had been presented and woe to you should you happen to break any of the rules. Everyone found the forms a bit demeaning, but for some, it was just another opportunity for office humor. Shortly after the barrage of training, management sent out an email regarding the condition of the staff bathrooms. In response, one brave employee had forwarded his version of the email to a select few colleagues, along with his creative embellishments. It read:

"I understand that I may only wipe my ass with 3-sheets of two-ply toilet paper per eliminating episode. The circumference of your eliminations shall not exceed the capacity of the drain to guarantee proper disposal in no more than one flush. Multiple flushes are an abuse of company resources. Furthermore, employees should either not wash their hands or, if they must, use only one towelette to dry their hands. Said towelette shall be properly disposed of in a trash receptacle. Opening the door with a towelette and unceremoniously dropping it behind the door is strictly prohibited. Please note that a fine will be imposed on employees caught not following this policy. Said fees will appear on your paystubs under the category "Pee Fee." The company considered TP Fees, Poo Fees, and Towelette Abuse Fees but decided that the administrative burden to categorize these fees was too high. Failure to observe our bathroom policy will result in discipline up to and including termination."

The email went viral and eventually found its way to management. Apparently, they didn't see the humor in it. It was the last email that person would send as an employee of Alz-Cura.

The tone in the company had clearly changed since before Jackie's medical leave. She initially thought it was the stress of the holidays, but it persisted after the New Year. The relaxed, friendly, trusting environment had changed to a cloying sense of suspicion and mistrust. People were on edge. Small infractions caused overly punitive responses.

The only positive for Jackie during her first three months back was the reception her clients gave her when she called them. As she had feared, Margo had done more harm than good. Not only was there a backlog of requests, but many requests her clients had made of her replacement had gone undocumented. Jackie was tempted to go to Cheryl and complain. Given the climate in the office, she chose instead to spend her time repairing relationships. If not for her clients, Jackie would have found precious little good to say about her job or her employer those first months back. While on leave, Jackie's greatest concern was going back on the road and leaving Ashley. Now, as odd as it seemed, she wanted desperately to get back on the road. Visiting her clients now seemed like a haven from the stifling, secretive, and suspicious climate that reigned supreme in the office.

She would get her wish when the following week, Cheryl called her into the office.

"I'm sending you to Maine next week, but we need to discuss the do's and don'ts," Cheryl said.

"Okay."

"Legal is still jousting with the DA's office over the release of information, so while the media has lost interest in the case, the State hasn't. You need to be careful about who you talk to and what you talk to them about."

"I know, I went to all the training sessions," Jackie replied, absently rolling her eyes.

"Don't get smart. This is different. You're wandering into the lion's den, and your most innocent statement might get misconscrewed by someone trying to have their 15 minutes of fame."

"Alright, what should I do?"

"First, no group meetings or meals where the public can

overhear you. If you invite docs out to dinner, book it for a private room, and be careful what you say when the waiters are in the room. Second, no discussing the case with anyone. Your standard response is to be, "I don't know anything about that."

"I DON'T know anything about it," she lied.

"Exactly why I told you months ago to keep your nose out of it. You good Catholic girls can't help but tell the truth once you know something. I don't want you having to go to confession to tell Father Bendover that you lied. When you get down on your knees, it should be for something more enjoyable than saying Hail Mary's and Our Fathers."

Jackie couldn't help but blush and laugh at her boss' penchant for irreverent statements.

"Finally, I need you to get close to Dr. Caron."

"What?" Jackie said in a shocked tone.

"Yeah, we're worried he might be playing a little loose with our clinical trials."

"Now, there's a shock," Jackie said sarcastically. "I told you he was dirty. Why not have someone from Research conduct an unannounced audit?"

"We want to handle this delicately. He's already a little on edge as a result of the legal case and media firestorm last Fall. No sense in driving one of our best Principal Investigators away with a formal audit and more bureaucracy and red tape."

"So, what do you expect me to do?"

"Make him comfortable. You know he loves to talk about himself. If you're nice to him, maybe he'll open up. Maybe he will divulge something, and then we can take the next steps."

"What do you mean, make him comfortable?"

"Just be yourself. Wear a dress. Have a glass of wine or two with him. It worked last time."

"Yeah, he almost molested me."

"Oh, don't be so dramatic. He tried to kiss you — big deal. I'm not saying fuck his brains out. Just get him to talk."

Jackie gave Cheryl a skeptical look.

"Jeez, Jackie, don't tell me you never used your sex appeal to attract someone's attention before. Here," Cheryl said, opening the top drawer of her desk, "put this in your purse. If he gets too frisky, a shot of this will do the trick." She tossed a small canister to Jackie. She caught it and saw that it was pepper spray.

"You've got to be kidding?" Jackie said.

"I carry it all the time. And by the way, Catholic girl, spray it in his eyes, not on his dick."

Jackie blushed and laughed again. Cheryl could sell anything.

"We need you to get him to talk. We can't have some cowboy doctor playing loose and compromising the integrity of our research. The last thing we need is an FDA investigation when Recallamin is about to take off not only nationally but internationally. You have a bright and rich future here, but you were right about Caron."

"Why would he talk to me if he's playing fast and loose with the rules? Wouldn't I be the last person he would want to talk to?"

"Jackie, Jackie, Jackie. You're so smart and so naïve. Appeal to him as a man, not a doctor or investigator. He'll talk."

"I still can't believe it will work."

"OK, trust me on this. Slutty works. If he doesn't respond to your charm, flash him some skin."

Jackie couldn't believe her ears but knew that Cheryl's sales techniques were edgy compared to her preferred approach.

"Cheryl, I don't know if I can do that?"

"Of course you can. Strategically uncross and recross your

legs while sitting across for him. Have him retrieve your accidentally dropped fork from under the table at dinner. Let your dress ride up accidentally in the car. Oops," Cheryl said in a salacious tone.

"You're serious."

"As a heart attack. Men will tell you their deepest, darkest secrets if you let them see your girl parts. And please, no granny panties. If you don't own a pair, get a thong. Red, preferably."

"You're incredible."

"Ya do what ya gotta do."

Despite Cheryl's sales pitch, Jackie's desire to be on the road again had dwindled. She was beginning to dread it. She wished her first business trip after her leave had been somewhere less controversial. Somewhere where a Dr. Caron didn't exist, and she didn't have to feign interest or flash her body parts to weasel some information out of him. Her mommy instinct also kicked in as the day to leave approached, and the thought of leaving Ashley began to gnaw at her. Stu and Jackie had also celebrated their 2nd wedding anniversary and Valentine's day, rekindling the epic lovemaking reminiscent of their college days. The only positive about the trip was that it was only two days. The company didn't want her first trip after her leave to be any longer, in deference to Jackie being a new mother. They recognized that their hottest commodity had to be coddled if they were to keep her happy.

It was with great reluctance that she handed Ashley over to her mother that early February morning and tearfully got into Stu's truck for the ride to the airport. Stu had offered to drive her to the airport, knowing that this would likely be an emotional time. She initially declined his offer but now was thankful that he knew her better than she knew herself. Stu was uncharacteristically quiet on the trip. Jackie asked him if everything was all right. He complained of a headache, writing it off to lack of sleep – a common condition both had suffered from since Ashley's arrival. She kissed him and stepped out of the truck. He opened the passenger window. Jackie, thinking he was going to say one last I love you, was met with words she couldn't believe were coming from his mouth.

"You aren't going there for work. I know better. Don't lie to me. You're going to destroy everything."

She couldn't understand why he had said this. She initially thought he was joking, although his tone sounded genuinely angry.

"What are you talking about, hon?"

"You know damn well what I mean," he said as he slammed his foot down on the accelerator, nearly side-swiping an airport shuttle before she had time to question him further.

Stunned, she stood at the airport curb, carry-on in hand, not knowing what to do. She tried to call him, but he didn't answer. When it came time to leave a message, all she could say was, "Hon, I love you. I don't know what just happened. Please call me." It was not in Stu's nature to be angry or jealous. She did not know anyone in Maine other than her physician clients. Stu knew how conflicted she was about making this trip, not to mention her disdain for Dr. Caron. So how could he think this trip was anything but business? As she made her way through Security and to the gate, she waited anxiously for his return call. When she boarded the plane, she held her cellphone in hand, praying to hear the familiar Kylie Minogue ringtone. She could not help but think of the irony that she was boarding United Airlines but feeling anything but united with the man who had been her world for the last six years.

Before they closed the airplane doors, she tried to call him again. This time, she left another message, "Hon, I'm so upset by what you said. I have to shut off my phone now, but I will call you when I land in Newark. Love you." She disconnected from her second message and shut off her phone. Tears began to well up, and she turned her head, feigning a look out the window to wipe any sign of tears from her eyes. She had not been anxious to take this trip in the first place, now with the unexplainable rift with Stu, she considered getting off the plane and not going. Just as she undid her seatbelt to leave, the plane jerked away from the gate, and the flight attendant began her safety briefing.

During her flight to Newark, she thought of all the reasons why this trip was a bad idea: leaving Ashley, Stu's outburst, inconvenient flights, Maine in February, having to wine and dine Dr. Caron. Landing in Newark, she turned on her phone, hopeful that Stu had left a message. She was depressed to find that Stu had not called, texted, or left a message. She picked up a coffee as she made her way to the connecting gate. Finding a private place in the waiting area, she tried to call him again, to no avail. "I'm in Newark. I guess you're probably at work. Call me when you can." She felt herself getting short with Stu as she left the message. No niceties, no, please, no love you. Looking at her watch, she was sure Stu was at work. She resolved not to call or leave him a message again. He was a big boy, and they had an almost idyllic marriage. There was no need for her to get desperate. She boarded the plane for the second leg of her journey, leaving her coffee untouched and abandoned at the gate.

On her flight from Newark to Portland, Jackie took inventory of all the things she may have said or done that could have caused Stu's outburst and found nothing. It had been a romantic Valentine's weekend that doubled as their wedding anniversary celebration. Jackie and Stu went to Danielle's. True to form, Stu had arranged for Jackie's dessert to come with a surprise - an envelope with a trip to Scottsdale and another clothes shopping spree. The trip would have to wait until April, as Jackie could not ask for time off so soon after returning from maternity leave. They talked mostly about Ashley and some about Jackie's upcoming trip. Stu had been upbeat about it, saying, "It will be good for you to get back in the saddle." They went to see the movie "Definitely, Maybe" after dinner. They had called Jackie's mother after the movie, and she said that Ashley had gone to sleep shortly after 8 p.m. Grandma Doris, delighted to have Ashley, couldn't stop talking about every little thing Ash did, including how her little lips would occasionally pucker while she was sleeping. After they got off the phone with Jackie's mother, Stu suggested a glass of wine before bed. Clinking glasses, they toasted to a successful date. After only one sip of their wine, they locked in an embrace. The kiss started in the kitchen. Things heated up considerably by the time they made it to the living room, and the grand finale occurred in the bedroom. Deliciously exhausted, they fell asleep in each other's arms.

Not finding any hint to what may have caused Stu's flare-up, Jackie started to inventory what happened between Sunday and this morning. They had gone to church on Sunday morning with Jackie's parents, followed by brunch at Momma's Diner. Other than complaining about a headache on Sunday night, Stu had been his old self – nothing to suggest any concerns. Stu felt better Monday morning, and Jackie made him breakfast before work. That evening, they cuddled in front of the TV until they retired at 10 p.m. Jackie got 3 hours of sleep before waking up to breastfeed Ashley. Even with interrupted sleep, Jackie woke up refreshed at 4 a.m. She quickly got ready, pumped some breast milk for Ashley, and dropped her at her parents' house. By 4:45, they were on the road to the airport. Stu had even found time to brew coffee for the trip.

She turned his words over repeatedly in her head, "You aren't going there for work. I know better. Don't lie to me. You're going to destroy everything." No matter how often she replayed the events of the last few days, she had no idea what could have caused such a reaction in Stu.

She arrived at the Portland Jetport, and Stu had still not returned her calls or messages. Although it was only mid-morning, she already felt exhausted. She needed to pick up her rental car and make a series of physician office visits in the Portland area before driving to Farrisport to check in to her room for the evening. She did her best to hide her concerns, but she found concentrating on her job and the physicians' questions difficult. For once, she was glad that her lack of attention could easily be compensated for. A flash of her smile here, a well-timed hand on a physician's arm there, or merely leaning over a bit, so her engorged breasts strained against her blouse would do the trick.

She finished her office visits and was anxious to get to the Farrisport Inn. She hadn't forgotten the warmth of the tavern or the delicious wine and lobster stew she had there now almost exactly a year ago. Her concern about Stu had shifted to anger. She couldn't understand why he hadn't called her back. If he was going to be that way, she was at least going to treat herself to a nice quiet and cozy dinner with a glass of wine or maybe two.

CHAPTER 42

C urt had dropped Caitlin and Cade off at the Children's Support Group. While his kids drew pictures and talked about their feelings, Curt went to the Back Bay Cove. It had become his therapy. For almost two hours, he stormed more than walked around the Cove. With each step, he found himself alternately cursing Darius Scott or praying to God for peace of mind. He completed two circuits around the 4-mile trail and had worked himself into a lather both physically and emotionally. He was quite certain that people he passed along the way must have thought that he was one of those deeply disturbed people you see talking to themselves on street corners. He got back into his car, his anger still raging and said a prayer: "God, I am so angry. Please send an angel to give me peace and understanding."

When he arrived to pick up Caitlin and Cade, they excitedly showed him the pictures they had drawn. Caitlin's picture had the whole family holding hands. He noticed that Caitlin had drawn angels hovering in the sky. Cade's picture was of him playing hockey. He did not know how this was therapeutic, but who was he to argue with the District Attorney's suggestion? Given the circumstances, he was reaching for anything that may be of benefit. He had been seeing Tim for nearly five months now. If he heard, "You have to learn how to take care of yourself" one more time, he was liable to punch old Tim right in the nose. Curt had quickly shifted through almost all Kubler-Ross' stages of grief when he suddenly downshifted to anger and was stuck there.

Curt tried to contain his anger and asked the kids if they wanted to go to dinner. That they wanted to go to dinner was the only unanimity they could muster. Curt listed six or seven restaurants. In what had become the norm, whatever Caitlin accepted, Cade rejected, and vice versa. Curt was growing intolerant of the kid's indecisiveness when they finally agreed on the Farrisport Inn. Curt thought this was a curious choice and when en route, the kids asked whether they could go to the toy store adjacent to the Inn. Now Curt knew the "real" reason and felt duped. He didn't need any fuel added to the fire already burning in him. All he had wanted was a quick bite to eat before returning home. He continued to pray for the angel that God had not yet seen fit to supply him.

They arrived at the Inn and Caitlin, and Cade ran down the hall towards the restaurant. He called to them to stop running to no avail. He picked up his pace and saw them stop abruptly to allow a woman to go ahead of them into the restaurant. At least they had manners, he thought to himself. He arrived at the hostess area, and shortly thereafter, the hostess approached.

"Table for four?" asked the hostess named Brittany with an eager-to-please lilt.

With that, the most innocuous question became a punch line for the woman and Curt as they realized the hostess's mistake. It was understandable. Curt and the kids had walked in just behind the woman, forming what looked like a traditional family of four. Between their laughter and the hostess' realization of her embarrassing miscue, what was impossible seconds earlier, was now possible. In the seconds that followed, the anger that Curt had felt and walked in with vanished.

"Can she eat with us, Daddy?" Caitlin and Cade asked in

unison when they realized what had happened.

Stunned by their immediate acceptance of a stranger and taken aback by her welcoming smile and stunning looks, Curt found himself asking, "Would you like to join us?"

After a pause that seemed to last minutes in Curt's mind, the woman responded,

"Well, why not?"

The interchange gave Brittany time to recover, and she quickly scanned the seating chart and grabbed menus and crayons for the kids. Brittany continued to apologize as she guided the newly formed group she had assembled in error. Determined to make up for her mistake, she took the woman, Curt, and the kids to a more private table by the fireplace.

Pulling Brittany aside out of earshot of the group, Curt asked softly,

"Errr, do you have another table, perhaps?" At the same time, he overheard the woman saying,

"Oh, thank god, a fireplace. I'm freezing."

Curt uncomfortably withdrew his request, "Oh, I guess we will be fine here."

Brittany, a bit confused, decided that this was just going to be one of those nights and quickly retreated to her station.

Curt pulled out the woman's chair to assist her into the seat, a chivalrous act she enjoyed but one only her husband usually performed. The kids, seeing their opportunity, quickly took seats next to her. Curt took his place across from the woman as the kids introduced themselves.

"I'm Caitlin. What's your name?". Before the woman could respond or Curt could pre-empt Caitlin and Cade's natural curiosity and naivety about social conventions, Cade blurted out,

"I'm Cade. How old are you? Are you married?"

Curt tried to cut the barrage of questions short, but before he could, the woman replied,

"My name is Jackie, I'm 25, and yes, I am married."

Curt had barely seated himself and was still wrestling with how he felt about having a woman other than his wife sitting across from him. He had successfully shielded the kids from his tryst with Chelsea, and this unexpected "family" gathering hit him like a Mack truck. Meanwhile, his kids had already interrogated Jackie and were extracting what Curt felt was information far too personal for their one-minute relationship. As Curt was formulating something less invasive to say, Caitlin said to Jackie,

"You're really pretty," exclaimed Caitlin.

"Why, thank you, Caitlin, so are you. You have the prettiest blue eyes."

"Yeah, Daddy says I got them from him."

Jackie laughed, and Curt blushed, still unable to gain his voice.

Curt could not catch up with the snowball that was rolling down the hill accumulating speed and mass. He was beginning to wonder if this had been a good idea when Cade skewered him with,

"My daddy is a lot older than you."

Caitlin piled on, "Daddy, isn't this just like when we would come here with Mommy?"

When Curt didn't immediately answer his daughter and shot her a pained expression, Jackie suspected that Curt must be separated or divorced from his wife. Thinking he may be sensitive to the topic, Jackie decided to avoid any questions about his wife or, was it, ex-wife.

Finally, finding his voice, Curt replied, "Jackie, it's nice to meet you. My name is Curt." He turned and addressed Caitlin and Cade. "Now, let's give Jackie some time to look at the menu. OK?"

"Oh, don't worry, I love your kids' questions. I have a baby daughter at home. I can't wait until she can talk and ask me questions," Jackie responded with a smile that devastated any resolve Curt may have had not to become enchanted by her.

His attempt to bring a hint of formality and slow down the avalanche of familiarity failed. Curt noticed the flames from the fireplace illuminate and dance across Jackie's face. Her brown eyes were already mesmerizing, but the glint of the firelight just made Curt uncomfortable. He grimaced.

"Is everything alright?" Jackie asked.

"Oh, oh, yes, yes," stammered Curt. "I just got a tiny cramp in my leg," he lied, reaching down to rub his calf to sell it.

Fireplaces had become his enemy. For most, they exuded warmth and charm. For Curt, they just symbolized the carnage and chaos that August 20th had wrought on his life.

For the next 90 minutes, Jackie and the kids conversed, punctuated by occasional interactions between Jackie and Curt.

"What do you do, Jackie?" Curt managed to slip in between his kids' questions.

"I'm a pharmaceutical rep visiting some of my clients here in Maine. And you?"

"I'm a partner in a healthcare consulting firm. I guess we're kinda in the same industry."

Before Jackie could respond, Caitlin interrupted.

"What's your baby's name?"

Jackie turned away and addressed Caitlin's question, "Her name is Ashley. Do you want to see some pictures?"

Both Caitlin and Cade gave an emphatic yes, and Jackie fired up her phone and shared pictures of her daughter. Caitlin oohed and awed about how cute Ashley was and how she wished she had a baby sister. Curt, not usually the silent type, listened, and watched. His kids became Energizer bunnies, transformed from children who had sulked for the better part of the last few months. They weren't only happy, they seemed over-joyed.

"What's your husband's name?" Caitlin asked, seeing him in one of the baby pictures.

"Stu," Jackie responded, painfully realizing that he had not yet called her back.

"He's handsome."

"I think so too," Jackie responded, trying to stave off the concern that was still eating at her from their morning interaction.

"Guess what, Caitlin?" Jackie asked to change the subject.

"What?" Caitlin responded with excited anticipation.

"We almost named Ashley, your name, Caitlin."

"Really?"

"Yep, we loved both names and had a hard time deciding."

Caitlin beamed, and Curt could see that both his kids were starved for the attention of a mother figure.

Curt knew they all ate dinner, but for the life of him, he could not remember anyone eating. The conversation consumed the time. The kids did most of the talking, directing questions toward Jackie or talking about their favorite subjects – horseback riding and hockey. Jackie graciously answered their queries and skillfully responded with questions that kept the kids engaged. Curt marveled at how they talked with one another. Conversations with his kids had been rare lately. Most of the interactions he had with his kids recently fell into the category of consoling, apologizing or fielding their frustrations. Now, his kids seemed happy. Surprisingly, he had to admit he felt happy too. He suddenly realized that perhaps Jackie was the angel he had asked God for as he stormed around Back Bay Cove.

As the waitress began clearing their dinner plates, Caitlin and Cade sprang into action. They did not want their time with Jackie to end.

"Can we order dessert, Dad?" both chimed despite neither finishing their Mac-n-Cheese dinners.

"You haven't even finished your dinner. How can you want dessert?" Curt responded.

Before they could respond, Jackie said, "Ummmm, what is your favorite dessert?"

"Crème Brulee," said Caitlin.

"Chocolate Cake with Ice Cream," replied Cade.

Once again, the train had left the station without Curt. The waitress came around to Curt, who declined dessert but ordered coffee.

"No, thank you," Jackie responded, "but maybe Caitlin and Cade could let me try some of their desserts?"

The kids' delighted and affirmative responses to Jackie's suggestion had Curt's head reeling. Sharing was not Caitlin or Cade's strong suit. Usually, the idea of sharing with anyone would cause conflict worthy of World War III.

Desserts arrived, and Curt watched as his kids excitedly pushed their desserts toward Jackie. They competed for which dessert Jackie would try first, and after that, whose dessert she liked best. By now, Curt knew she would have a diplomatic response and instead found himself watching her mouth accept bites from his kids' desserts.

"Yum" was Jackie's wide-eyed exclamation to both desserts.

Curt sipped his coffee, realizing that not only did his kids need a mother figure, but he missed sharing the joys and challenges of parenthood with a wife. It had been months since his dalliance with Chelsea. Now Jackie was creating a storm of powerful emotions that, like waves, crashed in on him.

As the waitress brought the bill, Curt and Jackie jousted briefly. Jackie reasoned she could claim her meal as a business expense. Curt wouldn't hear of it. The waitress, unfamiliar with this "assembled-by-mistake" family, gave the bill to Curt, who was already armed with his credit card in hand. While Curt paid the bill, the kids asked Jackie to accompany them to the lobby so they could show her something. Curt knew that they wanted to show her the moose head mounted on the wall - a source of his kids' endless fascination. He waved them away as he began to calculate the tip. Having dispensed with the bill, Curt paused before joining the kids and Jackie in the lobby. He took in the empty table with the carnage of shared desserts. He glanced uncomfortably at the fireplace and then back to the chair Jackie had vacated. Somehow, the topic of his wife had never come up. For this, he was relieved, but he wondered what Jackie must think. Although Jackie had only left a minute ago, he was surprised to feel the ache of missing her. He had arrived consumed by rage. How could he now feel nothing but longing? Longing for forbidden fruit. He didn't know whether to hug or curse hostess Brittany for her mistake.

Curt arrived at the lobby with Caitlin and Cade predictably stationed with Jackie under the Moose's head. Also, predictably, Jackie was either enthralled or just masterfully feigning her interest.

"I see you've been introduced to my kids' favorite thing about the Inn." Curt intoned.

"It's amazing," Jackie replied, "I have had so much fun tonight. Your kids are just a delight."

Curt didn't know how to respond. No one would have used "delight" to describe his kids of late. However, it was true. Tonight, they were a delight. While Curt knew it was all due to her presence, he surely couldn't divulge this to her.

"Well, you obviously have a way with kids. Ashley is lucky to have a Mom like you."

He had not meant to add that last part, but it slipped out. Jackie's eyes communicated that she appreciated and needed to hear the compliment. She was still suffering from guilt over leaving Ashley.

"Come on, kids, say goodbye to Jackie."

As if they had known each other for years, Jackie swept Caitlin and Cade up in a group hug. Curt did not need to hear her added encouragements to take care of each other and their Daddy. She had cast her spell long ago, and now she was just putting in more hooks. Curt went to shake her hand, but she moved into him and hugged him, saying,

"Thank you for dinner. You and the kids made it easier for me to be away from Ashley."

"Well, I think I have to thank you because I haven't seen my kids happier in years."

Jackie smiled. Then, as quickly as she had been associated with him at the beginning of the evening, she was gone. All but the sweet scent of her perfume left on his shirt from their hug.

Curt and the kids stood for a moment in the lounge, not sure what to do. Then like a flash, Caitlin had an idea.

"Let's go to the toy store and buy Ashley a toy."

"Yeah," said Cade.

Curt couldn't resist the idea. Thirty minutes later, they were giving Monty Moose to the front desk clerk asking him to deliver the stuffed animal to Jackie's room. Fortunately, only one "Jackie" was checked into the Inn, as Curt realized he hadn't learned her last name. Curt penned a note on the back of one of his business cards to include with the gift. They walked out of the Inn as huge snowflakes fell from the sky. Caitlin and Cade looked up and tried to catch them on their tongues. Curt looked up and said silently to himself, "God, thanks for sending your angel Jackie to us tonight."

CHAPTER 43

J ackie entered her suite and saw that room service had lit a fire in the fireplace and provided turndown service. She eased into a luxurious chair by the fireplace, its warmth protecting her from the cold February wind and snow outside. She was surprised that the last 90 minutes had caused her to forget all her concerns. She had somehow gotten lost in connection with three strangers at dinner. She could not believe that it served to suspend the anger and anxiety she felt from the morning. Somehow, they had managed to help her find a brief oasis in a desert of dread she had trudged through since Stu left her curbside at the airport. Little did she know that she had just shared dinner with the husband and children of the victim of the murderous event she researched that almost caused her to lose her job.

As reality began to wash over her, she wondered how she, or if she, should tell Stu about her unconventional dinner. While dining with virtual strangers was something Stu recognized and accepted as part of Jackie's job, she wasn't sure how he would react to this scenario. She never had reason to keep anything from him in the past. She would not have thought twice about telling him about this had they not had words before her departure this morning. Actually, it was more like HE had words for her. Inexplicably, his demeanor had changed, and she could not explain or find a cause for it. She continued to weigh how her dinner would play with him. She was certain it would not play well under the circumstances. There wasn't any reason to complicate things. It is not as if withholding this information was being dishonest. However, she and Stu had always told each other about everything. That she was debating this now represented a hurdle she never had to negotiate before. As the internal debate continued in Jackie's mind, her cellphone startled her from her reverie. The unmistakable "la la la la la" of Kylie Minogue announced Stu's call.

"Hi, Hon," Jackie answered in an upbeat fashion, masking any potential conflict that had just been running through her brain or anger she still harbored.

"Hi Boo, how was your flight?" Stu said as if nothing was wrong.

"Alright, but it was hard leaving you and Ash."

Before she could broach the topic of Stu's morning outburst, there was a knock on her door.

"Oh, hold on, there's a knock at my door."

She put the phone down and opened the door. Richard, the front desk clerk, stood holding a stuffed moose and a card.

"Ms. Deno? A gentleman and his kids asked that I deliver this to you."

"Oh, thank you, it's so cute," escaped from her lips. She did not have time to read the card, and as she closed the door, she realized that she had to make a quick decision about what to tell Stu. An innocent dinner with an older man and his kids would be one thing, but how would she explain a gift from them after the dinner? Even if the gift was for Ashley, this was getting messy. Had Stu overheard the interaction at the door? How would she explain that if she didn't tell the truth? The call with Stu had gotten off to such a good start; this could derail it if she weren't careful.

"Sorry, Hon, it was Room Service wanting to know if I

wanted turndown service," she lied.

"Oh, but what's so cute?"

"What?" Jackie asked as her heart jumped into her throat, and her face flushed.

Stu repeated, "I heard you say something about it being so cute." She was caught, and she thought for sure Stu could detect her pounding heartbeats through the phone.

"Oh, they serve these cute moose-shaped cookies to the guests," she lied again.

"Oh, that's nice," stated Stu, apparently buying her desperate recovery. She was flustered. She didn't know why she had lied, and she was determined to set things right. She couldn't go another day wondering about what had set Stu off or add to matters by keeping something from him.

"How did Ashley do today?" she started tentatively.

"Your mother said she did fine. Fussed a bit after her afternoon nap, but otherwise, she said she was a 'little angel.'"

Jackie could not help feeling a little pang of guilt. Was Ashley's fussiness a direct result of her absence? "Oh, that's good," she responded unconvincingly. "Hon, can I ask you a question?"

"You just did," replied Stu.

"Funny guy," she said, "but you didn't seem in such a good mood this morning. What was wrong?"

Jackie endured a silence that seemed unnaturally long and was about to ask Stu if he was still there when he said,

"I guess I was just upset that you were leaving. I had become used to you being home."

Anxious to have their discord behind them, Jackie accepted this explanation even though it did not feel right.

After some small talk, Stu closed with, "I love you, Boo."

She hung up and tried to feel like everything was once

again right in her world, but it wasn't. It all had sounded too hollow. She couldn't put her finger on it, but things were still not right.

She grabbed the moose and the card.

"For Ashley. Health, happiness, and blessings always. Curt, Caitlin, and Cade"

She started to cry. How could one uncharacteristic outburst from her husband make her feel as if her marriage was unraveling? Why did her accidental dinner and a twenty-dollar stuffed animal touch her so deeply? Once again, Stu's words haunted her.

"You aren't going there for work. I know better. Don't lie to me. You're going to destroy everything."

Her emotions were ping-ponging as when she had been pregnant. She started to second-guess whether she was the cause of Stu's outburst. Had she acted irritable and didn't remember or realize it? Had she somehow been insensitive? Forgotten something important?

She was too upset to think about going to bed. She started to fill the Jacuzzi tub and called room service to deliver a glass of wine. While she waited, she got antsy and tried to call Stu. She wanted to hear his voice again. She wanted to confirm that everything was all right. When she didn't get an answer, she reasoned that he might have gone to bed. She then called her mother. When she regaled Jackie about all the things she had done with the baby, how well behaved she had been, and how Stu came over for dinner and helped get Ash to sleep, Jackie began to feel better. The wine arrived just as she was ending her call. She slipped out of her clothes and into the tub. Twenty minutes later, the bubbles and the wine had worked their magic. Sleep came quickly after pouring herself into bed.

Jackie awoke with a start. Her heart was racing, and her pillowcase was soaked with sweat. The clock on her nightstand announced it was 2:47 a.m. She rarely had dreams, and she couldn't remember the last time she had a nightmare. This was too real, too frightening. She could not shake the horrific images. Her awareness that it had been a nightmare did nothing to dissipate her fear or the trembling. She knew the impetus of the nightmare immediately but couldn't believe how things had become so twisted. She felt she was with Ashley in the nightmare, but Ashley looked like Caitlin. Stu had come home, but Stu looked like Dr. Caron. Jackie asked him to light a fire in the fireplace so they could have a cozy dinner. She and Ashley carried dinner from the kitchen to the dining room only to find Stu had lit the dining and living room on fire. He was standing amidst the flames laughing, seemingly impervious to the fire. When Jackie screamed for Stu to get out of the fire, he reached for and grabbed Ashley, pulling her into the flames. That's when Jackie woke up.

It took all her fortitude not to call Stu at that very moment. She tried to understand why she had a nightmare. A therapist trained in dream interpretation likely could have made quick work of it, but she couldn't or didn't dare try to wrap her mind around it. She resorted to the simple explanation parents usually tell their children - it wasn't real. When that still didn't calm her, she got up and turned on a light. Then she turned on the TV. Finally, she went and got a drink of water. After about 15 minutes, her heart rate was back to normal. She had found additional pillows in the closet and replaced the sweat-soaked ones. She used the blow dryer on her hair and lay back down in bed, and turned off the lights but not the TV. She fell back to sleep and was not revisited by any more nightmares.

When she woke up, she felt like a freight train had hit her. Between the nightmare, the abbreviated sleep, and the dread she felt having to spend the day with Dr. Caron, she felt like an emotional and physical wreck. She trudged to the shower, letting the hot streams of water bombard her body, hoping it would wash away the frightening remnants of the nightmare and restore her physically. When she stepped out of the shower, she realized that restoration or not, she was seriously in danger of being late for her appointment with Dr. Caron. She forced herself to focus and get ready. Being late would not be a good way to start what was going to be difficult anyway – getting close to Dr. Caron and making him comfortable. She had hoped to call Stu but decided not to. She didn't want to sound rushed. Besides, she would be flying back home tonight when she and Stu could talk face-to-face. She grabbed a cup of coffee on her way out of the hotel, and by the time she arrived at Dr. Caron's office, the caffeine had lifted her energy level. It was time for Jackie to be on stage, and she finally started feeling she was ready for a command performance.

This feeling lasted only until Dr. Caron walked into his office. Jackie felt an immediate twinge like someone had grabbed her stomach and twisted it. She fought through it, stood to greet Dr. Caron, and almost lost her bearing as he masterfully converted their handshake into a hug.

"Jackie, it is so good to see you," said Dr. Caron, finally stepping back from the hug. "How are you feeling? How is the baby?"

Jackie didn't have to do much to make him comfortable. It was making herself comfortable that was going to be the challenge.

"Ashley's doing fine, and I'm feeling great, Dr. Caron," she lied, feeling like she was going to vomit at any second.

"Well, you're looking great, Jackie, but call me Steven. Sit down," he said, pointing to the chair she had recently vacated to greet him. "Now show me some pictures. I'm sure you have pictures."

Jackie pulled out her phone as Dr. Caron made his way behind Jackie's chair. She scrolled through her pictures, conscious of him leaning over her left shoulder. She could smell his aftershave and knew that from his vantage point, he could not only see the pictures but had a bird's eye view down her blouse. She could feel his eyes on her as she self-consciously scrolled past pictures she didn't want him to see. She felt as if she was being violated, and he didn't even have to touch her. She finally found some pictures of Ashley that were acceptable and felt his hand grip her right shoulder.

"She's beautiful, Jackie, just like her mother. Congratulations again."

"Thank you, Dr. Car..."

"Ah, ah, Steven, to you."

"Thank you, Steven," she said as his first name sounded unnatural and jarred her senses.

He finally let go of her shoulder and removed his lascivious stare down her blouse. He circled to his desk and sat down. Jackie crossed her legs, aware that she was wearing a skirt as Cheryl had instructed, and Dr. Caron's eyes were already tracking south of her face. Although she felt like saying, "Why don't you take a picture, it will last longer," she swallowed the urge and got down to business.

"Steven, first, I'd like to thank you for your support of Alzcura. You are our best client, and we want to be sure that you stay that way. Have you received the support and attention you've needed these last few months?"

It ached Jackie to open with this standard pitch knowing that A, it was a lie, there were far better clients, and B, it was unlikely Margo had done her job.

"Well, now that you're back, I think things will be just fine. How should I say this? Margo, your replacement, had limited skills."

"I'm sorry, Steven," she said, almost gagging each time she mentioned his name. "How were your needs not met?" she said as his gaze intensified when she uncrossed and then recrossed her legs.

"Well, I'm sure you heard about Inspector Adams visiting

me."

"Inspector Adams? No, I hadn't heard anything about that," she said, feigning the best look of surprise she could muster.

"Really? Doesn't anyone talk to each other at AlzCura? I'm interrogated by some investigator about a murderer and his mother who were both in one of my studies, and I hear zip!" he exclaimed, starting to get flustered.

Jackie was in Academy Award mode. While she was somewhat taken aback by his flash of anger, she knew that she might be able to capitalize on Margo's inept work. She uncrossed her legs, leaned forward on her chair, and reached out her hand to touch his. "Oh, Steven," she pouted, squeezing his hand, "I'm so sorry, this must be so stressful. I wish you could have called me."

"I know me too. My apologies, but your colleague Margo was useless. Even when she was here to visit, she was all questions and no answers. I finally asked her if I could speak to someone else, and she gave me Ms. Baker's number. I think she's your boss?"

Jackie nodded in acknowledgment and tried to hide the shock that Margo had visited Dr. Caron. Neither Margo nor Cheryl had briefed her about Margo's visit. She started to feel uneasy with ad-libbing and wondered what other surprises she might discover.

"Ms. Baker said she would handle it and that someone would contact me. No one ever did. I left messages for Margo, but I never heard from her."

"I'm so sorry, Steven," apologizing for the third time. "I wish someone would have told me."

She released his hand and leaned back into her chair, allowing her legs to linger slightly apart before slowly crossing them again.

He was like a cat chasing a flashlight beam. She could make him look wherever she pleased. As prophetic as Cheryl's words were, Jackie still couldn't get used to how disgusting, lewd, and shallow some men were. Even though the insight of Margo's visit confused her, and Margo and Cheryl had failed to brief her fully, she knew she had a job to do. She continued to indulge Dr. Caron.

"Well, maybe it's nothing. Have you heard from Inspector Adams or anyone else about it since?"

"No, but I gave him your number and Dr. Sheridan's name."

"Well, I will check with my boss and Dr. Sheridan when I get back to the office and give you a call if I learn anything."

"Okay, I guess it's good news that you haven't heard anything. Listen, I have a couple of patients I need to see. It will only take 30 minutes or so. Do you mind waiting here?"

"No, I'm perfectly comfortable, Steven," she lied and stood as he was moving to leave.

"When I get back, I'll take you to lunch."

"Okay, that sounds great," she said, although she would rather have had someone tear out her fingernails with a pair of pliers at that point. He gave her a wink, and she forced her best smile. The office door closed, and she gave a heavy sigh and relaxed for the first time in over an hour.

Dr. Caron did not return in 30 minutes, but Jackie wasn't complaining. The less time she had to spend in his company, the better. She called Stu, and she was surprised when he picked up.

"Hi, boo," he croaked, not sounding at all like himself.

"What's the matter hon, you sound awful. Are you at work?"

"No, I'm just a little under the weather. I'm staying home today."

"What's the matter?"

"Just a splitting headache. Maybe a fever."

"Do you think it's the flu? It is the flu season. Did you take something?"

"I took a couple of Tylenol. I had the flu shot when I saw the doctor a few months ago. I'm just going to rest until I have to pick you up tonight."

"Hon, I can call my mother. I'm sure she wouldn't mind picking me up. Besides, she can bring Ash to the airport. I miss her like crazy."

"Okay, Boo, I'm sorry."

"Don't worry hon, I'll be home tonight, and then I can take care of you."

"Sounds good. Love you," he managed to say before a bout of coughs erupted.

"Go back to bed. Love you too."

She ended the call and immediately called her mother, who said she was only too happy to bring Ashley to the airport to pick Jackie up.

"And Mom, I just got off the phone with Stu, and he sounds awful."

"Do you think I should go over and check on him?"

"No, I think he'll be alright. He just took some medicine and is going to sleep. Best to keep Ash away from him, so she doesn't get sick too."

"Okay. So, when should I be at the airport?"

"My flight arrives at 8:30."

"Okay," Jackie's mom answered and then started talking to Ashley. "Guess who is coming home? Mommy! Yes, mommy is coming home."

"You should see her face."

"Let me talk to her," asked Jackie.

Jackie's mother held the phone up to Ashley's ear.

"Hi, honey, it's mommy. Mommy misses and loves you. Do you miss me?"

Jackie strained to hear anything from her daughter but only heard rustling in the background.

"Oh, Jackie, I wish you could have seen her reaction. She turned her head toward the phone and raised her little hands. She's so precious." Her mother gushed.

Jackie ached to be back home with Ashley and Stu.

"Thanks, Mom. I better hang up and get back to work. See you tonight. Kiss Ash for me."

"Will do."

Dr. Caron's 30 minutes extended to an hour, and Jackie began to get restless. She started to peruse the stacks of papers, journals, and files that occupied nearly every horizontal surface of the office. Nothing particularly interested her or caught her attention until she found a folder labeled "Darius Scott." She paused, recalling that Cheryl had sent her here specifically to uncover any shady business in which the good doctor may be involved.

When she opened the file, she was surprised to see a brief letter from AlzCura signed by Dr. Sheridan.

"Dear Dr. Caron:

Thank you for your letter of August 21 regarding Participant #378487. I agree that this participant fits the criteria for being lost to follow-up and should immediately be removed from Study #RCAM1004. Please follow the protocol we agreed upon regarding how to process such participants and their records. If you should receive any queries regarding this individual or his participation in this clinical trial, please contact me immediately by phone. Please phone in any future participants who meet the lost to follow up criteria as we previously agreed. Thank you for your continued support.

Sincerely,

Dr. Asa Sheridan"

Before she could read further or close the file, the office door opened, and Dr. Caron stormed in. Jackie turned toward him as tactfully as possible, trying not to let a look of surprise or guilt cross her face. She smiled, and as he started to apologize, she realized that he had either had not seen her reading the file or was putting on a very good act.

"Are you ready to grab some lunch?"

"Yes, I'm famished. I didn't have breakfast."

"I need to speak to Rebecca briefly, and then we can go."

"Okay."

He stepped out, and Jackie debated whether she should attempt to read more of the file or just close it. What she had read had concerned her, but she had not had time to digest the contents. Perhaps reading more would give her some context. She was about to return to reading the file when she heard Dr. Caron coming down the hall. She flipped the file shut and stepped away from his desk just as he reentered.

"Let's go get you something to eat. It's not good for a nursing mother to go without nourishment."

Somehow, every time he spoke to her, it felt like he was violating her. How did he know she was nursing? While she could appreciate her OB doctor saying such a thing out of genuine concern, from him, it sounded just like an excuse to talk about her body. As they exited the office, he placed his hand on her back, ushering her out the door. Her skin began to crawl, as the placement of his hand was a bit lower than she thought appropriate and a bit firmer than necessary. He opened the passenger side door for her. Although self-conscious about how to get into the passenger seat without giving him a show, Cheryl's crass words revisited her, "flash him some skin." Predictably, her dress rode up, and she fought the immediate urge to fix it. She looked up, and he was holding the door with his eyes clearly on the prize. She could hardly restrain herself from bursting into a tirade about what a pig he was when he interrupted her thought.

"Don't forget your seatbelt. When you care about someone, you belt them," he said, chuckling at his lame play on words.

She had no choice to reach for her belt, allowing him to stare longer and watch as the shoulder strap found a home between her breasts. She couldn't help but wonder how many times he had done this with other women.

"All set," she said, hoping to compel him to shut her door finally.

"Watch your elbows," he said as he shut the door.

"Yeah, and why don't you watch my elbows instead of my boobs and everything else," she whispered sarcastically to herself as he made his way around the car. Before he got in, she pulled the hem of her dress down.

Dr. Caron got in the car, and Jackie flinched as he looked to be reaching for her thigh. Instead, he put the manual transmission into reverse. Looking down, she started to curse Cheryl for making her wear a skirt. Even though she had adjusted her dress, her thighs were still visible, and Dr. Caron's hand was just inches away on the stick shift. To make matters worse, he kept his hand on the stick shift all the way to the restaurant. She didn't remember him driving that way the last time she drove with him, and she was on edge the whole time. She could hardly pay attention to what he was saying. She was a bundle of nerves, and her mind focused on everything but what Dr. Caron was saying. Suddenly, she realized he was talking about a concern he had about a new clinical trial.

"What did you just say?" she said, knowing this would tip him off to her being distracted.

"I said, I'm a little worried about the Recallamin3 trial."

Although thrown off-balance, she did her best to ask a leading question hoping that he would give her more information.

"What exactly worries you, Steven," adding the overly familiar first name in hopes that this would encourage his continued openness.

"Well, I could understand Recallamin2, including participants over 40, but including participants who are between 20 and 40 years old seems a bit early. I mean, I'm all in favor of aggressive prevention and treatment, but this even seems overly aggressive to me."

She was stunned. Why hadn't Cheryl briefed her on this? Inside she was boiling mad but needed to maintain her composure and draw more out of Dr. Caron. It was going to be a challenge, not knowing anything but what he told her. She dreaded the possibility that he would ask her a question about the trial. She proceeded as cautiously as possible.

"Have you talked to Dr. Sheridan about your reservations or any other physicians who are participating in the trial?"

"Well, it was Dr. Sheridan who talked to me about it, and as far as I know, there is only one practice in Buffalo that has signed up. I don't even know if I can get my IRB to sign off on it. It's a Phase II study, and they normally only approve Phase III studies."

"Is there anything I can do to help you get more comfortable with the trial? Or information I can get for your IRB?" she ventured, hoping it didn't lead to any detailed questions about the trial.

"No, Dr. Sheridan said I should talk with him if I had any reservations. I have a call scheduled with him later this week."

"Okay, let me know if I can do anything for you," she offered in as genuine a tone as she could.

"Thanks, Jackie, I appreciate that," he said, looking at a point below her chin with an expression that seemed to be saying, "Oh, you can do something for me, alright!"

Fending off his stares, his undoubtedly lewd thoughts, and feeling ill-prepared were draining her emotionally. She had another 4 hours in his company, and she didn't know how much longer she could carry on the charade.

They sat down for lunch, and Jackie was thankful that the table was in the middle of a crowded restaurant. Hopefully, this would make it less likely for him to get grabby or leer at her, although she was beginning to wonder if he had a conscience at all. After they ordered, she excused herself to the lady's room, figuring that 5 minutes not being with Dr. Caron was 5 minutes without Dr. Caron. She freshened up her makeup and realized as she rummaged through her bag that she had forgotten to take the pepper spray canister that Cheryl had given her. She looked in the mirror and smiled as she remembered Cheryl's instructions about where to spray him if he got too frisky. She realized that she had to change her attitude to survive the next few hours and potentially get more information out of Dr. Caron. As disgusting as he was, she was going to have to pour on the charm. She rededicated herself to work him into such a frenzy that he would feel compelled to divulge any secrets he was hiding. That or he might be the first man ever to die of blue balls. She undid another button on her blouse, spritzed some perfume between her breasts, and applied a redder shade of lipstick.

As she walked back to the table, she purposefully exaggerated the swing of her hips. She could feel his eyes on her but refused to meet his stare until she was halfway back to the table. Then she locked tightly on his eyes and gave him her best smoldering smile and a flip of her hair.

"Did you miss me?" Jackie leaned over the table, making sure he got a good view down her blouse.

For once, he was speechless.

"What's the matter? Cat got your tongue, Steven?"

"I, I, I just..." he stammered.

"I'm not used to you being at a loss for words," she picked up her fork to start picking at the salad that had arrived. She accidentally dropped her fork - a nod to Cheryl's suggestion during their meeting about how to squeeze information out of him. After almost losing her job by being too nosy about the murder case on her first day back from leave, she felt compelled to follow her boss's advice.

"Oh, Steven, I think it fell under the table."

He ducked under the table to get the fork and saw her legs parted and red thong panties that barely qualified as clothing. He returned topside flustered.

"Did you find it?"

His face was flushed. "Yes, I did...I did. Yes, I found your fork," he stuttered, showing her the fork in his hand.

He motioned to the waitress with the fork, and she immediately understood his gesture.

Jackie had him so ruffled she almost started to pity him. The waitress delivered their lunch, interrupting her command performance temporarily.

"Ummm, this looks great Steven, I'm starved," she exclaimed.

"Jackie, why are you doing this?" he caught her by surprise as she had just taken a bite of her sandwich.

"Doing what?" she replied after swallowing. Her face flushed, and she rushed to dab her mouth with her napkin hoping it would hide the tell-tail sign she felt embarrassed and caught.

"Nothing, forget it. Enjoy your lunch, Jackie," he said, but his demeanor had changed.

Jackie began to wonder if she had overdone it. Although Dr. Caron didn't seem to have a conscience, could her aggressiveness have scared him off? Before she could continue her introspection, he spoke.

"I'm concerned, Jackie."

"Concerned about what, Steven?" employing his name to try and regain the connection between them that had been momentarily lost.

"About the company you work for."

"Because of the Recallamin 3 trial?" she fished.

"Yes, but more than just that."

"More than that?" not having to feign her surprise.

"Well, it's more like I need to tell someone something, and I don't know who to go to."

As soon as he said it, he regretted saying it. "No, Jackie, I don't want to talk about this here. I have a call with Dr. Sheridan this week. I'll talk to him, I guess."

"You can talk to me, Steven."

"I better not."

"Why? Is it a big, dark secret?"

"No, but let's talk about you. What does your husband do?" he backpedaled abruptly, trying to change the subject.

"Stu works for the Department of Transportation. He's a Maintenance Supervisor."

"Does he like what he's doing?" he said in a non-committed way. Jackie could tell that he was trying to avoid the discussion he had almost begun.

"I guess so. I mean, it's not as important as what you do, Steven. Why did you become a doctor?" she said, trying to spin the conversation back to him.

"I didn't want to be a doctor at first. I got a business degree, but then my grandmother got Alzheimer's, and I decided to become a doctor to see if I could cure her."

"Did you?"

"No, she died a couple of years ago, before Recallamin was approved."

"Do you think it would have helped her?"

"I don't know. Maybe when she had mild symptoms, but in the end, all she did was sit in her wheelchair and groan."

"How devastating that must have been," Jackie said, almost starting to feel sorry for him again.

"My grandmother died from Alzheimer's almost a year ago, and Stu's grandfather has it and is in a memory care unit," she said, realizing that she was divulging more personal information than might have been warranted.

"I'm sorry, Jackie," he said, almost sounding human.

They finished their lunch and drove back to his office. This time, there was no inappropriate staring, and he steered clear of any contact at all. When they walked into the office, Rebecca handed Dr. Caron a note. He read it.

"See, this is exactly what I'm concerned about," he almost shouted.

"What's that?" Jackie asked.

"Another one of my patients has liver failure..." he began but then thought better of continuing.

"I really can't say, Jackie."

They went back to his office.

"I'm sorry, Jackie, I'm going to have to see that patient who just was admitted to the hospital. I wouldn't do this unless it was critical."

"I understand, Steven," she feigned disappointment although she was leaping for joy inside.

"Thank you, Jackie. I'm so glad you're back," he said, extending his hand.

His formality surprised her. She fully expected she might have to fend off a groping hug. She extended her hand to meet his.

"Thank you for your time and lunch, Steven. Please don't hesitate to call me if your call with Dr. Sheridan doesn't answer all your questions."

"I will, Jackie. Have a safe trip back. I'm sure Ashley misses you."

He left the office, and she collapsed in his office chair, feeling like her world had just gone all topsy-turvy. Her head was swirling with so many questions. Then there was Dr. Caron. How the dangerously entrepreneurial physician with his mind and eyes perpetually in the gutter could suddenly seem vulnerable, caring, and human threw her. With nothing but questions churning in her head, she drove to the airport even though she would be two hours earlier than she needed to be. She needed time to digest all that she had taken in during her visit. She made a mental note to write down all the shocking revelations she had had during her visit with Dr. Caron.

On top of that, she still had unfinished business with Stu and the outburst that had prefaced this visit. Her head was too full. She consciously focused on her driving as all her thoughts and feelings threatened to overwhelm her. She didn't know what all these puzzle pieces added up to, but she was determined to put them together. Right now, however, they were just a blur.

CHAPTER 44

C urt and the kids left the Inn happier than they had been in a long time. The kids' animated conversation about Brittany's mistake, Jackie joining them for dinner, and whether Ashley would like the stuffed moose filled the drive back to Campion. While the kids chatted, each trying to outdo the other, Curt repeated his silent prayer thanking God for sending his angel Jackie. He reflected on his turbulent emotions before the transformative dinner. They now felt months instead of hours ago. He couldn't believe his prayer had been answered with such immediacy. Although he didn't pray often, when he did, he was used to getting a different answer than expected, having to wait, or never getting an answer at all. If anything had taught him, he didn't hold the blueprint to his life; August 20th had certainly driven that point home. This prayer response, however, had him thinking that God may have finally started listening to him.

"Daddy, did you think Jackie was pretty?" Caitlin asked a loaded question.

"Yes, she is very pretty," he responded, knowing what question would likely follow.

"I think you should marry her," Cade cut off his sister's follow-up question bluntly.

"Well, Cade, she's already married."

"But if she wasn't married, would you marry her?" asked Cade.

"Marriage is for people who know each other well, Cade. It takes more than just a quick dinner together to get to know someone. Your mother and I knew each other for almost two years before we got married."

It was the proper parental answer, yet he couldn't help daydream of what it would be like to look across the dinner table and see Jackie every night.

The mention of his mother silenced Cade but spurred Caitlin to continue what was beginning to feel like 21 questions.

"I thought she was nice. Do you think we will see her again?"

"Probably not, Caitlin. It was just by luck that we ran into her today. She lives in New York and only comes to Maine occasionally."

When he looked in the rearview mirror, Caitlin had disintegrated into tears.

"Oh, honey, don't be sad," but it was too late. Between sobs, Caitlin whined,

"But I liked her. She told me she wished I could see Ashley. She said she would like to see me ride Freckles. Can't we see her again?"

She was at the point of no return. She turned her head into the backseat and wailed. Cade, despite his tender years and long history of conflict with Caitlin, scooted over in the backseat and put his arm around his sister.

"That's okay, at least we got to meet her," Cade said, sounding more grown-up than he was. "Maybe we will see her again. Huh, Dad?"

"Yes, Cade, anything is possible. And thank you for caring for your sister. I'm proud of you."

Cade's inexplicable compassion for his sister caused tears to well up in Curt's eyes. Caitlin regained control of herself and, wiping her tears away, turned, and hugged her brother.

"Thanks, Cade," she said.

There were precious few magical moments in life, and yet, Curt felt blessed to experience several in the course of the evening. Tears overflowed their banks, and he resolved never to doubt the power of prayer again.

They arrived home, and Curt got the kids into bed. As he sat on the couch, contemplating the evenings' events, he started to add up all the things that had to occur for them to meet Jackie at that particular moment in time.

If the kids had chosen a different restaurant, they wouldn't have met. If he had hit a different number of stoplights in Portland, they wouldn't have met. If he had driven faster or slower, or if the kids hadn't run down the hall at the Inn, they wouldn't have met. If the waitress hadn't made a mistake.

Then he realized all the "ifs" that must have brought Jackie to that very spot at that moment and knew that God must have had a hand in this evening. He wouldn't soon forget her, but he knew that he would not likely see her again. Even if he wanted to get in touch with her, only knowing her first name, that she had a daughter named Ashley and worked for a pharmaceutical company in New York wasn't much to go on. Nevertheless, in an evening designed to be therapeutic for the kids, he also found some salvation from the crushing anger he had been feeling.

Over the next few weeks, life for Curt and the kids started to come together again. The kids finished their Support Group, and Curt's outlook on things had so improved that he discontinued counseling sessions with Tim. Spring was around the corner, and Sam and Curt worked feverishly on the work the Maine Employer's Group on Healthcare contract had brought them. They had needed to hire two additional consultants, and Loribeth got a promotion. In turn, she hired an assistant. The firm had doubled in size, and they leased adjoining space to accommodate the new staff.

No longer haunted by nightmares or thoughts of careening into the path of an 18-wheeler, Curt's life seemed as back to normal as it ever had been in the last eight months. The kids were in a good place, and between Caitlin's emerging equestrian skills and Cade's hockey prowess, there was little free time for anyone.

One afternoon out of the blue, Curt got a call from DA Wydman. When the DA conveyed the news, it seemed inconsequential. Curt had come to terms with Calli's death, and the inability to answer the question of why Darius had done it; no longer seemed so critical. He didn't care anymore. The DA seemed to be exercised by the information, and Curt struggled to make sense of it or find why he should expend any emotional capital on the matter. DA Wydman reported that Elvira Scott's autopsy lab tests had come back positive for the same suspicious and unidentifiable substance found in Darius' tissue samples.

"Can't you see Curt," fumed DA Wydman, "there might be a causal link. A link that might explain why Darius was driven to kill your wife."

"But Elvira didn't kill anyone Will," said Curt. "Even if there is a link, how does Elvira's death prove anything about why her son killed Calli? And if you can't identify the substance, what good does that do us?"

DA Wydman didn't have good responses to Curt's questions.

"We're trying to identify the possible source, Curt. Darius and Elvira were enrolled in a clinical trial sponsored by a drug company in Buffalo, for whom the principal investigator was Dr. Steven Caron. We subpoenaed Dr. Caron and the drug company for more information."

The mention of Dr. Caron's name piqued Curt's attention momentarily, but he still didn't feel like devoting much attention to the news.

"And what did you learn?" he asked half-heartedly.

"We learned from Dr. Caron that Darius was lost to follow-up and that Elvira was on that same track. Dr. Caron also informed us that the blood work done on them was analyzed at a regional lab and that the drug company maintained all the results. Dr. Caron's files didn't contain much because most of the information is centralized with the drug company."

"What's so sinister about that?" Curt continued to try to find the import of the DA's explanation.

"Nothing, but if we can get our hands on the information the drug company is holding, it might tell us something. If Darius and Elvira's blood work didn't contain this suspicious substance before the clinical trial and did after enrollment, we might be able to establish a link."

If Curt hadn't been a member of an Institutional Review Board and familiar with how clinical trials were conducted, perhaps he may have found this argument compelling.

"Do you have any proof that they even got the study drug? Most studies randomize who gets the study drug. How do you know they both received it?"

"We don't. But when they release the information to us, we will find out."

"And you're sure that the lab work that was done will be of sufficient detail to be able to determine if they had this substance in their system?"

"No, but it's the only chance we have."

"Sounds like a pretty slim chance, Will. When did you request information from the drug company?"

"Three months ago."

"Three months ago? What's taking so long?"

"The drug company's legal department is stalling. They're giving us a bunch of legal mumbo jumbo about proprietary information, patient privacy, blah, blah, blah."

"Listen, Will, I appreciate you calling me. You have been a real stand-up guy through this whole process. I've got to tell you, though, I've moved on. There are just too many ifs. If the drug company shares the information. If the lab work was of sufficient detail. If their blood didn't have the substance before the study. If they both received the study drug. And who's to say they didn't obtain the substance through some other means, even if you do get the answers to all these questions?"

"I understand, Curt. I know it must seem like a wild goose chase to you, but we must investigate this to the end. Your support could help us."

"What do you mean, my support?"

"Just a letter to the drug company."

"If a subpoena isn't causing them to cough up the information, why do you think a letter from me is going to change anything?"

"It won't necessarily, but having a human face behind our request may help."

Curt laughed. "I'm sorry, Will, I work in healthcare, and I've just never known drug companies to have a heart."

"Let me make myself a little clearer. It would be helpful if you filed a complaint letter to them. Maybe add something about going to the FDA or taking legal action."

"Whoa, now that's a little different request, Will. I'm not comfortable doing that as thin as this possible link seems to be. Unless more compelling evidence comes to light about how this study drug potentially caused that monster to kill my wife, I don't feel up to starting some crusade."

"That's just it, Curt. Without your support, we may not get

the evidence."

"I'm sorry, Will. I have just come out of the darkest place I've ever been and am now just starting to feel back to normal. I don't want to go back there."

"Okay, Curt, I understand. I didn't mean to upset you. The State is just worried that if there is a link, there may be thousands of individuals taking this medication. We must protect the public."

"I'm not upset Will, as I said, I appreciate all you've done. By the way, I also want to thank you for recommending that Support Group. My kids loved it, and it helped them immensely."

"I'm glad to hear it, Curt. Listen, if you change your mind, you know how to reach me, right?"

"Right."

"And if we do receive more information, you're okay with me calling you?"

"Yes, Will, you can call me."

After they ended the call, Curt chuckled. The great and powerful State legal system was asking him to help them take on a pharmaceutical company. They were grasping at straws if they had to come to him. He went back to work and didn't give the call or the State's crusade another thought until later that night.

CHAPTER 45

A rriving at the Portland Jetport, Jackie made a beeline for the Ladies' room to change clothes. The outfit that Cheryl had suggested may have served its purpose earlier, but now it just made her feel naked and embarrassed. After changing into a conservative business suit, she breezed through Security and found a quiet corner near her gate. She finally had some uninterrupted time to consider everything that had transpired in the last 48 hours. She took out a legal pad and started to write down all the things that had her concerned.

1. Stu's outburst and subsequent lame explanation

2. The accidental dinner with Curt and his kids and how to explain it and the stuffed moose

3. Her terrifying nightmare with mixed identities and Stu pulling Ashley into the fire

4. The curious letter from Dr. Sheridan in Darius Scott's file

5. Margo's visit to Dr. Caron and other information that Margo and Cheryl had withheld from her (e.g., Recallamin 3)

6. The concerns Dr. Caron had about the Recallamin 3 clinical trial

7. Other concerns Dr. Caron had about the company

that he felt he needed to tell someone about but couldn't

8. Dr. Caron's sudden change in demeanor at the restaurant and humanness and formality for the remainder of her visit

9. Dr. Caron's flash of anger when they returned to the office about another one of his patients having liver failure

She looked down at the list and retook inventory, making sure she hadn't missed anything. Satisfied that she had captured all the revelations and loose ends, she forced herself to consider them one at a time.

While she had previously accepted Stu's explanation for his outburst, she remained unconvinced that it was just that she was leaving. His words just didn't fit any context she could relate to their relationship. Jealousy and mistrust were just the furthest things from Stu's nature. She strained for other possible causes and landed on his headache that morning. Maybe he had been starting to feel sick the day before. He was rarely ill, so she didn't know how he behaved when faced with illness. She remembered some of her girlfriends saying what "big babies" their husbands were when they were sick. Still, she couldn't believe that a headache or perhaps the onset of the flu could spur the words he had said. She found some comfort in their subsequent phone conversations. He did say he loved her, and there were no more outbursts. She toyed with the idea of just forgetting it ever happened, but she knew she wouldn't be able to. She decided that the only way to reconcile this was to be with Stu and have a heart-to-heart conversation. This would have to wait until later tonight or maybe even tomorrow. She placed a question mark next to the number 1 item on her list.

The accidental dinner had been the only bright spot in the last 48 hours, and she fondly reminisced about her connection with Caitlin and Cade. It had cured much of the anxiety she had about being a mother. Curt had been curiously quiet and appeared a bit uncomfortable. Caitlin had divulged that they used to have dinner there with Curt's wife, but that was the extent of her knowledge about Curt's personal life. She did have one brief exchange about his being a healthcare consultant and his involvement on a local Institutional Review Board. She was confident that his IRB involvement probably included the review of AlzCura protocols. He may even know Dr. Caron. Her attention to the kids, however, had limited exploring any of these possible connections with Curt. Maybe it was just the serendipitous dinner together, but it somehow felt right and necessary. She struggled to understand her feelings. She felt a connection to the kids and could have easily taken them home with her. Her feelings about Curt were much more complicated. He was a mystery, and while she wasn't attracted to him per se, something about him stuck with her. Had it been pain or longing in his eyes? She couldn't tell. He had been an old-school gentleman, pulling her chair out, encouraging his kids to show manners at the table, insisting on paying for the dinner. These behaviors all reminded her of Stu. Her hugging the kids and Curt after dinner had just come naturally. An innocent gesture of caring - nothing more, nothing less. Less natural were her feelings after she left them. She found herself missing them. Like there was unfinished business. She thought that maybe it was just missing Ashley and Stu, but it seemed more than that. She placed another question mark at the end of #2 on her list. So far, she wasn't making much headway in her quest to find some answers.

The delivery of the stuffed moose just confirmed for her that the accidental dinner had a meaning that extended beyond just the sharing of a meal. That it had arrived while she was on the phone with Stu had been somewhat inconvenient and uncomfortable at the time. So much so that she had lied to Stu for the first time in their relationship. Now, that timing seemed to support the connection she had felt to Curt and the kids. Perhaps she had been as therapeutic for them as they had been for her. She resolved to tell Stu about the dinner and the moose. She would also apologize for the lie she told him. It would be difficult, but the words she used to say to her college girlfriends seeking relationship advice echoed in her head.

"If you can't be honest with the person you love, who can you be honest with?"

Next to #3, she wrote, "Tell Stu the truth." Finally, she had one item on the list for which she had a clear but complicated answer.

Jackie shuddered as she forced herself to recall the nightmare that had terrorized her out of her sleep 12 hours earlier. The passage of time hadn't blunted the emotional impact of the imagery or the outcome. While the mixed-up identities of Caitlin for Ashley and Dr. Caron for Stu confused and bothered her, she was better able to rationalize where the elements of the nightmare had their genesis. The gruesome details of Darius Scott's heinous acts that she had read on the Internet at work had had an impact. That Cheryl had threatened her job security shortly after that probably only cemented the monstrous acts in her head. The connection between Darius Scott and Dr. Caron was transparent. Apart from Dr. Caron's recent humanness, both men had generated fear and disgust in her. The connection between Caitlin and Ashley was also understandable. She could not get herself to think about what came next – Stu pulling Ashley into the fire. Obviously, the murderous fire played a role. She had also sat next to the fireplace at dinner that evening. She felt her heart starting to race again, and she quickly tried to move her thoughts to a happier place. Unsuccessful, she got up and bought a bottle of water from a vending machine. After taking a few sips, she returned to her chair to move on to her next concern, leaving her dream interpretation incomplete. She placed another question mark on her list.

The letter she had found from Dr. Sheridan to Dr. Caron was curious. The first thing that struck her was Dr. Sheridan's reference to Dr. Caron's letter of August 21st. Not only was that the day after Ashley was born, but she also seemed to recall that that was around the time that Darius had burned down that house and killed that woman. She couldn't remember the woman's name, but that didn't seem important. She could always surf the Web again and find her name if it became necessary.

The next odd thing was Dr. Caron had asked Dr. Sheridan about whether Darius met the criteria for lost to follow-up. From her internship days at AlzCura, she knew that Principal Investigators didn't need the Medical Director's permission or approval to designate a patient as lost to follow-up. The concept and the definition weren't complicated, and Dr. Caron wasn't new to research. Why Dr. Caron needed to consult Dr. Sheridan raised red flags. Also, Dr. Sheridan's insistence that Dr. Caron use the phone to communicate also seemed strange. If anything, in research, people usually erred on the side of more documentation, not less.

Finally, Dr. Sheridan either had written the letter himself, or one of his two assistants had failed to add the customary notation at the end, indicating who typed it. If he had written the letter himself, this would be truly out of character. From Jackie's experience, Dr. Sheridan rarely wrote his own copy of anything, let alone typed it himself. He had a team of PR types who would draft letters, memos, reports, and presentations for him. In turn, he would review these drafts before signing off, but not always. His assistants were even proficient in signing Dr. Sheridan's signature. Most people in the company didn't know this. Only those who had worked closely with Dr. Sheridan knew that most correspondence that went out under his name was not really generated or necessarily signed by Dr. Sheridan. Jackie wished that she had had time to go through the rest of the file. This one letter just raised questions and suspicions.

Add to this her concern about Margo's visit to Dr. Caron and the clinical trial she didn't even know existed. That Margo didn't mention her visit was somewhat understandable; she wasn't the sharpest tool in the shed. That Cheryl didn't brief her about Margo's visit, its outcome, or the Recallamin 3 trial had her questioning Cheryl, her employer, and her status within the company. Cheryl had always been so open with her and had always stressed the importance of thorough preparation. Why wouldn't she have briefed her on these things? Also, AlzCura was usually so good about communicating with their reps, knowing that if they knew about the latest and greatest information, they could better serve their clients. It seemed highly unlikely that they introduced a new trial during her leave, and there would be no evidence of it in her email, on her desk, or on the bulletin boards. When there was a new trial, a pharmaceutical rep would have to be dead not to know. Jackie was halfway through her list, and the exercise seemed to be producing more questions than answers. She drew another question mark on item #5 and forced herself to consider the next issue.

Dr. Caron's concerns about the Recallamin 3 trial seemed reasonable to Jackie, which had thrown her. She hadn't shared many feelings in common with him, and that he was expressing a level of concern and conscientiousness had her confused. Even more confusing was Dr. Sheridan's involvement. That Dr. Sheridan had a phone meeting with Dr. Caron to discuss his concerns was odd. Did it have something to do with Margo's visit? Maybe she had passed along his concern? If so, then why again wasn't she briefed about it? She was starting to feel overwhelmed and put the list and the legal pad away. The physical act of putting the list away could not, however, stop her mind. Minutes later, she pulled the list out again and continued.

Dr. Caron had genuinely seemed vulnerable, distressed, and desperate when he had expressed concerns about the company and wanted to tell someone about it. That he quickly back-pedaled and clammed up only made it more curious. What could be so bad as to cause an egotistical, overconfident physician to cower under the weight of some unspoken concerns? Was it Inspector Adams' visits? Did he know something that neither he nor anyone at AlzCura was telling her? She had been so sure about Dr. Caron's lack of ethics. Cheryl had even admitted as much in their last meeting. The questions that this visit had generated and Dr. Caron's sudden humanness and concern made her doubt her former assumptions about him and question the integrity of her employer. She shook her head in disbelief. Perhaps that was Dr. Caron's game. Maybe that was his way of deflecting unwanted attention. If the spotlight gets too hot, like getting a visit from an investigator, play the victim and point your finger at someone else.

Dr. Caron's leering at her womanly qualities may have been natural given her wardrobe choices, and yet, he had become surprisingly more professional and gentlemanly as the visit progressed. Maybe becoming more blatantly and aggressively sexual was a turn-off to him? Maybe he only likes to take advantage of women who are shy or seemingly unattainable. Was Cheryl, right? Show him your girl parts, and he'll talk? But he hadn't talked, and it didn't seem in his nature to suddenly get a megadose of decorum, morals, and manners. The more she dug into her list, the more confused she was becoming. Two plus two were not adding up to four.

Then there was anger when he learned another one of his patients had liver failure. What was that all about? It wasn't a condition that she recalled showing up in a significant way in the study data. Yet, it was the way he said it that had her concerned.

"Another one of my patients has liver failure," he said, followed by a quick refusal to talk anymore about it. Was he hiding something? Maybe it wasn't even about patients in Alz-

Cura trials, and he realized that he shouldn't be divulging information to her. What a shock, another question followed by only more questions.

The gate agent announced that her flight to Newark would be boarding shortly, interrupting her thoughts. She was only too happy to pack her list and legal pad away again. Her initial attempt to make sense out of the last 48 hours had only succeeded in raising more questions.

CHAPTER 46

C urt arrived home from work in a great mood and with excited anticipation for the evening activities. He was dropping Caitlin off at the stables and then taking Cade to his final hockey game of the season.

Caitlin was now spending 3 hours every Tuesday night, Friday night, and Saturday afternoon at the stables. She had a cadre of friends there, and Chantel had taken her under her wing and was grooming her to ride in some of the town parades in the summer. When Caitlin wasn't riding Freckles, she was talking about riding Freckles. She pampered Freckles, often spending more time grooming him than riding him. When she did ride him, it was as though they were one. Despite her diminutive size, she knew just the positions and body pressure to apply to make him respond as required. She had quickly graduated from walk, trot, canter and was now navigating low jumps. She was a natural, and to Curt's delight, his daughter's smile never left her when she was riding or thinking about riding, which was pretty much always.

Cade had become quite an accomplished skater and had worked his way into the first line. While he could skate circles around most, his stickhandling and shooting skills were only average. His coach had talked to Curt about enrolling him in a summer skills camp in Canada. Unfortunately, the coach had said this within earshot of Cade, and ever since, he had been begging and pleading to have his father sign him up. The camp was one week in length and hosted by a former NHL player. In addition to the substantial cost, it meant Cade would need to sleep at the camp, away from his family. Although Cade tried to convince him otherwise, Curt wasn't sure that Cade could tolerate being away from home that long. The deadline for signing up was fast approaching, and he knew he would have to decide soon. For now, he was just happy that both his kids were seemingly happy.

The evening was a success. Cade scored a goal to help his team to victory, and Caitlin was so happy after riding that she even found a place in her heart to ask her brother about his hockey game.

"Did you win tonight?" she asked before he had a chance to inform her.

"Yeah, and I even scored a goal?"

"That's great!"

"How was Freckles?"

"Awesome. We jumped a 3-foot jump today."

"Wow, I wish I could have seen that," said Cade, genuinely impressed.

"Dad, I think we should celebrate," Caitlin lobbied.

Although it was late and it was a school night, the wonder of their positive exchange made him bend the rules.

"So, where do you want to go to celebrate?"

"The Farrisport Inn," they both sang in unison.

The kids' usual difficulty selecting dining options had descended into an obsession with the Inn after their dinner with Jackie. This would be their second dinner in the month following meeting Jackie.

"Again?"

"Yes, maybe we'll...."

"I know, I know, maybe we'll meet Jackie there," he answered for Caitlin.

"You never know, Dad."

"Yes, and I might win the lottery tomorrow too!"

Despite his weak protests, he secretly had no problem with their suggestion. Not only did he love the food, but he also didn't mind the idea that perhaps he might win the lottery and see the woman who, with one magical dinner, changed his outlook on life.

They arrived at the Inn, and fortunately, the table that they had since claimed as "their table" was available. They sat in their assigned seats and left Jackie's chair by the fireplace open. Curt's discomfort with the fireplace was replaced by the memory of how the light had danced off Jackie's face. They ordered their same meals and desserts. The kids ate all but one bite of their desserts, certain that doing otherwise was bad luck. While Jackie didn't appear, the ritual seemed to perpetuate the feelings from their evening together.

The meal and the late hour caused the kids to fall asleep on the way home. Curt, not wanting to wake them, first carried Cade and then Caitlin up the three flights of stairs to the apartment and their rooms. Exhausted from the effort, he fell into bed, content that he and his kids seemed to have finally recovered from the horrific roller-coaster ride they had experienced over the last eight months.

He awoke with a start at 4:27 a.m. Sweat-soaked and gasping for breath, he wondered if he was having a heart attack. He couldn't distinguish the events still fresh in his head from the present. It all seemed like one horrifyingly contiguous event. He knew his kids were dead, and if he didn't act quickly, he would be next. Part of him didn't care anymore. Why continue to live when everything he ever lived for was gone. Paralyzed by the loss, he lay back, awaiting his fate. When nothing happened, and all but a roaring silence enveloped him, he propped himself up on his elbow and hoped beyond hope that this had just been a nightmare.

Kicking his covers off, he jumped out of bed, not able to move fast enough to confirm whether his kids were still alive. He half expected to meet his demise as he opened his bedroom door but granted a reprieve; he stormed into Cade's adjacent bedroom. Instead of charred remains, Cade slept peacefully. He had to touch Cade's face to confirm he was alive. When Cade stirred and turned over, he moved on.

He stumbled out of Cade's room, sure of the acrid smell of burnt flesh. Whispering no, no, no, he padded with urgency to the front bedroom. His mind couldn't deal with the loss of his princess. Pausing at the door, he was unable, or perhaps unwilling, to open it. If she were gone, he would have no choice but to put himself and Cade out of their misery. He almost went to the kitchen to get his sharpest knife without opening the door. He wished he had a gun. It would be quicker. Easier. He steeled himself against what he expected to see and opened the door slowly. To his surprise, no smoke and no smell, just the angelic face of Caitlin illuminated by her horse carousel nightlight and tainted only by a line of drool from her mouth to the corner of her pillow. He closed the door and flopped onto the living room couch. The dream had been a geriatric version of Night of the Living Dead. Thousands of zombie-like creatures were escaping from nursing homes and overrunning the community, torching homes and people. One by one, Curt had watched the carnage. It wasn't until the zombies approached the apartment and entered Caitlin and Cade's rooms that he sprung to action, but it was too late. He was on a treadmill, moving as fast as he could but getting nowhere. The screams of his children as they erupted in flames woke him.

Now recalling the horror his mind had wrought, he searched for meaning and causation. Yesterday had been one of the best days for him and the kids. Why this nightmare now? Then it occurred to him - the call with DA Wydman. It had surprised him. It had brought back all the memories of feeling tortured by the unanswerable questions. Why did he do it? Did he know Calli, or was it just random that he bought his murderous supplies where she worked? What caused his actions and death? Perhaps that is what dredged up the recurrence of this nightmare. Then he recalled the words DA Wydman had spoken after he had discounted their continued investigation.

"The State is just worried that if there is a link, there may be thousands of individuals taking this medication. We must protect the public."

It hadn't registered with him then, but it had registered with his subconscious. The thought of the thousands and soon to be millions of people taking what was now becoming one of the most frequently prescribed antidotes to Alzheimer's made him shudder. Could there be a link between the vaccine and the violent, crazed behavior and death? Could his refusal to write a letter to the drug company be endangering others, those getting the vaccine and their potential victims? The questions seemed preposterous, but it wasn't uncommon for medical science to discover some unintended consequence of a popular drug or some drug interaction that caused harmful effects. Perhaps the State's concern was not so far-fetched. Did he want to be responsible for the untold numbers of people who could suffer because he failed to write a simple letter?

Too late to go back to sleep, he fired up the coffee pot and prepared for his day - a day that would change his life forever.

CHAPTER 47

When Jackie arrived in Newark, she tried to call Stu. When he didn't answer, she assumed that he was probably sleeping. She left a message on his phone.

"Good morning, sleepyhead. Betty Sue misses you. I hope you're feeling better. I'll be home soon. Love you."

She was anxious to get home, and even the short layover in Newark was making her restless. She called her mother.

"Hi, Mom," she said brightly.

"Hi. You haven't arrived, have you?"

"No, Mom, I'm just calling between flights."

"Oh good, I was worried I might have gotten the time wrong. 8:30, right?"

"Right. How's Ash?"

"She's been a little angel. She started fussing, and I just gave her a bottle. You know, I don't think I want to give her back."

Jackie laughed. "I know, being away from her has been torture. I may have to quit my job, become a full-time Mom, and have Stu take care of us".

"Speaking of Stu, I brought over some chicken soup for him this afternoon. He still wasn't feeling good."

"You didn't take Ash with you, did you?"

"Why, yes, I did. And I let Stu hug and kiss her," her mother said sarcastically. "No, silly, I had your father watch her while I went over. You know, it hasn't been that long since you were a baby. I haven't totally lost my senses or motherly instinct."

"I'm sorry, Mom. I guess I'm just a worried first-time Mom."

"And I'd be concerned if you weren't."

"Okay, I will see you at 8:30 then. Love you."

"Love you too."

She boarded the plane for Buffalo, anxious to hold Ashley and eager to be home to take care of Stu. On the flight, she wondered if she should let her mother keep Ash overnight. She didn't want her to catch anything from Stu. The thought of going another night without having her baby didn't sit well. She reasoned that if she kept her away from Stu, everything would be fine. Then she realized that Stu might give her something that she could pass on to Ashley. Hadn't Stu said he only had a headache? That's not contagious unless he has some other symptoms. He had coughed on the phone. She fought this back and forth battle in her head for the better part of the flight. On the one hand, her brain argued for responsibility and prudence. On the other, her heart asserted that it was more important for Ashley to be with her mother and vice versa.

Her heart won the argument the moment she saw Ashley in the car seat as her mother pulled up to the arriving passenger pick-up zone. Although Ashley was sleeping, it didn't deter Jackie from unbuckling her and picking her up before she got in the car. Rousted from her sleep, combined with the unexpected temperature change from a warm car to the blast of winter air, caused a predictable response.

"Well, some mother you are! You're not even here a minute, and you've made your baby girl cry."

Jackie hardly heard her mother as she hugged Ashley, slipped into the passenger seat, and closed the door. Ashley quickly quieted down. The recognition of her mother displayed in her eyes and her little reaching hands. Nothing else in the world mattered in those first few minutes. Her mother was finally able to get her attention.

"Jackie, I can't drive until Ashley is in her car seat."

Her mother's statement felt like a slap across her face. Having to put Ashley back in the car seat and not being able to hold her for the 30-minute ride home seemed like cruel and unusual punishment. She relented and, rather than shock Ash with another blast of arctic air, lifted her over the front seat to her mother in the backseat. Safely bundled back in the car seat, Ashley soon fell back to sleep.

Jackie's mother made the ride home tolerable by talking endlessly about Ashley. Their conversation would have sounded bizarre to anyone who had never brought a human life into the world. Jackie and her mother thoroughly discussed and interpreted all of Ashley's gestures, babbling verbalizations, and body movements while Jackie was away. Her sleeping patterns, mealtimes, and even the appearance of the gifts Ashley left in her diaper were also topics of discussion. If Jackie's mother weren't driving, she would have likely shown her the 300 pictures she took of Ashley during her 36-hour visit. The 30-minute drive flew by, and they agreed that Jackie's mother would bring Ashley to her room while Jackie checked on Stu if he wasn't up and around. Jackie opened the door.

"Hon, I'm home. Hon? Are you up?"

Not getting a response, she motioned for her mother to bring Ashley to her room while she quietly entered the bedroom to check on Stu. Not wanting to wake him, she left the door open slightly to allow a sliver of light into the room. Stu was sleeping soundly, and Jackie bent over and kissed him on the forehead. She was shocked when her lips met something cold instead of Stu's warm forehead. Had she kissed an ice pack?

"Stu?" she asked. When she didn't receive a response, she reached for his shoulder and shook him. Again, her hand met something cold, and his body moved oddly. She drew back and flailing to find the bedside lamp knocked over an unfinished bowl of chicken soup and a bottle of Extra Strength Tylenol on the nightstand. Finally, finding the switch, she illuminated the room.

Jackie's scream filled the house, and the sight of his unnaturally pale skin with a bluish hue made her gag. Her mother appeared at the door.

"Jackie, what's..." she didn't have to finish her sentence.

"Call 9-1-1," Jackie screamed.

Ashley was now crying in the background. Jackie's mother dutifully made the call as her daughter decompensated in front of her, and her granddaughter decompensated behind her.

"Stu, you can't leave me," Jackie pleaded.

"Stu, oh, God. Noooooooooooooooo," she screamed.

"Stu, please don't leave me."

"Noooooooooooooooooo."

When her screams brought no response, and she couldn't bear to look at the body that no longer resembled the strong, vibrant, and loving soul mate who had carried her across the threshold two years earlier, she crumbled to the floor, wailing. Within minutes, her crying subsided, replaced by a stunned, faraway look. She didn't or couldn't move, paralyzed by the suddenness in which her life was changed. Jackie would not remember the arrival of the paramedics or her father 15 minutes later. She wouldn't remember much of the next few days. Stu was dead, and the paramedics didn't even attempt to rescue him. He had been dead for at least a couple of hours.

Doris and Jack brought their zombie-like daughter and inconsolable granddaughter to their house. Jackie and Ashley shared the room that used to be Jackie's when she was growing up. Doris fed Ashley and put her in the crib that Jack had moved from their bedroom. Jackie lay in her childhood bed, not sleeping but continuing to stare and not move. Doris sat in a chair in the corner of the room, occasionally checking on Jackie, not sure what to do for her daughter. She hoped that just being present would help, but she didn't even know what her daughter was experiencing. To Doris, it was almost as if her daughter was dead. Nothing emanated from her, no emotion, just the blank stare and her motionless body.

Jackie's parents would make all the critical decisions over the next 48 hours. They tried to involve Jackie, but she was unresponsive. They finally stopped asking her, worried that they were making matters worse by trying to make difficult decisions in her state of shock. The paramedics informed them that the Medical Examiner would need to do an autopsy since no one had witnessed Stu's death. This came as a relief and offered a modicum of hope to the questions swirling in their heads about how Stu, a healthy young man with no significant medical history, could have died.

Jackie didn't eat, sleep, or show interest in Ashley for the first 24 hours after finding Stu. Worried, Doris started to feed her daughter broth. She also forced her to get up encouraged her to breastfeed Ashley by placing her in Jackie's arms. Ashley responded enthusiastically, but initially, Jackie sat staring as if nothing was happening, not even acknowledging her daughter's presence. In a few minutes, Jackie started to realize that Ashley was in her arms, suckling at her breast. The connection was therapeutic, and with each feeding after that, Jackie began to recover the motherly instinct she had temporarily lost. Doris also got Jackie a prescription for Ambien, and for the first time in almost two days, Jackie slept.

When Jackie woke up the next day, she was staring into the bloodshot eyes of Sunny. Jackie's eyes showed recognition, and she reached out to Sunny, who promptly leaned over and hugged her.

"I'm so sorry, Jackie."

"Thank you, Sunny."

If her mother had not been there to witness it, she wouldn't have believed it. Her daughter was back. Jackie sat up as Ashley stirred in her crib.

"Sunny, could you bring Ashley here?"

Sunny was glad to oblige and, wiping tears from her eyes, picked up the little fussing bundle, and transferred her into Jackie's waiting arms. Sunny started crying again as she watched Jackie feed Ash.

"I'm so glad you're here, Sunny. This is so hard."

"I don't know what to say, Jackie. I just knew I needed to be here."

"Thanks. What day is it?" Jackie shouted suddenly.

"Sunday."

"Sunday?"

"Yeah, what day did you think it was?"

"I don't know. I kinda lost track of time."

Jackie started to get a little agitated.

"Where's Stu?"

This question stopped Sunny and Doris in their tracks, and before they could respond, Jackie got more agitated.

"Where is Stu?" she screamed, startling Ashley, who came off her breast and started to cry. Sunny grabbed Ash while Doris moved in to try to calm her daughter, who by now was trembling like a bowl of jello as tears began to flow.

"Honey, relax."

"Is he buried? Did I miss the funeral?"

"No, honey, the funeral is tomorrow. Relax."

She started to calm down, but this type of anxiety attack and outburst would haunt her for some time. Eventually, she would get a prescription for a sedative to help her calm down during these episodes. Before that, however, she needed a prescription for an anti-depressant. As the protective shield of her initial shock abated and the full realization of her loss washed over her, it threatened to drown her.

Perhaps most devastating and debilitating was the heartbreak and realization of Ashley's loss. Ashley would never remember her father. Never have him present for her first step, first word, or any of life's significant milestones. She would never feel his strong arms around her when she needed comforting or consoling. Never hear his laugh.

Every time Jackie would think about this, she would grieve all over again, for both of them. It made her recovery more difficult and lengthier. She couldn't imagine what would replace the chasm that Stu's death had left in her heart, soul, and mind. He had been so central to her life that his absence left her feeling anchorless. She was adrift in a sea of uncertainty with no signs of land or a safe harbor.

Sunny's presence helped. Sunny represented the one true friend that Jackie and Stu shared. Some of Jackie and Stu's best times together were when they were with Sunny, and her being at Jackie's side now was comforting. For several days, Sunny kept by Jackie's side. Not only did Sunny not want to leave, but at times, Jackie forbid her from going. Sunny had become a surrogate Stu, and not having Sunny around her made Jackie anxious.

Stu's funeral at St. Paul Church was a blur to Jackie. All she would remember of the ceremony was Ashley crying and being passed in front of her between her mother and Sunny to quiet and console her. Jackie, surrounded by family, felt numb and alone. Although the church was almost full, Jackie would later report not having any recollection of who was there. Nor would she recall the dozens of people who approached her after the funeral with their condolences.

As she stood in the first pew with Sunny and her mother, all she could do was stare at the casket that occupied the space where they had recited their marital vows. She felt the vows were flawed. Til death do us part was wrong. Death parted nothing. She still loved Stu, and she couldn't let go. She had taken an extra dose of her sedative that morning, and she didn't like the feeling. Outwardly she felt like an emotionless robot moved from place to place. Inside, and hidden from all others, was an emotional storm that felt locked in with no hope of escape.

People would describe her demeanor during the funeral as composed when, in fact, she felt like she was falling apart from the inside out. The sedative just masked the turmoil. Jackie wished she had not taken them. She wanted to fall apart, felt as if she was, but the medication hid this and prevented her from giving voice to the despair she was feeling. It was wrong. At one point, she remembers having the urge to just leaving the pew, open the casket, and crawl into it with Stu. He was the only one she wanted to be with right now. He was the only one who could understand. She probably would have done so if her legs didn't feel cemented in place.

Her mind could not link or hold two thoughts at a time. The mental faculty of thinking of what she wanted and then taking steps to pursue that end were gone. It was almost as if someone had hit the "Pause" button on her brain. When she had thoughts, they were singular thoughts, disconnected from any line of reasoning or ability to act or respond. The sedative had just made her feel more helpless. The only so-called benefit was that it allowed her to exist in the public eye without suffering the potential embarrassment of decompensating in front of everyone. Appearances, wasn't that all-important in today's world? She had lost Stu, and now the sedative was stealing her humanness. She could feel anger boiling inside her, locked in the pressure cooker of her body with no ability to vent.

Somehow, after the funeral service, she was transported grave-side and once again, amidst a crowd, felt alone, disconnected from her body, and impervious to any incoming information. Sunny and her mother were there to prop her up, but she only remembered wondering why she was standing there. This was just a bad dream, and when she woke up, Stu would be there. It wasn't until they drove past her house to her parent's house that things started to sink in. The sedative was beginning to wear off, and the pain and the reality started to flood back in. Stu, the man who had held her heart, soul, and dreams, was dead — buried in some meaningless, cold, dark place. The grief was too much to bear, and as she crossed the threshold of her parent's home, Jackie collapsed.

"Stuuuuuu," she wailed. "Oh, Stuuuuuu," disintegrating into sobs so violent that Sunny had to encourage her to breathe so as not to pass out. It was 15 minutes before the sedative Sunny gave her kicked in, and they were able to lead her to her childhood bed. She slept for 16 hours, drained from the emotional upheaval and numbed by the sledgehammer sedative.

When she woke up the next day, and Sunny brought Ashley to her, Jackie felt on the other side of the chapter in her life that had included Stu. She felt a strength emerging, a purpose that had left her for the last few days. Ashley needed her, and she would need to show her the love of two. Every motherly act felt like a tribute to Stu. As if she could somehow convey to Ashley the love of her Daddy through her every action. She refused the medications her mother offered her that morning and resolutely made plans to "go home" despite her parents' urging her to stay with them for a few days. As quickly as she had crumbled into grief-struck dependence, Jackie's independence now rose like a Phoenix. Her transformation from one day to the next was so instantaneous that most around her didn't believe it. They kept waiting for her resolve to crack throughout that next day, but it didn't.

If Jackie had any reservations about moving back into the house, she hadn't been in for nearly a week; she didn't show it. While Ashley stayed with Jackie's mother, she and Sunny marched into the house that morning and spent the day cleaning. Remnants of Stu's last days in the house still existed. Dishes he had used. Clothes that he had worn. Leftover Chinese he had stored in the fridge. Sunny kept waiting for the weight of these things to get the better of Jackie, but if anything, they seemed to fuel her recovery. She grew stronger and more determined throughout the day.

Jackie walked into the bedroom she used to share with Stu. There was no bedding removed as part of the coroners' investigation. Police tape lay balled up unceremoniously next to a wastepaper basket. Jackie made a mental note to call the Coroner's office and noticed Sunny staring at her.

"What?" Jackie asked Sunny.

"I don't know. I just thought this might be a difficult room for you to be in."

"There are more good memories here, Sunny, than bad," Jackie exclaimed to Sunny's surprise.

"You're incredible."

"Not really, girlfriend. It's just that I know Stu would want me to be strong for him and Ashley. That love is stronger than anything else."

Seconds later, it was Jackie consoling Sunny as she erupted into tears.

"What's the matter, Sunny?"

"I'm just so sad for you and Ash," she sobbed. "I have never known anyone so in love. You were so perfect for one another." Sunny buried her head into Jackie's shoulder. It was Jackie's turn to be strong for Sunny.

Sunny slept with Jackie her first night back in the house. Jackie and Ashley slept better than Sunny did. When Jackie woke up, she was surprised to see her buxom blond friend next to her in bed.

"Good morning, Jackie."

"Good morning, Sun...oh my god, where's Ash?" Jackie jumped to get out of bed.

"Relax. She's fine, Jackie. She slept through the night, just like you. I checked on her several times."

"You look like you haven't slept," Jackie said, settling back into bed.

"I may have nodded off once or twice, but no, I didn't really sleep. I must look like a wreck."

"Do you have to go home today?"

"I do Jackie, I'm sorry."

"Don't be sorry Sunny; you've been here for a whole week. I feel guilty about you using all your vacation time."

"Stop it. Will you and Ash be OK? I can see about changing my flight if you need me to stay."

"No, Sunny, we will be alright. I need to get my life in order. The sooner I get back to work and figure out how to get through my days and nights without Stu, the better for Ash. When's your flight?"

"1:30."

"You should get some sleep before your flight."

"No, I can sleep on the plane."

"Wanna get breakfast?"

"Sounds good."

Ashley started to cry. "I guess Ash wants her breakfast first," Jackie said, popping out of bed. Sunny showered and got ready while Jackie fed Ashley. When Sunny came to relieve Jackie and stay with Ash, Jackie showered. While showering, Jackie realized that her morning routine was going to change considerably without Stu or Sunny there to stay with Ash. She went through the motions of getting ready, all the time taking inventory of how she would have to change two-person to one-person processes. On top of her profound loneliness now sat the challenges of single parenthood.

CHAPTER 48

Jackie drove Sunny to the airport after breakfast at Momma's Diner. While holding Ash, Jackie and Sunny hugged and could not hold back their tears. Jackie promised to visit Sunny, reminding her that she still had the travel voucher and shopping spree that Stu had given her for her birthday.

On her way back from the airport, she called Cheryl to say she would be coming back to work the next day.

"You sure you're up to coming back?" Cheryl asked.

"Yes. I need to."

"And you have arrangements for the baby?"

"Yep, other than getting her ready in the morning by myself, my mother will still be taking care of her during the day."

"OK. Well, stop in to see me first thing tomorrow, and we can talk more."

Jackie hung up and felt better, knowing that she was going to get back into a more normal routine the next day. She wasn't good with her free time. It caused her to overthink, and that usually led to thinking about Stu, which often led to sadness. As she was just about to pull into her driveway, her cell phone rang.

"Mrs. Deno?"

"Yes?"

"This is Dr. Jacobson from the Coroner's Office. Would you have time to come by today?"

"Yes, what is it?"

"Well, I'd rather speak with you in person. What time today would work best for you?"

"I'm available now."

"That will be fine. I'll see you soon."

A sense of foreboding settled in the pit of her stomach as soon as she hung up. During the last week, she and many others had often questioned why Stu had died. Somehow, when she received the Coroner's call, the concern about how Stu died had left her mind. The call was like a punch to the solar plexus, knocking the wind out of her sails. She called her mother and asked her to take Ash so she could run a few errands. She knew her mother would likely want to be with her to receive the coroner's report, but Jackie felt like this was something she had to do on her own.

Upon entering the Coroner's office, she immediately started to question her decision to do this alone. What if she couldn't handle the information? Her legs felt rubbery, and she was relieved when the receptionist encouraged her to take a seat in the waiting area.

"Mrs. Deno?" said a tall, graying man with glasses dressed in corduroy pants and jacket.

"Yes," Jackie replied, somewhat surprised to see a doctor wearing something other than a white lab coat.

"I'm Dr. Jacobson. Thank you for coming in. Let's go to my office."

Although well-practiced in visiting and speaking to doctors, something about this visit felt different - uncomfortably different. Winding their way to his office, she pushed away thoughts about what Dr. Jacobson had to do to Stu to arrive at the results he was about to share. Her legs were getting rubbery again, and as she took a seat in Dr. Jacobson's office, he could tell she was uncomfortable.

"Would you like a bottle of water, Mrs. Deno?"

"Yes, please."

Reaching into a mini-fridge behind his desk, he handed her a bottle. She twisted off the cap and took a drink. His kind gesture and the cool water settled her somewhat, and she prepared herself for what she might hear.

"Mrs. Deno, first, I'd like to say I'm sorry for your loss."

"Thank you."

"It is never easy losing someone you love, and losing someone so young is even harder."

Jackie could feel tears welling up in her eyes. She once again questioned her judgment about coming here alone.

"I'd like to ask you a few questions before I tell you my findings. Would that be OK?"

"Yes, of course."

"When was the last time your husband saw his doctor?"

"He went to his doctor a few months ago for a physical and his flu shot."

"Were there any unusual findings from his physical?"

"Not that I'm aware of," Jackie responded, starting to get nervous about the nature of his questions.

"Did Stu have any illnesses or physical complaints over the last few months?"

"Not until the weekend before he died. He complained of a headache Sunday and stayed home from work one day complaining of a headache."

"Any other complaints or symptoms? Did he have a fever? Vomiting?"

"I was away on a business trip, but when I called him, he just complained about the headache. He did cough some while he was on the phone. I don't know if he had a fever or vomiting." Jackie started to feel guilty about not having been more observant or insistent about Stu taking his temperature or going to the doctor.

"Did he take any medications either normally or for his headache?"

"He didn't need medications normally, but he told me he took Tylenol for his headache."

"Was he taking Tylenol regularly or perhaps taking high doses?"

"No. As I said, he rarely took medications."

"Did your husband drink alcohol heavily or take any illegal drugs?

"No. He drank occasionally and never took illegal drugs."

"Did you notice anything unusual about your husband in the last few months? Behavior changes? Mood changes? Changes in his interests or energy?"

Suddenly, Stu's words that morning at the airport came flooding back in.

"Yes, the day he brought me to the airport, he got angry for no reason. Just out of the blue, he yelled at me and drove off before I had a chance to find out what was bothering him."

"And this was out of the ordinary?"

"Yes. Stu and I never fought and never argued. He never raised his voice to me before."

"Did you ever learn why he did that?"

"When I finally spoke to him, he said it was because I was leaving, and he had become used to me being home."

"Do you often travel for your job?"

"Yes, and he never had a problem with my traveling before.

This time, however, it was the first trip after my maternity leave. I had been home for a few months" Jackie started to feel tears welling up in her eyes again.

"I'm sorry, Mrs. Deno. I know this must be hard for you to recount and relive the last few months. I just want to get some context to my findings."

"So, what did my husband die from?" Jackie pleaded.

"Alright, let me tell you first that my findings are preliminary. I have sent tissue samples to a regional lab that has more sophisticated equipment. So, what I'm telling you now may change based on what they might find."

"OK."

"Your husband appears to have died from some kind of bleeding in his brain. What is unusual about it is first his young age and second the amount of bleeding and tissue damage."

"What do you think caused it?"

"That is where I'm stumped, Mrs. Deno. I have never seen this type of brain bleed, even in elderly patients, let alone a young, seemingly healthy individual. He did have some evidence of liver failure. That is why I asked you about Tylenol, alcohol, and drug use. I want to get his medical records from his doctor. Would you agree to have them released to me?"

"Of course."

"Okay, I will have my assistant give you the form to complete on your way out. Do you have any questions?"

"I have nothing but questions. Did you find anything else?"

"No, other than the brain bleed and evidence of liver failure, your husband appeared to be healthy. I wish I had more answers for you. Perhaps the regional lab and his medical records will provide some answers."

"Do you have any idea how long it will take the Regional

Lab to get their results?"

"I hesitate to say. They tend to take 2-4 weeks. I have asked them to expedite their examination, given the unusual nature of my findings."

"Thank you, Dr. Jacobson."

Jackie completed the release of information form on her way out of the office. When she got into her car, she allowed herself to feel all the feelings that she had kept bottled up in Dr. Jacobson's office. The tears did little to wash away her concerns. All the questions Dr. Jacobson had asked her haunted her. Some had made her feel guilty for not being there for Stu when he was sick. Others raised questions as to how transparent Stu may have been about his health. He was not a complainer, and if not for her insistence, he would not likely have gone to the doctor for that physical and flu shot. Was he potentially hiding concerns from her?

After feeling so positive about moving forward earlier that day, she now thought she had taken two steps back. She was sentenced to an additional 2 to 4 weeks of not knowing and of people asking her questions about how Stu died. One thing Dr. Jacobson had said had hit her like a freight train - evidence of liver failure. When the doctor had said that, her mind recalled Dr. Caron's outburst during her recent visit. She wrote it off as a coincidence, put herself back together emotionally, and prepared to go back to work the next day.

CHAPTER 49

Cheryl marched into Dr. Sheridan's office directly after having received the call from Jackie announcing that she would be returning to work.

"Asa, what are we going to do about Jackie?"

"I think we have to do what we talked about doing last week after I spoke to Dr. Caron."

"So, you still think that keeping her on or reassigning her is more dangerous than letting her go?"

"Yes. Dr. Caron is spooked. If Jackie picked up on any of his reservations, she is too smart and too ethical not to consider going on a crusade that might implicate us. Having her here with access to information is just too risky."

"What if I feel her out tomorrow and see what she knows? She's too honest to keep anything from me. If she divulges anything that may reflect poorly on us, then I can cut her loose."

"No, bad idea. If you cut her loose after she sings, she will immediately know why and that will most certainly fuel her suspicions. She needs to think her performance was the cause."

"So, impropriety with a client it is."

"Yep."

"And what if she claims wrongful dismissal and gets Dr. Caron to support her?"

"Let her. Dr. Caron won't come to her defense. I've made certain of that."

"And just how did you assure that he wouldn't come to her defense?"

"It's called my Margo strategy."

"You sly dog Asa."

"He squeals or moves to support Jackie, and we post all the photos of him doing the nasty with Margo on the Internet, and his marriage and career are toast. Besides, dismissing Jackie will set her back a few notches. I doubt she will have the wherewithal even to consider fighting us. She's a smart and pretty girl who will need a job to take care of her baby, not a legal battle. She'll land on her feet and never give us another thought."

"I hope you're right," Cheryl said as she left Dr. Sheridan's office.

CHAPTER 50

Jackie successfully navigated the morning routine alone and got to work, anxious to focus on something other than her loss. Dropping her bag at her cubicle, she went to Cheryl's office.

"Good morning, boss," Jackie said as cheerfully as she could.

"Good morning, Jackie, come in, take a seat," Cheryl instructed while shutting the office door.

Jackie noticed that there was another person in the room who she recognized as someone from Human Resources.

"Oh, I'm sorry, Cheryl, I didn't know you were in a meeting."

"I'm not Jackie. I asked Mel to join us because I have to let you go."

"What?" Jackie gasped. "Why?"

"Jackie, we have evidence of improper behavior with a client, and our rules and consequences for this are crystal clear – immediate termination. As it is, we waited for you to come back from your bereavement."

"Improper behavior with whom?" Jackie was stunned and searching for answers.

"We received a complaint from Dr. Caron."

Before Jackie could catch her breath and think to respond, Cheryl continued.

"Mel has your final check and some forms for you to complete. A Security Guard will then accompany you to your desk so that you can pack your personal items, and he will escort you off the premises. There are very strict rules related to your termination that forbid you to divulge company or proprietary information or to contact clients. Mel has an agreement that clearly outlines these rules. If you abide by them, AlzCura will provide a neutral reference to any future employers. Should you not follow these rules, we will divulge the reason for your dismissal to prospective employers, and depending on the infraction, may take legal action against you. Is that clear?"

Jackie couldn't catch up with Cheryl, and her mind reeled. "I...."

"I don't need your answer now, Jackie, but read the paperwork Mel has, sign it, and I will send Security up. Best of luck, Jackie."

With that, Cheryl left Jackie in the office with the HR representative, who systematically reviewed the paperwork. Jackie tried a couple of times to engage the HR person in a conversation about the grounds for dismissal, but she didn't bite.

"Mrs. Deno, the Termination Agreement spells out all the details of your dismissal and expectations about your behavior and communications. I cannot say any more. I will give you a copy of all the forms for your records. A copy of our grievance and appeals process is also included should you wish to contest this action."

Ten minutes later, a security guard appeared, his body nearly filling the doorway. After Jackie had signed all the required forms, he escorted her to her cubicle. Several empty boxes had been left for her use. Trembling, she could not believe that this was happening. She couldn't understand why Dr. Caron would have filed a complaint. She was wondering how she was going to make the mortgage payment and take care of Ash without an income. She was embarrassed to be standing there with a Goliath of a man protecting the company's assets as if she was some criminal. Stu's death and now losing her job was a one-two punch that put her on the canvas. She was devastated and searched for answers and support, but she had precious few options.

She didn't even remember how she navigated the drive home. Alternating between swimming in tears, feeling numb, and a wave of growing anger, all contributing to her amnesia. As she pulled into her driveway, she wondered what in the world she would do next. She entered her empty home, wandering from room to room. When she got to Ashley's empty bedroom, her cell phone rang. Debating whether to pick it up, she realized it was the Coroner's office. She answered in as calm a voice as she could muster.

"Mrs. Deno, this is Dr. Jacobson. Is this a good time to talk?"

Although it wasn't, she lied, "Yes, this is a fine time."

"You may want to sit down. Did you know that in addition to the flu vaccine, your husband also enrolled in a clinical study when he visited his doctor?"

"No, I didn't."

"Well, he did. His doctor did genetic testing on Stu and found he had the Alzheimer's gene. Stu signed a consent form for a Phase II study involving a vaccine called Recallamin manufactured by AlzCura. Didn't he mention it?"

It was as if someone had gored her in the stomach, and she fought to keep the contents of her stomach where they were.

"No, he didn't mention it, but I'm familiar with the vaccine. Why do you think this is important?"

"Well, it might not be anything, but study drugs are experimental, and if he got the study drug, it might help explain what killed him. I am requesting information from the manufacturer to unblind the study to determine if Stu received the study drug. I just thought it would be important for me to tell you. Would you rather I not update you until I have something definitive?"

"No, no, thank you, Dr. Jacobson. Please do continue to keep me updated."

They hung up, and she pondered what he had said. As she looked across Ashley's room, she spied the stuffed moose that Curt and the kids had sent up to her room. A bolt of lightning struck her, and she knew what she needed to do.

CHAPTER 51

C urt entered the office, greeted Loribeth, and asked what his calendar looked like for the day.

"It's pretty clear. You have a couple of phone meetings later this morning and in the early afternoon."

"Ok, thanks. I may have to leave mid-afternoon if I can get a meeting with DA Wydman, so please try to keep my calendar open if you can."

"OK, that's a name I haven't heard in a while. Don't mean to pry, but anything new? Just tell me it's none of my business if you'd rather not say."

"No problem, LB. He called me yesterday and asked me to write a letter to a drug company. I declined yesterday, but now I'm rethinking it."

"Why write a letter to a drug company?"

"Well, the State is trying to investigate if there's a link between a study drug they manufacturer that Darius and Elvira may have taken and their behavior and deaths. The drug company is stalling, and they think a letter from me might compel them to share more information."

"Wow, sounds like crime novel stuff. Why are you reconsidering writing it?"

"At first, the State's case just sounded so weak and lame. I didn't think it was worth my time. Then something DA Wyd-man said to me triggered a nightmare I had last night. That has me worried that perhaps there is a link, and if I don't try to help the State, thousands of people might be harmed by the drug."

"Geez, your life is obviously more interesting than mine out of work! What was the nightmare about?"

"I'd rather not relive that thank you very much, but can you do me a favor?"

"What's that?"

"Call over to the hospital and see if they can courier over the IRB materials from the SMILE and SMILE2 trials. I want to refresh my memory about the study drug before I consider writing the drug company."

"Sure thing, boss."

Curt grabbed a cup of coffee and trooped to his office. No sooner had he sat down and LB rang him on the phone.

"Curt, there's a Mrs. Deno on the line for you?"

"Did she say what the call was about?" he asked, not recognizing the name.

"No, but she seems upset. Should I take a message?"

"No, if she's upset, I better take it."

LB transferred the call, and Curt answered.

"This is Curt Barnes; may I help you?"

"Curt, this is Jackie," said the woman in obvious distress.

"Er, Jackie?" he questioned, the name still not clicking.

"Jackie, we had dinner together with your kids at the Far-risport Inn a few weeks ago."

"Ohhhh, Jackie. Now I remember. How did you find me?

"Your business card. You wrote a note on it that accompan-ied the stuffed moose you sent up to me for Ashley. Thank you, by the way."

"No problem, but what's the matter? You sound upset?"

"I am. My husband died two weeks ago, I just got fired, and I need your help."

"Jesus, Jackie, that's awful. How can I help you?"

"Actually, I think we can help each other. I didn't know it when we met, but wasn't your wife murdered by Darius Scott last August?"

"Yes," he replied tentatively.

"Well, up until today, I worked for the drug company that sponsored the clinical trial in which Darius participated. Are you aware that the State of Maine is trying to establish a link between the drug and Darius' behavior and death?"

"Yes, as a matter of fact, the DA on the case called me yesterday. He wants me to write a letter to the drug company because they are stalling. Their case is pretty weak as far as I can tell."

"Well, it might just have gotten a bit stronger," Jackie replied, "Rather than try to do this over the phone, I think we should meet. Would you be willing to have dinner with me at the Farrisport Inn again?"

"Absolutely. What can I do to prepare?"

"See if you can get the DA and anyone else you may know who knows the case. If there is a connection, and I think my firing may be evidence that there is one, then we can expect a war. We're going to need firepower. Let's say this Friday at 7 p.m. Can you call the Farrisport Inn and reserve a private room?"

"I'd be happy to. Jackie, I'm so glad you called and me and sorry for your loss."

"Thanks, Curt. You were the only person to whom I felt I could turn. What luck that you gave me your business card. I'll see you on Friday."

Curt felt like electricity was running through his body after he got off the phone with Jackie. He called the Inn and made reservations for Friday at 7 p.m. Not knowing who else he would be able to get to attend, he reserved a private table for four.

Jackie hung up with Curt and planned her next steps. That AlzCura had taken her job away from her was not what was propelling her forward. It was the possibility that AlzCura had contributed to Stu's death and perhaps many more that prompted her actions. If she had to, she would sell her house and move back in with her parents to get to the truth. For now, their savings and Stu's life insurance would help her get by. She called the airlines and booked a flight for Portland, Maine, on Friday. She decided not to tell her parents about losing her job just yet. She said to them that she had a business trip to Maine at the end of the week and wouldn't be back until Saturday evening. They were all too happy to take Ashley for a couple of days but cursed Jackie's employer for being so insensitive for sending her off on a business trip so soon after her loss. If they only knew, she thought!

CHAPTER 52

C urt didn't dare tell Caitlin or Cade about his upcoming dinner with Jackie. Friday's dinner was strictly business, but he knew that it was now much more likely that Caitlin and Cade would eventually have an opportunity to see her again.

Curt arrived at the Inn. Seeing the lobby empty, he asked the front desk person to call Jackie's room to tell her of his arrival. While waiting, DA Wydman arrived, and they took seats by the lobby fireplace. Jackie made her entrance, and as she approached, Curt wondered about etiquette for greeting her. Before he could resolve this question, Jackie gave him a broad smile and moved to hug him. He obliged.

"Jackie, it's so good to see you again," as the scent of her perfume and the press of her body brought back memories of their serendipitous dinner.

Jackie, at a loss for words, could only tighten her hug subtly as tears welled up in her eyes.

"Oh, Jackie, I'm sorry," Curt responded when he recognized she was barely holding it together. As she unsuccessfully tried to prevent her tears from falling, he couldn't help but react to her vulnerability. He hugged her again and held her. Jackie returned the hug and let her tears wet the shoulder of his jacket.

"I'm sorry I'm such a wreck," she said, finally able to push away from Curt after their prolonged embrace.

"Totally understandable, Jackie. You've been through a lot. Let me introduce you to District Attorney Wydman."

DA Wydman moved to shake Jackie's hand and quickly instructed her to call him Will. As Jackie apologized for her emotional state, he offered words of condolence as Curt tried to recover from the unexpectedly intimate greeting. For the hell she had been through the last few weeks, she looked surprisingly good. Frankly, she looked great, and he found himself immediately enchanted by her once again.

"Are we ready to go to dinner?" Jackie asked, seemingly recovered.

"Actually, we're waiting for one more," Curt announced. "He should be here soon."

No sooner had he said this, and the front door of the Inn opened. Jackie's stomach rolled upon seeing him, and she had all to do to keep from vomiting. He was the last person she expected to see.

"Dr. Caron, I'm so glad you could make it," cheered Curt, who introduced him to DA Wydman and was about to introduce him to Jackie when Dr. Caron took over.

"Oh, we don't need an introduction. Hi Jackie, good to see you again," stretching out his hand.

"Hello, Dr. Caron," she said in a cold, mechanical way. She felt certain everyone could detect the bewilderment in her eyes and the roiling in her stomach.

"Jackie is my Pharmaceutical Rep at AlzCura," Caron said to DA Wydman and Curt. "I'm so sorry to hear about your loss, Jackie."

She nodded, once again unable to verbalize a response. His expression of sympathy did nothing to thaw the iciness she felt towards him. When he had said that she "was my Pharmaceutical Rep," she almost jumped in to correct that she was not

HIS anything. She started to feel tears approaching, brought on this time by anger, not despair. How could someone who just cost her her job stand there and act as if everything was all right?

They departed for the dining room all the while, Jackie wondering if she should excuse herself from the meeting. The thought of having dinner with Dr. Caron was unimaginable. How would she hold it together? She wished she had briefed Curt more thoroughly during her call earlier that week. It was her fault; she had instructed him to invite whomever he thought could help. How did he know that he had invited someone she couldn't stand, and who was ethically challenged? It was like inviting the enemy into their meeting.

As luck would have it, Brittany greeted them at the hostess station with her singsong "Table for four?" question, reprising the role she had played in Jackie and Curt's first meeting.

Not even Jackie's apoplexy, given Dr. Caron's presence, could stop her and Curt from glancing at each other and erupting into laughter. DA Wydman and Dr. Caron looked at them and wondered whether they had missed something.

"Inside joke," Curt said, "we'll tell you later."

The momentary comic relief propped Jackie up, and Curt's warm and reassuring smile helped steel her against the turmoil that she was struggling with inside.

Brittany led them to their private room, and Curt made a point of pulling Jackie's chair out. Jackie smiled, caught in the middle between her affinity for Curt and her animosity for Dr. Caron, who took a seat opposite Jackie. Initially glad that he had taken the chair furthest from her, she dreaded that it was the best-positioned chair for making eye contact. After the group settled in their chairs and the waitress had taken their drink orders, Dr. Caron, as if he had been reading Jackie's mind, stood up.

"Excuse me, gentleman. I think to make this a comfortable

and productive meeting, I first need to address Jackie."

Surprised, Jackie couldn't imagine what he could say to calm the storm that had renewed itself in her stomach, which was now joined by tightness in her chest, making it difficult for her to breathe.

"Jackie, I don't know what your former employer told you about me, but don't believe a word of it. I know I may have made you uncomfortable in the past, and for that, I'm sorry. I'm on your side and now know that your employer was playing both of us against each other. When they learn we attended this dinner together, they will make both of our lives very difficult. I am sure they will smear my name and reputation. Unfortunately, I did some things for which I am not proud, and that will likely come back to haunt me, but I'm through living a lie. You have been nothing but professional in our relationship. I know that these few words may not clear the air between us, but I hope they put us on the right path. I want to help you and Curt, as well as the many people who will be harmed in the future if we don't succeed in uncovering the truth about AlzCura and their so-called miracle drug Recallamin. Please forgive me."

Shocked, Jackie considered his apology and stammered. "I, I forgive you, Dr. Car…"

"Steven, remember? Please."

"I forgive you, Steven," Jackie said as her uneasiness with using his first name and his presence began to evaporate.

"Thank you, Jackie," he said, taking his seat.

Wydman and Curt looked lost. Dr. Caron continued.

"I'm sorry, gentlemen. I will certainly be helpful to our cause here tonight. However, I'm afraid you will learn some unseemly things about me, some that Jackie has already deduced or experienced. I just needed to set the record straight, so Jackie knew where I stood."

The waitress arrived, bringing their drinks. The group fell silent and considered their menus. Curt proposed a couple of appetizers, and the rest readily gave their consent. Upon the waitress's departure, they resumed their discussion.

"We have a lot to cover," started Curt, "I would like to suggest that DA Wydman."

"Will," interrupted the DA, "It sounds like we may have a long night, and I suggest we all get comfortable using first names." The group nodded its approval, and Curt continued.

"OK, Will. I suggest that Will update us on the State's case, and then we can all fill in the gaps as best we can to see what, if anything, we can do in response."

Will updated the group on where the legal case stood. They were surprised to learn that the State's impetus for continuing this investigation was fueled by complaints originally raised by Elvira Scott that were now carried forth by the National Alliance for the Mentally Ill (NAMI) and the State Office of Advocacy (SOA). Both groups felt the State was not investigating the concerns vigorously enough and were pushing the AG's office to take their investigation to the FDA.

"Elvira Scott may have been as crazy as a loon, but had she not filed those complaints, we likely wouldn't be sitting here today. The pressure NAMI and SOA are putting on us caused me to call Curt recently to ask him to write a letter to AlzCura. We think that Curt may have greater success in compelling them to open their books on Darius and Elvira Scott, as both were found to have the same suspicious and unidentifiable substances in their systems. As additional motivation, I was hoping that Curt's letter would threaten to go to the FDA if they didn't cooperate."

Curt broke in, "I'd like to interject Will, that I'm reconsidering your request. I didn't know then what I know now, and I suspect that what Jackie and Steven may have to say tonight may further strengthen my resolve to write the letter."

"Thank you, Curt. I took no offense when you declined. It was quite understandable, given the hell you've been put through. I understand you want to get on with your life and not live in the past. You also pointed out some of the vulnerabilities in our case. Hopefully, some of those loopholes you identified will get closed tonight."

The waitress entered with the group's appetizers, momentarily interrupting the conversation. Realizing that they had not consulted their menus, they paused and made their choices.

As the waitress exited, Dr. Caron continued, "I can tell you with certainty that AlzCura has hidden and misreported complication data on their Recallamin trials. I've had several patients who had to be admitted to the hospital with symptoms of liver failure. Each time, I called AlzCura and reported the complications, and not once have I seen these complications reflected in their quality data reports. I thought at first AlzCura's approach to complication reporting was innovative. They paid me to report complications by phone, claiming that reporting them on paper was time-consuming, more costly, and a barrier to reporting. Now I think it was to try to prevent a paper trail."

"Did you keep records of your calls to them?" Will asked.

"Yes. I made a notation in my office records each time I called them. That and my office phone records to their 800 number specifically reserved for complication reporting should be pretty solid evidence."

"Great, Steven. Anything else that we should know?"

"Do you have all night?" The group chuckled, "AlzCura also holds potentially damning evidence close to the vest."

"How do you mean?" asked Will.

"All the lab work is done by a regional lab. This was another reason I was initially attracted to the AlzCura trials. Not having to be responsible for the lab work associated with clinical trials reduces the strain on my practice. Unfortunately, what I subsequently learned is that it introduces the possibility that they may withhold information that I would typically get. Also, several study subjects were removed from the study for "exclusionary conditions identified post-approval."

"What does that mean?" Curt asked.

"Exactly what I wondered," responded Dr. Caron, "When I asked for specifics, they never provided them. All they would say is that they had found pre-existing conditions in these study subjects that should have excluded them from the study. This was highly unusual. I now suspect that it was their way of removing subjects that might taint obtaining favorable study results."

"Does AlzCura know that you harbor these concerns?" asked Curt.

"Unfortunately, yes. I had a call with Dr. Asa Sheridan last week and probably said more than I should. I complained about all of it. The radio ad scripts they had me read. The lack of information I got from the regional lab. The curious procedures around Lost to Follow-Up patients, the cases of liver failure, the"

"Wait a second," Jackie interrupted, "AlzCura gave you the scripts for those radio ads?"

"Yes, didn't you know that?"

"No," Jackie said louder than she intended, "I heard those ads on my first visit to Maine and thought they were unethical and told my boss about my concern. She said that the company was not in the business of policing how you marketed your services and never let on that they were our scripts."

"Like I said, Jackie, they've been playing us. Do you want to know where I got the money to pay for all my branch offices?"

"Don't tell me," Jackie started.

"Your company helped me finance them, not without strings, I may add. Their rationale seemed to make sense at the time. They wanted to deal with one physician to get the clinical trial saturation they needed in Central Maine and reduce variation in following their protocols rather than try to get a dozen physicians onboard. Over time, they wanted me to help influence my physician colleagues, not only in Central Maine but in Portland and Bangor. Of course, now I know that they just wanted a young, naïve, energetic physician who was hungry to build his practice. Before I knew it, I was succumbing to their less than ethical practices, and they had me by the balls, excuse my French."

"Is that legal to finance your offices?" DA Wydman asked.

"No, it's not, but AlzCura didn't finance my offices directly. They have a Board member or two highly placed in the Banking industry. I applied for a loan at the Bank AlzCura suggested, and voila, as long as I played ball with AlzCura, they would forgive my loan. The moment I balked or make any noise, the loan would come due with interest."

Jackie sat perplexed at the table until Curt addressed her. "Jackie, it looks like you've seen a ghost."

"I'm shocked. Here I was thinking Dr. Car, I mean Steven, was playing fast and loose, and all the time, he was just a puppet for AlzCura. I guess I was a puppet for them too. They even sent me here last time to see if I could get you to talk about how you were bending the rules."

"Yeah, and I made the mistake of telling Dr. Sheridan that I had talked to you about my concerns about Recallamin 3. That's what probably spelled your doom, Jackie. I was under strict instructions not to voice any concerns to anyone but Dr. Sheridan. "

"If that were the case, then I would have spelled my own doom shortly after your call with Dr. Sheridan. I was just about to go in and tell Cheryl all about your concerns about Recallamin 3, the liver failure cases, the letter from Dr. Sheridan in Darius Scott's file."

"You saw the letter in Darius Scott's file?"

"Yes. I'm sorry, but Cheryl wanted me to dig for dirt on you, and when you left me alone in your office, I found it."

"Yes, the letter I had written to Dr. Sheridan got me in a lot of hot water. His response letter, which you read, was cordial. The phone call that preceded it was anything but."

"I was also surprised when you told me Margo had visited. What was that all about?" Jackie probed.

"That was apparently a test that I passed. Margo tried to use her persuasive powers, if you know what I mean, to see if I would squeal about anything. While I didn't succumb to her incessant questioning, I did give in to some more base behavior with her. I suspect AlzCura will find a way to use that behavior against me. Apparently, some Pharmaceutical Reps at AlzCura are coached to wear provocative attire and to drop their forks during meals."

Jackie blushed and felt a stab realizing that Cheryl had set her up. No wonder Dr. Caron's demeanor had changed after she had dropped her fork at lunch. He had seen that act before. It tipped him off that she was there to try to extract information from him. The whole charade Cheryl was playing was designed to perpetuate Jackie's assumption that Dr. Caron was breaking the rules. When, in fact, her employer was behind it all and was only using her to make sure Dr. Caron kept his concerns under wraps.

A cadre of wait staff entered the room and synchronized the presentation of the group's dinners. With Dr. Caron's recent revelation, Jackie made a conscious attempt to grip her silverware tightly. How embarrassing would it be to drop anything, even by accident, now?

"Steven," Will began, "it seems clear that AlzCura is ethically challenged – to put it mildly. However, our case rests on trying to establish a link between the study drug with Darius Scott's erratic behavior and subsequent death, as well as Elvira's death. You're the only physician in the room who can speak knowledgeably about the potential effects of this drug. Perhaps we should shift gears and determine whether we can strengthen our case in this regard."

Jackie answered before Dr. Caron could respond.

"Excuse me, but from what I know of the autopsy results of Darius and Elvira Scott, they sound suspiciously like those of my husband – massive brain bleed and evidence of liver failure. Stu was in the Recallamin 3 trial, and before my last trip here, he complained of headaches. While he didn't torch anyone's home, his behavior did change. He snapped at me when he dropped me off at the airport. Totally out of character."

Mentioning her husband's name felt like a dagger to her own heart. She wished Stu had consulted with her before agreeing to participate in the trial. Of course, why wouldn't he trust a clinical trial from the company his wife represented? Yet, if he had consulted her, it would have raised red flags because she had never heard of the Recallamin 3 trial.

"Thanks, Jackie," replied Will. "I didn't mean to suggest that you didn't have important information to offer this case."

"No offense taken. I just wanted you all to know the similarities."

"That's helpful because it weakens the whole hereditary argument. We now have another case with similar symptoms and sudden death, which is not related to Darius and Elvira Scott."

"Will," Dr. Caron began answering Will's initial question to him. "I appreciate your confidence in my medical knowledge. However, the simple fact is that until we can confirm that Darius, Elvira, and Stu received the study vaccine, it is almost impossible to establish a definitive link. Either AlzCura voluntarily unblinds their study results, or we get the FDA to compel them to do so. We already know their position on voluntarily unblinding their study results. The question is, can we provide the FDA with enough evidence of adverse reactions or deaths from study subjects to gain the FDA's support?"

"I guess I was wondering if you think it possible for this vaccine to cause the behaviors and deaths that we know about? Is it physiologically possible?" Will probed.

"Absolutely. Medicine is full of examples where a drug, thought to be beneficial and safe when tested under controlled circumstances, is subsequently found to be harmful. Even through the arduous FDA approval process, there is no way to be absolutely certain about the long-term effects of a drug or how it will perform when interacting with other drugs or substances. That's both a blessing and a curse."

"How so?" Will urged.

"The blessing is that the FDA and the medical industry know that medications cause adverse reactions and death. The curse is that most people take multiple medications, so the evidence that one medication is the culprit has to be pretty compelling to have the FDA investigate. We mustn't also forget the curse of economics and politics. Big Pharma means big money, and there isn't bigger money than in a potential cure for Alzheimer's. The political stakes for the FDA to investigate and potentially halt production of a drug that the public wants and needs are extraordinarily high."

"So, we're fighting a losing battle," Will said dejectedly.

"I'm not saying that. I'm just saying it won't be easy. We must all be committed to seeing this through. It will likely take years and lots of resources."

"You mean money," Curt clarified.

"Yes, that and other parties willing to join the crusade. There's no telling how many other physicians AlzCura has in their pocket that, like me, are just itching to get out from under their thumb. It's a risky business, though, because they will not only try to ruin my reputation and my livelihood. They will try to do the same with all of you."

"Eventually, if we're right about the damaging consequences of the drug, the evidence should speak," Curt replied hopefully.

"I have to wonder, just how many coffins we'll have to bury before the FDA sits up and takes notice?" Will pondered.

"First things first," Curt interjected, "Knowing what we know, do we think we can assemble the resources we need, and are we willing to dedicate the time needed and risk attack from AlzCura?"

"AlzCura has already started their attack on me," Jackie replied. "They've fabricated improper behavior with a client as the cause for losing my job. They've threatened to ruin my reputation if I speak to any clients or AlzCura employees. They're dirty, and their vaccine was probably responsible for Stu's death. I'm all in."

Dr. Caron took the floor.

"As I said before, my being here and divulging my concerns to Jackie will undoubtedly bring on AlzCura's wrath. I'm ashamed of the things I did and can't live like this anymore. I can refute AlzCura's allegations against Jackie. I have records of multiple patients who have suffered similar fates as Stu that never surfaced in the research. I have no choice but to fight. I'm in for the long haul."

DA Wydman then took his turn.

"I'm a public servant obligated to investigate and, if necessary, prosecute the complaints and allegations brought by Elvira and now some powerful consumer groups. I don't have a choice. I'm in."

Curt looked around the table, recognizing that no one had

folded. His life had finally turned the corner. He and the kids had returned to that mythical state of "normal." Agreeing to join this initiative meant jumping back into the fray and putting a big target on his back for AlzCura. He knew that this would not only affect his life but could bring unwanted attention to his company. Then there were the kids. How could this affect them? He hesitated.

"Curt," Will spoke, interrupting his thoughts. "I know this must be a hard decision for you, but let me advise you. AlzCura already knows if Darius, Elvira, and Stu received the vaccine. Frankly, if we're right, they probably have many other examples they're trying to keep under wraps. AlzCura already knows you're a potential enemy to their cause. Even if you choose not to join our little crusade, the moment AlzCura starts feeling the heat, they will take a scorched earth approach."

Curt winced, and Will, realizing his poor choice of words, apologized.

"I'm sorry, Curt, I shouldn't have used those words, but when AlzCura's kingdom is under siege, you can be certain that they will aggressively protect their profits."

Will's choice of words reignited Curt's vision of Calli's brutal murder and the free-floating anger that had tortured him for the last six months. He realized that joining the crusade could finally channel his rage towards a goal. He had given up trying to answer the question of Calli's murder. Didn't Calli deserve his full effort to answer that question? And what if AlzCura's vaccine was killing others? Could he live with himself knowing that he hadn't taken the opportunity to try to stop it? In a moment, he knew what he needed to do.

"I'm in," he declared, slamming his fist on the table, rattling the dishes, and startling the rest of the group. When they recovered from his emphatic gesture, the group erupted into a spontaneous cheer. Raising their wine glasses, they all proposed a toast.

"To restoring my integrity and saving innocent lives," announced Dr. Caron.

"To eliminating greed and bringing criminals to justice," intoned DA Wydman.

"To Stu, whose love always inspired me, and for Ashley, who needs a mother who isn't afraid to stand up for what is right and good."

All eyes shifted to Curt, whose eyes had misted over.

"To Calli, Caitlin, and Cade," his voice cracked as he raised his glass with the others. "I do this for you and for the table for four."

As the group's glasses clinked, Curt and Jackie's eyes met, and a deeper understanding of what he had just said passed between them. The crusade was just beginning.

❋ ❋ ❋

Thank you for reading Table for Four, the first book in the series. Enter the following web address to reach Amazon sales page to purchase Dying to Recall, the next book in the series.

https://readerlinks.com/l/1350868

ACKNOWLEDGEMENT

My parents both died from complications of Alzheimer's Disease. Before their downward spiral from this devastating disease, they lived long, productive lives. They endured unimaginable hardships growing up, yet survived and emigrated to America to build a better life for themselves and their children. They instilled in me values for which I will be forever grateful. Thanks, Mom and Dad. This first book in the series is for you.

When you've lived 62 years, you invariably recognize two facts: 1) a lot of people helped you get here, and 2) there is no way you can list or adequately thank them all. However, I would like to recognize and thank a handful of people who were instrumental in helping guide and inspire me. Teachers like Sister Nora in grade school, Marilyn Rubald in high school, and Annette Reiser, Dr. Howard Rome, and Dr. Vernon Weckwerth in graduate school. All were uncommon educators that were not only effective teachers but also gave me direction in life and inspired my best efforts as a human being.

I wouldn't be where I am today without colleagues and mentors like Edwin Harlow, Lynne Yauger, Doug Crabtree, Shelley Peterson, Dr. Shawn Dufford, Jill Fainter, and Dr. Eric Ramos. You are not only the best leaders I have worked with but also some of the most caring and genuine human beings I know.

On a practical level, publishing this book was made possible by Mark Coker, founder of Smashwords. Thank you for giving aspiring writers an easy path and vehicle for getting our words and voices heard. I am also grateful to Tatiana at Vila

Design for her expertise, responsive service, and captivating book cover that captures the essence of this story.

Last but certainly not least, my friends and family who have anchored and encouraged me and helped bring purpose and joy to my life: Lori LaChance, Lindsay Long, my children Tori and Nick, my sister Renie Alverson, and my ever-faithful dog Tekka. Thank you for your boundless love and support.

A portion of the proceeds from this book and the other books in this series, including *Dying to Recall* and *Memory's Hope*, will be donated to the Alzheimer's Foundation of America (AFA). AFA's mission is to provide support, services, and education to individuals, families, and caregivers affected by Alzheimer's disease and related dementias nationwide and funding research for better treatment and a cure.

BOOKS IN THIS SERIES

Table for Four
A 3-book series about a Pharmaceutical Company's discovery of a cure for Alzheimer's disease that has unforeseen and ominous consequences.

Table For Four: A Medical Thriller Series Book 1

A blockbuster Alzheimer's cure. A murder and unexplained deaths. Two aggrieved parties meet by chance. Will they expose the truth, or die trying?

Dying To Recall: A Medical Thriller Series Book 2

A suicide, a break-in, an ominous warning. Is it a coincidence? Or have Jackie and Curt unleashed the wrath of vengeful pharmaceutical executives?

Memory's Hope: A Medical Thriller Series Book 3

The case against AlzCura intensifies until the FDA's shocking response to the data. Will the guilty parties walk, or will they be brought to justice?

BOOKS BY THIS AUTHOR

Table For Four: A Medical Thriller Series Book 1

A blockbuster Alzheimer's cure. A murder and unexplained deaths. Two aggrieved parties meet by chance. Will they expose the truth, or die trying?

Dying To Recall: A Medical Thriller Series Book 2

A suicide, a break-in, an ominous warning. Is it a coincidence? Or have Jackie and Curt unleashed the wrath of vengeful pharmaceutical executives?

Memory's Hope: A Medical Thriller Series Book 3

A suicide, a break-in, an ominous warning. Is it a coincidence? Or have Jackie and Curt unleashed the wrath of vengeful pharmaceutical executives?

Aja Minor: Gifted Or Cursed: A Psychic Crime Thriller Series Book 1

Aja has disturbing powers. She feels cursed, but the FBI thinks otherwise. Will she stop a serial rapist and killer or become his next victim?

Aja Minor: Fountain Of Youth: A Psychic Crime Thriller Series Book 2

Aja Minor goes undercover. The target, an international child trafficking ring. When her cover is blown, the mission and her life are in jeopardy.

Aja Minor: Predatorville: A Psychic Crime Thriller Series Book 3

Solving a surge in assaults and missing children is Aja Minor's next test. But when the hunter becomes the hunted, will she get out of Predatorville alive?

Old Lady Ketchel's Revenge: The Slaughter Minnesota Horror Series Book 1

No one truly escapes their childhood unscathed. Especially if you grew up in Slaughter, Minnesota, in the 1960s and crossed Old Lady Ketchel's path.

Hagatha Ketchel Unhinged: The Slaughter Minnesota Horror Series Book 2

Twenty-four years in an asylum is enough time to really lose your mind. And arouse one to unleash the dark and vengeful thoughts residing therein.

Hagatha's Century Of Terror: The Slaughter Minnesota Horror Series Book 3

What does a crazy old lady in Slaughter, Minnesota, need on her 100th birthday? Sweet revenge, of course.

Loving You From My Grave: A Wholesome Inspirational Romance

He ran from his past. She's held captive by hers. Could love set them free, bridge their differences in age and race, and survive death?

Little Bird On My Balcony: Selected Poems

A collection of poems that speak to the love, loss, longing, and levity of navigating young adulthood.

Adilynn's Lullaby: Poems Of Love & Loss

A collection of poems about love and loss that provide hope and inspiration during some of life's most difficult times.

ABOUT CHRIS BLIERSBACH

Chris Bliersbach is originally from St. Paul, Minnesota, and now lives in Henderson, Nevada.

Follow him on Amazon, Facebook, Goodreads or join his mailing list at cmbliersbach@gmail.com